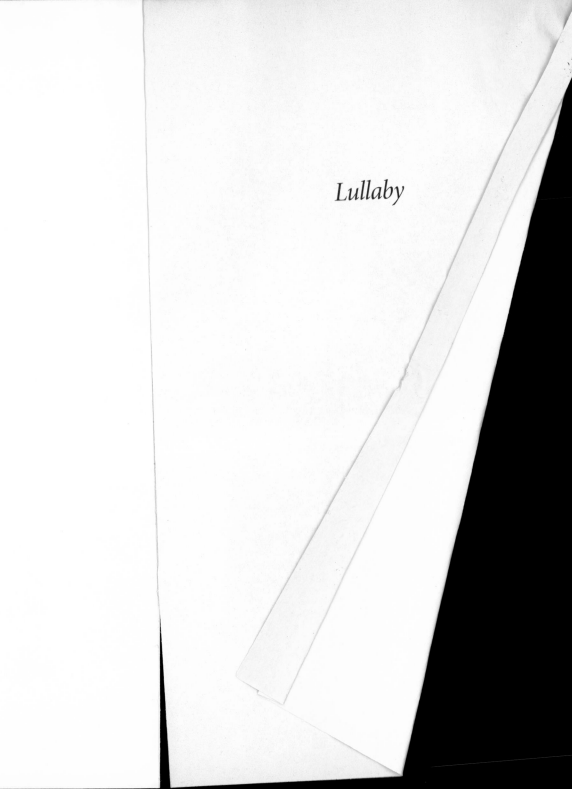

Lullaby

Lullaby

CLAIRE SEEBER

Thomas Dunne Books
St. Martin's Press
New York

This is a work of fiction. All of the characters,
organizations, and events portrayed in this novel are
either products of the author's imagination or are
used fictitiously.

THOMAS DUNNE BOOKS.
An imprint of St. Martin's Press.

LULLABY. Copyright © 2007 by Claire Seeber. All rights
reserved. Printed in the United States of America. For
information, address St. Martin's Press, 175 Fifth
Avenue, New York, N.Y. 10010.

Extract from *Bad Friends* © Claire Seeber 2007. This is
taken from uncorrected material and does not
necessarily reflect the finished book.

www.thomasdunnebooks.com
www.stmartins.com

Library of Congress Cataloging-in-Publication Data

Seeber, Claire.
    Lullaby / Claire Seeber. — 1st U.S. ed.
        p. cm.
    ISBN 978-0-312-55577-1
    1. Mothers of kidnapped children—Fiction. I. Title.
    PR6119.E43L86 2010
    823'.92—dc22

                                        2009037453

First published in Great Britain by Avon, a division
of HarperCollins*Publishers*

First U.S. Edition: January 2010

10 9 8 7 6 5 4 3 2 1

To Fenn, Raffi and Tim, without whom this book would never have been written.

PROLOGUE

Later, I couldn't think whose idea it had been to visit the Tate that day. I did remember we'd been talking about going for ages, months even, and how pleased I was when Mickey finally took a rare day's holiday to spend with us. I remembered that we thought we should do something more interesting than trotting round the local park behind Louis's pushchair for the millionth time that month; that I was happy it would just be us three for once as we caught the train into town.

So whose fault did that make it when my whole world fell apart?

CHAPTER ONE

It was the kind of summer day so hot you feared another's clammy touch – a sticky August afternoon that made me long for cool, cool, sliding rain, and I was quietly cursing Maxine as I tried to rid the bag of all the sand, the eternal grains that tumbled softly from folds of muslins and stained-forever bibs. She'd brought home half the beach from her trip to the seaside last week, and everything had gone all gritty, trickling into Louis's lovingly prepared food that he'd just refused to eat. I was starting to feel flustered as I tried to escape the soft, pale powder, but it was in my mouth and eyes now and I pulled a face and spat it out, and felt my good mood begin to fade.

I took a deep breath and then one more. It was stupid to get upset, I told myself, I was just tired, and Louis didn't even know, he didn't care; he'd nodded off above his mango mush now anyway, so resolutely I shut the bag. An exhausted-looking woman in horrid green tie-dye removed her screaming daughter from the postcard racks opposite our table, pulled the toddler past us, Picasso prints falling like confetti in their wake. The child slumped hard to spite her mother, an awkward deadweight dragging her small heels, livid squawking face clashing with her yellow Miffy vest. Middle-aged art lovers looked on unamused and unafraid to show it (they didn't want domestic dramas disturbing their special day out, no thanks. Not when they'd caught the early train up to town, a copy of *The Times* tucked neatly under their arm; not when they'd splashed out on Chardonnay and smoked-salmon sandwiches for lunch). I tried to catch the mother's harassed eye to smile my sympathy, smile this brand-new maternal solidarity that – apparently – now included me. That still astonished me, every time it happened. But she'd already gone. I sneaked a quick look at the for-once-actually-sleeping Louis – and for a moment, just for a tiny precious moment, couldn't help but bask in the rare glow of *my* child being quiet and well-behaved.

In front of a great poster depicting *Religious Revelry* a young couple ran into each other's arms, hugging happily before a naked Adam and Eve. Friends or lovers, I wondered idly – until the boy, quite beautiful beneath his frizzy hair, slid his hand inside the plump girl's silk waistband. She sighed with visible pleasure and wrapped herself around him, twisting her body like the serpent round the apple tree.

And I thought about last night, about the early hours of today, and I smiled again, smiled to myself this time, and felt quite strangely shy, remembering Mickey's steady hand on me this morning for the first time in months. I looked about for my husband. Perhaps this was it; perhaps things would be the way they were before. I took a slow deep breath and tucked my hair behind my ears. Perhaps now, I thought, and this was what I truly prayed for, perhaps soon I'd stop feeling like some kind of pretender. I glanced back at the baby; I felt my heart contract. My confidence with him was slowly growing every day.

I contemplated the rather bad drawing I'd just done of Louis blinking up at all the lights and then glanced quickly at Mickey's plate. And then, since he still wasn't back from wherever he'd wandered off to now – the toilet, I thought he'd said this time – I shoved my sketchbook away in favour of his leftover cake. With a sort of frenzied guilty pleasure I was trying to scoff the chocolate bit, the bit with all the icing on, when I felt an unexpected hand upon my tired shoulder.

God, she made me jump! Her skin was so cold it felt weird, like it almost burnt me through my thin cotton top. I jumped at this stranger's familiar touch – like, really jumped I mean, jogging my cup, sending the coffee splashing, scalding, down my white skirt. But she was unperturbed; she didn't seem to see the impact she had on me at all.

'Your baby,' she gestured to the pushchair, to my sleeping son. I smiled politely, but actually I was thinking about my skirt, the fact I had to wear it for the rest of the day, the fact that it was now ruined.

'He's beautiful. It is a boy, no?' She'd removed her hand now, bending towards Louis. Normally I would have been flattered, ready to proudly stand and coo together, but for some reason this time I couldn't. She was too near me, near us, and something about her ice-blue stare unnerved me. I tried to move my chair away imperceptibly, but now she'd got between me and the baby. I didn't want to cause offence but she was starting to give me the creeps. I mean, she was perfectly respectable-looking. Rake-thin, I noticed straight off – like you do when you have pounds of baby weight to shift. Youngish, expensive summer dress; a racehorse stance. Attractive enough, I supposed, in a blonde, shiny sort of way. And yet, and yet – I couldn't explain it. There was just something about her I didn't like.

My reflexes were slow; nappy brain was taking its fuzzy-headed toll.

'Yes. Yes he is – a boy. Louis.'

'Hi, Louis. You're so bonny.' She had a faint accent I couldn't place, and this last word seemed wrong somehow. It clattered clumsily to the ground, incongruous from someone so obviously not British. She stroked my baby's little moon cheek and his eyelashes fluttered. I felt myself go tense, my hands clenching instinctively. He made little sucking motions in his sleep, his mouth all soft and sweet. Oh look, I nearly crowed, his Touché Turtle face. My heart did a funny flip.

'Sorry,' I said, and I tried not to sound rude, 'do I know you?'

'I don't think so,' she replied, 'though it's quite strange, now you say it. Your face does look – kind of familiar.' She smiled, moved down to Louis again.

'Please,' I said, too fast, 'don't wake him.' Inside I was

6

shouting, *Don't touch my son!* But out loud I just said, 'It takes ages to get him off to sleep.' Later I hated myself; thought I was stupid to have been embarrassed because I felt protective, the reserve of the British. But right now I did nothing except gape at her.

'Though people, they always say that, don't they? It is one quite annoying thing, I find.'

'What is?'

'You know – "You look just like someone else – my sister, my old friend."' With a dazzling smile, head on one side, she mimicked 'people'.

'Oh, I see. I don't know really.' I stood up, flustered. 'We must get going actually.' I was dropping nappies, muslin, wipes, scooping them up, pushing away from this confident stranger who made my skin prickle. Willing Mickey to hurry up.

She moved away, then turned back again.

'Excuse me.' With a little smirk, she pointed to my top. I looked down; it was rucked up above my bra from where I'd fed Louis earlier.

'Oh,' I said foolishly. A burning flush crept up my chest, across my face. Hastily I pulled my T-shirt down, tucked myself in. She swung a large bag over her spiky shoulder.

'Enjoy the exhibition,' she called as she went.

'Thanks,' I said to her departing back, but I wasn't thankful. I was simply humiliated. 'Silly cow,' I muttered. Right on cue the baby woke with a high-pitched squeal of indignation.

'I quite agree, darling,' I crooned to him. Kissed him, patted him, walked him up and down to calm him. Finally, just as I was starting to wonder where on earth he'd got to, Mickey sauntered slowly round a corner, pushing his thick hair back from his dark deep eyes, and there it was. The familiar rush of lust, of anxious desire. I was like a maddened moth, a crazy, mad old moth banging against the light. When had I lost myself?

Mickey apologised half-heartedly, took the baby from me for a cuddle, holding him with ease against his lithe frame. Bumped into someone he knew from work, he said, forgot the time. I felt a sudden twinge of schoolgirl satisfaction as two chi-chi Italian women raised eyebrows over my handsome husband, and I smiled at him, and leant up for a kiss. But he didn't seem to notice as he hummed to the baby – I thought I recognised the tune from the show we'd been to see last night – so I feigned interest in my skirt instead.

'Look at it,' I groaned, 'it's ruined now.' I smeared the stains round uselessly with a baby-wipe.

'I told you not to wear white, you daft eejit,' he said, but his attention was still a little off.

'It wasn't my fault actually. This weird woman made me jump.'

He wasn't listening, I could tell.

'Anyway, it's the only decent thing that fits right now.' I tried not to sound moany. Mickey jiggled the baby on his knee. Thank God at least he seemed interested in Louis today. He glanced at the stain that I was still fussing at.

'You're just making it worse.' He nodded towards the gallery. 'Let's get on now, shall we?'

'Are you grumpy cos I ate your cake?' I joked as I packed up.

'I couldn't care less about the cake.'

'Are you sure?'

'Sure I am. Forget the fecking cake.'

Did he look bored? Don't say it, I thought. Remember this morning. But somehow it spun out anyway.

'You think I'm fat, don't you? I *am* losing the baby weight, you know.' I pushed the cake crumbs behind the menu card. 'It's coming off now.' I wrinkled my brow at him. '*Do* you think I'm fat?'

'Jessica – for God's sake! I'm not even going to dignify that with a response.'

I looked at him; I smiled hopefully. He took the bait; he smiled back. 'All right then. You're beautiful.' Then he went and spoilt it. 'It doesn't matter about the weight.'

How quickly it could escalate from nothing if we let it. For a split second I hesitated. Then I raised a hand and tentatively stroked his cheek. Mickey caught my hand in his; he turned it over pensively. He looked back at me; he could be so inscrutable. Then slowly, very slowly, he kissed the palm. I felt my own pulse quicken. Carefully he twisted my wedding ring around so the fat diamonds sat at the front again.

'You should have a new diamond for the baby. One of those – what do they call them? Eternity rings, is it?'

'You've got me so much stuff already. You don't need to buy me any more.'

'Well, I might just want to, might I not?'

I heard the bite in his tone and acquiesced. 'You might. You're always so generous. But the main thing is,' I smiled at him, 'the best thing is, you're here. It's been so long since we've done something all together, all three of us, hasn't it? Something special, I mean.'

He put Louis back in the pushchair. 'Too long.'

'And I've been dying to see this exhibition, haven't you?' Why was his approval always so paramount? More so than anyone's had ever been.

'I have to say, I don't like Hopper's style very much.'

'Oh.' Quietly I absorbed this. He did Louis's straps up; I watched his long fingers at their work. 'Don't you really?'

'What?'

'Like Hopper. Or are you winding me up?'

'No. I really don't.'

Sometimes, you know, I longed for the free and empty days. For my freedom from this hold that he had over me.

'Pedestrian crap. More your thing, you know.'

For the days before the old Jess had slipped away. I chucked the used wipes in the bin. But he caught my eye and he relented; leant in to kiss my forehead.

'I didn't mean it nastily. I'm just tired, Jessica. Working too hard to keep you in those diamonds, hey?'

I didn't want all the presents; they made me rather nervous. I was happy just with him. And it was true; he did look exhausted, dark shadows staining his pale skin, his sharp cheekbones more prominent than usual.

'I'm sorry. Ignore me. I just need some sleep.'

You and me both, I thought glumly as Mickey kissed the top of my head, walking off before I could respond. He said something else I couldn't quite catch – took Louis with him, I saw with some relief. Lately he hadn't seemed quite so besotted with his son, which had taken me by surprise. Perhaps slowly our roles were reversing; as my love for Louis grew, did Mickey become a little disinterested in him? Maybe he felt a little less needed, that was what worried me now. It was another reason this day together was so long overdue.

'What, Mickey?' I called. 'What did you say?' But then some small beardy bloke got in between us, tripping over the pushchair that was trailing bags. I caught the man's arm to steady him, apologised like it was my fault, and then Mickey was gone already, pushing the baby proudly. He stalked away like the cock of the walk, so upright as he led the way into the gallery.

I untangled myself from Beardy and I followed them. They were already out of view. I looked at the pictures, but I didn't really see them. They all seemed to be out of focus, like we were under water or something. I had this nervous feeling in my tummy, like when you've drunk too much coffee. Then I remembered that woman. Something about her niggled me, but I couldn't think what.

Something had woken me with a start that morning, and for a minute I didn't know where I was. Dragged from a death-like sleep, that unique new-parent sleep. And I'd drunk too much the night before; not used to alcohol these days, so my head was feeling groggy. I suppose it was about five, cos the planes were coming in to land. I listened for the baby, but for once he was quiet, and so I just lay there for a while. I thought about last night; drinking champagne with Mickey at the Royal Opera House, like we'd done on our first real date last year. Last night I'd worn the new dress Mickey had bought me for my birthday, deep pink and deep cut and terribly sophisticated, darling. During the second act he'd surprised me – leant over in the box, regardless of his clients, and whispered I was beautiful. He'd lifted my hair to kiss my neck and I'd bit down on my lip; bit down my dormant desire. But truly the best bit in all this heat hadn't actually been that kiss, nor the swaggering singers or the multicoloured costumes of this last-minute treat. Nor was it the tragic love story I'd lost myself in on a rare and longed-for night off from all the baby talk. It wasn't even Mickey's hard-won approval. No, it had been the air-conditioning in the Royal Opera House. Oh, the sheer relief of that coolness licking round my melting limbs for a few hours.

Mickey rolled over, muttering something inaudible, then went back to sleep. I stopped thinking about *Madame Butterfly* (Mickey said he'd prefer Wagner any time – but his corporate clients lapped up the champagne, which was all that really counted; and I'd loved it, almost crying when the poor heroine died for her son's sake, though I didn't let Mickey see). I started worrying pointlessly about other things, like you do in the small hours when there's absolutely sweet Fanny Adams you can do about any of them, as my Nana would have said. I remember worrying about why I was awake when I had the rare chance to be asleep, but that just made me more restless; even more alert. Then I worried about going to the gallery that day and Mickey getting annoyed because I didn't like some picture or other that he revered. I thought, I must remember not to ask any silly questions. For some reason that cringe-worthy time at Greg's dinner party when Mickey had got so cross with me drifted through my head; I'd flip-pantly called my husband a Brit, and God, how deep those touchy Northern Irish roots were dug; how quickly he was riled. I'd tried to make a joke of it, but that only served to make things worse; I'd looked hope-fully at Greg for some support that never came, though later my hostess caught my eye knowingly across the candles and the coq au vin. With no reprieve, I'd kicked myself under that dining table, and still Mickey had refused to speak on the journey home because appar-ently I'd made him look stupid in his own rage.

Eventually I shoved the mortifying scene from my mind, and then I just lay there listening to the planes, imagining all those tiny passengers suspended high above the ground, above a toy-town London, and how sad they must be to be nearly back. The bit I always used to dread, coming home again. Until Mickey. Until Louis came…

I was just dipping back into that half-world between sleep and consciousness when Mickey rolled back towards me and cupped my breast, a sore breast swollen with milk, blue-veined as a road map. I tensed. Everything was so different now. I held my breath; his other hand stroked down my hip bone slowly. However much I prayed that he'd go on, I still wanted him to stop. I lived in fear that he'd discover how much I'd changed in the past six months. Mickey opened his eyes lazily and, in the half-light, looked into mine, his all slit with sleep still. He put his hand up to my cheek and stroked his thumb across my mouth.

'All right, big eyes?' he whispered. I nodded, shy; felt the kick of lust that I'd suppressed when Louis arrived.

'God, you're sweet, Jessica,' he groaned, tucking a curl behind my ear. Then he gathered up my hair in the nape of my neck and, pulling me to him, kissed me gently. I was about to mutter that I hadn't cleaned my teeth yet, but before I could speak he drew me against him and kissed me harder now, like he hadn't in a long time, and finally I let go. The dawn heat slid down me like melted chocolate, and I forgot my fear, my anxiety, my very different body. I just felt the utter longing I always felt for him. I dissolved into him; I let myself enjoy it.

And afterwards he fell back to sleep and finally light began to bleed around the heavy curtains I hated so, and in the end I thought, sod it, I might as well get up and have a cup of tea; an hour to myself before the baby wakes up. And then of course the baby woke up.

It was funny, because after that odd woman and my poor ruined skirt, and all those peculiar nerves, I suddenly found myself enjoying the exhibition.

I turned a corner into one room and there was a little painting of a woman just leaning out of a window, looking off into some kind of field, and I suddenly felt all sort of, I don't know – serene. It's a good word, serene. All the anxiety of earlier started floating away, and I just stood and contemplated the picture. Like, I forgot where I was, forgot all about my baby fat and how flipping tired I always seemed to be, and that Mickey and I had been bickering recently. And instead, I felt really happy, like I was where I was meant to be, with my son whom I'd finally come to love so much, and the husband whom I still longed to get to know. Who loved me really – even if I did once call him British; who'd made love to me this morning just like the old days. The not-very-long-ago days. And then I thought, I just want to be with my little family now, and before I walked off I thanked that woman in the painting. I know it sounds quite soppy, quite strange, but I did. I thought, yeah, that's it, that's why we come here, and look at art, etc. – because it puts a different perspective on our lives. Lives that seem so humdrum sometimes.

And I looked around for Mickey and Louis, so I could share my grand thoughts with them. Only they weren't in sight. I thought they must be ahead of me, and I walked on through the next rooms, but they weren't there either; so I retraced my steps, thinking Mickey must have gone back to look at a picture. He could be a real slow-coach, Mickey, sometimes. I'd known him to stand in front of one painting for a quarter of an hour, whereas I'd just get bored, wanted to keep moving, on to the next thing.

Only he wasn't there. He wasn't anywhere in the

gallery. My heart started to beat a little bit faster, but I thought he must have just gone out; perhaps Louis was crying and I didn't hear; they're probably in the small exhibition shop, buying postcards. So I rushed to check, but he wasn't there either. Or in the café. And now I started to feel a cold sweat prickling above my lip. He could be changing the baby. Or maybe down in the big shop on the ground floor. Perhaps he'd gone back into the exhibition, gone round the other way, and I'd missed them. So I explained to the po-faced woman on the door that I'd lost my husband and my baby and could I go in and look. For a minute she seemed dubious because I didn't have my ticket any more, like I was lying to get in for free, and I thought, *she's going to be a real jobsworth about this*, but something about my manner must have convinced her that I was telling the truth, because she finally let me. Fruitlessly, I looked. Oh God, I looked so hard, so hopefully.

And then suddenly I felt a big rush of relief, and I thought, *Of course, you silly cow, just ring his mobile –* why didn't I think of that first? But with a sickening lurch I realised that my phone was in the back of the pushchair, that my bag was hanging over its handles, that I had nothing on me, no phone, no money. Nothing.

For the next forty minutes I hunted around that enormous building. Up and down escalators I went, barging past happy, chatting tourists like some mad woman; in and out of lifts. Like some stupid scene from a French farce. Up to the members' room to see if Mickey had blagged his way in there for a view over the Thames and that wobbly bridge. Typical Mickey. He'd be sitting in a deckchair on the roof terrace, sunning himself above the grey river, above the half-empty pleasure boats, Louis blowing bubbles next to him. Showing off to all the girls.

But there were just scruffy academic types discussing art, pushing worn-out specs up spindly noses, flip-flopped students sharing cappuccinos, well-bred ladies with little else to do but lunch. No Mickey. No baby. And all the time I was hunting, I was preparing what to say, how I would tell Mickey off, how I would cuddle Louis, how we'd laugh about it later. But eventually as I felt more panicked I started to get angry, and I stopped thinking about laughing, and started thinking about shouting.

Suddenly, coming up the main escalator for about the fifth time, I saw my pushchair. Oh God – the surge of relief was immense, overwhelming. Whooshed through me and made my knees shake for a minute.

'Louis,' I croaked. Thank Christ! My heart soared – until I saw this strange man lifting my son high into the air, chucking him under the chin, spinning him round above his head, and the baby was laughing, giggling, and they both turned round, and it wasn't Louis. It wasn't my pushchair. And then I felt sick, sicker than I could ever remember feeling, sick to my stomach, like they say; sick right down to the soles of my aching feet.

Please, Mickey, you fool, please just be here this time, I silently intoned, going back downstairs again. People were starting to give me funny looks. I was gritting my teeth so hard my jaw hurt. I was so furious now, furious that he could be so inconsiderate, that he could just vanish like this and not even think about me. So furious I was nearly crying with frustration. It was so bloody typical. And I was furious with everyone else here too, for having such a nice time, for not being worried and frantic like me, for not being the ones who'd lost their family. For not being inadvertently alone.

They must have gone for a walk. Of course! I went running outside, and I mean properly running, through the crowd I went. Past the sweet burning smells of the peanut stall, past the bloke with his silly bird whistles, running through shots badly framed by indignant Germans, who tutted, and humble Japanese who cast their eyes down at their cameras rather than complain. Gulls wheeled above, crying mournfully for scraps, and I nearly sent some small girl's ice cream flying because I was looking around for Louis all the time I ran.

'Sorry, darling, I'm so sorry.' I wanted to reach down and hug her just for the touch but her parents were glaring at me like I was some sort of nutter, so I turned and headed back inside.

I was out of breath now. My chest hurt, and my inhaler – I scrabbled for it. It was in my missing bag, of course. I must not panic. I sat down for a minute on a leather pouffe thing and, head in hands, tried to collect my thoughts. To be practical. I searched my pockets – I had 6p in change, my train ticket and a baby sock. Just one little bobbly sock. I thought about reversing the charges – could you do that to a mobile?

I thought about ringing my sister, getting her to phone Mickey. I found a guard and asked about payphones.

'Downstairs,' he said tersely, waving a vague hand.

'Is there a missing persons' point, a meeting point or something? A Tannoy? I've lost my husband,' I said. 'He's got my baby, you see. Our baby.' Was I having trouble forming words? He didn't seem to understand me. Frankly, he looked bored.

'Walkie-talkie,' he mimed eventually, gesturing off into the distance. I tried to pull myself together. This was ridiculous. People must get lost here every day, it was so vast, so bloody anonymous. I thought about Louis and that he must be getting hungry by now, and I felt my eyes prickle, fill up with tears. I decided to go and find the payphones before I started wailing right there in the middle of the Tate Modern, and then I saw this nice friendly man who looked official, holding a walkie-talkie, and coming towards me.

'Everything all right, miss?' he said, and I used every fibre of my being not to cry. He was such a nice man, he had hair growing out of his ears in little tufts just like my granddad used to, and his nose was a bit red as if he liked a whisky now and again, and he let me use his own mobile phone to ring Mickey, and I was so relieved; and in the end I stopped the tears before they came.

Only the phone just rang and rang. I looked out at St Paul's, at that great dome, and I prayed again. Really hard. I tried to ring three times, and the first time I got the number wrong because my hand was shaking so much. The next time, it just rang and rang until the voicemail picked up and Mickey's disembodied voice floated down the airwaves. I left a rambling message that started off angry and ended up pleading. 'Please,' I said, 'just ring this number back, quickly.' And then the third time, it was dead. Mickey's phone line had gone dead.

CHAPTER TWO

The rattle of the train battled the hiss of my tight breath. I automatically reached for my inhaler again, but of course it was still missing. Just the sock, the bobbly little sock, and a fingernail of fluff.

In the carriage, which stank of pee, I tried to relax, but I couldn't sit back even for one small second because I was squeezed into the corner by the world's largest man. He sweated on me all fatly, pores oozing in the stifling heat, squashing his huge nylon leg fully along my thigh, but I didn't care. I crossed my arms over my poor bosoms that were as hard as crash helmets now, and I willed the train on with every piece of me, because by now I was quite sure that Mickey was back home; would be there when I arrived; that Louis was safe; and I banished thoughts of his tearful little face firmly from my mind. I stamped them down and replaced them with his fuzzy-peach head, his chubby smile.

And all the way I played that stupid game, the one I played incessantly as a kid. I was gambling with myself, making promises I couldn't keep. If that bald man got off at the next station, Louis would be home; if that woman turned her page before the old lady beside her nodded off, Mickey would be so apologetic, would kiss and hug me and beg for my forgiveness, and I would be serene, oh yes, serene, bestowing a gracious kiss.

And when the train pulled into Blackheath, I was like the kids from my old school, the daredevil ones; like Robbie used to be. Like I used to be. I jumped before we even stopped, running beside the still-moving train, about to fall. I was falling but then I caught myself and righted myself, and before I hit the tarmac I was running safely again.

I had sat in the Tate until I could bear to sit no more. The nice man, whose name was Mr Norland, let me ring my house – but the answer-phone picked up. I left a brief, burbling message, told Mickey to stay put if he came home, and then Mr Norland suggested tea. When he heard I had no money, he pressed handfuls of warm change into my hot, damp hands and propelled me to the café.

And so I sat alone and waited, sat very still and watched the world go by. My drink went cold, left a scummy tidemark on the shiny china as happy tourists bustled round me. People joined my table and left again. One couple had a muttered row about what film to see that night, and the bloke got really quite irate and went all pink, so I looked the other way and tried hard not to listen.

A brisk German lady in a khaki cagoule sat beside me eating carrot cake, and then forgot her postcards.

I called after her but she'd already gone, so I wiped a blob of buttery icing from the bag, and thumbed through her selection. She'd bought the one of the woman looking out over the field, the one I liked so much, and it made me want to cry again. But I didn't. I wouldn't cry. I just kept searching for Louis in the crowds and kicking myself for letting them vanish from my sight.

An hour passed, the slowest of my life. Mr Norland came to say his shift was over, but his colleagues had my details. And then, very gently, he suggested that perhaps I should go home.

'Can I borrow your phone again?' I asked, and one final useless time I rang Mickey's mobile and home. Still nothing whatsoever on Mickey's line, and just my silly jolly voice at home, with Louis's gurgle in the background recorded for all time.

'They must be on their way back home, d'you think?' I said, and Mr Norland nodded and shakily I thanked him, stuck my chin in the air, much braver than I felt. As the sun slid down the creamy summer sky, I headed out for home.

Exploding into the dawdling rush-hour crowd the train had just spewed out, I pushed up through the village like a bullet from a gun. Natalie from my antenatal class waved merrily from outside the pub, her posh pram tucked all safe behind her, but I wouldn't stop to talk; I couldn't talk. On and up the hill I forced myself until I hit the great humid heath. Normally I'd feel relief here, pause to savour the space surrounding

23

me, but there wasn't time for any of that now. I desperately needed my inhaler to breathe in this stagnant dusk, but at least the house was in view, and the light was on in the front window, and I promised God that I'd do anything, anything whatsoever, I'd never swear or lie or row with Mickey ever, ever again if he could just be home with Louis and everything would be normal once more.

I rang the bell. I could hear voices – thank Christ, there were voices! But no one came. I rang again, stuck my finger on the gold-plated doorbell that Mickey hated, kept swearing he'd replace, and I left it there until eventually the talking stopped. A silence fell, and that unnerved me more. Then footsteps pattered down the parquet floor, and the front door swung open – and it wasn't Mickey at all. It was just the cleaner, Jean. I pushed past her into the house I so rarely called my own, past her into the kitchen, but I could see, oh God I saw, that no one else was there.

For a moment I nearly lost control. I put my head back and I almost howled 'Louis? Mickey?' Resounding silence met me.

'Mickey, is he here? I heard voices?' I croaked, leaning over the table, head bowed, trying to catch my breath. Sweat trickled down my back uncomfortably; the air hung thick around us and I knew the answer before it came.

'No, dear, I haven't seen him, I'm sorry.'

I stared at her. 'But – the voices?'

'The radio was on. I've switched it off now.'

Apologetic, timid voice, breathy as a child's. White hair blending into chalky cheeks, my 'diamond' Jean might have spent her whole life underground. I knew she was a diamond because my neighbours told me so when I moved in. Only I'd never really felt that she was mine, you know. Jean belonged to the old regime.

'When did you get here?'

'Oh, I'm not quite sure, dear.' Jean's timekeeping was always a little hazy; a true hourly-paid conspirator.

'Please do try to remember.'

My frantic tone seemed to drive her backwards. 'I was late from Mrs Hamilton's today, on account of her delivery, you see.' A whisper, very fast, as if I might scold her; her pale face working hard. 'I got here about three, I think. Is everything –' she gulped at me like a goldfish out of water '– is everything all right, dear?'

'Have you answered the phone at all? Are there any messages?'

'No, dear. Well, actually,' nervously she paused for thought, 'actually, I did hear your voice on the machine, dear, when I was coming in. No one else, though, I don't think. Not since I got here anyway.'

My chest contracted painfully. I scrabbled in the drawer for my spare inhaler, fingers curling round it gratefully like a drowning man's. I breathed the spray in, and then very carefully I replaced the lid. With a huge effort to keep my voice from trembling, I tried to explain.

'I'm just a bit worried because I got separated from Mr Finnegan and the baby at the gallery, where we've just been, you see, and I'm not sure – well, it's just –'

25

oh God, it hurt me to admit it '– I just don't know where they are right now, that's all.'

That's all.

'Oh dear. Oh well, I'm sure they'll be back soon, won't they?' She looked at me with hope.

I ignored the doubting inner voice; I said quickly, 'Yes. Yes, of course they'll be home soon.' She was still waiting. 'I'm going to make a few calls now, see if I can track them down.'

'I'll get on then, shall I, dear?'

Her heels tapped busily away as I searched through the junk on the kitchen table for my address book. Then I sensed a shadow in the hall. My head snapped up.

'You could try ringing his office, Mrs Finnegan. Do you think – perhaps he needed to pop in there for something?'

'Yes, good idea, Jean. I'll do that.'

She smiled proudly, and tapped off again.

So I sat rigid as a tent-peg at the table and dialled Pauline's direct line. She'd know where he was, surely, if anyone would? Leaden with exhaustion, I laid my head down, closed my eyes for just a second as I listened to the ring.

'Pauline Gosforth is out of the office. If you need to reach Mickey Finnegan, please call Jenny Brown on extension four six five seven.'

Fuck! I redialled. Three rings in, friendly Jenny answered, thank God. She offered to check Mickey's diary.

'You know, I've got a feeling he did have a meeting

this afternoon. I was a bit surprised actually when he said he wasn't coming in.' She was enthusiastic. Did she feel complicit in something now, helping the boss's wife? 'Hang on, can you?'

I waited, stared unseeing at the folder of negatives Mickey had chucked on the table late last night when we'd got home. '*Idyllic Ideals, Romantic Retreats*' the italics boasted, all swirly typed and grand. I clicked a pen between my teeth, up, down, up, down, up…

An eager Jenny was back on the line. 'Yes, I thought so. Four p.m. drinks at one the Aldwych with Martin Goldsmith from Genesis. It's a massive new account. Mickey must have forgotten when he took his day off.'

For a moment, the relief rendered me speechless.

'Hello – Mrs Finnegan? Are you still –'

'Sorry. Yes.' Slowly my brain kicked back in. 'Thanks so much, Jenny. How stupid of me. I knew it'd be some-thing like that. He's just – he's so useless at recharging his phone, it must have run out again.' I took a deep breath. 'I just panicked when I couldn't reach him.'

'No problem. He's always a bit all over the shop when Pauline's away, isn't he?' She giggled shyly, as if she'd slightly overstepped the mark.

Yes, I agreed, of course he was. Lost without the indomitable Pauline, head of Mickey's stable of capable women.

I was about to ring 118 for the hotel's number when a car pulled up outside. I went running to the front window, skidding across Jean's sparkling hall. Mickey! It was Mickey – it must be him.

But it wasn't – it was just a delivery for next door.

27

Wine. Boxes and boxes of wine piling up beneath their sagging buddleia as they laughed and joked with the driver; as I prayed for my son's return.

The phone rang and my stomach swooped. Finally! I dashed back across the hall again. It would be him now, out of his meeting, slightly pissed, buoyant about sealing the deal on a huge new account. I could practically hear Louis chuckling down the line –

But it was Jenny. She sounded apprehensive.

'Um, Mrs Finnegan, I just checked Mickey's voice-mail. There was a message from Mr Goldsmith wondering where Mickey had got to. I've just spoken to him and he – well, he did wait apparently, for over an hour. Mickey never turned up.'

The most important thing was not to panic.

'Oh. Oh, right. Thanks, Jenny. Will you –' I forced myself to say it '– can you let me know if you hear anything else please?'

The most important thing was to remember to keep breathing.

'Of course, but I won't be here much longer. Shall I just quickly ring the hotel for you and double-check?'

'Please,' I accepted gratefully. 'I'd appreciate it. Thanks, Jenny.'

I hung up, paced the floor, chewing my lip. I checked the answer-phone. Nothing but me, and then the plumber, whose call I'd been awaiting for weeks.

Jenny didn't ring back.

I stood in the middle of the house, which had never felt so alien and cold, despite the day's raw heat, and wondered what the hell to do next. I must keep moving or terror would take over. I kept trying to think what I'd forgotten, replaying the scene over and over as Mickey had wandered off. What had he said that I hadn't caught? Louis's face cartwheeled through my head; how he must be crying for me now, his sooty lashes separating into damp little spikes, his bottom lip curling out to sob his little seagull cry. He wouldn't understand why I wasn't there, why I'd abandoned him, and would Mickey pick him up and comfort him like he should? Of course he would. Wouldn't he? Was Mickey even there – and then I stopped, clawing my palms with my own nails at the horror of my thoughts. Oh God, it was all my fault; I should never have let Louis leave my grasp.

So I did it. I did what I'd been holding back from ever since the start. I dialled 999, and when I got through I said, rather frantically, that I had missing people to report. Missing persons. My missing baby.

But of course the police thought I was ridiculous, though they were too polite to actually say it. An officer with a smoker's wheeze talked calmly to me; he seemed quite patient but I couldn't concentrate on what he said; I was imagining his stained teeth, I was jumping on ahead. When he said it was too early to call them missing, I asked quite tersely, 'How long do they have to be gone to call them missing then?' and he said something about twenty-four hours but as it was a baby they might make it earlier, but not this early, eh? And he tried to laugh with me, but why would I laugh? And so he coughed instead, and cleared his throat and said, 'Friends, family? Have you checked with them?'

A match flared down the line. I thought of my father-in-law, going slowly senile in a care home west of Belfast. Of Mickey's only sister Maeve, pregnant with her fifth child on the Californian coast. Tentatively, Stained Teeth went on.

'I should ask, madam, did you argue with your husband today?'

I wondered dimly whether he'd count almost-rows about chocolate cake and being fat, and so I replied, 'Yes, well sort of, well – actually no, not really. Well, not about anything serious, you know. Just a silly sort of row.'

And there was rather a fraught pause, in which I felt quite daft, and then the policeman said he'd take my details anyway, though he was sure it would all be fine, but just in case … and when I said goodbye, I knew the policeman thought I was just being neurotic, only I wasn't, you know, I really wasn't. It's just that deep in the pit of my stomach I felt that something was wrong, very wrong, and what I really wanted to do was scream, but I didn't, because that's not what we do. Not what I did then, of course.

Blindly I stumbled to the bathroom. I splashed my face with freezing water and then I leant back and shut my eyes. I needed to have a plan, that's what I needed.

I went up to Louis's room. Shaded by the old ash tree behind the house, it was cool in there, very cool and silent. I felt a sudden urge to lie on the floor, prostrate myself beneath the dangling star mobile, but I pushed the impulse down. Instead I walked across the big white rug with all the blue giraffes on, and walked up to Louis's cot. And though I could see he wasn't there, though I knew he couldn't be there, I stood for a minute looking down. I held on to the cot bars very tight, and then I moved his soft bear to the end where I always laid his head. To where his head had left a little dent. I walked out very fast.

Outside Mickey's study I stood for a moment, feeling like a five-year-old awaiting her dad's approval; took one deep breath and pushed back the door.

Dust danced in the slatted light the blinds threw forth as the evening closed in outside, and the room smelt kind of weird. Of my husband, perhaps; a familiar, rather sensual smell. Like some kind of clumsy spy I rifled through the diary on his desk, turning the pages ever quicker – but hope faded fast. Today hadn't warranted an entry at all. I pulled down the huge Rolodex that lurked on the shelf like some great metal spider, next to Mickey's scotch. It made me realise suddenly how dry-mouthed I was; I looked quickly over my shoulder and then unscrewed the lid, took a swift gulp of the fiery liquid. It brought tears to my eyes – but I had another slug anyway. Fortified a little bit, one by one I began to call his friends. I rang everyone whose names I recognised, and then those I'd never heard of. The people I reached were most polite – polite and rather disconcerted. And of course no one could shed any light on Mickey's whereabouts, although, as Greg said with a great woof of a laugh, trust the old bugger to vanish without a trace! Probably down the boozer. I had another go at the scotch and resisted telling Greg what I really thought of him. The Mickey I knew never did 'boozers'.

Finally I rang my sister. I took the handset, kicked Mickey's door firmly shut behind me.

'Honestly, Jess, I'm quite sure he'll walk through that door any second now.'

Was there a trace of exasperation in her tone? 'Leigh, I haven't fed Louis since about two and it's nearly seven now. My boobs are about to explode, Mickey's phone's dead, I can't think where he'd be, and the police already think I'm insane. Yeah, I'm sure he will walk through the door soon, but if I don't do something in the meantime, I really will go stark raving mad.'

A voice behind her muttered; Gary, no doubt. She covered the receiver to muffle him. 'It's a bit early to start panicking, Jess.'

'I'm really trying not to, believe me. I just want the baby back here, that's all. I don't understand where they've gone.'

'Look,' her sigh was almost inaudible. 'Do you want me to come round and keep you company while you wait? I can if you want.'

I wished she sounded like she meant it. 'It's up to you,' I replied, 'but I wouldn't mind the company.'

'He's probably, I don't know. Gone for a drink with a mate.'

'What – with Louis? Why?'

'Oh come on, Jessica. You know what Mickey's like. I mean, it's usually you who's saying –' Her sentence hung heavy, open-ended in the air.

32

'What?' I hunted for hope in her words.

'You know. He likes to do his own thing, I thought.'

'Not like this, though. This is a bit odd, even for him. Isn't it?'

'I don't want to speak out of turn.' She was cool. She'd been cool for weeks.

'Please, Leigh. There isn't time for this now. Just say what you mean.'

'Yes, well, normally I would, Jessica. Only, since the other day when I said you'd lost your bounce a bit, I seem to remember that you told me –'

I nearly laughed. 'You made me sound like a shampoo commercial, that was all. Anyway, look, it's not important now, is it?' I was as level as I could manage. 'If the girls don't need you, would you mind – will you come round, just for a bit?' She said she'd try.

Alone in the kitchen's gathering gloom, I contemplated my sister's words. Perhaps she was right. Perhaps I was over-dramatising things. Oh God, I hoped so. I mean, I should have been used to Mickey's erratic behaviour by now. He hated being tied down, you know, liked to come and go as he pleased, that type of loner thing. I stared at the white wall opposite, where the huge picture of a four-month-old sleeping Louis hung, the photo Mickey had taken while I lay on the sofa in the nursery, knackered from the newness of it all, watching my feather-haired son sleep. And I looked at that photo and I remembered that I was happier then than I'd ever been. I remembered how I thought that after all the recent months of angst I was finally at peace.

Jean popped her wispy head round the door and said she was going now, and I started to look for some money when suddenly it came to me. Of course! Why the hell hadn't I thought of this before? I cursed myself for being so slow as I scrabbled on the table for the handset I'd just flung down, and I sliced my finger on some of Mickey's sketches that weren't filed, but ignored the dripping blood as frantically I dialled my own mobile phone. I pictured it flashing bright in the pushchair pocket where I'd left it, my phone with a little photo of a day-old Louis on the user screen.

And it rang and rang and I was praying, *Mickey, answer it, please answer it,* but it just kept ringing – and then suddenly, just as I was about to give up, to sink back down, somebody answered. Someone answered my phone. Whoever it was didn't speak, but I could hear them breathing, and somehow it didn't sound like Mickey, though how the hell I could tell, I didn't know. But someone was on the end of my phone, and so I said in a quick tight voice before I started screaming, I said,

'Hello, who is this? Can you hear me? Mickey –' but then, before I could say anything else, whoever it was hung up. They wouldn't talk to me. They just switched off my phone.

CHAPTER THREE

Leigh arrived as I was putting the phone down after talking to the police again. I watched the elephantine manoeuvres of her huge car as she tried to park and I thought of Mickey scoffing rudely at my sister, at her burly husband. What does she need that tractor for, he always said – just to do her shopping? Mall rat, Mickey called her, Bluewater rat.

Her perfect streaks swayed precisely up the path, and as I let her in I was trying not to gibber. I told her the police were coming over soon, they finally seemed to be taking notice, and she put an arm around me and suddenly I was crying; and I found I couldn't stop. I dissolved into tears so hot they scalded me because I was chilled to the very bone. And in the middle of all this horrible emotion, Maxine arrived home. She trod lightly into the room, as done-up as a Christmas tree, and randomly I thought I really must help her out sometime, teach her not to look quite so obvious.

Then I was thrust back into my hideous reality as I sensed how thrown the girl was by my tears. She looked

35

away again, as if she was embarrassed – only I'd never, not in the three months she'd been here – known her to be thrown by anything. Maxine was the kind of girl who would walk stark naked from bedroom to shower every day if she could get away with it, the kind of girl who didn't mind who got a jolly good eyeful. Early on she'd paid the price for her insouciance, though, reckoning without Mickey's foul morning temper: he'd finally bollocked her as I listened with some relief behind the bedroom door. He gave her short shrift indeed about her skimpy little towels – although apparently she'd just shrugged.

Leigh took Maxine into the other room as I attempted to pull myself together a bit. I got through a packet of tissues, and my eyes were all puffy and sore, but eventually my wheezing calmed. After a while they appeared in the doorway together, Maxine towering over Leigh, her shadow all lengthy down the hall.

'I'm sure Mr Finnegan, he will return soon, no?' she said. 'I just come back to get my purse, but – *si tu veux* – you want me to stay?' and her funny plasticine face almost trembled with the effort. And I saw her crooning to Louis in French, rocking him gently to and fro, so natural when I'd been so scared at first, crushed beneath the weighty terror of my new responsibility. I shuddered at my jealousy as she sang him old songs like 'Frère Jacques' and he beamed up at her; remembered painfully how my tummy had squirmed and I'd felt like such a failure. Now the guilt lacerated me, and I clenched my fists as all my petty jealousies came back to punish me. If Louis could just come home now,

Maxine could sing to him anytime she liked and I'd never ever feel envious again.

And then another car pulled up outside and beeped, once, and then again, and I rushed to quiet it because of the baby, and then I remembered the baby wasn't here, and I rammed my nails into my palm again, and then I thought perhaps it might be Mickey, so I threw the window open, but it wasn't, it was just Maxine's date. He beeped again, all arrogance, dark brows and silly phone headset as he tapped an impatient gold-bracelet rhythm against his shiny red car, and he wouldn't catch my eye though I was sure he saw me, but slicked his hair back in the mirror instead.

'Oh no, Maxine. Don't worry.' I sniffed hard, hating the fact she'd seen me cry. 'New bloke?' I said, too brightly. 'Nice motor. But whatever happened to the lovely Leo?' and Maxine flushed beneath her peroxide hair, and muttered something about him still being around. The fug of perfume that she left behind her probably belonged to me. With discomfort I remembered that sometimes – often, if I was honest – I'd felt left behind, by Mickey, by my friends, even by Maxine – jealous of their exciting, carefree lives, my freedom truly finished by motherhood. I was tied to Louis and the house. But someone else had Louis now – and I'd kill them for that tie.

Leigh got me a glass of water, and then she changed her mind and found some brandy instead, which I'd never normally drink – but now I downed it in one.

'You might want to sort that out, Jess,' she said rather

37

stiffly, and I realised that my poor over-full boobs had leaked all over my new T-shirt, staining it. What with my dirty skirt I was looking a right old state. Not that I cared.

'Go and get changed. You'll feel better. I'll hold the fort,' she said, but I shook my head.

'I can't. The police –' I mumbled. But she prodded me upstairs anyway and stuck me in the shower, where I leant against the tiles and sobbed and sobbed, watching the blue-white milk dribble from my swollen bosom. I looked over at the framed sketch of Louis I'd only hung the other day – a sketch I was quite proud of for once – and I felt like I was unravelling, like one of Louis's teddy bears all my stuffing was coming out and I was deflating in a little limp pile, and suddenly I wanted to howl, like I'd been ripped apart.

I cried till I simply didn't know what to do with myself any more. The only thing in the whole wide world I wanted now was to hold my baby, and I'd never want for anything again, never let him go again, never take my eyes from him, never curse the sleepless nights – if he could just come home now. I fought the feeling that this was all my fault, my just deserts for those first bad days.

And then just when I felt like I couldn't cry any more, Leigh came in. And I didn't mind, even though we'd never been the type to wander nude in front of one another, because I guessed the police had finally come. I looked at her face and suddenly I was scared, but before I could speak, she said in a gruff voice,

'Put something on and come downstairs. Quickly,'

and the urgency of her tone shot through me like a
red-hot poker in my guts, and before she could go on
I leapt out of the shower and grabbed her arm. I must
have pulled the skin too tight because she winced and
I said, 'What? Tell me now, Leigh – what is it?' and she
said, still in that funny voice, 'They've found Mickey.'
And I felt a kind of relief, just for a second, but then
I said,

'Mickey? What about Louis? Where's my baby?' and
she couldn't look at me, she wouldn't look at me; she
just handed me my dressing-gown and then turned
away and went towards the door. And whether it was
the brandy meeting emptiness and Mickey's scotch, or
me moving too fast, or just the pure, pure horrid shock
– but I passed out – went down like a tree, apparently.
For a while I knew nothing, which, as it turned out
later, was bliss.

CHAPTER FOUR

Louis was crying; I could hear him. He was crying quietly; still, I shouldn't be so lazy. I must get out of bed and see to him. But something pressed me into the bed. I struggled hard against it.

Awake. It was dark outside, and my head was throbbing badly. Louis wasn't here; I was mistaken. The cries I heard weren't Louis's cries at all; they were the gentle coos of pigeons hiding in the eaves. A deep pain clamped my body, squeezed the air slowly from my gasping lungs.

Gradually, Leigh came into focus. She was gazing out the window, the wide-open window, the curtain ruffling gently in the lazy breeze. A woman I'd never seen before sat near my bed. It seemed like they were both waiting. I looked away, listened to the light summer rain, rain that carried smells of dust and the honeysuckle that clambered up the sill, spindly fingers beseeching. I lingered in those last seconds of not knowing.

*

Only once before in my whole life had I almost fainted. Only once. It was just after I'd had Louis, and we were leaving hospital for the first time, me clutching this child they insisted was mine, who I had to care for. I held him like a piece of precious crockery, terrified I'd drop him. God, Mickey looked so proud as he shepherded us out, but I – well, I was still stunned. Shell-shocked by the dramatic turn my life had taken in the labour ward, my baby coming four weeks early but thankfully all right. Finally privy to the terrifying secret all child-bearing women know and hide; the mothers' club I'd lingered outside anxiously as I grew ever bigger, peering in, wishing fervently for someone to guide me in and tell me I could do it. (Leigh was no good – she'd elected Caesareans even before celebrity culture made it cool. And my mum – well, she was my mum. No practical use at all.)

As we reached the car, I staggered, my legs unexpectedly fragile from lack of use, a little like a foal's. With some sixth sense, Mickey felt I was going to fall; he caught me as I stumbled, wrapped his arms around his son and me before we hit the ground. In silence we stood there for a moment, this new three, and Mickey held us tenderly. I was bemused by this new concern, quite frankly – it was so un-Mickey like. Then he took the baby from me and whisked me back inside. This time he carried Louis, clamped tightly to his chest. And I was happy that he took him.

Shock, the midwives said. Nothing to worry about. A bit of blood loss; a traumatic birth; a baby that came too early, scaring us all badly for a short while. I stared

41

at them, uncomprehending. A trauma I worried might do me in for good.

Until then, before this, I'd always thought fainting was a kind of glamorous thing to do – and even Shirl, my best mate, couldn't call me that. I might be small in stature, but I was tough. Skinny, languid girls with translucent skin, like old-fashioned TB victims, you know the type – they were the ones who should collapse. Not me. Much as I might have fancied being languid, I was the kind to make a cup of sweet tea, to just get on, you know. I'd always had to, I'd never had a choice. Only now Louis was gone I could be tough as you like, but all the tea in China wouldn't heal this massive hurt.

I sat bolt upright and I asked – though I was scared to ever hear the answer – I rapped out, 'Where's Louis? Tell me where he is, please,' and the police lady came over all concerned but practical, just like they must get trained to be. She moved nearer, and she took my hand, but I shook her off. I was already quite sick of strangers' sympathy.

'For God's sake, just tell me,' I persisted, and nausea washed over me.

I have always thought how easy and yet how hard it must be to be the official bearer of bad news – you know, coppers, doctors, that type of person. The relentless certainty that you convey despair; the constant devastation of once-happy lives. Easy because you give, and, God forbid, you don't receive. Forever thankful it's not you, do you grow hardened by leaving grief behind, until you learn to sleep sound again at night?

This mop-headed girl didn't look like she was yet used to doling out distress. I stared at a tiny vein that curled blue beside her eye. She started to talk, and still I studied her thin shiny skin, like it could block out all my pain.

'We don't know, Mrs Finnegan. We're not sure where Louis is right now.' She tried to take my hand again. 'Your husband was taken to St Thomas' Hospital about an hour ago. I'm afraid he's been quite badly beaten; he's still unconscious. He's being checked for the severity of his injuries, but the good news is he's stable at the moment.'

Her gentle touch felt gritty on my skin. Quietly, Leigh moved to me, handed me some kind of drink.

'But he was found alone.' She took a breath. 'I know how hard this is, Mrs Finnegan, but you need to try and keep calm. I'm afraid we do now have to say your son is missing. Officially missing, for now, at least.'

Missing. My son was missing. Louis – his solid little weight, his chubby wrists where the fat folded over itself. His dark fluffy head, his guffaw when you tickled him, his double chin when he fell asleep sitting upright in his chair. Louis was missing. Mickey was badly hurt. The policewoman started to talk about search-parties and perhaps a helicopter; I watched her mouth open and close as I sat stock-still; still except for the glass I twisted in my hands. Simply paralysed by fear.

Suddenly Leigh screamed. 'Christ, Jess, what have you done?'

Dully, I looked down. My hand was streaming blood; the glass cracked clean in two. This morning I'd lain

43

here, first in Mickey's arms, then cuddling my Louis, wishing lazily for more sleep. Now there was no baby. No baby anywhere; just bright red streaming blood.

Everything went slow. Leigh fetched me plasters while I got dressed, very tentatively, as if I had a migraine, like I might shatter into a thousand pieces if I moved suddenly. Then I went downstairs with the police-woman, who was called Deb, and got into the patrol car, and I could feel all the neighbours having a good old gawp, and for a minute it took me back to my lost childhood. It just wasn't the kind of street where people got taken away in police cars, if you know what I mean. I sat in the back and Deb's colleague turned to try to comfort me but I ignored him because nothing could comfort me now, not ever, not until I got my Louis back.

Leigh tapped on the window and I could see that she was trying not to cry herself.

'Please, Jessie, try not to worry too much, babe,' she said, but we both knew her words were futile. She took my hand, my sore and icy hand, and held it for a minute. Then she sniffed, and pushed her hair back hard, regaining control; said she'd follow in her own car, she'd lock up and meet me at the hospital. I don't think I even answered her. I just stared ahead as I was driven through the darkening summer streets, back the way I came this afternoon, back when I still had some hope. Back through dirty London town I went, and, all the time I travelled, I wanted never to arrive.

CHAPTER FIVE

Pluck a single hair from your head and you might notice that it twangs, reverberating deep inside your brain. Through the dim neon-lit corridors of the hospital I followed a uniformed back and I felt like I was that little hair, like someone was pulling me so tight I might just go snap at any moment. And as I walked, I ducked from the images the hospital-smells hurled at me; I was ducking and weaving from memories of my dad, so that by the time we reached Intensive Care and Deb rang the entry-bell, I was shifting from foot to foot like some prize boxer before the big fight.

It was impossible for me to imagine Mickey in any vulnerable state. It wasn't part of the equation. Outside the locked door, Deb smiled reassuringly, but I was terrified of going in. It wasn't a rational terror, like you might expect; it wasn't about the extent of Mickey's injuries, or the pain he might be in. It was, if truth be told, more a fear of seeing him inert, exposed. Unable. Mickey was never *unable* to do anything. He strode through life as if movement and decision were his life-force. It was what I'd come to accept in the short time we'd been together. It was what swept me along, what took me unawares from the moment we first met.

A nurse eventually opened the door and Deb explained who we were. She looked exhausted, this nurse, but still her almond eyes were all compassion as she ushered us in. In the dim light beyond the door everything was deathly quiet. Everything was deathly.

'I'm afraid he's still unconscious, but all his vital signs are good,' the nurse said quietly. Then, 'Come,' and she laid a gentle hand on my arm. She was the first person whose touch I didn't flinch from today.

Outside a small room stood another policeman; he nodded gravely as we passed and I was yet more disturbed. The nurse's shoes squeaked softly in the silence.

And through the door there was my husband, my elegant husband, and he looked just like he was sleeping – except he had all sorts of tubes sticking out of him.

'Just a precaution,' the nurse said, following my gaze to the machine that seemed to breathe for him, and I stopped at the foot of the bed and just stared. Dark hair swept back from his face, Mickey was as pale as the moon. One eye was horribly bruised, sealed entirely shut; down the other cheek a slash had been lovingly stitched. It was the shape of a big tick – Nike would love him, I thought disjointedly. He was bare to the waist, Christ-like, his sore arms splayed out as far as the narrow bed allowed. His chest was covered in bruises. In fact, except for the machinery, he looked like some old oil painting that he'd hate and I would probably love, and I stifled a hysterical laugh that bubbled up inside.

'He may be able to hear you, Mrs Finnegan,' the nurse said, gently propelling me forward. 'It's a good idea to talk to him, let him know you're here.' I just gawped at her. Deb muttered something about a minute on my own, and the nurse said she'd page Mickey's consultant. Together they squeaked back across the shiny linoleum, and I strained to catch their muffled whispers in the corridor and wished I wasn't here. I wished I was out there, whispering with them.

Alone, I felt horribly uneasy – as if I was being watched. Was Mickey watching me? Eventually I forced myself nearer the bed, and very carefully I placed my hand on Mickey's pyjama-clad leg. Gingerly, like his leg might snap from any pressure.

'You'd have a fit if you saw what they've got you in,' I said. I started to laugh, which quickly turned into a wheeze, and then I stepped closer still and said, right into his shut-down face, I demanded,

'Mickey, where's Louis? You've got to wake up, cos Louis is gone. What did you do with him, Mickey?' and I heard my voice go sharp and shrill, and I had a sudden urge to pummel him, but before I could Deb was back beside me, and she held my arms down and I wasn't laughing any more. Tears rolled down my cheeks and my nose was running, streaming snot, but actually I wasn't going to cry, I was sick of tears, I was made of sterner stuff. Wasn't I? I pulled away from Deb.

47

'I'm fine,' I said. 'Thank you. Honestly, I'm fine.' But I caught the surreptitious glance she gave the nurse that said *Of course you are not fine.*

Sister Kwame made me tea so sweet the spoon practically stood up in all the sugar, and after she'd heard my singing chest, she found me an inhaler.

'He will be all right. You must have faith,' she said in her slow African lilt. I did feel a little calmer; there was a quiet dignity in her movements that somehow reassured me.

'I wish I did,' I said, 'but everything's so wrong.'

Before she could reply, Mickey's consultant bustled into the room. Small and red-cheeked, he reminded me a bit of a cartoon Noddy. The scans showed no apparent brain injuries, he said; it should just be a matter of time before Mickey woke. Any real danger now would be from undetected internal bleeding – unlikely at this point, they thought.

'He might even just be sleeping now,' he said, beady little eyes flicking to see if I believed him. 'But I'm afraid he must have taken quite a kicking.' Lovingly, he stroked his beard, contemplating something on a chart he'd plucked from the wall. 'A rib or two are broken, but we're pretty satisfied now that most of his injuries are fairly superficial.'

I winced at the thought of Mickey on the ground, at the idea of Louis watching his father being beaten. Bile rose in my throat.

'I think – sorry, could I sit down please.'

The doctor rattled on oblivious as Sister Kwame

fetched me a chair. 'Hopefully by tomorrow he'll have come round. I know the police need some info from the poor chap.'

The sister murmured something as she took the chart from him. He peered at me like I was an exotic specimen; his small cheeks as hard as apples. 'And you, are you all right? In shock, of course.'

Without waiting for a response he wrote out a prescription. 'Sister Kwame can raid the cupboard,' he winked conspiratorially. 'Any questions, just sing.' He tucked his pen behind a strangely small ear. Then he was gone.

Soon after that Leigh arrived with Gary in tow, and then Deb's detective inspector turned up to take me home. Sister Kwame gave me a printout on concussion, and some pills to keep me calm.

'I don't want them, really. Thank you.' I shook my head. I rarely took even an aspirin. I'd seen the power of pills over my own mother.

'Maybe it is best to have them just in case. Only take them if you really need them, yes?' Leigh pocketed them on my behalf.

There was some discussion about me staying in case Mickey came round, but I really couldn't stand the thought. I needed to get home. What if someone brought Louis back? The policeman, whose name I learned was DI Silver, said he'd drive me back home so we could talk; then Leigh complicated things by kicking up such a fuss about me being alone that in the end they suggested she come too.

49

'Stay at ours. That's the best idea, isn't it, Gaz?' She was decided, looking to her husband for his usual affirmation.

I shook my head again. 'No.'

'No?' She was surprised. 'Why not?'

'Just because, Leigh.' I was so weary now – too weary to fight with her.

'But – we'll look after you. You need to be with family.'

Family. My family had been suddenly disbanded. I was finally relaxing into having one of my own, a proper one, after all these years – and it was all gone. Swept away in a second. I turned away. 'I'm going home, and actually I'd like to go right now, if that's okay.'

DI Silver drained the Diet Coke he'd just clunked from the machine.

'I'd say that was fair enough,' he agreed mildly, and Leigh glowered at him. In the end Gary agreed to go back to the girls, and Leigh would accompany me. I slipped back into Mickey's room a final time. Staring at him, I couldn't shake the Christ-like image from my mind. So what did that make me, standing helpless at his feet?

'Please wake up, Mickey.' He didn't stir. 'I'm really scared. I don't know what to do,' I whispered, and then I kissed his hand quickly, his long-fingered hand which lay so frighteningly still. There were grazes on his knuckles.

'I love you,' I whispered, quieter still. Allowed to say in crisis what I never dared to in real life, what I'd hoped to hear every day at the beginning, until eventually he'd whispered it once into my hair in the still-ness of the night, just before I had Louis, so quietly I'd thought I might have been dreaming. It had been enough – for a while.

When I went back out, Leigh and Gary were muttering; they jumped apart like guilty teenagers. Not good at being separated, those two.

'Thanks for coming, Gaz,' I managed, and he shook his big blunt head at me.

'Don't be stupid, darling,' he muttered, and awkwardly he hugged me, following with a peck that ended in a painful clash of cheekbones. How poorly we all did affection.

'So, shall we?' Silver gently cleared his throat. He looked a little like his name. Salt-and-pepper hair and a suit that looked suspiciously expensive for a copper. Gum in his long, straight-lipped mouth; slightly hooded eyes.

'The car's this way, Mrs Finnegan, Mrs –?' He looked quizzically at Leigh.

'Mrs Hopkins,' she said, with a toss of hair.

In silence we waited for the lift, a gloomy trio, when I had a sudden thought. I sped back down the corridor to the ICU, ignoring the voices protesting behind me. This time Sister Kwame answered the door immedi-ately. She smiled enquiringly.

'You forgot something?'

'No,' I was breathless already. 'It was just – I just wondered,' I stuttered, 'what did Mickey – did my husband have anything with him when he came in?' She held me softly in her direct gaze.

51

'I mean, like a – a bag, or something. Anything really.' I trailed off uselessly. What was I hoping for?

'Nothing, my love, I don't think,' she said. 'He had nothing but the clothes he stood up in, as far as I'm aware. The police dealt with all that, you know.'

'Oh.' I felt a crushing disappointment. 'Oh well. Thanks.' I staggered a little as exhaustion snatched greedily at me. 'I just – you know. I just wondered. See you later.' As I turned back towards the lift, DI Silver appeared noiselessly at my side.

'Wait,' the nurse called softly, 'actually, there was one thing. I meant to give it to the police earlier. I'll get it.' She disappeared inside.

'All right?' Silver asked, and I detected a northern burr. I nodded stiffly, attempted a wan smile but my face had frozen. Sister Kwame reappeared. She handed me a see-through bag, which held a padded brown envelope, like the ones Mickey used at work for disks and negatives. I opened it with trembling fingers, shook the contents out. A passport slid into my hand.

CHAPTER SIX

Blindly, I clutched it, but DI Silver quickly eased it from my grasp.

'I'll need that, Mrs Finnegan,' he said smoothly. 'Fingerprints, you know, all that jazz.'

'Please,' I said, 'I just want to know whose it is. I don't understand why –'

He took pity on me; flicked open the back cover. Mickey, younger, scowling, stared out.

'Cheerful chap, your husband?' Silver said, but it wasn't a real question. I walked away from him, down the corridor, away from my unconscious husband. Away from my only link to Louis.

When I'd first met Mickey, he didn't smile for weeks. In fact, we hadn't really met at all; having just started my part-time foundation at St Martin's College of Art, his assistant Pauline hired me as a graphics junior. I knew it was my big chance – years behind my peers, I was ready to do anything to prove myself. Clamped to my computer, I watched Mickey come and go when he was in the office, although he never deigned to say hello. I'd watch him lounging behind the glass divide the few times he was actually there, hand-stitched shoes up on the desk, anxious minions darting in and out as he pushed his dark hair back distractedly and perused their work without a word. I watched him share his enthusiasms with his underlings, although his frustrations were often obvious. Most of all, I watched the girls in the office preen and flirt with him, always dressed best on the days he was expected in. He seldom responded to their wiles, but when he did, when he flashed a quick rare smile, his face was truly illuminated and, reluctantly, I saw what they saw – although I fought it. The only person he ever looked relaxed with was the sassy Pauline. He'd laugh with her like no one else and, bizarrely, his casual arm around her once made me feel quite jealous.

Finally, one afternoon I was called in to show Mickey some proofs I was working on. Ridiculous I knew, but my hands were shaking as I picked up my file. I'd worked so bloody hard for this; I couldn't bear to blow it. I was terrified of Mickey; that he'd discover I was a fake; that he'd see the truth and turf me out.

When I knocked, Mickey was on the phone; he beckoned me in and I hovered near the door. Waiting for his attention, I absorbed the room. No photos, no personal paraphernalia, just one exquisite orchid and what looked like a Tracey Emin original on the wall. He hung up without saying goodbye. How rude, I thought, but secretly I was impressed. It was just like they used to do in *Dallas* when I was small.

'I like her stuff.' I pointed at the picture.

'Do you?' Mickey was browsing through the proofs I'd handed him; he didn't bother to look up.

'She's a bit of a head-case, though, isn't she?'

'Is she now?'

'I think that's probably what gives her art its – you know. Its verve.'

'Is that right?' He did look up this time. He looked up and grinned right at me. Oh God. He was even better looking close-up. I rattled on. 'I like her spirit. Even though she always seems a little – damaged.'

I thought I caught a look, an almost wistful look, flash across his face. 'That's not necessarily such a bad thing, is it? Being damaged.'

I looked at him and he looked straight back. And for a second, it was very strange – for a split second it was like peering in a mirror. I felt a sudden blaze of recognition of something hidden in those dark eyes. And there was something else about him now, something I couldn't quite pinpoint right then. For a minute he seemed like he might relax his guard. I dragged my gaze back to the picture.

'Anyway, I wish I could draw like her.'

'Who says you can't?'

'Oh, I wish.'

'Do you not think she's a little – overrated?'

'If she's overrated, why would you have her work on your wall?'

'As an investment, mainly.'

But he was lying now, I knew. Masking himself. 'That's a bit depressing, isn't it? You should have art there because you love it, I think.' I was enthusiastic. 'Or because it allows you to escape, or stirs up something – you know, some passion. Some big emotion.'

'Is that right?' He was staring at me now. I had the uneasy feeling I wasn't meant to answer back. 'Well, perhaps I hate it then.'

'Do you?'

'No. But you might be happier if I did, mightn't you?'

I smiled nervously. He looked down at my work again. 'You know, these aren't bad –'

There was a pause. I realised he didn't know my name.

'Jessica. Most people call me Jess, though.'

'Jessica. In fact, these are very good. You've really understood the brief.'

I tried to hide my blushes; I was secretly ecstatic. 'Thank you.'

His phone rang. Answering it, he swung his leather chair around until he had his back to me. I waited for a minute then I realised that, apparently, the meeting was over. I gathered up my proofs and left; I was angry for the rest of the week. Meanwhile, he ignored me for the rest of the week, although one afternoon I looked up from the paste-up I'd been concentrating on, my tongue between my teeth, my tangled curls skewered with a lone pencil, and found his eyes burning into me through the glass divide. He smiled a very slow smile and turned away.

I went out most nights and drank too much with my new mates from St Martin's, finally living part of the dream I thought I'd been denied, crawling home to my bedsit alone and happy.

One evening I stayed late at work to finish a job that I'd been struggling with. An unseasonably warm spring was creeping towards summer and the office air-conditioning was on the blink. I worked on until I found myself practically expiring with heat, and then I stripped to the old petticoat beneath my jersey dress. Through the open window I could hear the bustle of a Soho evening: sirens wailing, chatter and catcalls, laughter and lovers arguing, cars and running feet and the jingle of rickshaw bells. I was so wrapped up in my work that when the door opened suddenly, it made me jump. Mickey, quiet as a cat, padded across the room, champagne in hand, a couple of major Japanese clients in tow, set to close a deal in his office.

'Sorry,' I stuttered, jumping down from my stool. I kicked the art-school project I'd been about to start work on as far under my desk as I could manage.

'Jessica.' He stared at my petticoat, then glanced at his clients. Very quietly he said, 'That's hardly appropriate for the office, is it now?'

Mortified, I scrabbled for my dress as the Japanese woman bowed her head towards me, sublimely elegant in midnight-blue; her short, rather haughty male colleague ignoring me entirely. I nodded back, horribly conscious of my unmade-up shiny face, my scraped-back hair; and I dived into the loo to change. When I came back, Mickey had shut his office door, and I felt a twinge of something, but I soon lost myself in my work again, looking up only to see him pour the woman a drink. Soon after that, I slipped out and home.

The next morning I expected a bollocking, but instead I found an envelope propped against my computer. An invitation for a Tracey Emin private viewing in Cork Street that night, a Post-it note attached.

'I'll meet you there at seven. Dress for dinner. Or wear your petticoat. Your choice. M.'

I went out for a coffee on my own, my hands shoved deep in my pockets while I paced the buzzing streets around the office. I didn't really do relationships. I had such a bad template, you see. And dallying with the boss: textbook mistake, surely? Or perhaps he just wanted to discuss art… Wandering up and down Broadwick Street, I ate some early strawberries that weren't quite ripe and avoided glancing at the saucy underwear in the window of Agent Provocateur. Avoided thinking about Mickey's slow smile the other day. What would someone like him see in me? We were worlds apart.

But when I went back into the office, against my better judgement, I pleaded a headache to Pauline. Was it my imagination, or did she have a knowing look about her? At home I lay on the sofa in front of *Richard and Judy*; I decided not to go. I had a neat vodka. Then I had one with ice. And then I dressed for dinner as best as I could in the ten minutes I'd left myself; anxious I wouldn't get there in time, anxious that I couldn't afford the kind of glamour Mickey was obviously used to. Anxious I was imagining a situation that didn't exist.

When I eventually arrived in an extravagant and

vodka-fuelled black cab, Mickey was slouched languidly against the wall outside. It was much chillier than yesterday, and I shivered in the breeze.

'Hi,' I said shyly. 'Sorry I'm a bit late.'

'Hi,' he said calmly, kissing my cheek and leading me inside. 'I like your plaits. And that's a nice coat. Very Anna Karenina. Though I think I preferred the petticoat. There was something very disturbing about you in it.'

'Really?' My insides felt all funny. I didn't tell Mickey I'd nicked that petticoat from my mum many years ago. I accepted the wine glass a waitress offered me.

'You looked about sixteen.'

'Oh. You like sixteen-year-olds then?' I looked up at him from below my fringe.

He smiled – not quite a cruel smile; more the smile of someone used to getting his own way. Not a very nice smile. 'That's not what I meant.'

'What did you mean?'

'You know, Jessica...' I liked the way he said my name, the slow drawl of it. I found myself holding my breath.

'What?'

'There's something about you I can't put my finger on.'

I looked at his long, thin fingers wrapped round his glass. The vodka was singing in my blood. 'How do you know?'

'How do I know what?'

'How do you know that you can't put your finger on it?' I prayed he couldn't hear my teeth chattering as adrenaline coursed round my body.

He laughed. 'You remind me of myself, I think that's what it is.'

'In what way's that then? Mean and moody?' I looked down coolly at my nails, but I didn't feel the least bit cool inside. I was sure I'd stepped too far this time; come Monday, I'd be collecting my cards. But he just laughed again.

'Sure, I'm not sure. Appearances are deceptive, they say. You're deceptive, that's what I think. You look like you need looking after, but – well –'

'Well, what?' I said, taking a long sip of the cold white wine to hide my nerves.

'I reckon you're one of life's survivors.'

I looked him square in the eye. 'Yes, well. I tend to generally survive.'

'And you're so different –'

'Mickey Finnegan, you old devil,' a red-faced fat man slapped him on the back. 'And who's this gorgeous young thing?'

I nearly choked on my drink but Mickey didn't turn a hair. Nor did he bother to introduce me.

'Charles. Back from New York already?' I half-listened as Mickey chatted to the art dealer for a while; looked around for the waitress for a refill. One of Emin's pictures on the wall behind them disturbed me, a sketch of a naked young girl. There was something very innocent about her, I thought, despite her nudity. Something sad. I peered closer; it was called *If I could just go back and start again*. Finally the fat man wandered off in search of further sustenance that he really didn't need, and Mickey turned back to me. I looked up at him flirtatiously.

'What were you saying? I'm so – different?'

A cloud crossed his face. 'Forget it.'

My own foolishness walloped me in the gut; I'd read things wrong. Quickly I changed the subject. 'Don't you think that print's a bit – tragic?'

I pointed behind him to the picture of the girl. He swung to look at it. 'Why?'

'I'm not sure really. It makes me think of my childhood for some reason.' God. I *must* have had too much to drink. But I caught that look again; the one I'd glimpsed in the office earlier that week. The one I'd recognised – and I realised what it was now. Sadness suddenly unveiled.

'Was your childhood not much fun then, Jessica?'

I shrugged. 'It had its moments.'

He reached over and stroked my naked earlobe. I caught my breath again. How could that little touch trigger the feelings that followed next? We wandered round the Emin together but I couldn't concentrate any more. I felt Mickey's presence at my side like a literal force of life, the energy emanating from him, despite his mood being darker than before. I saw something of me in him; some vulnerability he chose to hide – most of the time.

And afterwards we didn't even make it as far as the restaurant that he'd booked. The minute the taxi door closed behind us, Mickey pulled me towards him – and I didn't resist. I wanted him so badly now that I could barely think. I rarely relinquished my control to anyone – but this man, this man was very different. Slowly, very slowly, he unbuttoned the long coat that I'd done

61

up so tight. This time it was desire I shivered with.

'I've been wondering what's under here all night,' he murmured.

Under here was that petticoat – and nothing else at all. He ran his hands along my naked collarbone; I bit down on my lip.

'God,' Mickey groaned quietly. 'There's something about you, little Jessica. Something I want very badly.'

Then he told the driver to take us to the best hotel in town – his choice, Mickey said carelessly, and then he turned to me intently. He traced my mouth – my eager, swollen mouth – with his forefinger until I caught it between my teeth and sucked it gently. Mickey slid the other hand under my coat, across the silk, stroking the smooth flesh between my shaking legs. And then finally, just when I felt like I'd dissolve with pure anticipation, he pulled me to him again by my wildly escaping and most-deliberately-provocative plaits and kissed me hard, his teeth grazing my lips, and I kissed him back with an abandon I was glad to feel. I forgot the blackness of his earlier mood and yielded to the pleasure, prover-bial putty in the hands that slid hot and hard over the sliding silk of the petticoat, tracking my body through the thin material. I didn't even worry about the driver in front. I would have done it right there on the back seat, right there and then if he'd wanted to. I'd never felt like this before; completely floored by my own lust, so wanton and destroyed by it. Never in my whole life.

*

I didn't speak on the way to Silver's car, and when we got there I let Leigh go in the front though I knew the policeman wanted to talk to me. I just couldn't concentrate on questions; my head was whirring with possibilities. Mickey travelled a lot with work, but I couldn't think now if he had a trip coming up. Why the hell would he have his passport on him otherwise? My mind was a huge black hole churning the information round and round.

The big car purred effortlessly onto the deserted road. Anyone with any sense was tucked up safe in bed, safe from this sticky night. We circled the concrete monstrosity that crowned Westminster Bridge, crossed the top of Waterloo, heading south again. Two young girls stepped suddenly from the darkness onto a crossing, and DI Silver stamped on the brakes. We all lurched forwards as the teenagers giggled at their own daring, obviously drunk, bare midriffs milky under the fluorescent streetlights, navel rings a-glimmer. The policeman's jaw set.

'Bloody stupid,' he muttered. I leant my sore head on the cold glass of the window and listened to the crackles on the police radio. My swollen bosom throbbed agonisingly. In the front, DI Silver cleared his throat perfunctorily.

'Mrs Finnegan, I know you're tired, but you'll appreciate I must ask some questions. I need to take a statement from you when I get you home.' He caught my eye in the mirror, and held it. In the gloom his eyes were almost black. 'Until your husband regains consciousness, you're our only connection with your son.'

Levelly I held his gaze. I knew he was right, and I

was about to agree when suddenly the huge chimneys of the Tate loomed over to my left.

'Stop!' I shouted, and he slammed on the brakes again.

'For Christ's sake!' Leigh swore, pushing herself back from the dashboard. 'It's like the bloody Dodgems in here.'

'I need to get out,' I said, fumbling for the handle.

'Are you feeling ill?' she asked.

I shook my head impatiently. 'No. I just need to go there now.'

'Where?'

'Back to the Tate. I never should have left.'

'Jess, don't be silly. It's shut now,' Leigh said, turning in her seat.

'Not *into* the Tate. To the river. To where they found Mickey. Did they find him here?' I realised I didn't know. 'I need to make sure Louis is not – I mean, what if he's still here?'

'Jess, wait! I'll come with you,' but I was already opening the car door, scrambling out, running across the road. Leigh's voice faded quickly as a lone motorcycle whizzed past me, so close I felt the wind against my cheek, so near I heard the driver's curse. But I was infallible. I was running, back to where I'd come from today, back to where I'd last seen my son. Of course – this was right! Why had I ever left? I was mad; I should have stayed. I could have found him. I ignored the voices behind me, the shouts. I ran and ran, past the shuttered coffee stand, through the high, pruned hedges, until suddenly I hit the river.

I stopped for a second. I breathed in the dark night air. The city on the other bank looked magnificent, lit up like a great fairground in the sky. And somewhere here was Louis. Somewhere near –

I felt an arm go round me, a quiet, calm voice speak in my ear, a northern drawl. I realised I was shaking.

'Mrs Finnegan, I can assure you that our teams are out looking. They're scouring every corner of the city. There's no sign of Louis here, you know. And actually your husband was found some way away.' He turned me round to face him but I wouldn't meet his eye.

'We should go now, don't you think?' Gently he persisted. 'You're going to make yourself ill and you'll be no good to anyone. Let me take you home.'

I doubled over. I couldn't stand. I couldn't stand it. I'd never felt so helpless in my life. I was racked with pain in every little crevice, every part of me cried out for my only child. So this was mother love. It hurt like fucking hell.

'Please,' I begged, and I heard my voice crack hoarsely. 'Please, just let me look. Just for five minutes,' and he looked at me, and he must have sensed my desperation, because he did. He held my arm and we walked up and down and round and round for a bit, and I could feel him trying not to march me. And I could see that it was all tidy, that there was no baby here. My baby wasn't here.

But I couldn't bear to leave. I slunk out of his grasp and sunk down on the ground and I lay my head on the tarmac still warm from the day's sun. Tears slid down my face without sound. I put my hands flat down as if I could pick the earth up and spin it round my head, and I wondered what I'd done wrong to make me lose my son.

Eventually I let the policeman pick me up again; gently he brushed me down, like I was a child, a little child, and then he led me by the hand to the car where Leigh was waiting, smoking anxiously in the warm night. She saw my face and ground out her fag, offered me a rather grubby tissue, all lipstick-stained. Then she hugged me clumsily, and, awkwardly, I submitted. And this time I got in the front of the car, and took a pill that Leigh handed me, from Sister Kwame's bottle, and I answered all Silver's questions as he took me home.

CHAPTER SEVEN

Someone was calling my name, over and over again. I swam up to the surface. As I bashed against sedation's spongy crust, it was too late – I had remembered. Frantically I tried to burrow back down into oblivion, but oblivion had gone.

I covered my face with the sheet until eventually I was forced out by Leigh. She stood above me, steaming cup in one hand, pill bottle in the other, and I sat bolt upright in hope but she quickly said there was no more news, not yet. Mickey was still unconscious, Louis still not found – but not long now, eh? Leigh was carefully cheerful – over-cheerful in fact – and her make-up was perfect. She said DI Silver was back, downstairs, and he wanted to go through things again. And then the doorbell rang, and my stomach leapt. She went down to answer it.

'It's just Deb,' she called up and I sank back down again, forlorn.

I was befuddled. The bed was all wet; I couldn't think why. Then I realised that my milk was spilling out, the bed soaking it up. I sipped and burnt my mouth on the boiling drink, I clutched my damp knees and tried not to shake. Then I got up very suddenly and went into the glossy en suite with the roll-top bath and the shower so powerful it stung my skin every time I stepped beneath it, the bathroom that used to excite me so, and I threw up. I retched and retched until there was nothing left inside. I slumped over the toilet. I thought that I would kill myself if my baby was not alive. After a while I forced myself up off the floor; I wiped my face and cleaned my teeth.

I tried to think for a minute but my brain felt like the fuzzy bit when you can't tune a telly in. Then I picked up the phone and I dialled my mum in Spain. There was a hiss on the line like I was ringing outer space and then George answered, out of breath. I didn't tell him anything. Irrationally, I wanted my mother, but she was out, of course, probably playing bridge and drinking gin, or shopping for more headscarves. He was jolly old George and he made me want to cry again but I didn't, the tears had dried for now. Instead I asked that she ring me back as soon as possible, and then I went down to see DI Silver.

Leigh was fussing round him in a way that immediately put me on edge. I slopped more coffee from the pot on the side into my cup. My eyes felt hot and sandy as the policeman smiled at me, folding his used napkin very tight. It was rather a lopsided smile, out of kilter with his measured movements.

'The au pair?' Silver asked politely, placing the napkin

neatly on the table in front of him. I waited impatiently as he unwrapped a stick of gum. Last night, I wondered, why didn't I warm to you?

'Maxine Dufrais – is she here? I'd like to speak to her.'

I glanced at his plate, wiped totally clean; looked over at Leigh. She flushed. 'Eggs, Jess?' she asked, and turned back to the hob. I shook my head. The thought of food made me want to retch again.

'Is Maxine up?' I asked, and I tried hard not to see the pile of Louis's bibs folded neatly on the counter. Leigh moved herself surreptitiously to stand in front of them.

'Haven't heard her.'

I went out into the hall to call Maxine. Anything to get away from Silver's polite but probing stare. My head felt strange and woozy; I was puzzled that my sister was flirting with this stranger in my kitchen. Then I thought of Louis and how much I needed the stranger, and I shoved my discomfort down.

Maxine wasn't stirring apparently. I went up to the next floor and called again. Silence met me. Balancing precariously on one bare foot, I craned up through the twisting stairwell. I could just about see her bedroom door from here, up in the attic. It was very slightly ajar.

'Maxine,' I called again. Nothing. Muttering, I tramped up the attic stairs.

She wasn't there. The room smelt fusty, the bed was rumpled. God knew when it had last been changed. It was stifling already, and the bedside clock said it was only 8 a.m. If she wasn't getting up to help me, Maxine slept in for hours. She must have stayed out last night. I pulled back the curtain and threw back the little casement window to let some air in. A saucer of fag-ends rested on the ledge outside; presumably a boyfriend's. Mickey would have a fit; it was his smart Thomas Goode china. Wrinkling my nose, I picked up the once-white saucer, dislodging a bus-pass holder tucked underneath. The plastic was damp with dawn dew, so I wiped it on my dressing-gown and chucked it on the small desk beneath the window. But as I turned to go back downstairs, something caught my eye. As it landed, the holder had fallen open, and tucked inside was a folded page of passport photographs. Photos of my son.

I took the stairs two at a time, brandishing the shiny strip like some kind of trophy, thrusting them at the policeman, gabbling about the girl I'd welcomed into my home, paid to be in my home.

Calmly, Silver studied them. I began to bite my thumbnail. Then he pointed out the two photos that featured both of them: Maxine grinning, her squashy nose in profile, holding up my baby; Louis in green and white stripes, staring huge-eyed and surprised into the lens.

'She's his au pair. She's probably very fond of him, isn't she? I mean, he's a cute kid. Why not have photos taken?'

'Why hide them? She's got loads of photos of Louis. Her ex bought her some flashy digital camera, for God's sake. Why go to all the hassle of sticking Louis in a photo booth?'

Silver shrugged imperceptibly. 'Who says they were being hidden? Do you have any reason to suspect Maxine? You didn't say so last night.'

'Not really. But – well, where is she now?'

'Has she stayed out before?'

I considered for a moment, then nodded glumly. 'Yes. I suppose she has.' Quite often, if truth be told.

'So, honestly, why not have them taken? It's the kind of thing kids do to fill in time. God knows, babysitting can be quite dull.'

He was so horribly detached; I, on the other hand, so horribly desperate.

'Oh, and you'd know, would you?' I snapped.

'Yes, I would actually.'

'I don't think you're taking this seriously.' I poured myself a glass of water just so I didn't have to look at him, drank long and hard.

'Believe me, I am. Look, really, I don't mean to insult you, Mrs Finnegan. Have you any other worries about the lass? You must tell me.'

I didn't. Not a single one that came to mind right now.

'Are you concerned that –' he paused.

'That what?'

Silver twisted his gum packet between two fingers. 'That your husband and the au pair might be –'

'No!' I stopped him quickly. 'Absolutely not. It's never even crossed my mind.'

'So we'll wait until she's back and talk to her before we rush to any assumptions. Does she have a mob—'

'I'm sorry –' I was abrupt. He wasn't all that tall,

but still he towered over me. For a moment I saw myself like some scrappy little terrier yapping at a big sleek labrador. It riled me even more. '– perhaps you haven't noticed, but my son's still missing? I'm just trying to be useful.'

He took a deep breath. 'I realise that. And I want to know everything you think is relevant. So,' he rubbed his jaw, 'DC Whitely from Lambeth tells me that you reported an argument with your husband.'

I was thrown. 'I didn't.'

'Well, he seemed to think you'd rowed about something.'

'I never said that. It was just a silly, you know, disagreement about –' About chocolate cake. About hormones and insecurity.

'About?'

'About nothing, really. This isn't helping, DI Silver. It's irrelevant.'

'How can you be sure?'

'Because I am. If you really want to know, it was about me eating Mickey's cake. It wasn't, you know, *that* kind of row.'

'What kind of row? You've got to be honest with me.' I'd got his interest now.

'Please, you're confusing me.'

'Are you really telling me everything you know?'

I stared at him. 'How can you doubt that? Do you really think I'd hide anything?'

'I presume not, Mrs Finnegan.'

I rushed out of the kitchen. Leigh was reapplying her lip-liner in the hall mirror.

'What's wrong?' She tried to hold my eye, but I wriggled away. 'You need to calm down, Jess. You're going to drive yourself mad.'

'You calm down.' With supreme effort, I kept my voice very quiet and low. 'You calm down next time Polly and Samantha go missing. You come round and tell me how you feel, okay, Leigh?'

'Look, Jess, is this –' She stopped short.

'What?'

'Is this police thing, is it because – well, you know.'

Don't say it.

She did. 'Because of Dad? Because of what happened then?'

My fingers went white where I clutched the banister. I'd buried it extremely deep. 'It's not about anything apart from Louis, Leigh. It's *only* about Louis.'

'Are you sure? Cos you really need to chill out with that copper.' She jerked her head towards the kitchen. 'You need him on your side. He's only doing his job.'

'Is he? Why does he look at me like that, then? Like I'm a liar?'

'I'm sure he doesn't.'

'He does, Leigh. Anyway, whatever, I don't care. I'm going back to look for Louis. You two, you sit and eat my eggs. Why not? Feel free.'

I started up the stairs, and then I saw the copper's face come round the kitchen door, and, as my bosom throbbed, I was sure he smirked at the wet patch on my front. Something just went click. With a thud I thought of DC Jones, and I went flying back past Silver, my breath coming in big ragged gulps. The box of eggs was open, half full, on the side. I selected one, nearly crushed it in my hand. It was cool and smooth, and for a second I had the urge to roll it slowly down my scalding cheek. But I didn't. Instead, I lifted my arm and hurled it at the wall. It smashed with a glorious, satisfying crunch, a slick of yolk sliding down the shiny tiles. I took another, then one more. As my arm went back for the throw, a hand grabbed my wrist.

'Get off me.' I was gasping for breath, struggling to get free.

'Mrs Finnegan – Jessica. Please. You're hysterical.'

'I'm – if you don't let go, I'll – I'll have you for assault.' I freed myself. 'I can't believe you think I'm lying.'

'I didn't say that. Look, I know you're feeling terrible. But this isn't going to help. We need to work together, don't we?' He wheeled me round to face him. 'I didn't mean to offend you, really.'

'Why don't you tell me what will help?' I hissed, pulling away. 'No, actually,' and I could hardly get my breath now, 'I'll tell you, shall I?' I went very close to him, so close I could see the flecks of yellow in his hazel eyes. 'Just get my baby back. That's all that will help. Get Louis back for me, please. Before I go insane.'

'We will. We're trying.' Silver stood looking at me for a moment, and then he went away. I collapsed into the old wicker chair in the corner. Leigh bustled over, all consternation. The phone rang and my heart skipped. She bustled out again, and Deb slid into the room, no doubt sent by her incredibly sensitive boss.

'All right?'

This time I let her take my hand. The fight was seeping out of me, leaving me limp and broken.

'Listen,' Deb said quietly, leaning in. 'He can be a little blunt sometimes, I know.'

'Blunt? That's a polite way of putting it.'

She patted my knee sympathetically. 'But he's a really good guy to have on your side, I promise.'

'He thinks I'm lying.'

'He's just being thorough. No stone unturned, you know. Bear with him, okay?' I looked away, then nodded slowly. She smiled encouragingly. 'Now, Jessica. When you're ready, if you're feeling up to it, DI Silver would like you to do a TV appeal. Jog people's memories.'

He appeared silently in the doorway.

'Who was on the phone?' I found myself addressing the wall behind his ear.

'I think it's your sister's husband.'

'Oh.'

'Someone must have seen *your* husband, Mrs Finnegan, when he left the Tate. We're waiting for the CCTV tapes now, but the appeal is a really good idea. They usually generate a lot of public support, especially when there are kids involved.'

'Whatever you think,' I said dully.

'We need witnesses to the struggle Mr Finnegan must have had.'

'The struggle with who?'

'With – with whoever took Louis.'

My chest tightened further. Scrabbling for my inhaler, I caught the warning look Deb shot Silver.

When I'd recovered myself a bit, I asked them to

take me to where Mickey had been found. 'I want to check it for myself.'

'And you'll do the appeal?'

'I'll do anything, everything it takes.' I looked at him steadily and he looked back.

'Good lass.'

I nearly retorted that I was hardly a lass, but instead I said, 'I'm going to get dressed.'

'Great,' said DI Silver. 'Then Deb'll make you some toast, you need your energy, and then we'll go.'

I paused at the foot of the stairs. Leigh was still simpering down the phone.

'Oh,' I said icily, and for once I got to look down on Silver. 'Don't you do toast then?' I swept up the stairs and slammed my bedroom door behind me.

CHAPTER EIGHT

When I first had Louis and I went out without him, I used to panic. Not because I didn't want to be alone – the truth was I did, quite badly. And not that I got to leave him very often, but whenever I did, I'd suddenly remember him with a gut-wrenching lurch. I'd scrabble around desperately, wondering where the hell I'd put him. I'd be queuing for coffee, or buying a magazine, and my heart would suddenly stop. So quickly did I get used to being tied to this other little body that being alone – much as I did yearn for it from time to time – seemed strange, alien even. And each time the sense of relief when I remembered he was safe somewhere was overwhelming.

I waited for that wash of relief again; every time the phone rang or DI Silver's mobile chirruped, I clenched my hands, my stomach, my heart, and I waited for Silver to punch the air and shout, 'He's found.' But inside, really deep down in a place I daren't go, I waited for the words that would finish me forever. And I tried desperately to dispel the memories of the lust for my lost freedom I'd felt quite often since Louis's birth.

DI Silver and Deb took me to the street where Mickey had been found last night. Just an innocuous little alley on the way to Tower Bridge, dirty and grey in the cloudy morning light. I looked nervously for bloodstains, I craned my eyes for clues – but of course there was nothing. Just a pile of dried old dog-shit on the corner, and a week-old page-three girl idly flapping her wares in the sticky summer breeze.

And then we went back south to Lewisham, to the monstrous new police station, where Leigh awaited us. We trooped into a room where T-shirted men with TV cameras lay in wait, looking bored, and young women with expensive flicky hair and tight, anxious faces clutched microphones and notepads and checked their watches all the time. They reminded me of the squirrels that darted across our garden foraging for that last hidden nut, and I felt very alone as I waited to walk up onto the small stage, though DI Silver was with me. Before we took our seats, he gave me a reassuring wink, and for the first time I was glad that he was there.

'They're just doing their jobs, kiddo,' he murmured, reading my mind, 'you'll thank them in the end,' and then he adjusted his shirt cuffs almost imperceptibly, the smooth white fabric immaculate above his suntanned hands.

Leigh came up with us, as polished as ever, despite the air still thick as sludge; despite the fact I looked like I'd been dragged through forty hedges backwards. I shied away from the thought that Leigh was almost enjoying this. As a kid she'd had dreams of stardom;

she even went to stage school for a bit until my dad had finally gone, along with all our income too. I used to clap faithfully along to everything Leigh sang into her old pink hairbrush – but actually she was pretty rubbish, tone-deaf with two flat feet, my Nana always said, slipping me a fiver because she felt sorry for me. Because I never got the attention from my mum that Leigh and my little brother did.

But this time the attention was all on me, however hard Leigh might try, and really I didn't want it, all I wanted was my Louis back, and I tried not to whisper when I said what we'd agreed I'd say. Silver did his bit first, about the first twenty-four hours being crucial, and I tried not to think what happened after them. I pulled myself together and breathed deeply to stop the shake that travelled through my voice. I looked straight at the cameras, the flashes turning my eyes kaleidoscopic, sending diamonds of light spinning through the air. I was going to read something Silver's team had prepared for me, but in the end I simply begged. I said, 'Whoever's got my baby, please, give him back. I just want him back. Please don't hurt him,' and the idea that someone actually could made me feel like my brain might explode; it was filling up with cotton wool and everyone in the room suddenly felt so far away even though they were all staring right at me, and I was a tiny speck of nothing floundering in a sea of agony.

Then DI Silver put his arm around me and I smelt his lemony male smell that seemed too close, and he led me off the stage to a little room where someone brought me more sweet tea and I scrabbled in my pocket and clutched Sister Kwame's bottle of pills with relief.

I was forcing down a sandwich that, however hard I chewed, turned to sawdust in my mouth, when Deb entered the room. There was an urgency about her that I didn't like, which made that horrid sandwich stick right in my throat as I watched her gesture discreetly at DI Silver. His eyes slid over me before he crossed the room to her. Then another man with a funny little potbelly and thin slicked-back hair came in looking tense and worried and leant in towards his boss. Deb detached herself, came bustling over, wearing a false smile.

'Good to see you eating at last, Jessica,' she said, but by now I had stopped and was staring at the men behind her. She knew where my eyes were trained but she kept on anyway.

'Another cup of tea, love?' she asked, but I shook my head. I was drowning in the stuff.

'What is it?' I said, and I looked her in the eye. She nearly flushed but her training was better than that and she kept very calm and still, and just sat beside me. Leigh was still on her mobile as DI Silver came towards me and, for the first time since I'd met him, I could swear he looked rattled. Leigh kept laughing, a throaty kind of laugh that meant it must be Gary she was talking to, and I wanted to slap her but instead I stood up and went towards Silver.

'What is it?' I said, and I clutched his arm inadvertently. I nearly choked on the words. I didn't

80

want to ever hear the answer, but I asked it anyway.

'Don't panic, Jess,' he said. He'd never called me Jess before. 'Don't panic but I've got some news, and I'm not sure it's very good. Let's just sit down again.'

I held my ground. 'Just tell me. I'm not a kid you know,' but my hand was going sweaty where I grasped the fine cloth of his suit.

'Apparently someone's – a pushchair has been found. A pushchair and a bag,' he added, almost reluctantly. 'Can you describe yours to me please?'

'Louis's pushchair? Describe it again?'

'Yes please, Jessica. If you don't mind.'

'It's blue,' I whispered stupidly. 'Blue for a boy. It's that make –' but my mind was blank. I scrabbled for the name. 'Like the racing cars.'

The other policeman joined DI Silver. 'Was the bag you lost green?'

'No!' Relief flooded through me. 'Not green. His bag's bright red! That's not mine then, thank God. My changing-bag's bright red. With a – it's got a big zip across the front.'

The other man muttered something in Silver's ear.

'Did you have a handbag, Mrs Finnegan, when you lost your son? Another bag that was with him?'

'I didn't lose my son,' I corrected him, 'someone *took* my son. Someone's taken him.' My head was spinning; I stumbled where I stood. I whispered, 'Yes, I had a bag. A green bag.'

'Leather? With lots of pockets and a –' he looked at his notebook. 'A platinum tag?'

I nodded miserably. A birthday present from Mickey.

The most expensive item I'd ever owned; I'd been scared to even use it. 'Have you found it?'

The policeman with the potbelly cleared his throat. 'Looks like it, Mrs Finnegan. Not the red bag though. Just a green one. And a Maclaren pushchair.' Maclaren. That was it.

'Where?' I asked quietly. My world was finally caving in. Finally and irrefutably it was collapsing round my ears.

The policeman shifted from one foot to the other, tight little belly straining against his cheap striped shirt. 'On the river beach, down by Tower Bridge Pier.'

'And – and Louis?' I croaked, and my knees went weak. DI Silver held me up. Leigh had stopped laughing and ran to support my other arm.

'There's no sign of Louis, Jess,' Silver said. 'No sign at all. Which is a good sign, at this point.'

And I wavered for a moment. It was like being on a tightrope, high above a fatal drop. The way I looked at it right then was that there were two ways down. I could fall and go under forever: the obvious route perhaps, but it wouldn't help my son. Or I could do what I eventually did. I steadied myself; with every ounce of strength I had left I pulled myself up tall and I decided right there and then that if they hadn't found Louis, well then of course I would.

'So you've got nothing to report except a soggy bag then?' I said steadfastly, 'so that's okay then, isn't it?' and I walked away, past them, out of the door into the horribly beige hall, through the buzzers and the swing doors into the street.

*

I walked so fast that I lost myself in minutes. I didn't know where I was going but I went there anyway. I just wanted to be alone, to get away from all the sympathy, to dodge the prying, over-anxious eyes that watched my every move. I needed to clear my head but it was so hard to focus. So I just walked; wondering every second if I was near my Louis. I looked through every window, peered into every car, stared at women with babies until they seemed unnerved; stared at the babies, willing them to be mine.

At one point some leather-faced builder shouted, 'Cheer up, love, it might never happen,' and I went right up to him, so close I could see the sweat glistening like dewdrops on the curly chest hairs above his vest, and I said right into his surprised face, 'Yes, but you see, it already has,' and he shut up pretty flipping fast. I walked and walked and walked until I felt like I was going to drop. And when I couldn't walk any more, I found a cab and I went home.

CHAPTER NINE

When I got back it all went very crazy. They were all there – Leigh, Silver, Deb – but they didn't hear me come in because they were glued to the six o'clock news, to Mickey's cherished enormous television where an immaculate presenter looked both doe-eyed and serious, and talked about 'over twenty-four hours now'. Suddenly Louis's little face flashed up on the screen, and he wasn't smiling. Why hadn't they picked a picture of him smiling, I wanted to know. I didn't choose that photo, so who had? But then there I was, looking like some waif and stray, bedraggled and blotchy and absolutely stunned, like the proverbial rabbit in headlights. Beside me, the composed Silver looked horribly together. I should have brushed my hair, I thought illogically.

'If only Mum could see me now,' I joked, and they all turned round and started to fuss, and suddenly I didn't feel very well, my head was about to float right off. Deb made me yet more tea. I didn't even really like the stuff but I drank it like I knew it was my duty to, ate some digestives, and then I looked at Polaroids of the buggy that they'd found and my poor posh bag, and, with a sinking feeling, I knew there was no denying they were mine. I started to feel that bubble of hysteria again and so I made another joke.

'Mickey will have a fit, you know. That bag cost a bomb,' and then I caught Silver and Deb exchanging a look, and I said 'What?' again, and I wondered how much of this not-knowing I could take.

Deb said, 'Mickey came round.' But I didn't like the tense she'd used, and I interrupted her before she could go on.

'What do you mean "came" round?'

She replied, 'He's gone again.'

I stared at her until she rushed to correct herself.

'Gone under, I mean. Unconscious. Sorry – I didn't mean to scare you. Stupid of me. Sorry. He's fine, apparently, but he's out cold for now. Still, it's a good sign, isn't it?'

'Is it?' I said limply. Nothing seemed good right now.

'Mum rang,' Leigh said, smoothing her straightened hair nervously. 'I've told her the worst.' A ridiculous expression, I thought. I pictured my sun-raddled mother on her Spanish phone, gold hoops swinging as she leant to light another fag, her little monkey face working to absorb the news.

'How much worse could it get?' I said, and then, 'Don't answer that. Is she coming back?' I looked hopefully at Leigh, but she'd already turned away.

'She said she'll try to get a flight.'

That meant no, I knew; I felt my shoulders slump yet further. Then I noticed that Leigh was drinking wine. Mickey's wine no doubt.

'I'll have a glass please,' I said.

'Oh,' she said, blankly. Then, 'Do you really think that's a good idea?'

I quelled her with a single look, a death-stare that I perfected in my teens. I didn't use it very often, certainly not on my big sister, but now it worked. She clacked out to the kitchen in her spiky heels.

Silver started on about formally identifying the buggy and the bag, which was empty by the time it was found, and going to the hospital, and I was just saying that presumably it was a good sign that the baby-bag was missing because it must still be with Louis, someone must be using it, when suddenly the telephone rang. The noise sliced through the humid air like a knife through softened butter, and everybody jumped. I waited for a moment, and then I realised that of course it was my house, my phone, I was the grown-up here, so I guessed that I should answer it. I picked it up carefully, Silver watching me intently, and I said 'Hello' like I'd had a lobotomy. A familiar voice said hello back; a voice that had been silent for too long.

'Just seen you on the telly, Jessie darling,' and I nearly dropped the receiver right where I stood.

Leigh clacked back in, wine glass in hand, and mouthed, 'Who is it?' and I stared at her, not the death-stare this time, and I said rather helplessly, 'It's Robbie,' and she double-took, just like Stan Laurel would have done. She dropped the wine glass; it went slipping through her fake-tanned hand and smashed at our feet, one thousand shiny shards lying lethal in the evening sun.

*

86

On the heath outside my bedroom window a young family picnicked in the dying light. Their spaniel bounced round and round them in ever-shrinking circles, barking joyfully, while the mother laughed at something one of her children said, threw back her head like some old-fashioned movie star. Then her husband leant in to kiss her and I didn't want to watch any more.

The evening air was syrupy with heat, although the sun was nearly gone. Still damp from the shower, I pulled on an old red sundress that I'd had forever, shoved tissues in my bra to mop up the leaking milk, piled my dirty dark hair up on my head. Sister Kwame's bottle called to me from the bedside cabinet. My hand hovered over it. Silver was waiting for me outside. Resolutely I picked up Louis's photo instead. I sat on my bed clutching it, staring at him like I could conjure him back to reality by my sheer will.

I slid into Silver's car beside him; he was taking me to see Mickey. The roads were clear although the heath outside The Hare and Billet was packed with evening drinkers, laughing, flirting, ambling around the dehydrated pond that a lone duck floated on. Who were all these people living their lives so casually while mine collapsed?

Silver leant down and switched the police radio off, flicked the car stereo on. I hadn't seen him in his shirt-sleeves before and it unnerved me. He looked unfinished somehow. A mournful Billie Holiday sang of her lost love, and I raised an eyebrow at the policeman.

'Wouldn't have had you down as a blues man myself.'

I opened the window as far as it would go, my hair whipping my face in the sudden breeze.

'Really? What have you got me down as?'

I spat a curl from my dry mouth and considered him. 'I suppose you're a bit old to be an indie kid.'

He snorted. 'Just because I was born somewhere near Manchester doesn't mean I'm into Oasis.'

'Not really what I'd call indie, mate,' I said. 'That's a bit behind the times. But then you are Old Bill, I guess.' I nudged the police radio. 'Won't you get in trouble if you don't have that on? What if someone finds Louis?'

He shrugged. 'They'll ring if they need me. I wanted to have a talk. Uninterrupted.'

'Oh.' I shivered despite the heat. 'That sounds ominous.'

He shrugged again. 'Not really. Just hard to get you on your own.'

'Why would you want to get me on my own?'

'What I meant was, you seem a little cagey.'

'Cagey?'

'Yep.'

'Are you insinuating something again, DI Silver?'

'I don't know. Am I?' he replied pleasantly. God! He actually made me feel quite violent. Not trusting myself to respond, a sticky pause ensued. He drove with one hand on the wheel, the other propped idly on the window. Like a dying man I gulped in the air that skimmed the open window. We left Blackheath behind, dropped down from the genteel oasis my husband had brought me to, down to Deptford and New Cross. The

88

badlands, Mickey always called them, with a dry laugh, much more like Belfast, much more like where I'd grown up than where we lived these days.

A woman in a navy people-carrier pulled up along-side us, her older children squabbling across the baby in the back. Was Louis in a car like that? I began to watch every car intently, just in case we passed him. I was drifting off to Louis when Silver broke back into my muddled head.

'Correct me if I'm wrong, but I get the feeling that things might have been a little –' he paused '– strained between you and Mr Finnegan?'

'Oh you do, do you?' He'd wrong-footed me again. 'I didn't realise marriage guidance was part of the service.'

'It's not. It was just an observation.'

'Yeah, well, it's a rubbish one.' I folded my arms tight across my painful chest.

'Look, I'm just doing my job, Mrs Finn— Jessica. You don't mind if I call you Jessica?' He didn't wait for an answer. 'I have to know anything at all that might have an impact on Louis's disappearance.' He swore softly as a van cut us up. 'You must see that, surely?'

Something about this man's smooth confidence brought out the very worst in me. 'Yes, I do see that.'

'So if you can be as honest as you can, it's really helpful. And it won't go further than me, I swear.'

'How very reassuring.'

I got the benefit of his full smile then. His teeth were so ludicrously white it was like being caught in the blazing sun.

'Have you had those done?' I couldn't help myself.

'What?'

'Your teeth?'

Something new lurked behind the tightened smile. 'On a copper's wage? Hardly. Just good genes, kiddo.' Another pause. He looked at me expectantly. I grimaced back politely.

'So, you and your old man then,' he eventually prompted.

'What about us?'

'Tell me about it, please.'

'I must say, DI Silver –'

'Joe.'

'I must say, DI Silver, I'm not really sure why you think things were strained between me and Mickey, given that ever since you've known us, he's been out cold.'

'Well yes, there is that,' he agreed mildly. 'So why don't you tell me how it really was then?'

'Was?'

'Sorry. Is.'

We stopped at a red light. Stony-faced, I looked away from him. 'It's bloody-well fine, thanks very much. Absolutely fine.'

'When did you meet?'

'Early last year.'

'Where?'

'I did some work for him. He's got his own company. Graphics.'

'Doing well, judging by the trappings.' He pulled off with a jolt. Was I a trapping?

'He does all right.'

'And so you, you're a designer? An artist?'

'Hardly an artist, unfortunately, much as I'd like to be. I was an assistant. He was – I was going to train. I was studying back then. When I got pregnant, though, Mickey thought I should stay home with Louis.' With a nasty squeeze of guilt, I remembered how resentful I'd been at first about giving up my barely-begun career for motherhood. How when the real depression set in I begged to be allowed back to work. It had seemed so much safer than having full care of my own child.

He changed tack without warning. 'So it was a whirl-wind romance?'

I laughed despite myself. 'What is this – Mills and Boon? Christ, Silver, Billie Holiday *and* happy endings! Next you'll be asking if he got down on one knee.'

'Well, did he?'

'No, he didn't.' I could have sworn he was racing the car in the next lane.

'Lust, then?'

I twisted round to him as far as my seatbelt allowed. 'Excuse me, but what's this got to do with Louis? I don't mean to be rude, but what bloody business is it of yours?'

'Language, Jess!'

'-ica.'

'What?'

'Jess-ica. No one calls me Jess except my nearest and dearest.'

'Mickey then?'

'Mickey what?'

'Calls you Jess?'

'Maybe. Sometimes.' Mickey never called me Jess, ever. 'And maybe it was lust,' I rattled on, 'in fact it was. Definitely lust. Pure, unadulterated X-rated stuff. You know the sort of thing I'm sure.'

More to the point, I'd been seven months pregnant when we got married. The big wedding day I'd always dreamed of had been quite the opposite; it had been tiny and rushed without any family there, the fantasy dress a dreadful maternity affair. Intimate, Mickey said, kissing the top of my head; beautiful, he said, gently stroking my bump. The best bit was reaching the fancy hotel that night, a place called Blakes in Kensington, all very hushed and subtle. The present Mickey had bought me was waiting in our suite, beautifully wrapped – the Emin sketch I'd admired on that first evening in Cork Street. I'd been overwhelmed. It was the start of a new life, he said, for both of us. For the three of us, kissing my bump through my satin dress. I shivered with distress at the memory.

'And now, please can we not talk about this any more.'

He glanced at me, and rather tiredly sighed. 'This isn't for my own ends, Jessica. I'm trying to help you. It's all perfectly normal procedure. I'm just trying to find your son. I have to say,' indicating right, checking his mirrors zealously, 'I don't really get your reluctance to tell me things, I'm afraid.'

I took a deep breath. 'It's – well, it's –'

'What?'

'I just find it a bit hard, that's all.'

'That's quite obvious.'

'Because it's my private life, I guess.' I was trying, honestly I was.

'Yeah, I appreciate that. But it's also your son.'

'Yeah, I know.' I was so plugged up, so used to erecting barriers, so frightened of the police from old. How could I explain my reticence to this stranger? I watched the ugly shop facades flash by. A streetlight pinged on. I'd never caught that moment before.

'I'm sorry,' I said quietly. 'I just – I've got a bit of a thing about coppers.'

'Not a good thing, I presume?'

'No, not a good thing. A pretty bad thing really.'

'And I don't suppose you want to expand on that?'

'Not really. Not right now, if you don't mind. I'm, you know, still dealing with it.' I was only just realising that – despite it being over ten years ago.

'It's just that if you're too clammed up, Jessica, it might come across as a little – odd.'

'What do you mean, "odd"?'

'Like you might be hiding something.'

'For God's sake! I'm not.' Hiding something. I thought about my dad. Friday nights at the dog-track in Walthamstow – he'd give me a quid to put on my favourite, and I'd spend my winnings on penny chews and Spangles – though, thinking back, I couldn't possibly have won as often as he made out. Watching the horses together on a Saturday when my mum took Leigh to tap class, cheering on his dead cert, squeezing his hand so hard in the hope that he'd laugh and call me his Gripper Girl. Riding his mate Jack's old pony

Mildred bareback in the fields behind our estate with Robbie, while my dad and Jack smoked over by the gate and talked 'business', before I fell off Mildred when they weren't watching one day and lost my nerve. I thought about the times much later; about the eternal wait for the rare and precious letters; about the hot and angry tears I cried into my pillow when the others were asleep. I remembered begging my mum to take me to see him, pleading and pleading until she finally snapped. I remembered with a shudder the visits where we weren't even allowed to hug, where my dad tried to remain chipper as he clasped my eager little hand – he'd always combed his hair for me specially, but he'd got so very thin, and he coughed such an awful lot that I was always really worried. With good reason, it turned out.

'Jessica?'

I struggled back to now. 'Nothing to do with Louis anyway. Why would I hide anything?'

'Talking about your private life – it can feel intrusive, I do understand that.'

'Yeah. I'm not used to it, that's all. We weren't very good at – you know – feelings in my family. It's – it feels weird.' *I* felt weird. Inertia was creeping over me. 'Like being on some crap chat-show.'

'Yeah, well, *Richard and Judy* this ain't, kiddo. I'm just trying to get some idea of exactly what we're dealing with. You're sure there's nothing else you should have told me, anything at all that might throw any light on this?'

'No, nothing, I keep telling you.' I was having trouble concentrating, could feel my eyelids fluttering. I tried to focus on the road.

'It could be someone close to you; it could be you were a particular target. It's very likely to be maternal bereavement. And by the way, we're checking Maxine out now. I know you were worried about those photos, but there still seems no apparent reason to –'

His voice became a drone as we slid to another stop. My brain had turned to mud. The most terrible ennui spread through my bones, torpor like I'd never known before. I felt carsick, heartsick, truly Louis-sick. I stuck my head out the window and breathed as long and hard as I could. How many pills had I swallowed before we left? And suddenly there it was, flapping on the dirty pavement, among the fast-food wrappers and the fag butts, the newspaper billboard that screamed my business to the world.

'BABY SNATCHED – DEAD OR ALIVE?'

'Please,' I said indistinctly, 'I don't feel very well.'

He pulled up so fast he practically smacked my lolling head on the windscreen, pushed me out and dragged me onto the pavement. Then he held my tumbling hair back as I gagged into the gutter. When I thought I must have finished, he handed me a cotton handkerchief to wipe my gasping mouth.

'It's ironed.' I clutched it like my life depended on it. 'You ironed it.'

'Someone did, kiddo. Better now?'

'I feel a bit odd. Sort of – woozy,' I whispered, and I staggered there against him on the pavement.

'I'm not bloody surprised. Have you eaten anything apart from a few biscuits since Louis disappeared?'

I couldn't remember really. I shook my head. Food

when my baby screamed for me and I couldn't help him?

'It's not that anyway,' I said hollowly. 'I think –'

'What? You think what?' He leant in to hear me, but the smell of his aftershave made me retch again. Down the gutter grate I could see a shiny penny among all the muck.

'Too many pills,' I managed in the end. My mouth was furry, the words stumbled across my heavy tongue, thick like a slab of dead meat. Thick with misery. I rested my full weight on him. Why bother standing any more?

'For Christ's sake!' He practically picked me up and threw me in the car. 'Like how many pills?'

'Dunno. Lost count. Not used to them.' I was falling away, falling into a pit with sides so slippery that I couldn't grasp them. I would go and join Louis now; he needed me. My head snapped back as we screeched off in a blare of horns.

'Just stay awake, Jessica. Stay awake.' He yanked my face round to him. 'Do you hear me? We're nearly at the hospital. Don't go to sleep, okay?'

My chin banged my chest. 'Don't have to shout,' I slurred.

He put the radio on loud and I forced my eyes back open. Newspaper print swam before them, wrote itself across the road. Dead or alive? Dead or alive? Dead or alive, *deadoralive*, dead and gone, *goinggoinggone, gone, gone, gonegonegonegonegone*.

CHAPTER TEN

I didn't mean to do it. I wasn't trying to die. I was just trying to stop the pain.

When I had Louis and the postnatal fog finally dispersed a bit, when the terror of intimacy began to fade, the terror that something terrible would happen to him, I let myself love him properly. I stopped panicking that he was mine and that I'd break him; allowed myself to relax a bit – and slowly I began to feel like I was six again. The feeling you get on Christmas Day as a kid, when you wake and you lie there for a moment and then you remember something great has happened, there are presents to be unwrapped. So I'd get up and wander into Louis's room and see his face light up, hear his chuckles and his squeaks as he waved a hand about, a fat little hand that was mine to hold. And I loved him more than anything right then, he was all my Christmas Days rolled into one.

I woke up in a hospital bed, and I didn't know where I was. But I did know it definitely wasn't Christmas Day. I looked round and my friend Shirl was by my bed, she took my hand and squeezed it, and I was so pleased to see her that one fat tear rolled from my eye. She pulled some tissues from the box beside her, pushing them into my hand, and for a minute I held that hand like I would never let it go.

'Any news?' I croaked eventually, my throat feeling like it had swelled up tight as a straw. She bent her head to hear me.

'News?' I implored again, and she shook her head sadly.

'Still no Louis, I'm afraid, not yet, sweetie, anyway,' she said, like it was painful to actually speak it out loud. Then she brightened slightly. 'But Mickey's awake, I think.'

'What day is it?' I asked, and I clutched her hand even tighter.

'Wednesday morning,' she said, and I started to do the maths. Almost two whole days since I'd seen Louis. Forty-eight hours: a lifetime.

'Why didn't you call me, babe? I saw you on the news last night and I nearly had a bloody heart attack.'

I stared at the ceiling. Then I looked at her. 'Because you were the one person I knew who'd have no idea where Mickey was.'

She smiled a rueful kind of smile. 'That's true enough.' A beat. Then before I could ask: 'They haven't found Louis, but apparently the phones have been ringing off the hook. That tasty copper's going to come and see you soon. Hundreds of calls they've had, he reckons. Char man, someone's gotta know where the lovely Louis is.'

'Don't suppose you've heard from my mum?' I asked

quietly, and I tried to sit up in the bed. 'Ow! God, my belly hurts.'

'Yeah, well, it will, it's been pumped.'

'Pumped?'

'Yeah, pumped. As in overdose.'

I looked away. From my bed I could see the corner of the London Eye, like an enormous Ferris wheel. 'Nice view. You'd pay a lot for this in a hotel.'

'Jessica.'

'What?'

'You know what.'

'I didn't take an overdose, Shirl. I didn't. I just took – you know. A few too many pills.'

'Come on, babe. I don't think I've seen you take a pill in my whole life.'

'Yes, well. You know. Needs must.'

A nurse bustled in with a vase of flowers. 'Aha!' she said, all false jollity and skinny little plaits. 'Awake at last, Miss Sleepy-head?'

Yes, I thought, awake at last. Unfortunately. 'Nice flowers,' I murmured politely. Then I looked at Shirl.

'What?'

'You don't really think he's tasty, do you?'

'Who?'

'Silver.'

'In that sort of – what would you say? Debonair sort of a way. Don't tell me you haven't noticed it, my girl.'

'I've got more important things on my mind, actually, Shirl.'

'Yes,' she sighed sorrowfully, 'I suppose you have.'

*

The night that Louis was conceived Mickey and I fucked with a ferocity that threatened to overwhelm me; a savagery I'd never experienced with anyone before. We'd been eyeing each other for weeks, unsure since that first and last time, after the Emin exhibition, pacing the office floor between us like the cagey tigers in that song. I wanted him and yet he scared me; I wanted him but I wasn't giving in to it. He filled me with a strange dread I couldn't face; he reminded me of sorrows that I'd fought to escape. He skated on a surface I couldn't pierce; something darting beneath – something too dark to fathom. He chose to hide his vulnerabilities, and he did it very well – most of the time.

That second night Mickey took me to the ballet in Covent Garden. We saw something called *Coppelia*, which was about dolls and a toyshop and was what Mickey called 'frothy', and I thought it'd be silly and I'd be bored stiff, but actually I loved it. Gene Kelly and Fred Astaire were old favourites of mine – how many wet afternoons had Leigh and I spent dancing around the cluttered living room to 'Singing in the Rain', sending my mum's glass animals flying with our umbrellas. Old musicals were one thing, though – I thought Fonteyn and her crowd were way beyond my ken. But once I'd overcome the nerves I dared not show, I really enjoyed the sheer splendour of the whole event – the over-dressed posh people, the champagne in the interval, the novelty of the plush red theatre. Mickey by my side, so handsome, so charming and attentive now.

Afterwards he took me to a restaurant so expensive they didn't bother with prices on the menu, where women whispered through the door in silken clothes more costly than my rent, where the men were swollen and sanguine in their wealth, clicking for the waiters. Mickey hand-fed me oysters, which I hated, and caviar, which I loved, the salty eggs popping across my tongue – food I'd really only dreamed of. Asparagus and rare steak and cherries dipped in chocolate followed, but my heart was in my mouth throughout the meal and I soon found I'd lost my appetite. Out in the spring breeze Mickey bought me wild roses from a sweet-smelling stall on Piccadilly – so many I could hardly hold them all. Then he whistled for a taxi and sucked the blood, red as the roses that I clutched, from where I'd pricked my finger on the thorns. He took me home to Blackheath for the first time; let me into his own world a little, let his mask slip just a bit.

Mickey went to change his shirt and pour us both a drink, and I'd made my way outside into the cool night air, to admire the lush garden. By the back door I passed a faded photo of a small boy in dungarees. He was laughing at the camera, a front tooth missing, a cheeky grin below his pudding-basin hair, pigeon feathers tucked behind each small ear, Red Indian style.

'Who's that?' I asked, pointing behind me as Mickey came out into the night. He didn't turn to look.

'My big brother, Ruari.' I felt his fingers tighten over mine as he passed me a glass.

Later, Mickey put on some music and danced me slowly round the kitchen. I leant against his chest; I drank in his heady smell.

'Your brother. Where is he now?' I asked quietly, but I think I knew already. He let me go.

'He...' he took a sip of his whisky, moving away, 'he died. Quite soon after that was taken. He was only eight.' A muscle jumped in his cheek.

'Oh God. I'm so sorry, Mickey.'

'So am I. He drowned. Fishing. Determined to get the biggest one, stupid bugger. Hopped school that morning.' He downed the rest of the drink in one, and wandered back out onto the porch steps. I waited, watching him. I think, for a while, he forgot I was there.

'We were best mates, you know. But I wasn't with him that day.' He was talking to himself now, leaning over the railing, staring into the darkness. 'Some things – some things you never recover from, do you know what I mean? My ma never did. It killed her in the end.'

I walked out to him, slid my arms around him, rested my head on his warm back. I could sense his heart beating through the soft cashmere of his sweater. I wanted more of this man. However much I kept fighting it, as he opened up a bit, I began to fall.

In the morning I woke sated, utterly spent, and yet still he came for more. I was limp and yielding in his hands, sticky with lust, half-asleep, basking in abandonment as his fingers played me like some instrument constructed purely for his pleasure. He looked down at me with an intensity I'd never known and I yearned for more – finally, utterly lost. So didn't it make sense that the best sex of my life should bring me my son? Unbidden, initially unwanted – but irrefutably there, hurled suddenly into existence.

The hospital insisted I see a psychiatrist. According to them, I'd attempted suicide, and no matter how hard I denied it, they weren't going to budge. I tried everything I could to put it off until eventually the only thing left was pleading to see Mickey before I spoke to any other doctors, and reluctantly they agreed.

The ICU was as quiet as ever as Sister Kwame took me in to see my husband. Despite the sun that shone so bright outside the shuttered windows, it was completely dim in here, church-like in its reverence for the sick.

'He's sleeping now,' she murmured, looking down at him with fondness. 'Why don't you wake him, my dear? Just do it gently, yes?' Then she vanished, starched skirt whispering, left me standing alone there by his bed.

Mickey's bruises were starting to change colour now, purples starting to yellow just a little round the sides like some over-ripe exotic fruit. Tentatively I put my hand out and softly stroked the skin around his sore eye. He stirred a little and I resisted a strange urge to press down hard.

'Mickey,' I said quietly, after a while. He muttered incoherently and rolled his head from side to side. He was breathing without the machines now and his mouth twisted in discomfort. Pain flashed across his face and I wondered where he was, what world he walked. And then suddenly his eyes snapped open. I stepped back in shock.

I steeled myself. I tried to be the strong person I once was.

'It's me, Mickey. It's Jessica,' I said, and I leant down to him a little, as if he was a child. 'How're you feeling?'

For a moment he just looked at me blankly and I saw nothing behind his eyes. Panic filled my chest, pressed against my lungs. Oh God, I've lost my husband too, I thought. We stared at one another and then slowly, very slowly, he brought one scraped hand up to touch my face.

'Jessica,' he whispered, and I could have sworn I saw a tear glinting in his sore eye. 'My Jess.' He took me unawares. 'I'm so pleased to see you, darling.'

I swallowed, nervous, stroking his hand while I racked my brain for something sensible to say. His face contorted again, like he was struggling to remember something gone. Then he said, 'How's Louis? I can't wait to see him. Is he here?'

The bile rose again, burning my damaged throat. What the hell did he mean? I clenched my fists and bit my tongue; I turned from the bed. I fought the impulse to run away. Instead I found a chair, pulled it slowly up to sit beside him. I took a deep breath and then I said it. 'Louis is missing, Mickey.' I couldn't spare him my pain. I couldn't do it on my own any more.

'Missing?' He tried to sit up. 'What do you mean, "missing"?'

I felt my chest contract again as I stared at him, searching for the words. I knew he needed comfort, but I didn't know where to find it.

'I mean missing. Gone. Someone – someone's taken him. Don't you remember *anything*?'

He shook his head slowly, and the tear that had been pooling in the corner of his dark, swollen eye finally escaped. I watched with horrified fascination as it tracked down his cheek and hit the scar below, seeped through the neat stitches that puckered there. Then it was lost.

'Louis has been missing for almost – for two days now. He was with you when he disappeared.'

He looked back up at me blankly.

'You had him.' My voice was climbing. 'I lost you both, don't you remember that at least?' I was sweating now.

There was an unearthly pause.

'I think I remember a train,' he said then, almost hopefully, brow knitted with anxiety; the effort it took tangible.

'Yeah, well, we went to the Tate. To see the Hopper exhibition. I lost you both in the gallery. The next time I saw you, you were here, and Louis –' I couldn't bear to say the words again '– Louis was missing. I haven't – no one's seen him since. Apart from five hundred nutters, apparently.'

'Five hundred nutters?'

'Yeah, five hundred bloody nutters. The nutters phoning the police since the appeal.' He still looked blank. 'I can't believe you can't remember.'

'The appeal?'

'I've been depending on you, Mickey. On you remembering what happened.'

'For pity's sake, Jessica. I –'

One of Mickey's machines began to beep loudly, fighting his words for supremacy. Sister Kwame padded to his side and fiddled with it for a while. Then she took Mickey's pale hand in her own dark one, circled his wrist.

'And you?' he whispered, but his eyes couldn't quite connect with mine. 'Are you all right?'

'Oh yes, I'm grand,' I said numbly, 'to coin your phrase.'

The nurse spoke softly. 'His blood pressure's rocketing. I think he needs some calm, my dear.'

Calm? If only there was some to give.

'Mickey, I've got – I'd better go. You sleep. I'll see you later.' I stood up. 'But please,' I implored, 'please, while you're lying here, you must try to remember. We've got to find him quickly. The police are outside. They're waiting to talk to you. You've got to think – don't you remember anything at all?'

Slowly he shook his head, and I fought to contain a growing rage – and yet I supposed I was being unfair. It wasn't his fault – was it? At the door I looked back. He looked so pathetic, so broken and so utterly unlike my Mickey, so mournful lying there, that suddenly all the anger dissipated; love and pity took its place.

'I'll come back tonight, okay?' I said. But he was staring away now, lying very still. Only his fingers moved, plucking at the sheet over and again. I went back to the bed and kissed him gently on the forehead.

'Get some rest, darling,' I crooned, and I wondered if this was how it'd be. Mickey could be my baby, now Louis was gone. Then I walked resolutely from the room before I went quite mad.

Deb was waiting in the corridor. 'Are you feeling a bit better? How's your husband? Good to talk to him at last, I'll bet!' she said cheerily.

'There's something wrong. That's not my husband,' I said, moving off towards daylight as fast as I could. I heard her footsteps quicken as she followed me, tried to catch my arm.

'What do you mean, not your husband? I don't understand. Has there been some -'

'No, sorry. It *is* Mickey,' I stopped her. 'But it's not – oh, I can't explain. Not the Mickey I know.'

'What do you mean?'

'It's like he's gone all – all sort of odd. Retreated. And he can't remember anything.'

'Oh, I see. Well, come on now, Jessica. Give him a chance. I mean, he's had a huge blow to the head, hasn't he, and a terrible ordeal I'm sure –'

'A terrible ordeal,' I repeated, parrot-like. 'Yes, I suppose he has.' I pushed open the door to the corridor before my thoughts turned any darker.

*

Shirl was sitting in the canteen with DI Silver. They looked a little too cosy for my liking, her afro glittering invitingly above a green bandana as her head tilted towards him. Was she telling him my secrets – the ones he wanted to know? Sometimes I wanted to plunge my hands into her sparkly hair like Louis did; today I just stood at the table-head and gazed at her. My stomach really hurt now.

'Blimey, babe, you look terrible. Sit down. I got you a coffee,' she pushed it towards me, 'but I think it's probably cold by now.'

'Glad to see you've recovered. How're you feeling, kiddo?' Silver asked lazily, and I nodded, all wobbly, to indicate that I was fine, horribly aware that last time I'd seen him I'd been retching in the gutter. He stood up and stretched, and I plonked myself down in his seat. I thought how wan and insignificant I must look beside Shirl. Washed out like over-skimmed milk.

'And how's your old man?' He straightened his tie using his reflection in the window. I took a tentative sip of the coffee. It was stone-cold and foul.

'All right, I think', I muttered, 'but his memory's gone all weird.' I put spoon after spoon of sugar in my cup. 'He didn't even know that Louis was missing.'

'Ah well,' said Silver, 'give it time. He's had an almighty knock on the head, poor lad. I'm going to see him now, if that scary nurse'll let me in.'

His words singed me. 'We haven't *got* time, though, have we?' My voice came out too loud.

'Sorry – what do you mean?' His smile didn't falter.

'Time. You said give it time. But we haven't got time. I haven't got time anyway. I mean, what's happening? Surely there's been some kind of development?'

'You mean, what's been going on since you've been out cold?' Finally his smile was fading.

'It was a mistake,' I mumbled, abashed.

'Yeah. Easy one to make.'

'Please,' I looked him directly in the eye, 'it really was. I'm sorry if I – you know, if I scared you.'

He held my gaze. 'You did. Anyway, forget it. We've got a couple of good leads, but I need to interview your husband first. I'll be in touch.' He picked his mobile and his gum up from the table. 'Just be more careful next time, okay? You gave me a nasty fright.'

'You can say that again,' Shirl chimed in treacherously. Silver melted into the motley canteen crowd. 'Still, no harm done, hopefully,' Shirl went on. 'What do you want to do now, sweetie?'

My skimpy summer dress rippled in the fierce air-conditioning and I shivered. 'I guess I should go home.'

'Okay. Let's get out of here,' she said. 'I hate bloody hospitals anyway, they give me the creeps.' She pushed me gently forward as she squeezed round the Formica table, towards a waving Deb. 'I'm sure that nice policeman'll come and tell you what to do soon.'

'Great,' I muttered and stomped off towards the car park. 'I can't wait.'

As it happened, I didn't see Silver again that day. Deb drove Shirl and me home, and I trembled in the back and tried not to vent my frustrations. Deb kept assuring me that the amount of calls the appeal had prompted was entirely positive, and teams were working through them to rifle out the hoaxes from the genuine.

As I opened the car door outside the house, I heard voices calling my name. They were getting louder. I flung myself onto the pavement, tripping over my own feet.

'Louis!' I cried, righting myself – turned straight into a pack of photographers, TV cameras. The press.

'Jessica, how are you feeling?'

'Is there any news yet?'

'What's happened to Mr Finnegan?'

Deb put an arm around me; Shirl appeared at the other side.

'Gentlemen, ladies, please. Mrs Finnegan needs peace and quiet right now. There'll be another press call at Lewisham in the morning.'

Deb propelled me through the throng into my house and slammed the door. The voices kept up their clamouring for a while. Deb looked concerned.

'Okay?'

Leaning against the closed front door, I nodded.

'I'm sorry, Jess. They have no respect for privacy, that mob. Let's move out of the front of the house for now.'

'They're doing their job, I guess.' But I could hardly bear to think of that moment when I'd thought it meant my son was back; of the pure sheer joy I'd felt so fleetingly. I buried my face in my hands.

'I'll put the kettle on.'

'I'm fine, honestly.'

Shirl said she'd run a bath for me while I went upstairs to change. As I opened my bedroom cupboard to retrieve my dressing-gown, a sheaf of papers fell out of the folder I kept tucked in the side of the shoe-rack; the folder of things I didn't want to lose – my passport, my wedding certificate, my hard-earned exam results. Sketches of Louis; a few of a sleeping Mickey I'd done on holiday in Mauritius – our only holiday together before the baby – that weren't good enough to show him. A rare photo of my dad, a smiling youth on horseback, from the days he'd hoped to race professionally, spiralled slowly to the carpet now.

Fear crawled up my back and sat heavy on my shoulder, pricked across my skin in tiny little barbs. No one ever went in this cupboard except me, not even saintly Jean, but it was quite obvious now that someone had moved things round. The bedroom door banged behind me and I started.

'Sorry, sweetie,' Shirl said, 'I didn't mean to scare you. I just brought you some juice.'

'Someone's been in here, Shirl.' Frowning, I scooped the photo up.

'Who's that? Roger? Lord, isn't he young and handsome? Look at him on that horse, very la-di-da.'

'Hardly', I said distractedly, 'he was just the groom. Before he got too tall to race.' I turned the photo over and over in my hands. 'Shirl, this is serious. I'm sure someone's been in here. I always leave that folder right –'

'Listen, babe,' she took my hands and made me look

111

at her. 'You're in the middle of the world's worst nightmare. You're bound to be all jumpy, your imagination's bound to be playing tricks, you know? You've got to try and chill a bit. Come, I've run you a nice bath.'

I stuffed the folder into the back of the wardrobe and followed her to the bathroom, listening to her waffle as she tried to buoy me up. Jean had probably hung some of my clothes up, hadn't she, dislodged things accidentally? Reluctantly, I agreed. But despite the day's relentless heat, despite the bath, I couldn't get warm.

As we'd left St Thomas' Hospital earlier, Deb had tried to steer me past the papers in the hospital shop, but too late – I'd spotted myself on the front of nearly every one; wide-eyed in a grab from the news conference, looking a little like a lamb who'd lost its flock. Beside me was invariably a rare picture of Louis, Mickey and me, all smiling and carefree.

And despite Shirl's cheerful chatter now, all the photos of lost children I'd ever seen grinning on the news kept flitting through my mind. I ducked beneath the water time and time again, but their faces followed me. The innocence behind their toothy smiles, the ignorance of what came next; that their tragic destiny meant they'd never age past that photo – frozen forever in that time. Louis hadn't even got as far as having a toothy smile.

And just when I was battling not to succumb again to the utter desperation that drilled my very bones, the doorbell rang – only this time I didn't leap up in hope. I dragged myself from the bath and down the stairs, praying it might be good news. By the time I reached the kitchen, there he was, safely ensconced, like he'd been there for years, beer in hand, ash-laden fag in the other. It wasn't news about Louis at all. It was Robbie.

CHAPTER ELEVEN

When we were little, my brother Robbie was like my baby. I protected him from the world as best I could, but in the end my best no longer worked. By the time I'd got away from home, left it as far behind as I dared, he was being sucked under by a side of us that I'd attempted to stamp out.

We were so similar, Robbie and I, inheriting a streak of something from my dad that lucky Leigh had dodged. Blonde, blue-eyed Leigh resembled our mum; Robbie and I, dark tousled little devils, were freckled clones of our beloved dad. We rough-and-tumbled, fought and laughed; learnt to ride our bikes together, round and round the estate, ran riot in the local playgrounds, nicked Pacers and lollipops from the corner shops – needed no one but each other. We taunted poor Leigh mercilessly when she started dating. 'Ooh ah, lost your bra, left it in Gazza's car,' we'd chant when she slipped into the bedroom after another night of snogging Gary in the Coronet's back row, collapsing into giggles at our own daring when Leigh slammed the bathroom door shut to get some privacy. Robbie and me. Where one led, the other faithfully followed. Inseparable kids – distracted by our wayward dad.

In our teens Robbie began to move with the wrong crowd – a very bad crowd. He was my mother's favourite, and my dad was gone for good now; no man to haul my brother up. Mum never stopped Robbie from doing anything; never reprimanded him, never punished his increasingly destructive pranks, until eventually he lost all sense of control. I tried to reach him, but, despite my best efforts, by the time I was twenty and putting myself through night-school to get the exams I'd failed before, we'd lost touch for the most part – every number he gave me disconnected when I rang, every former mate disenchanted.

Dreams of being a drummer led to nothing but the dole. Occasionally he worked Soho club-doors, until one day I went to see him at his latest haunt and he'd just gone, packed up and left, no forwarding address. No forwarding address! He was on the bloody run; he didn't intend being found.

I was broken-hearted but unsurprised, exhausted by constantly bailing him out, excusing him to Mum. He was bad for my bank balance and my brain, but he was still my little brother, and I loved him with a passion I'd felt for no one else. Not even for my dad. A few years ago I got a larky postcard from Goa, and it made me laugh out loud to imagine him bearded and beaded, dancing on the beach like some old hippy fool. And I felt a stab of envy that he'd got so far: to places I'd always dreamed of but had never actually seen. But, most importantly, at least he was alive. Then nothing – until now.

'All right, sis. Beautiful as ever,' he said indulgently, dragging on his scraggy roll-up which tumbled ash onto the terracotta tiles. He got up to hug me. 'You've done all right for yourself, I must say. Congratulations.'

I fell into his embrace, absorbing him for a long and quiet minute. Then I pushed him off, although the bigger part of me wanted to keep holding tight.

'Sis?' I said, incredulous. 'You're not in Albert Square, you know. It's not flipping *EastEnders*, Robbie.' I went to the fridge to pour us both a drink, playing for time. My heart was beating very fast. I was shocked, confused, overjoyed, in fact, I thought – but above all else, I was cross. Five years of pent-up hurt throbbed through my brain.

'You said you weren't in the country when you rang. You said you saw the news on satellite.' I poured the juice very carefully, sliding my eyes towards him. I'd spent so long dealing with his disappearance I didn't know how to cope with the real Robbie now. He looked apologetic at least, smiling his charming little smile. The fact he was missing a front tooth rather ruined the effect.

'Yeah, well, you never know who might be listening, do you?'

'Don't you? Blimey, Rob. This is the real world, not Tarantino.'

'Taran— who?'

'You know. *Pulp Fiction*?'

'Oh, right. The real world, is it? God, Jess, your

116

life's more dramatic than mine's ever been right now.'

'Maybe. But not through choice.' I gulped the cool liquid, my throat still sore from having my stomach pumped. There were so many things I wanted to ask him; so many things rattling through my aching head I didn't know which to choose. I selected a real winner.

'I mean, where've you bloody been for the last five years, Rob, you bastard?'

He shrugged, sitting down again, grinding out his fag-butt in a saucer.

Shirl came in and screamed.

'Lord, Robbie, what have you been doing with yourself, man?' She sucked her teeth. 'You look like you could do with a good bath.' She sniffed the air. 'Smell like it too. Have you been smoking in here?'

I grinned. She was nothing if not maternal, my best mate Shirl.

'Char, what about your sister's asthma? Have you no thought, man? You're as bad as that husband of hers. Always doing jus' what you want.'

I let that go.

'Nice to see you too, Shirl.' He raised his arms in mock submission. 'Sorry. Won't do it again, I swear.'

'You can say that again.'

'I won't do –'

Shirl quelled him with a look. I turned back to my little brother, attempting to harden my heart. Where Robbie went, invariably trouble came too.

'So, like I said, what *do* you want?' I sat next to him at the table; I couldn't stop staring at him. 'Leigh's going to do her pieces, you know that, don't you?'

'Aw, Jess, don't be like that, darling.' He tried his puppy-dog eyes on me and I couldn't help but smile. 'I've missed you. And Leigh.'

I'd missed him too, quite desperately at times, but he really didn't deserve to hear that straight away. It was what he traded on, Robbie. Old good feeling for the good old days. Then he spoilt it all. 'I'm worried about my nephew.'

'Rob, you've never even seen your nephew. I doubt very much you even knew you had one until you saw the news. Did you?'

He had the good grace not to lie. He twisted one of his earrings through its hole and back again. 'I knew you were married, though.'

'Really? How?'

'Mum must have told me.'

'When did you ever speak to Mum? She never told me.'

I stared at him; he looked a little sheepish.

'Only the once. She must have forgotten to tell you.'

'Forgotten to tell me?' I looked at him; I didn't know who to blame. In the end, I let that go too – for now. 'So,' I prompted, 'why are you really here?'

'I've come to help.'

I grimaced. Robbie had helped no one but himself in years. He'd been the kind of kid who didn't pull the wings off daddy-long-legs himself, but stood and watched while others did. I sighed wearily. 'I appreciate the offer, but I don't really need your kind of help, Rob, I don't think. I just need to find my son.'

'Yeah, well, I can help you look, can't I?'

'Robbie, half the Met are looking. Where are *you* going to start?'

He shrugged, running nicotined fingers through greasy hair. I thought I could see his hands shaking a bit. He had a name tattooed across the left one – *Jinny*, I thought it said. He slumped against the dresser, his shadow wavy down the dusky hall.

'I'll look anywhere I need to. Christ, Jessie, I'm your family. We've got to stick together at a time like this.'

Shirl laughed quietly. 'That's a good one. Like you've always stuck by Jess, you mean?'

Robbie's mobile phone rang. He looked down at the number and scowled, shoved it back into his pocket.

'Don't you need to get that?'

'No.'

The ringing stopped. Then it began again.

'Someone's persistent,' I said. 'They must really want you.'

He snatched up the phone. 'What?' he growled. Then he darted outside the back door, phone clamped between multi-pierced ear and leather jacket, rolling yet another fag. 'Yeah, yeah, all right. I'm there now,' I heard him say. I wondered who knew he was here.

Deb had melted discreetly away when Robbie had arrived. Now the doorbell went again, voices muttered in the hall, then Leigh walked in. She saw Robbie outside on the back steps; she stopped dead in her tracks. And I was right. She completely did her pieces.

Later, when Robbie had gone, limp in the wake of Leigh's wrath, leaving a mobile number that I didn't

119

expect to work and another hug that, despite all my mixed emotions, I was overwhelmed to relax into for a second – was glad to get, in truth – the hospital rang again. They'd worked out that I'd scarpered without ever seeing the shrink; they asked me to go back tomorrow for a 'quick chat'. Then Deb came in and said that they'd got a few leads on the calls they'd had, and I tried to feel some optimism, I really did. She said that they wanted me to appeal again tomorrow, and that it wouldn't be long now before Louis was back.

I knew I should go back to see Mickey now, but the thought made me feel rather sick. When I spoke to the nurse on duty she said he was asleep, and so I sat down with Shirl and a bottle of wine but the drink just made me feel ill. I switched on the computer and started to surf the net. I was looking for something reassuring about how much time could go by and stolen babies would still be found safe and sound, but the only statistics I came across were sparse and scary. Eighty per cent of babies were found within three days, and if they weren't – well. Over and over again I read how crucial the first forty-eight hours were in the investigation – the most crucial. It was another slap in the face. Fear mounted in my chest until I had to log off.

I was knackered but I knew I wouldn't sleep, so I tried to watch some silly soap that Shirl had on. I couldn't concentrate. The 100,000 British kids who went missing every year whirled round my mind like fairground waltzers. Where were all those poor lost children? Hidden in cupboards, stashed in cellars, bedsits, existing under the arches in Waterloo and Vauxhall, round Liverpool's cathedrals and Birmingham's Rag Market? Images of the Austrian teenager locked in a stranger's cellar for her entire childhood, the American boys absorbed into a new family not far from their real homes floated back to me. The horrifying fact that these poor stolen kids had seemed to almost love their captors. I flicked channels dispiritedly, looking for something to distract me.

'Shall I see if I can find one of those travel shows you like?' Shirl prised the remote control from my hand.

'No, don't worry about it. Sorry. Am I annoying you?'

Mickey was so scathing about television – it was so trite and vacuous, he'd scoff, for the entirely brain-dead, that I rarely watched it any more.

The soap was back. I stared blankly at the screen as some blowsy blonde ran off with her stepfather, leaving her kids behind. Heartless cow. I bit the skin around my thumb – and then I had a thought.

'I'm going to make some posters of Louis. Some missing posters.' The word 'missing' bounced painfully round my brain like the pinball in a pub machine. I jumped up, trying to slam it away.

'You mean like people put up for their cats on lamp-posts?' Shirl looked bemused. 'Surely the police are doing all that kind of thing, aren't they, babe?'

'Louis is hardly a cat, Shirl.' I rushed over to the chest where we kept our photo albums, and dragged the doors wide open.

'I didn't mean that, silly. I'll give you a hand, shall I? I'll find a pen.'

An expensive blue album fell onto the floor, '*BOY*' emblazoned across the front in gold. I'd bought it just after my second scan, when they told me and Mickey I was expecting a boy. I'd watched my baby's foot flying through the unearthly air on that ultrasound machine and I'd felt the first flickers of the most profound love. I'd said goodbye to Mickey, who'd gone back to work, and then I'd wandered round the shops in a haze. I'd spent a fortune on tiny babygros and jumpers and clothes, and then I'd hidden them all away, waiting with growing excitement for the birth of my son: before the cosh of postnatal hormones whacked me over the head and left me reeling.

I picked up the album. I hadn't stuck a single photo of Louis in yet – I never seemed to have a spare second any more. Piles of pictures of the baby were stacked haphazardly on the shelves, and I felt another surge of guilt. For not bothering to officially record my son's short life. For failing him as a mother, yet again. I gritted my teeth and picked a recent photo; I drank in his serious little stare; the next one where he'd begun to blow a raspberry with excitement at the camera – a trick he was so proud of.

And then Maxine arrived home. Her swarthy new boyfriend dropped her on the doorstep and they had the gall to have a long smooch right there, not minding who could see, and then I watched him saunter down the path to his car. A foreign flag I didn't recognise fluttered from the back window. Anger flooded my veins. I hadn't seen Maxine since I'd found the photos of Louis in her grubby little room.

I shot into the hall as she opened the front door. Key in hand, Maxine stared at me as if I was some odd animal she'd never seen before. Was I imagining it or did she actually seem nervous now?

'Why did you take those photos, Maxine?' I demanded.

'Photos? What photos?' she shrugged.

'The passport photos of Louis. The ones that were hidden in your room. What have you done with him?' And I began to shout. I shouted incoherently, shouted for all the times she'd made me feel inadequate, for every time she'd taken the baby from me and he'd stopped crying and smiled happily up at her, for every deliberate flash of her long legs in front of my husband. I shouted for all the guilt and all the pain and all the times I'd not known what to do with Louis – and she, she just kept looking at me now like I was mad. And finally I ran out of steam, ground to a halt, and she said, quite calmly, 'I don't know what you talk about. Why should I not take photographs? We go shopping; I see the photograph place. I want a picture of me and *le bebe*. It's just something for me. You know, because I love him.'

And I stared at Maxine, just like she had stared at me when she'd come in, and I knew that it was true. She did love him; I'd seen it and I'd smarted with jealousy and fear, but it was why I'd let her stay, why I hadn't fought Mickey to get rid of her. I'd needed her expertise; her unruffled knowledge. The truth was, I'd thought Louis had needed her as I recovered from my early depression, recovered both my brain and my courage.

'I just get the photos for myself. For – how you say – for my wallet?'

I thought of Silver's words when I'd found them in the first place, and finally I surrendered. 'Yeah, all right, Maxine.' I took a deep breath. 'Sorry.'

She shrugged again. 'It's okay. I am sorry for you, really. I will help you if I can.'

'Thank you.' I went back into the sitting room and slumped on the sofa holding the photo of Louis that I'd chosen; holding it to my heart, feeling foolish, feeling utterly empty. I kept glancing at the picture of his beaming face.

'In the morning, I'll go to Blackheath and get it photocopied,' I told Shirl carefully, and she smiled and offered me an éclair she'd nicked from my stash in the freezer. Normally I loved them, but the image of Mickey's chocolate cake in the Tate haunted me and I couldn't face it now. Shirl put something quiet and ambient on the stereo and offered to give my shoulders a rub, but I didn't fancy it. I knew I'd never relax. I half-listened as Maxine skulked around the kitchen, then went up to her room with the inevitable can of cold baked beans (her peasant roots were embedded deep, Mickey had always said, whatever her aspirations to climb the social ladder) and a copy of *Hello!* that I'd sneaked past Mickey a while ago.

In the night I woke and couldn't sleep again, thought longingly of pills, but I'd flushed the remainder down the loo. I supposed that was for the best. And then, as I finally slid towards the dreams that went some small way to protect me, I remembered something I hadn't checked. My eyes snapped open as fear sidled back into the room and my heart began to race. I put the bedside light on; forced myself out of bed and half-crawled to the cupboard where I kept my things. I cursed my own stupidity as I slid my hand down beside the shoe-rack, past the plastic folder, to my dad's old boot-bag where I kept Louis's precious things. I drew it out and with trembling hands scurried through the contents. The first photos, the wrist-band from the hospital, his birth certificate…and then, thank God, the passport I'd only just received back for him. I flipped it open and studied his tiny little image, barely visible in the half-light. Then I buried the bag back into the cupboard, deeper than before, and carried the passport to bed, slipping it carefully beneath my pillow.

As I finally fell towards sleep again, Mickey's own passport flickered through my brain. I hadn't asked him why he'd had it yet… Then darkness overtook me and chucked me back into oblivion.

Someone woke me by shaking me so roughly that I thought I was being attacked. Still deep in sleep I lashed out, until I finally connected the voice repeating my name over and over with that smell of lemon, not quite so pungent this time. I sat up all confused, peered through the gloom at Silver standing by the bed.

'What is it?' Oh God. I pulled the duvet round me, felt my skin itching with pure fear.

'Get up,' he said urgently, 'I've got some news – some good news.'

I hurtled out of bed but he was already gone. I pulled back the curtain to let the streaky dawn light in, tugged my old dressing-gown on, tripping over my own feet in my rush to get downstairs. In the kitchen, the copper with the little belly, DC Kelly, was drinking coffee from a cardboard cup, eating something toasted from a greasy bag. He nodded politely and kept munching.

'What is it please?' My voice was all taut with stress.

Silver pulled a chair out and shoved me in it, shoved a fresh stick of gum in his mouth. He had faint scratches across one cheek.

'This one you're sitting down for, kiddo.'

'What's going on? Have you found Louis? Is he –'

He cut across my words. 'No, sorry, it's not quite that good. But,' he looked jubilant, like he wanted to punch the air triumphantly, 'he is alive! We've got definite proof that he's alive.'

If I hadn't been sitting, I would have fallen. 'Of course he's alive,' I whispered. 'Why wouldn't he be?' But still I felt relief crash through me like the sea, sucking all the air from me on its tide.

'So where is –' but I couldn't breathe again. I scrabbled around in my pocket for an inhaler but there wasn't one. I gestured frantically at the drawer. 'Inhaler, please,' I wheezed, and Silver delved around until he came up with my lifesaver. He plonked a cup of steaming tea in front of me, ladled sugar into it and ordered me to drink. Deb came into the kitchen with a package she gave to Egg-belly; smiled blearily but encouragingly at

126

me. Egg-belly disappeared into my living room, leaving a sickly smell of melted cheese in his wake. Silver called me through.

'Come in here please, Jess.'

I sat tentatively on the sofa, desperately tried to stop my hands trembling as I clutched my tea to me. The dawn air was already humid, but I still searched for warmth. Deb, next to me, patted my knee reassuringly, and I resisted the urge to fling my arms around her and sob into her flat bosom. DC Kelly knelt by the video on the floor, leaning so far over that a great expanse of white flesh was exposed above his builder's bum. He switched the machine on, the sweat rings saucering his underarms. And there, suddenly, almost larger than life on Mickey's plasma screen, was Louis, blinking, bewildered but alive, absolutely definitely alive. He was lying next to a copy of yesterday's *Daily Mirror* that bore our photo on the front.

My tea scalded my leg, splashing down over the white sofa that scared me each time I sat on it.

'See,' I said hysterically, never taking my eyes from the screen, from my son's perfect cherub face, 'white's so impractical.' I was gibbering with joy, clutching at Deb next to me. 'He's beautiful, isn't he? I told you he was.'

'Yes, Jess, he is. Absolutely beautiful.'

'Thank you. Thank you,' I murmured. 'Beautiful. He looks okay, doesn't he?' I gazed at Louis on the screen, at my son, thanking a God I didn't believe in until now. Then the camera moved away from his little hands that chopped and whisked the air – his helicopter arms, we

127

used to say so fondly – moved from his wispy feather-head, his softly folded double chin, and panned down to a note scrawled in chalky capitals on the flagstone floor beside him.

'NOW YOU'VE SEEN ME, LEAVE ME BE. I AM QUITE SAFE' was all it said. A ghostly light flickered across the message again and again.

'What the fuck does that mean?' I snarled. Desperately I looked around, at Silver, at Deb, at Shirl who'd just stumbled into the room rather indecently clad in just a T-shirt, afro akimbo from restless sleep. I was looking for some explanation.

'What do they mean, leave me be? Leave *who* be? Louis? Why would they think I would do that?' My words were running out, my chest crackling like an old lady's. 'Why would I leave my own son be? Oh God. Where is he? You need to find him now.'

'Breathe, Jess. Just keep calm and breathe.' Silver stepped towards me as Deb handed me my inhaler again. 'That's what we've got to work out, kiddo. What these people want.'

'What *do* they want?' asked Shirl.

'What people? Who the hell are they?'

'We're working on it, believe me. They haven't asked for anything yet. This doesn't seem to be a traditional kidnap. There's no ransom demand, not yet. No demand for anything, just this one, to be left alone. It might suggest a more – well, a more psychologically disturbed case than we first thought.'

'Disturbed?' I whispered.

'Very often young babies are taken by women who

are desperate for babies; who have been thwarted somehow.'

Deb clocked my face. 'They nearly always care for the child impeccably.' She squeezed my arm.

'Nearly always?'

'Always.' Her vein flickered.

'They've got to be kidding. They've got my son and they think I'm going to leave them alone? Just leave him there? They're fucking mad.'

The video suddenly ran out, the rattling white noise at the end made us all jump. I clutched Silver's arm.

'Can you rewind that please? To the bit – to where Louis is again.'

Tears streamed down my face, my nose was running, dripping down my chest, mingling with the tea on my kimono. Shirl tried to thrust tissues into my hand but I was crawling towards the TV screen where I traced my son's face with my fingers. I saw him smile. He smiled! My heart snapped in two. He was happy enough to smile – but he was happy without me. All my guilt compounded to thump me in the gut: this was my punishment.

'Where did you get this?' I croaked.

Silver was standing behind me now. 'It was sent to Scotland Yard on a bike,' he said.

'On a bike?' Shirl repeated, incredulous.

'A courier's bike. It was dropped off in the early hours. This is a clone, the original's with forensics. We're tracing the courier company now; the package was signed for at the Yard. We're going to find him, Jessica.' He was so near I could feel the heat from his body on my back. 'I promise you we'll find Louis.'

'Please,' I whispered, 'can you just give me a minute on my own.'

'Sure,' Shirl said. She herded them all out. I fumbled for the remote control and when I found the pause button, I stopped it on Louis's smile. I sat and stared at him. Numb with shock, I just stared at him.

Some time later, Silver made me jump again as he trod silently back into the room.

'Are you all right?' he asked quietly, sitting on the sofa behind me. 'I know it's a shock. But it's good to see him, kiddo, isn't it? It must be a relief.'

I tore my eyes from my son's image that juddered on the screen, turned to Silver, who was followed by an anxious Shirl. 'There's something, DI Silver, that I should have mentioned earlier.'

'Oh yeah?'

'When I got back from the hospital yesterday, from, you know –'

'You know what?'

I cleared my throat nervously. 'From, you know, my accident.'

'Ah yes. Your accident.'

'Well, I'm sure someone had been in my room. Going through my things.'

I had his attention now. 'Really? Like what things?'

'Well, the folder where I keep my papers for one. I've checked for Louis's passport, and it's still there, but all the papers – they were out of order.'

'Right.' He frowned. 'You should have told me straight away, you know.'

'Sorry.'

'It's my fault,' Shirl chipped in, embarrassed. 'I told her she was imagining it.'

'Right,' he said. 'Well, next time, come to us, okay, Jessica? That's what we're here for.'

'Of course. I will. I should have told you anyway, I realise that now. It's my fault, not Shirl's.'

'Yep, well, it's got to be your responsibility to keep us informed. I'll get the fingerprint lads up here again.'

I flushed. 'Right.' Standing, I found myself at eye-level with the welts on his cheek. 'Been partying?' I said without thinking.

'That's right,' he muttered back, so only I could hear. 'With a little wildcat. She whacked me this morning when I woke her.'

I flushed redder still, and turned quickly away – but not before I caught Shirl's raised eyebrows, the makings of a grin on Silver's tanned face. And as I couldn't think of an apt response, I went upstairs and got dressed instead.

As soon as I knew Louis was alive, every vestige of anger with Mickey finally fizzled out. I rang the hospital to break the news, but he was still sleeping and they didn't want to wake him. Sister Kwame was back on duty and she was polite and pleased to hear the news, though she seemed a bit distracted. Then I rang Leigh, just back from the gym. She was still cross with me about Robbie.

'I don't understand why you let him in.' I heard her light a fag.

'I didn't. Deb did.'

131

'Yeah, well,' she took a deep drag, 'he's bloody lucky he didn't get arrested right there and then.'

'Oh Leigh,' I said, 'you don't even know if he's in trouble now. Give him a break.'

'Jessica, Robbie's always in trouble. You're such an easy touch when it comes to that boy.'

'Yeah, and you're too harsh. He says –' I debated whether it was worth repeating. 'He says he wants to help.'

She laughed scornfully. 'And you believed him? God, Jess, there's one born every minute.'

'Did you know he'd spoken to Mum?'

'When?'

'A while ago, apparently. Before I had Louis. He said he knew I'd got married.'

'No. No, I bloody didn't know. Why wouldn't she have told us?'

'I don't know. I can't work it out. I mean – well, when it comes to Robbie and her, you never can tell.'

She inhaled crossly. 'Yeah, I suppose. But whatever, it still doesn't mean you should trust him.'

'Look, Leigh, I know he hurt you, but right now I don't know who to trust. Or what to do. I'm – I feel like I'm hanging on by the skin of my teeth.'

Another drag, another exhalation. Her voice softened. 'You're doing brilliantly, Jess. Just hang on in there. We'll have Louis back before you know it.'

My eyes filled. 'Yeah, well, I just hope you're right. All the statistics say that if a baby's not returned within the first forty-eight hours – well,' my voice cracked. 'And it's been three days now. If he doesn't come back –'

'What?'

'If anything happens to him, Leigh, I won't – I couldn't bear to live.'

'Jessica!' Shock flooded her voice, 'Don't you dare talk like that!'

'Why not?' I stared at the floor. 'It's the truth.'

'Jess, you're a fighter, babe. Come on.'

'I'm tired of fighting now. I've been fighting all my life. I thought this was meant to be the good bit.'

'Look, nothing's going to happen to him. What did that note say? He's safe, thank God.'

'Yes,' I said bitterly, 'but he's safe with someone who's snatched him from his own mother. So how safe is that?'

CHAPTER TWELVE

I slipped out of the house when Deb was using the bathroom. Shirl had gone to work and I was meant to be going to the hospital for my own appointment but I honestly found the idea horrendous. I wasn't sitting down with any therapist, thanks very much, and pawing through my private life. I wasn't that mad – yet. I put on an enormous pair of dark glasses and Mickey's old baseball cap, and shrugged myself down into my poncho, though it made me sweat. Just in case Silver was having me followed.

He was sitting at the counter with a pint already half drunk, a whisky chaser by its side. He looked haunted and older than his years, and I felt my heart yearn for him, for all he could have been. I cursed my father silently, I cursed the hurt he did us back then, the scars he left, however often he said we were his darlings. I thought of Robbie following my dad like some small shadow, and my heart went out to him now. Illogically, perhaps I still wanted to protect him, just like I'd done back in those crazy mixed-up days.

On cue, Robbie looked up and smiled at me, and I heard him order a drink. I was touched that he remembered my favourite – but my sentiment quickly went crashing to the ground when he looked appealingly at me for cash – could I pay? I pushed Leigh's harsh words from my mind and obligingly fished some change from my shorts.

'Blimey, Jess, you going incognito now?'

I smiled, sort of, and took the glasses off. The pub was dark and there were few drinkers so early in the day.

'I'm not meant to just do one without letting the Old Bill know where I am. I just fancied a little peace and quiet, you know.'

'Don't blame you,' he said, and offered me a roll-up. I frowned. He grinned goofily. 'Oops! Sorry, Jessie. I didn't think. Mind if I do?' But he'd already lit up. He spat tobacco from his tongue.

'Just blow away from me.' I perched on the stool beside him, taking a sip of the vodka that slid down very nicely, tracing a warm path past my aching heart. 'I haven't got much time,' I said, and he checked his watch. It was cheap and scratched and I said, 'Remember those fake Rolexes Dad got us that time? From Greasy Wilf on East Street?' and Robbie grinned and I felt an affinity with him I'd almost forgotten, that made me glad – until he said, 'I flogged mine actually. Some old dear bought it when I swore it was real.'

'Robbie!' I admonished, but I was hardly surprised.

'What? She was a mug with too much money. Anyway, I was, you know, down on my luck.'

'You've been down on your luck since you were sixteen, according to you.'

He downed the end of his pint. 'Fill her up, mate, can you?' He shoved the glass at the rotund barman. I shifted a little closer. There was a scrap of paper on the bar beside his tobacco; various phone numbers for someone called 'General' scrawled in Robbie's terrible writing, next to some sums, big figures being added together and divided.

'Robbie, what's been going on? I –'

'You what?'

'I missed you.'

'Blimey, Jess, don't go getting all silly on me now.' But he chucked my chin just like our dad used to.

I blushed. 'I'm not. Tough as old boots, you know me.' I took another sip of vodka to steady myself. 'I still don't understand why you've been hiding out for so long, Rob.'

'I haven't. I've just – I've been away.'

'You mean –'

'No, not that kind of away. Away away. Abroad away.'

'You'd better ring Mum. She's been worried sick.'

'I have now. Now I'm – not away.'

'I bet she was pleased.'

'You could say that.'

I struggled with an envy I'd known since Robbie first came home from hospital in my mother's ecstatic arms. A boy at last – just like she'd always wanted. She'd never forgiven me for not being one, that's what I'd always thought.

'So, where was abroad?' I asked after a pause.

'Asia mainly. Bit of South America, but mostly Asia. Thailand most recently. Bangkok's a fucking banging city.'

I thought of sun and sea and exotic smells; of travellers and backpacks – a whole world I'd longed to explore. I thought of five-star Mauritian luxury – the furthest I'd ever been. The all-inclusive Mickey had insisted on when I was three months pregnant: the overwhelming opulence. We hadn't been allowed to venture far out of the resort. All very nice, thank you, but not really my idea of travel. I'd been planning to see a bit of the world when I'd finished my art course. Another ambition thwarted by my unplanned pregnancy; another thing I'd initially been fed-up about – another nail now in the coffin of my tearing guilt. Now I'd happily live in a shoebox under Lewisham Bridge with Louis, never go anywhere ever again, if he could just come back. I stared at my brother.

'And you didn't think to let us know you were all right?'

He pulled heavily on his roll-up. It wilted pathetically in the heat.

'I sent you a postcard, didn't I?'

I snorted. 'Yeah, right. One in five years. Thanks very much. Very reassuring. Most considerate. And how come you rang Mum and not me?'

'When?' He looked cagey, hunched his shoulders. I looked at him properly for the first time today. Despite the temperature outside he was still wearing the old leather jacket, sweating very slightly. Droplets skittered and beaded across his pale and clammy forehead. I realised just how ill he looked, and I felt a surge of panic.

'Robbie, why've you let this happen? We were always so – so –' But I couldn't finish the sentence. He was no better than my dad, no more reliable. There was a horrible pause. I felt us drifting from one another, like every blood connection had been severed long ago. I'd tried and tried to rein it in, but I had to recognise I'd failed. My life had gone one way and his – his went down the drain, it seemed. Down the drain to 'fucking banging Bangkok'.

'Jess,' he said, then seemed to think better of it, and downed his whisky instead.

'What?' I encouraged. He wouldn't look at me. 'What were you going to say?' I asked again, impatient now.

'Nothing.' The leather creaked as he ground out the roll-up, gave it up at last. Then, 'Are you happy?'

'Oh yeah, ecstatic. Never been happier. What do you think, you idiot?'

'I don't mean right now. I don't mean since – since, you know, Luke got taken –'

'Luke?' I slid from the stool, my anger swelling. 'Are you kidding me? You say you came because you're concerned – but you don't even know my baby's name. You can't even remember his name.'

Too late, he saw his mistake; grabbed my arm to stop me going. 'Louis,' he corrected hurriedly, 'I meant Louis, of course. Sorry. Are you happy with Louis, you know, normally? And with your old man?'

I drained my drink, then I stepped up to him and took my brother's clammy face in both my hands. I looked right into his glazed eyes; they slid away from mine.

'Rob, you're wasted, aren't you? Absolutely fucked. God,' I dropped my hands in despair, 'I didn't realise how wasted till just now.' I chewed my thumbnail, thinking on my feet. 'Look, Robbie, I'm happy to help you, I'll do anything I can – but only if you promise to help yourself too. Robbie?'

But he wouldn't meet my eye again, just beckoned to the barman instead. So I turned away. I had to. I walked away from my brother, the baby who I had protected for so long, who didn't want to help me but wanted something from me, despite my own desperation. As I passed back into the sunlight it blinded me, and I fished for my sunglasses again. I racked my brains to think what I might have that he needed. I really wished I knew.

I was halfway back up the hill before I changed my mind. I saw a woman with a pushchair a bit like mine ahead of me, and I started to stalk behind her. As she neared the heath, she stopped to let her toddler out to walk. He dropped something, his pink beaker, rolling into the gutter. The child wanted to retrieve it; the mother wouldn't let him. He began to stamp his feet and squeal; she grabbed his arm too roughly and pulled him away so his knees dragged on the ground.

'Hey!'

She stopped and turned, her brow knitted.

'You're hurting him,' I said.

'Oh yes? And what's it got to do with you?' She was

well-spoken, her clothes straight out of Boden. Her hands tightened on her handbag.

'Everything. It's everything to do with me. You should never hurt a child,' I whispered. 'You should be glad of what you have.' I picked up the beaker and handed it to the tearful child. His warm little hand curled round the cup, and I resisted the temptation to scoop him up and run.

Instead, I turned around and ran back down into the village. Robbie was still skulking at the bus-stop on the other side of the road. I skidded to a halt before he could see me, stepped back into the doorway of Lloyds Bank opposite. The bus pulled up. I thought it would be too difficult to follow him, but he was at the head of the queue, and went straight upstairs. Panting in the sticky heat, I sprinted across the road and through the doors just before they closed. I curled up in the back corner of the lower deck.

The streets we travelled towards town were hot and noisy and thick with fumes. We passed the private gym Mickey and I belonged to, and I thought wistfully of the ice-blue pool. It was one extravagance I hadn't argued with when Mickey added me to his membership. I loved swimming, was good at it – much better than my husband, who, cat-like, hated getting wet. I thought about how if Louis was with me now I'd probably have taken him there today to escape the heat; his little tummy swelling above his swimming nappy, clapping at the water, splashing and splashing with delight as I laughed, as he chortled at his own cleverness. My stomach lurched just like the bloody bus.

On the Walworth Road Robbie got off, and I plodded after him, dodging between big black women with bags crammed full of fruit and veg, around scrawny pensioners with skinny ankles and tartan shopping trolleys, thick coats on despite the burning sun. Eventually Robbie dropped down into an estate on the edge of Elephant and Castle, not all that far from where we grew up. Who did he know here these days? I dreaded to think. He crossed the kids' playground, stopping to roll a fag; then he leant against the flaking yellow bars of the roundabout and made a call.

He waited, smoking. Five minutes later, a pretty young black boy with short dreads cycled up on a Chopper. He skirted Robbie, they laughed at something, and then Robbie jumped off the roundabout and walked with the boy, who lightly held my brother's shoulder to keep his balance. I followed them until they reached a flat that was partially boarded-up, on the ground floor of the estate. A fat white man sat outside on a bashed-up deckchair that had seen better days, reading an old *Sunday Sport*.

'Stevo in?' I heard the black boy call. The man shrugged, then jerked his thumb behind him.

'Give him five minutes. Annette's in there – if you know what I mean.'

Some manful leering followed, and I shuddered. A hairy bloke in a white vest rounded the block next to me, holding a pit-bull straining on a metal leash. My heart began to thud. The man carefully chose a spindly tree near me and threw a rubber ring onto a branch, began goading the dog to jump up and reach it.

141

An emaciated girl came out of the flat in a tiny skirt, zipping up a tracksuit top, her legs mottled and twig-like. She started laughing vacantly, blatantly wrecked, as she crashed into Deckchair Man.

'All right, darling?' He slapped her scrawny arse, leering at the other men – at my brother and his mate, but they'd lost interest now. They were heading into the flat themselves. Another youth approached; spotty and pale, he held himself as if he was freezing, shaking despite the heat.

I didn't think that my baby was in there. I smelt the desperation in the stagnant air: I just knew they must have come for drugs. Behind me, the little dog was still throwing his thick body up at the ring, increasingly frantic to reach it.

I was about to slope away when a young black girl with braids rounded the corner of the block that flat was in. She was shaking her head in time to music from her earphones, pushing a new pram although she looked barely fourteen. I tensed; my heart began to drum so loudly I was surprised they couldn't hear it. I strained to see the baby. But the pram was empty.

The girl was heading for the flat Robbie was in. Deckchair Man watched her approach, her ebony midriff taut and flat beneath her yellow bikini top and her gold chains, his fat pink tongue practically lolling on the ground amid the fag-butts and the Tennants Super cans. She disappeared into the stairwell; I heard her knock and the door crash shut behind her, and I began to run. I knew the baby was here – my baby. I ran faster than I'd ever run; as if my life depended on it – as if Louis's did. I sprinted past Deckchair Man.

'Oi,' he shouted, but I got to the door, a great metal plate, and I began to bang on it. I made two tight fists and I smashed them on that door, screaming my brother's name, screaming my baby's. My hand began to stream blood from my old cut. I kept on banging.

'Robbie,' I howled, 'let me in, you fucker. I know Louis is in there. Let me bloody in.'

Deckchair Man lumbered up behind me just as I heard the bolts inside slide back. He seized my hand, my bleeding hand, as it went back to strike again – but then the door opened and my brother stood there, backlit by the sun streaming through the tiny toilet window behind him. He was framed in pure light like a saint depicted in stained glass. Like the Angel Gabriel in the Annunciation, I thought deliriously, about to deliver my baby to me. I held out my arms.

'For Christ's sake, Jess.' He reached forward and grabbed my wrist. Then he saw the blood. 'What the fuck have you done to her?' he hissed in the other man's face.

'Nothing, it's nothing,' I moaned, launching myself forward, so I stumbled. 'Is Louis here? Where's Louis?'

Robbie slammed the door behind me, slammed it in the other man's face. 'Shut up, will you, you bloody nutter,' he hissed at me now. 'Pull yourself together.'

The black girl appeared in the hallway.

'Where's my baby?' I panted, gasping for breath. 'What have you done with my baby?'

She sucked her teeth at me. 'You wanna take care who your bredren accusing,' she spat at Robbie.

I broke free of my brother, pushing past the girl into the room at the end of the hallway. Some of the windows were draped with old bedspreads to keep the light out; two were boarded with planks of wood. There was no furniture at all, just a stack of boxed DVD players right up to the ceiling and an old mattress in the corner, filthy and stained. Music throbbed through the wall from next door – and the pram stood in the middle of the room. As I moved towards it, the girl brushed past me, holding something to her. Holding a baby – a lifeless little baby. I gagged; I moved towards her like I was sleep-walking. In her arms she held a doll. It was only a doll. The girl placed it very carefully in the pram, and covered it with a thin blanket.

I ran back out into the hall, and pushed on the other door that was closed. I could hear low voices, low beneath the music. The door opened a crack. The black boy sat on a bust-up old armchair; the skinny youth and a bloke with a peroxide Mohawk, all covered in tribal tattoos, shared a sofa so old they had both sunk down backwards into it, their four knees almost higher than their heads. The boy was lighting something made from an old Coke can, inhaling deeply, manically. Like his life depended on it. A crack-pipe, I realised with a hollow thud. The youth had his eyes shut, scratching at his arm ferociously. The peroxide man looked at me and raised a dark eyebrow. He was preparing something in his lap.

'Was that you doing all the shouting?'

'I'm looking for my baby,' I whispered.

'Well, he ain't here,' he said calmly. 'And you wanna keep your mouth shut. We'll have the filth round here with all that noise, and we don't want that now, do we, love?' I shook my head soundlessly. 'So why don't you fuck off now. Okay?'

Robbie came up behind me. 'I think you better go, Jess.'

I slithered through his grasp, back to the pram.

'I just want to know, why are you wheeling a doll around?' I asked the girl, but I knew now she couldn't help me. 'Don't you have a baby?'

She was getting ready to leave, slotting her stereo into delicate little ears that poked through her plaits. She stared at me, then she turned the doll over and unzipped its back. A long, fat slab of something black, almost chocolate-like, poked out between cotton-wool stuffing.

'A bit of blow for the boys, all right, nosey-parker? And you wanna keep your questions to yourself, ras. Know what I'm saying?' She sucked her teeth again, and tucked her doll back in very carefully. Almost lovingly.

Robbie propelled me to the door.

'Come with me,' I pleaded. 'This is a hell-hole, Rob, and you know it.' My eyes filled with tears, I grabbed his hand. It was very cold. 'You don't belong here. Come and stay with me if you want. Please don't stay here. I could use the company, you know.'

His eyes slid away from me. 'I got some business to finish up,' he said, very quietly. I felt the shame burning from his thin frame. But he wasn't going to leave, he really wasn't. He leant down and kissed my cheek. 'I'll call you, okay?'

As I hurried back through the estate, biting my lip with anger and pain, the man with the pit-bull was still there; the poor little dog almost out of its mind with

145

frustration. It hadn't reached the rubber ring. It wasn't ever going to.

Deb was waiting for me at home like some clucky mother-hen. She pointed out that it was long past time to go to the police station, that I'd been ages, and I caught the chiding note that crept through her voice.

'Are you my chaperone now?' I asked tiredly, slumping in an armchair. I couldn't bear to tell her about Robbie. I didn't want anyone to know how far my brother had fallen.

'No, of course not, Jessica, I'm just here to make sure you're all right. I'm sorry.' She pushed back her hair. 'Do you – do you need some space?'

Immediately I felt all mean. 'I'm only joking, Deb,' I said quickly. 'I'm just so tired, and scared, and it's still so bloody hot. It makes me ratty. I'm very grateful to you, honestly.' I realised suddenly how much I'd already come to take her for granted, how little I knew about Deb's own life. But she was reticent about it; not keen to share her personal views. I didn't even know if she had a boyfriend.

Her mobile phone rang. I was staring aimlessly out the window at the man who mowed the heath, making perfect circles with his big mower, when an urgency entered Deb's voice. She hung up, straightened her collar in the mirror.

'We're late. The boss is a little – riled.' I thought she was just nervous of upsetting Silver. They all seemed to idolise him, his team. Or maybe they just feared him. I hadn't worked it out yet. Outside, the press was down to one disinterested bloke with a camera, a flask and a copy of the *Mirror*. They were bored already. Deb bundled me into the car in such a hurry that I realised something must have happened.

'What's wrong, Deb?'

She shot me a rueful look. 'It's the Tate's CCTV. There's a glitch on the system apparently.'

'A glitch?'

'It skips ten minutes an hour. Unfortunately, the ten minutes must have been when Mickey left the building. There's no trace of him on the tapes.'

'Fantastic.' We travelled the rest of the way in silence.

At the station, I was whisked along to do my press-conference thing again. The fact that I'd seen Louis now made things both a little easier and a whole lot worse. I kept thinking of some other woman bustling round him, acting like he was all hers. I couldn't focus on the faces merging before me, and I couldn't seem to articulate my desperation. Silver was talking and then some moley-faced journalist with long, lank hair and hipster jeans stood up and introduced herself.

'Lynn Werthers, *Evening News*. I'm so sorry for your loss. It must be terrible to join the numbers of bereaved parents that –'

I sensed Deb frown beside me; Silver adjusted his tie minutely. My heart started galloping like a runaway horse.

'What do you mean?'

'Sorry, *Ms* Werthers,' Silver cut across me curtly, placing his cool hand on top of mine on the table. 'Bereaved is hardly the correct term in this instance –'

The journalist goldfished for a minute before flushing bright red, the livid stain joining her moles like children's dot-to-dot. She didn't try to redeem herself; she sat down very hard. Despite myself, I clutched Silver's hand like it was a lifeline. It was so hot, so stifling in the room I could practically smell the individual sweat of all these strangers, see it rising off them like steam, and panic was stamping through my brain now. *Bereaved*, the stampede spelt.

'Please,' I interrupted another journalist who was asking for yet another description. I leant forward into the microphone, which made it screech. My voice cracked above the static. 'Please, whoever you are, just give me back my son. Three days is long enough. He needs his mother. I need him. I can't – I can't live without him,' and then I got up and ran out of the room too fast. I whacked my elbow on the door, so hard it jarred my teeth.

Deb tried to calm me, to reassure me that things were really going well, honest. Waiting for Silver, her voice faded in and out as I nursed my throbbing arm. She told me that the phones had been red-hot; there were some promising leads. Eventually Silver appeared at the end of the corridor, drink-can in hand, with a young redhead in uniform. I willed him to hurry up as Deb droned on. Why the hell was he taking so long? The girl was simpering at him in a way that made my skin itch, rubbing her foot coyly down the back of her own leg. After a good few minutes, she wandered off and Silver strolled down to us.

'Now, Jessica, I have a little question and I want you to answer it like the good lass I know you are.'

Sometimes, you know, he was so cocksure, so sanguine, he made my blood boil.

'I'll do my best.' Still, deep down, I craved his re-assurance more than anyone's when it came to my son. He was always so unflappable, and his motives seemed so – pure. Unlike most of the men in my life up to now.

'Good. Deb told you about the CCTV cock-up. Unfortunately there's no trace of Mickey or Louis leaving the building, although we can see you all arrive together.' He swigged the end of his drink, then lobbed it in the bin. A feeling of foreboding was building in my chest. 'But there are several images of you going in and out of the main entrance, alone.'

'Several?' I was confused.

'In your original statement, you said you went outside just once.'

'I did, that's right.'

'Well, on the tape it's at least twice.'

I shook my head like I was going mad. 'It was just once, I swear.'

He looked at me very hard. 'And you're quite sure?'

'Yes, I'm absolutely sure.'

Deb shifted uncomfortably from foot to foot. Silver rubbed his earlobe thoughtfully. 'Right. Well, we'll leave it at that, for now.'

For now. I changed the subject to what I'd been waiting to ask.

'Who are these people that say they've seen Louis?'

149

I tried and failed to sound calm. He looked down at me, repeated much of what Deb had said. 'I can't tell you everything for operational reasons, you understand. But you mustn't get too excited. There are a lot of crack-pots out there. You do know that, don't you, kiddo?'

I slumped back in my chair despairingly. 'First you lot spend days telling me to think positive about all the calls you've got, now you're saying they're all mad.'

'I realise how frustrating you must be finding this. But it's all good really, Jessica, what's happening now. I know it's hard to believe, but stick with us, okay, kiddo? We're sorting the reconstruction as we speak.'

I stared over his head; I felt the bloody tears begin to needle my tired eyes. God. Not again.

'Deb, you need a break. Go home, get some rest.' She started to protest but he waved her off. 'I'll get Jessica back. We need a chat anyway.'

Ten minutes later and I was in his car again, the eternal passenger. He offered me a very shiny apple, which I declined. He bit into it hard. Juice hit the dashboard, splattered my arm with a strange intimacy. It was so hot outside that the heat shimmered above the road in glistening waves.

'We're making definite progress.' He flicked the core out of the window. 'And I do understand that all this waiting must be doing your head in.'

'I just want to do something useful – but I don't know what.'

He looked down at me, the expression in his hazel eyes veiled. 'Let me buy you a quick drink and we can talk about it.'

'I should be seeing Mickey really,' I said, but it was rather half-hearted.

'Oh should you?' he said levelly. Guilt suffused me yet again. I was drowning in the stuff. I guessed it was quite obvious by now that I was hardly playing Florence Nightingale.

'I don't – I'm not very good at hospitals,' I muttered.

'No, well, they're not the most cheerful places usually.'

There was a long pause. My hair tickled my face in the breeze. 'It was – it's just my dad, you see,' I offered eventually.

'I see,' he said. A pause. 'What happened to your dad?'

'It just – it made me go a bit – you know. Funny about them. Spent so much time there when he – um, when he died.' I rarely let myself dwell on this; a part of my life too painful to bear. 'My mum couldn't face it, you see. Used to make me go instead.'

'Nice of her.'

'Oh it wasn't her fault really. She just couldn't cope with him, you know, being so ill. And I didn't mind. I was glad to have him on my own, I suppose. And he used to make me laugh so much. Doing impressions of the nurses.' I smiled fondly at the thought.

'How old were you?'

'About ten or eleven, I think.'

'Bit young to be hospital-visiting on your own.'

There'd been far worse things the three of us had had to do at that age. I shrugged. 'Not really that young. Robbie used to come sometimes. And I loved my dad, you know. I hadn't seen him for a while when he got sick. Lung cancer. Too many fags, you know.'

Oh God, how much I'd loved that cheeky bloke. I pulled the sunshade down swiftly, fished around like I had something in my eye. The unshed tears made them look a strangely glassy green. Silver glanced briefly down at me. There was something irrefutably solid about this man. He made me feel safe in a way Mickey never did. No hidden angst of his own. None that was obvious to me, anyway.

'Well, nice drive in all this heat, just what you need. Bit of fresh air, clear your head.'

'I wish it would,' I said wistfully. Waited a beat, forced myself to ask.

'So, how many of these "crackpots" say they've seen my son?'

Did he suddenly look a little less sure of himself? 'They all say they've seen him. But the sightings that we're taking seriously, that we're acting on right now – well –'

'Yeah?'

'Three.'

I nearly choked. 'Three! You *are* having a laugh.'

'Three's good, you –' He caught himself mid-sentence.

'You what?' I asked.

'Nothing,' he finished rather lamely. 'DC Kelly's gone to interview them. Look, they're all in the same area, which is a real positive. It's about realism now, and a – well, a touch of optimism.'

'Is that what they teach you at police academy?'

He laughed, and I smiled listlessly. 'Yeah, that's right. Good old police academy.' He turned the music down a bit.

'So where are they?' I said.

'I can't tell you yet. But I will soon, I promise.'

'Can I meet them?'

'Not until we've got something concrete, no. Just trust me, kiddo, okay?'

'Okay,' I said.

Silver took me to a pretty old pub on a green about twenty minutes into Kent and bought me my second vodka of the day, and some crisps. Then he decided I should eat something more substantial, but I declined politely, so he ordered us something 'to share'. Food still made me think of cardboard at every chew; my vodka slipped down much quicker than the Ploughman's that eventually arrived, but under Silver's watchful eye I tried to eat. He, on the other hand, just chewed his eternal gum and drank some diet drink.

'Didn't you fancy a pint?' I felt myself wilting at every mouthful. A huge sheepdog slavered over my bare feet with a hot, lolling tongue.

'Not while I'm on duty,' he said rather tersely, and I looked up at him. He didn't catch my eye. I resisted the urge to kneel down and bury my face in the dog's soft back.

'My kids'd love this place,' Silver said, chucking a lump of cheese down for the dog. On the green a straggling band of ten-year-olds were playing a tempestuous game of rounders, overseen by a bossy little boy with freckles as hot as the day.

'Kids? Plural?'

'Yeah. Got three,' he said, and something like remorse flitted across his face. He didn't elaborate. I waited for a moment.

'Will you – do you want to tell me about them?'

'Some other time, kiddo.' He chucked the dog some bread, which he pushed around with his great damp nose and then rejected. 'I'll just say, though, I do understand what it's like to love a child. I really do.'

I stared at the ground miserably. An ant was struggling to carry a crumb twice the size of his own tiny body. He was just about managing.

'You know you asked about my dad,' I said quietly, still watching the ant.

'Yes.' Silver didn't push.

'He was a nice man, really. He just couldn't quite keep on the straight and narrow. He was – he did quite a bit of time.'

'I guessed he might have done.'

'He broke my mum's heart in the end.'

'What about your heart?'

I looked up, surprised.

'It sounds like you were very close.'

I swallowed hard. 'Yes, I suppose I was. We were. I think – no, I know I was his favourite. We had a sort of bond. I don't know why really. It was just there. And – my mum hated that, you see.'

'That's a shame.'

'He got a long sentence, the last time. Then he got sick. They let him out in the end.' I felt my mouth go dry. 'To – to, um, die. You know. In the hospital. And

154

when he did die, my mum wasn't there. She was – she was up at my school seeing my headmaster. I'd got in a bit of trouble, you know.' Sticking up for hot-headed Robbie, I seemed to remember, who'd punched another kid in the playground for teasing him about his jail-bird dad. I took a swig of drink. 'And she never really forgave me for that, I think. For keeping her from my father, at the end.'

The freckly boy slammed the ball way out across the green, to copious whoops and cheers. Silver clapped him heartily.

'Good lad.' Then he looked at me again. 'Go on.'

But I couldn't really. I remembered crawling into my mother's bed the night Dad had died. She'd let me lie beside her, she'd even held my hand as she smoked into the early hours, zonked out and coughing. I was so frightened that something would happen to *her* now, I clutched on tight until I finally fell asleep. I was late for school that day. The next night I'd attempted to climb in again – but she'd turned over, turned her back and told me to please go away, all right, love. I'd shuffled back to my bunk above Robbie; I'd never tried again.

The ant had disappeared now.

'You know, I just keep wondering,' I pushed the sweating pickle round the plate, 'what would drive someone to steal a baby?'

He looked at me.

'*My* baby,' I repeated fiercely. 'I mean, they must be mad. Mustn't they?'

'Not mad, I don't think. More like desperate.'

In silence, we both contemplated the possibilities,

until Silver excused himself and went to pay the bill. I thought about the weeks after Louis's birth and flinched. I drained my drink but I couldn't block the memories, the relentless bloody memories that were crushing me. Shouting at the screaming baby when he wouldn't feed, terrified he'd starve; my bosom a flaming tennis-ball of fire, suffering from mastitis, desperate to stop the pain, afraid it'd harm my son if I did. My tears: the stream of endless, terrified tears; feeling there was no one to turn to, to ever tell me what to do, to assure me I was doing whatever I did do okay. Leigh occasionally turned up to see us, dispensed a bit of advice that I'd fall on like a starving woman, but she was done with babies by that time. And anyway, she didn't really do boys. Too much trouble. She preferred her girls – and her beautician. My mum flew over once, but she spent most of the time wandering around, spaced-out, in awe of Mickey's house, and shopping for things she couldn't get in Spain. I dug the palms of my hands into my eyes.

'A penny for them.' Silver swiped his car-keys from the wooden table. I jumped.

'You don't want to know, I promise you.'

He looked at me closely. 'Are you okay?'

'Just got a bit of a headache, that's all.' I trailed after him to the car.

My bosom throbbed emptily; my guilt stalked me like a great black shadow. The kids on the green were screeching with laughter in the fading light. I didn't look back.

CHAPTER THIRTEEN

The next morning, I finally gave in. The German psychotherapist had very shiny hair, that was the first thing I noticed. Coppery bright as a new penny coin, the light from the ceiling bounced off it. To shield my eyes against the gleam, I stared instead at the carved wooden Buddha sitting plumply in the corner, oddly out of place among the yellowing leaflets about HIV and stress.

Actually she seemed quite nice, the therapist, quite genuine, but I wasn't going to get sucked in. I was noncommittal, monosyllabic in the main. Mostly I was fascinated by her centre-parting – it was so straight. She managed to ascertain that no, I wasn't really suicidal; no, I didn't have a death wish; yes, I was just desperate for my son back. She said that four days of enforced separation from your child was bound to destroy anyone. Yes, I was suffering from the worst kind of guilt imaginable – the feeling I had failed my son – although of course I hadn't, she hastened to add. That my postnatal depression had been quite normal, that thousands of women suffered from it, a lot of them untreated. That it didn't mean I was a bad or unfit mother, or that I deserved this fate. I nodded blankly to show I understood all this, while she said that yes, it was quite natural in the circumstances to feel this way, and then she suggested, rather tentatively it seemed to me, that if I needed more medication I should give the pills to someone 'responsible' to hold on to for me.

'Like who?'

She looked slightly perturbed, pushed her rimless glasses up her small nose with one neat movement. 'You have someone to lean on a little, Jessica? It is vital at this time, *ja*?'

No, I wanted to say, there's no one I really want to lean on, no one I'm really allowed to anyway – but I just wanted to get the hell out of there, so I agreed. I said what I thought she wanted to hear.

'Yeah, of course,' I said, 'there are lots of people around. My best mate Shirl, my sister Leigh.' And there were. I had lots of friends and all sorts of well-wishers getting in touch. It was just that I felt like a battered little island in a ferocious sea, under relentless elemental attack. So absolutely and utterly alone, despite the crowds. I smiled slightly. That was probably what she would like to hear. But I couldn't bear to admit it.

'What makes you smile now, Jessica?'

'What?'

'You're smiling a little now.'

I shook my head. I waited. Eventually she continued. 'And your parents? The baby's grandparents?'

I shrugged sadly. 'Mickey's mum and my – my dad

158

– are both dead. Mickey's dad's senile, unfortunately, and my mum's in Spain. She lives there now. I think she's coming over, she's meant to be. I hope so, anyway.'

'That's good, no?'

'Well, yes.' I thought about it. 'Actually, it's a bit late in the day really. I would have liked it if she could have come straight away. But she's not that well.' I thought some more. 'And the thing is, honestly, she'll be about as much use as –'

'As?'

'I don't know. I can't think how to say it politely.'

'Don't be polite then. Why should you?'

'Cos she's my mum?'

'I'm sensing a lot of hurt here, Jessica. So, tell me, she'll be as much use as what?'

'As a slap in the face.'

Her face almost lit up. I cursed myself.

'A strange analogy, no?'

'No, not really,' I said, rather crossly. Well, she'd asked me to say it. But I knew it was dangerous to let my secrets out, and I hated analysing with a passion. Boyfriends had always loved the fact I didn't do deep chats.

'She's just a bit – out there, if you like,' I said. 'My mum.'

The therapist stared at me expectantly, until I felt obliged to say some more. I muttered, 'Well, you know, she's – she's had a hard life. I don't blame her for anything. I guess it's just sort of – wounded her. She was never very good at showing love, you see.'

'Ah. I do see, yes.' Finally. I sat back. She'd got what

she wanted. The therapist breathed a great whistling breath of understanding over her immaculate teeth. I wondered if she shared a dentist with Silver. I didn't like the way his name kept cropping up in my head. I resisted the urge to ask her to please explain the mother thing to me, because I certainly didn't see, couldn't see in fact, had never really seen the truth between us. Whenever I needed my mum, she wasn't ever there, and she never really had been. Simple as that.

The therapist wanted to talk about Mickey. I didn't.

'This makes your despair worse, no, Jessica?' she asked, all pat, and I nearly laughed with frustration. 'You are fearful for him.'

Yes, I was fearful, but more of him than for him. I was fearful that he felt like such a stranger since his injuries. I was fearful that I found his vulnerability so odd. Like a snail, he suddenly seemed to me, stripped of its shell. Soft and utterly defenceless. It frightened me – and worse, I was violently ashamed of these new feelings.

There – I'd finally admitted it. My head snapped up to look at her. Had I spoken aloud? She sat patiently, watching me still, so I guessed not. Anyway, if we went down the Mickey path, we'd be here for hours. We could get on to why I'd married him, why he'd chosen me when every girl in the office was panting after him, was I actually good enough for the man? What I was most fearful of, in truth, was that if the floodgates opened, the flood would never stop.

'You are angry with him?'

'I was.'

'I think it is an absolutely natural reaction. To hold him responsible, even if he wasn't.'

'But I've dealt with it.' She stared at me. 'Really, I have.'

I thought of telling her about my premonition – the premonition I'd had when Louis was first born four weeks early. I'd sat in the hospital, tucked away in the private room that Mickey had insisted we'd have, even though I protested, rather delirious from all the drugs, that I'd quite like the company of all the other mothers out on the ward, to make some new friends. But I'd held my baby in my arms when he came out of the incubator and I'd felt the most unexpected, the most huge, the most gargantuan surge of love. It was quite breathtaking; it knocked me nearly sideways. And I was terrified as it bowled me over, swept me in its wake. The only love I'd felt anywhere near this before was for my dad, for my little brother – and look what happened there. They'd both gone and deserted me; left me all alone. And I knew, I knew in that moment in that bed clutching my new love, that I could never trust this feeling, this pure emotion that was stronger than anything I'd ever felt. I knew then that this tiny person with his little tortoise face, his scrunched-up soft skin, his wise old eyes that already seemed to know a thousand things, his warm body like a puppy, bunched-up and not yet unfurled, clinging to my chest as though his life depended on it – I just knew right then that something bad might happen to him, and I wouldn't cope, I couldn't cope without him now. I'd fall apart and die. And after that realisation followed the terror and the sleepless nights, the struggle to breast-feed, the hormones rampaging at the heart of it – the knowledge that I loved my baby too much to see straight any more. To be an able mother.

A long time later that panic finally subsided and I learnt to trust the love; to go with it and not keep battling. But I'd been right, hadn't I, all along? It was too perfect, that love, to keep on going unspoilt.

In the end, I didn't mention it. She'd think I was mad, madder still than I must already seem, discussing postnatal premonitions. And as soon as I could, I made my excuses and left. I reckoned she must have got her paperwork on me all filled in by now; I promised to call her if I felt like I was about to lose control again. She held on to my hand as she gave me her card; asked me to ring her any time, and I managed to resist the temptation to fall on the floor and admit I didn't have a clue how to keep on coping. Just about coping. So instead I squeezed her hand back very gently.

And actually, I did want to see Mickey now. I might be finding his vulnerability hard to fathom, but I had questions and I wanted answers. Something had been going round my mind since the other night.

I sat by Mickey's bed and held his hand. His breathing was shallow and he was back on the oxygen. Sister Kwame hovered and, despite her calm smiles, I felt an underlying anxiety I hadn't sensed before. They were waiting for the consultant with the little ears.

'Has anything come back to you?' I tried to sound as level as I could but Mickey must have seen the

162

desperation in my eyes. He shook his head and winced.

'Oh, Mickey.' I clutched his hand a little tighter. 'Are you still in that much pain?'

He grimaced. ''Fraid so,' he muttered.

'Can I do anything?' I plumped up his pillow helpfully, but when I'd obviously just made things worse, I gave up again. He tried to get comfortable, and I waited for him to settle again, until I couldn't hold it any longer.

'Mickey, why did you have your passport on you?' I blurted out. He looked confused; forgotten, my hand slipped from his.

'When?'

'When they found you – after Louis – after you were attacked.'

'God only knows. I wish I could remember.' There was a pause. His brows knitted. 'My passport, you say? Are you sure?'

I nodded, didn't trust myself to speak.

Then relief crossed his face. 'Sure, I always have my passport on me, don't I?'

'Do you? Why would you?'

'For work. I don't know. I had some big cash transaction for some trip I guess. There's nothing odd about it, Jessica.' For the first time since he'd woken he sounded like the old Mickey. Impatient. Slightly on the edge. My heart did a tiny somersault. Glutton for punishment, me; it was what I both liked and hated about my husband: his certainty; his utter refusal to suffer fools.

'If you're so worried, ask Pauline.'

'I will. I think she's still away though. No one's got hold of her yet.'

Sensing my discomfort, he reached for my hand again. The least-affectionate man in the world. I knew I should revel in this new Mickey, but actually I felt like I was on a rope bridge, trying to get a footing and slipping, constantly slipping, swinging above the heads of normality.

'The police never mentioned it, you know.'

'What?'

'The passport.'

'Yeah, well,' I drew my shoulders back, 'there's lots of things those coppers seem to forget.'

He laughed softly. 'I'd forgotten how much you hate them.'

'I don't hate them,' I said, although I remembered talking into the early hours with Mickey when we were first together, more than a little drunk, not knowing I was pregnant, telling him about my parents, about my shattered teenage dreams. About DC Jones. I thought of Silver now. 'I just don't really trust them. You know why.'

He squeezed my hand. 'Yes, I do. But come on now, Jessica. Don't wind 'em up. You need them on your side.' He coughed and winced again. The Irish tang was more pronounced than usual. 'Our side, I should say.'

Our. Only I didn't feel like there was an 'our' right now. There was just me.

DC Kelly had interviewed the three 'crackpots' – with little success, in my eyes. Deb, permanently by my side these days, opened the door to him. Wearing the same sweat-stained pink shirt from yesterday, the poor man was obviously exhausted. His little belly was even diminishing a bit, though the dried egg-yolk on his tie did nothing for his appearance.

He explained that of the three calls they'd taken seriously, one could definitely be discounted, because she'd turned out to be a constant caller to the police. The other two, however, both down in East Sussex, had said similar things to one another – but there was still really nothing conclusive. One was an elderly lady: she'd been weeding her front garden when she'd seen a metallic-coloured car pull up, driven by a blonde woman who looked harassed and 'frightened', the lady said. Apparently the woman had been reading a roadmap, and had then made a call from her mobile, a young baby screaming in the back the entire time. The old lady had remembered it because the woman looked so worried and so helpless, like she had no idea at all what to do with the crying baby, and was practically shouting down the phone, though it was impossible to hear what she was saying. The woman had then tried to give the baby a bottle, and though the old lady hadn't been able to see properly into the back, she got the impression the baby wouldn't take it, kept pushing the milk away.

I didn't feel amazingly optimistic about any of this news. 'Every new mother looks worried and frightened, don't they? I know I did, all the time,' I said gloomily.

Deb smiled reassuringly. 'I know it's not much, but the second witness saw a similar sort of thing. It means there's better odds.'

The other guy was a student at the local college. He'd been stopped by a woman in a silver car, a baby crying in the back, asking for directions. She wouldn't open the window properly, and the child was obscured by sunshades, so he didn't get a good look. But he'd thought it was particularly odd, because the woman kept looking away from him while they spoke, although he'd decided it was because she was so worried about the baby screaming. She asked for the road to London, and he remembered very little about her other than she'd had a huge coat on, which was odd, considering the weather, and sunglasses, and he thought she might have had an accent, though he found it hard to describe. Possibly American, he'd said.

'So now what?' I asked helplessly. I was horribly aware it was already forty-eight hours since the Louis video had been shot.

'We're trying to ID the woman. A local newsflash is asking any women matching the descriptions to come forward to be discounted. We're trying to trace the car. I know it's not much, but it's better than nothing.'

'Where's the boss?' I asked casually.

'He's following up other enquiries,' was all Egg-belly said, and I left it at that.

Since DC Kelly had left, I'd lost the will to live. Deb had a rare night off, and Shirl was out with some new bloke. I went online for a bit: I was going to set up a 'Looking for Louis' website, and I wanted to do some research. I surfed the net for yet more stories about missing babies, desperately seeking reassurance that they were all returned safe and sound – but it didn't seem to be the truth at all. I read some old news reports on famous cases where bereaved women or women who couldn't conceive had stolen babies. Some had been found again – some many years later. Some hadn't. Worse still, a few had actually been discovered dead. I stared in abject horror at the face of a tiny baby boy who'd eventually been found in a drain. Hot tears sprang to my eyes for that little life, and terror mounted again, thudding through my chest – so when the internet connection went down, perhaps it was for-tuitous. I thought about running screaming down the road, banging on every door I came to looking for my son, but in the end I knew it wouldn't help.

I slumped in front of the TV, vaguely listening to some expert drone on smugly about damaging toddler day-care, babies' faces flitting through my mind, flicking through one of Maxine's glossy magazines trying to dispel them. There was a picture of some foreign super-model at an awards show 'only forty-eight hours' after delivering her second child, looking svelte and rested. She reminded me of someone. Listlessly I flicked on through. Then I turned back to the model. Heidi what's-her-name. With a huge great lurch, I realised who it was she looked like.

I jumped up to find the phone. How could I have been so flipping dense? The stranger at the gallery who'd scared me so. The weirdo at the Tate. Tall and blonde and foreign – just like the woman in the car. The woman with the baby.

*

As I rushed across the hall on a hunt for the phone handset, a great breeze flew through the house; somewhere upstairs a door slammed shut. There was a bang followed by the tinkle of glass breaking, a picture dislodged by the gust, I guessed. 'Great,' I muttered. But I wouldn't be distracted from my task now; I kept on towards the phone.

And then I heard a footstep, followed by a soft curse, from somewhere up above me. I froze; only my stomach kept rolling on with fear.

'Maxine?' I called tremulously after a second. But I was sure she was at college this evening, and anyway no one replied. The phone was within my sights now; as I picked it up a small bead of sweat dripped as if in slow motion onto my shaking hand, ricocheting onto a black tile on the floor. I switched the button to get a dialling tone – and then I heard the voice.

At first I thought it was a crossed line but, listening, I quickly realised there was someone speaking on my own phone. Speaking on my phone, in my own house, in a tongue I didn't recognise. Adrenaline swept through my body; I moved swiftly towards the front door and then, with hand trembling on the latch, I shouted down the receiver, 'Who the hell is this?' There was a stunned silence, followed by a click as one party hung up. The other cleared his throat before beginning in broken English, 'Excuse me, Madam, this is Gorek Patuk.'

'Who?'

'Maxine's friend.'

'Maxine's friend?' I repeated foolishly. 'Where exactly are you, Gorek?'

'Upstairs,' he said, as if it was quite normal. 'I am upstairs.'

'Oh, I see,' I said, trying to collect my thoughts, although I really didn't see. 'Well, could you please get off my phone and come downstairs. Right now.'

'Right now –' he began, but I snapped off the handset before I could hear any more and stood at the foot of the stairs, drumming it against my hand. A surge of fury chased away my fear until it had completely gone – though afterwards I thought perhaps I should have been more frightened. Now I just felt cross.

He slouched down the stairs, jangling his car-keys in one hand, as innocent as the day he was born, though thankfully with more clothes on.

'Hi,' he said cheerfully, which rendered me entirely speechless for a second. 'I was just waiting for Maxine, okay?'

'How did you get in?' I asked him, and I held out my hand for my phone. He came very close to me and his eyes were black as night. 'Maxine, she give me her key. Okay?'

'No, actually, it's not really okay.' For some reason my knees had gone a bit wobbly. I put my hand out to steady myself on the banister, but he was too quick for me. He slid his hand around my wrist to support me; his skin was very hot.

'You all right?' He looked right into my eyes and I found I couldn't answer. I was utterly disconcerted now. 'I wait in the car for Maxine. I give her the key back. Thank you for the phone.' He picked up my other hand and slipped the sweaty handset into it. I breathed in his smell, a strange musky kind of scent. Then he was gone.

And it was only later, when I'd collected myself a little more, when Shirl finally came home and found the note Maxine had left reminding me she'd gone to Cambridge for the night with her English group, that I realised the whole time we'd spoken, his blue-tooth mobile receiver was clamped to his well-oiled head. So then why did he need to use my phone?

CHAPTER FOURTEEN

Early the next morning I waited anxiously for Deb to arrive, to tell her about Gorek, to ask her what I should do. She was running unusually late, so I paced the house putting things in piles and then moving them again rather pointlessly until Shirl finally appeared, half-dressed and yawning. She was all nervy about her meeting later with a big new gym in town.

'I've gotta look smart, and you know me, babe. I don't really do smart.' She dangled a white shirt from one hand rather pathetically; it looked like the archetypal dishrag.

'Give it here. I'll find the iron.' Glad to have something to do, I ironed while she squatted on the floor, sorting out her massage oils. Catching our reflection in Mickey's huge designer mirror, I nearly managed a wry smile behind the ironing board.

'What?' Shirl looked up from arranging the small bottles.

'Nothing. I was just thinking – this wasn't quite how I saw things when we were seventeen.'

'What – you in a big posh house ironing my shirt?'

'Me in a big posh house perhaps.' I thought about it for a minute. 'No, neither of those things.'

'Or me going out to work and you being a stay-at-home –' Too late, she stopped herself.

'Mum,' I finished for her, quietly.

She shrugged. 'I guess I always saw you as the one that'd get away.'

I had a sudden vision of Shirl and me behind the art room, both with school skirts barely past our bums. Shirl smoking, me with my Walkman that my Nana bought me when my dad died, sharing a pair of headphones, listening to Shirl's tapes of Marvin, laughing at *Viz*. Of us lying on the scorched grass outside the canteen the year we did our GCSEs; me sketching Shirl in the back of my maths book (never enough money for the fancy sketchbooks that I craved); Shirl's everlasting legs eliciting admiring glances from every boy that passed. Glances from Robbie's gang – when Robbie put in a rare appearance at school. No one looking at me, not really, not so that I ever noticed. Shirl telling Robbie he was thick for running with that crowd. Me poring over the glossy travel brochures that I'd pinch from Thomas Cook in the precinct in my lunch-break. Dreaming of being anywhere but on our estate. Leigh in the sixth form, all blonde and perfect in her uniform, poker-straight hair and pale pink lipstick, the other girls in my year so admiring of my sophisticated older sister. Leigh leaving to do a typing course on Oxford Street, very grown-up in her stilettos, engaged to Gary on her nineteenth birthday. Me determined not to go down that path. Planning my getaway. Always planning. Planning to go to art school; my art teacher giving me extra time in the evenings because she said I had talent. Imagining myself in long woolly jumpers and black berets, drinking cheap red wine and absinthe till four in the morning with intense and glowering male artists, with girls who used cigarette-holders and spoke like Audrey Hepburn and said 'darling' a lot. Messing up my exams because I got involved too fast with a boy who broke my heart as I searched for some kind of substitute for my dad. Something, anything, to fill the gaping hole in my heart. Dealing with the nightmare that took place at seventeen, when the police came knocking again, even though my dad was long gone. Not going to art school because of my mum. Because she couldn't cope with life any more on her own – not after the police raked it all up again. Because I had to get a job; had to earn some money to stop her going under; because Leigh and Robbie were gone. Ending up behind the counter in Thomas Cook in the precinct, the place I'd imagined booking my great travels in, not other people's cruises or caravans or their two weeks in Benidorm. Wearing a horrid nylon uniform and not a stripy arty jumper at all, nor a natty beret. Hardly what I'd planned. Not what I'd planned at all.

'Damn it.'

A bottle slipped from Shirl's hand, the oil spilling across the floor in a greasy little pool. A smell of oranges pervaded the room; it made me think of Christmas. I stared up at Louis on the wall just for a moment; we hadn't even had a Christmas together yet. I checked the clock for the umpteenth time this morning. Come *on*, Deb. I turned Shirl's shirt over very carefully.

'I didn't think I'd have kids by now. Not before thirty, you know. Not ever, necessarily. Not after my mum and dad.' I tried not to dwell on the fact that it hadn't been part of the plan in any way; at the initial anger I'd felt at being trapped by my own stupidity.

'No, well, I didn't think you'd know what an iron was either, but you do. God, I think my flipping lavender is off.'

Silently I thanked her for not reminding me of my early maternal failings; of the sobbing wreck I momentarily became. 'I didn't really until Mickey.'

'That figures.'

'Though Jean does most of the ironing these days.' I caught myself. This time Shirl smiled.

'Listen to you, lady of the manor.'

I blushed. 'I sound like a wanker, don't I?'

'You sound like you, babe. Never the latter.' She slotted her oils very carefully back into their compartments. 'Only sometimes you do sound a bit like –'

I finished the second cuff without looking up. 'Like?'

'Like *him*.'

'Well, that's natural, isn't it?'

'Is it?'

'I mean, he's a strong character.'

'I'll say.'

The tip of the iron caught my inner wrist, burning the thin skin there. 'Ow. Bloody hell that's hot. Oh God, where's Deb?' I handed the finished shirt to Shirl. 'Do you know what gets me the most? Apart from feeling

174

crap when I think of all the times I wanted to go out dancing instead of sitting in with Louis every night.'

'All new mums feel like that sometimes.'

'Do they?'

'Of course they do. They'd be lying if they said they didn't. And actually,' Shirl put the shirt on, 'actually some of them just go and do it. Some of them never stay home with their kids.' She didn't say it but I knew she was thinking about my mum.

'The worst thing is all this waiting all the time. It's this constant feeling that I'm absolutely bloody help-less. That it's all out of my hands.' I leant down to unplug the iron, the rant building in my chest. 'That I could hunt and hunt and hunt for Louis, that he could be right nearby somewhere, but that unless that person who's got him slips up, you know, like, lets someone see him by mistake, or actually changes their mind, I won't have a hope in hell of knowing.'

Shirl hung her bag over the back of the armchair and hugged me. 'You're doing the best you can, babe. Don't beat yourself up about it.'

'I'm trying not to, but it's bloody, bloody hard, Shirl, you know. I keep thinking of what I could have done to stop this happening.'

'It's not your fault, Jess. None of this is your fault. Know that, girl. Okay?' She kissed my forehead, catching sight of the clock as she did so. 'Shit, is that the time? I'd better get a wiggle on.'

As Shirl left ten minutes later, banging the front door behind her, the photocopies I'd made of Louis's picture, which had sat waiting on the hall table, fluttered in the breeze. One floated slowly to the floor; I pinned it beneath my bare foot. I looked down at Louis's little face; I seized the phone and rang Deb again but she didn't answer. In the kitchen I found sellotape and scissors in the drawer, grabbed my bag and left Deb a message saying I'd be back soon.

I tramped across the baking heath, attaching a picture to every lamppost and road-sign that I came to, fighting the feeling I was wasting my time entirely, ignoring curious stares from passing strangers. One man slowed and wound down his window, gazing at my still-swollen boobs. I felt a lewd remark brewing so I gave him my death-stare until he shot off in a blast of diesel fumes. And every house I passed I wondered whether Louis was inside. I worked my way down the hill into Greenwich, ending up outside the library on the High Road with my last photocopy. I stuck it to the bus-stop outside the entrance of the next-door language school. My poster looked utterly pathetic, already curling in the heat, Louis's little face staring out all blurry, my big bold pleading letters all wonky beneath – '*MISSING FOR NEARLY SIX DAYS*'. Did I honestly believe that anyone would ever respond?

I was so hot by now that my hair was damp and my chest was tight. I'd forgotten my inhaler again and I couldn't face the walk back in the rising heat, so I slumped on the little plastic seat in the bus-shelter and waited for a bus to take me home. Near me a group of foreign students chattered excitedly, drinking lemonade from green and shiny cans and jostling each other dangerously next to the busy road. On the group's periphery a dark young woman wearing a headscarf and an awful lot of layers for this temperature was hovering, a small baby in her arms. She held it rather gingerly, I thought, my stomach swooping the way it did every time I saw a tiny child who might, just might, be mine. I craned for a look – it was a girl with a big birthmark on her face, gold studs in her shell-like ears. Then a red car pulled up just past the bus-stop, music thumping from the open windows, and the woman raised an uncertain hand at the driver. He jumped out, swaggered to the pavement, wearing some kind of uniform. I realised with a jolt that it was Gorek. Of course, it was Maxine's school that I was outside. I leant back into the bus-shelter. I didn't want him to know I was there.

Some of the group greeted him half-heartedly; they seemed polite rather than affectionate, I noticed. But he ignored them anyway; headed straight to the woman, taking the baby from her with absolute authority, tickling her so she began to giggle in that bubbling infectious way only babies can. He held the baby up high above his head then and the mother began to panic, stretching her arms out for her daughter, saying something to Gorek I didn't understand, her mouth turned down, all grim. For a moment he held the child up higher still, out of the woman's reach, taunting her deliberately. I stood – then sat again, sat on my hands instead. I resisted the temptation to intervene.

Eventually Gorek passed the baby back, pinching her cheeks hard as he did so – too hard, so the baby's lip began to curl and tremble. Gorek was gabbling fast in his own tongue, just like last night, the woman nodding in reluctant agreement as he got out his wallet and handed her a wad of notes, pinching *her* cheek this time, so hard his fingerprints remained behind. And just as Gorek ran down the stairs into the school beneath the library, my bus finally pulled up.

All the way home I felt uneasy. Was the baby Gorek's? Did Maxine know about that woman? But when I got back to my house, Deb was there and my mother was on the phone and it pushed all thoughts of Gorek from my mind.

My mum wasn't coming. She'd finally found the bottle to tell me; she definitely wasn't coming. I couldn't say I was surprised, but I was shocked at how sad I felt. She suddenly sounded old on the phone, and I was trying to comfort her, though deep inside I was shouting *How could you let me down right now?*

'Jessie, you understand, don't you, love?' she implored, and I sniffed and raised my chin like I had when I was ten, and replied, of course I did. Her heart was bad again, she told me, the doctor said she really shouldn't fly. I swallowed the temptation to say that we all knew there was little wrong with her silly heart apart from all her nerves, but it was obvious that would be the end of her today, so I pushed it down and tried to smile instead.

'Perhaps, when the baby's back,' she said, and there was a little tremor in her voice, 'perhaps you'll bring him out to see us?'

'Of course I will, Mum.' This was how it always was.

Why should it be different now? Poor fragile Mum, sunk under the weight of my feckless father, destroyed by the very love of her life. Held together by her children, who couldn't bear to let the whole thing dissipate, trying for some semblance of normal family life. My baby was missing, presumed kidnapped, and my mother was planning holidays with him in the sun.

There was a pause. I could feel her working up to something. There was a jangle in the background, and I saw her gold-looped arm as she raised her gin and tonic to her mouth, drinking to find the courage.

'Robbie rang,' she said. A pause, and then a gush she just couldn't hold back. 'My little boy. Thank God, I said to George. Just when you least expect it. All this time, and then – well, I thought he was really ... really gone this time.' Perhaps she finally sensed the insensitivity of this sentence because she stopped for a moment; then spoke again very fast.

'I think he needs some money, Jess. I don't want to ask you to sort it out, especially now you're looking for the baby –' she said it like I'd put him down and absent-mindedly forgotten where '– but Robbie says he hasn't got a bank account right now. I think – I imagine cos he's been abroad, would you think?' She sipped again, then rattled on. 'Georgie said we can lend him some. I must say, I was so relieved when he agreed.'

Lend! To Robbie? My patience was wearing thin. I thought of him on that estate in Elephant the other day, his dignity all gone.

'*Give* him some, Mum, you mean,' I said, with a small sigh.

'What?'

'Give him money. Not lend. You know perfectly well you'll never get it back.'

'Oh, Jessica. Don't be like that. He's – he's your little brother.'

'Yes, Mum, and I'd do anything for him, you know that. I'm only stating fact. It's just, Mum, I've been wondering –' I stopped.

'What, love?'

'Well, don't you think it's a bit odd – that he's just turned up like this? Out of the blue? Just when every-thing's so terrible?' I had voiced the thing that had been niggling me all this time. The thing I didn't want to say to Leigh, because I knew she'd already jumped to worse conclusions than I ever could.

'He said he saw you on the telly, Jessie love. He said you looked so sad he had to come. You know how soft he is deep down.'

I almost fell for it; I really wanted to. But still I strug-gled with the jealousy of years gone by. However much I loved Robbie, it was hard to accept my mum loved him more than anything. Much more than me.

'Well, I've been sad for years that he just disappeared, and he never came back then. We've all been sad, haven't we, Mum?'

'Yes,' she admitted, 'I have been very sad. But', she brightened, 'he's back now, come to help you find the little baby.'

'Is that what he told you?' There was a long pause. 'Mum?'

'Something like that, yes.'

'Mum, what's he said? Has he said anything else about Louis?'

I waited as she lit a cigarette. I thought she'd given up.

'Mum!'

'What?'

I heard the clink of ice down the receiver, then a sip. A very long sip.

'You're not being straight with me, Mum, I know you're not. You need to tell me what Robbie said. You can't always cover up for him.'

'Don't be silly. Of course I wouldn't. All your brother told me is that he wants to get Louis back.'

'But why is he so desperate to? He's never even seen the baby.'

'How can you ask that, Jessica? Louis is his blood too.' Sometimes I thought my mum was stuck in Sixties' gangster London; that she thought life was like the Krays' had been. 'He loves that baby like you do. Blood's thicker than water, you know.'

I resisted the urge to scream very loudly; was about to tell her about her son's fall from grace, but she rambled on regardless. 'And actually,' I steeled myself for some great imparting of wisdom, 'actually, I want to send Robbie some money straight away, you know, tide him over while he gets a job. While he helps you.'

I raised my eyes to heaven.

'Mum, you didn't even tell me you knew Robbie was okay.'

'When?'

'He said he spoke to you last year sometime. He knew that I got married.'

'Did he? I don't remember.' She was lying, and we both knew it. 'Anyway, look, you talk to Georgie. You can sort out the money thing together.' As usual she abdicated all responsibility.

'Mum –'

'And try not to worry too much, lovey. I'm sure everything will be just fine. Hang on in there, okay?' I could practically hear the relief wash through her voice as she handed the phone over. For some reason, she wasn't going to admit she'd talked to Robbie last year.

'Jessica!' George's jolly tones crackled down the line. I loved George. He was like the big silly bear from that kids' programme *Rainbow*; just what my poor damaged mother needed after the disaster that was my dad. And George took care of her, which meant finally Leigh and I didn't have to worry so much any more. But still, he wasn't my dad.

When I got off the phone, Deb was waiting to take me to the police station. She looked very hassled and hot, and I wanted to ask her where she'd been this morning, but I got the feeling this wasn't the time. Every day until Louis was found I would have to do the police press conference; Silver said they were imperative in order to stay in the public's consciousness. Today he met me before I went up on that stage, to discuss the woman at the Tate. I hadn't seen Silver since our drink, and I felt suddenly quite shy. He was rather abrupt, the police artist in tow.

'Why didn't you remember before, Jessica?'

'It didn't seem important.'

'I keep telling you, everything's important.'

'I just forgot.' I stared down at my feet, a slow flush creeping across my face, feeling like I was in the headmaster's office. He looked quizzically at me.

'What do you mean, you forgot?'

'I didn't really think much of it at the time. I mean, she gave me the creeps, this woman, but she was quite, you know, normal. Well, I thought she was.' The internet reports from last night began to clatter around my head. 'Normal' women so unhappy they did something mad.

'Go on.' He was trying to keep the impatience from his tone. 'Define "the creeps", can you?'

'She was just a bit sort of – full-on. Like she kept going on about how bonny Louis was.'

'Well, he is,' said Silver.

'Yeah, but I thought – she looked kind of familiar, but then she said she didn't know me. And she just got a bit – close, that was all. You know, like when people invade your space.'

'Familiar?' he prompted.

'Well yeah, but I never worked out why. I don't think I did know her. She just had one of those faces.'

'Could you describe her again?'

'I'll try.'

'Good,' Silver said. 'You go with Mitchell here and do just that then. Better to be safe than sorry, I think. Shame you didn't remember before, kiddo.'

I was shocked at how upset I was at his reprimand. He strolled off before I could mention Gorek and I decided that in the circumstances it could wait. I shook off the peculiar feeling that I'd begun to crave Silver's approval now, and followed the artist into another room. I'd brought Maxine's magazine to show him; he promptly made some bad joke about supermodels not needing to nick babies when they could afford to buy them, and Deb coughed loudly and pulled a face at him.

He shut up and drew quite fast, tapping his pencil ferociously against the table when I found it difficult to describe her exact features. I kept getting muddled with flipping Heidi-in-the-magazine, and the final image didn't really convince me. Still, it was a start. Then Deb took me into the conference room, where I joined Silver on the platform. There certainly wasn't going to be any hand-holding today. He sat beside me, absolutely cool and calm, as I faced the usual barrage of flashes and questions destined to make my head ache. Then a rather spotty youth stood up.

'Chris Thomas, S.E. News Agency. Glad to hear your husband's on the mend. I just wondered, are the police considering the possibility of child-traffickers? I've been covering a story about a Moldovan gang who've been known to operate in this area. There are various rumours about snatching kids to sell to wealthy child-less couples –'

My top lip lifted up and back, like an animal about to snarl for its life, but before I could speak, Silver interrupted him, smoothly glossing over Spotty's words.

'It's something we're definitely looking into. But we're following a few other leads right now. The feeling is it's likely to be rather more domestic than your scenario. Any more questions?'

184

But I was shaken to the core. Baby traffickers? They'd never crossed my befuddled mind. Silver began to give a description of the woman spotted down in Sussex, asking for more eyewitnesses to come forward. He asked people to be especially vigilant; to report anyone with babies in any sort of suspicious circumstance. Then he called the conference to an end.

'Same time, same place tomorrow, guys – unless there's any change in news. Thank you.'

Then he said he'd drive me home; Deb would meet us there. I was haunted by images of swarthy-skinned, pirate-type men with gold teeth and heavy accents snatching Louis from his pushchair and running to the ports with him, wads of money jammed in stone-washed denim pockets.

'Do you think there could be any truth in what he said?' I asked nervously as Silver pulled off. I puffed rather desperately on my inhaler. Dark clouds sagged with unspent rain, the air still thick and soupy. God, I wished this weather would break; there was nothing left to breathe.

Uncomfortably, Silver looked less certain than he had in the conference room.

'We've certainly been aware of these gangs that he mentioned – but the scenario doesn't really fit in your case. Why would they target you in the Tate? They work much closer to home generally. And there's usually some connection with the family first.'

A horrible thought had been speeding through my brain since Spotty had stood and spoken.

'Maxine's new boyfriend. He was alone in my house

last night, using my phone to call abroad.' Silver's head snapped round. 'He said Maxine let him use her key but she's been away so I couldn't ask her. I didn't like it anyway. It was kind of creepy.'

'Why didn't you tell anyone?'

'I was going to mention it to Deb, but she was late this morning.'

'It's not really fair to blame Deb, Jessica.'

'I'm not.' I was feeling increasingly flustered. 'I didn't mean that. It's just – this morning I saw the same bloke with a baby. I thought – I thought it might be his daughter, but I'm not sure. And he had a strange flag flying from his car that I didn't recognise the other day. He could possibly be Moldovan, I suppose. I don't know anything about the place,' I said in a very small voice. I looked hard at the oily shimmer that rose from the road.

'Maxine told me she didn't have any one boyfriend. She mentioned someone called – something French, I think.'

'Leo? Yeah, but she's a bit of a – a goer, you know. I've mentioned it, I'm sure. The night Louis went missing this bloke came around for the first time, came to pick her up in a sports car.'

A blare of horns as we swerved out too far across another vehicle's path.

'Christ, Jessica! Why the hell didn't you tell me this before?'

'*You* questioned her.' I was panicking now. 'You said there was nothing to worry about. I told you about the photos in her room and –'

'This isn't about the bloody photos. You should have made sure we knew about any strangers around the house. I have asked you time and time again. What with the woman at the Tate and now this –'

He pushed me over the edge I was balanced so precariously on. 'Hang on! Why do you keep blaming me for all the things you miss?' I thumped the window angrily. 'You're the copper, aren't you? You're the ones doing the questioning. I'm trying to make sure you know everything but it's just – it's all been so full-on, and with Mickey in the hospital too, well, it's really hard to think straight at the moment. God, please don't try to make me feel worse than I already do.'

I felt him struggle to compose himself. I'd never seen him so disconcerted. 'Okay, you did tell me about the woman. Only, not immediately.'

I was about to snap, when he held a conciliatory hand out. 'But you're quite right, Jessica. I am the copper. I'm sorry.'

My head was throbbing. 'I'm sorry if I messed up, it just didn't occur to me. I've only seen this bloke Gorek a couple of times; it's just, well – last night he really freaked me out.'

'Forget about it, kiddo. It's just a bit – frustrating to realise that I don't have all the facts when –'

'She has so many bloody boyfriends I can hardly keep track –' I was choking on my words. 'God, Silver, I can't bear it if something I didn't mention has made things worse for Louis.' Hysteria was building; I tried to hold it down.

'All right, kiddo. Calm down, okay?'

'Don't call me kiddo, please. I really hate it, it's so – so bloody patronising. What if that bloke has got Louis, Silver? What then? Whose fault will that be?' I groped at the door handle. 'Let me out, please.'

'Don't be stupid.' He snapped the central locks on.

'I just need to be on my own for a minute.'

'I don't think you do, you know. You're panicking.'

I couldn't really speak now; I just kept stuttering, 'Just let me out right now, please, just let me out. Let me out or I'll –'

'You'll what?' He pulled the car over onto the small road across the heath. I fumbled with the door again; he leant across and grabbed my arm. I could smell him, smell the sweat under the perpetual aftershave, see the grey under his tired eyes, the yellow flecks in the hazel irises, the silvery hairs in the close-cropped dark hair, feel each finger on my skin. We were so near each other, the adrenaline pumped through me and I felt my stomach lurch strangely. I stared at Silver for a second that stopped and hovered in time, and then I tore my eyes from his. I turned back to the door and muttered 'Let me out, please' again, and finally he did. He unsnapped the locks and I hurled myself out, pulling out of his grasp, stumbling over my own feet, running and then nearly falling, and then righting myself on that arid heath, the parched grass beneath me, the huge sycamores towering above, dripping with insects' honeydew.

I was practically crying with sorrow and frustration as I heard him call my name, just once, and I nearly looked back at him but I couldn't bear to, I could hardly bear to see how shaken he was, when I was relying on him so completely. And I was realising he was only human, and I didn't want to know that right now, because I was coming to depend on his warm solidity, and I felt like I was betraying Mickey, but most of all my Louis, and that this unbidden feeling of some kind of need for him was the most ridiculous thing of all. As I walked across the heath towards home, my breath came harsh and ragged as I repeated over and over again, 'I'm sorry, Louis, sorry, Louis, I'm so sorry, my little baby,' dashing the hot tears from my eyes.

Silver didn't follow me.

As my house came in sight I made out a man walking from the front door, behind Maxine. Nearing, I saw it was Egg-belly, and he was ushering my au pair to his car. Silver was taking this seriously then. I tramped across the pavement outside as the big car backed out of the drive, and Maxine's round eyes swum over me. She didn't look particularly perturbed, but then that was Maxine for you, tightly woven into a tough but silken sheath.

Deb was waiting anxiously in the kitchen.

'Are you all right?' she asked, peering closely at me. I was so hot and sweaty my dress clung like a second skin, and I felt an exhaustion that crept its greedy tentacles into my very core. I opened the fridge. 'I'm fine, honestly, Deb.'

'DI Silver just rang. He left a message for you.' Deb shoved a bit of paper into my hand as I drank half a bottle of cold water straight down in one go, feeling almost triumphant. He was going to apologise. Then I read the note. I didn't understand what it said.

'What does it mean?' I passed it back to Deb.

'Ring him and find out, why don't you?' She handed me the phone.

Silver picked up straight away. 'Do you remember where Mickey was the night before Louis disappeared?' he asked, and his voice was flat. He definitely wasn't about to say sorry. I thought longingly about the time before everything went wrong, back when I was just Louis's mother and not a crime statistic.

'He was meant to be working, but actually we went to the opera.' It sounded terrible in the context of things now. Was it really only a few days ago that I had only small worries like whether I was too fat? And why the hell hadn't I been at home with Louis, instead of enjoying a night out – albeit rare. Instead of – the guilt drenched me yet again – dashing out the door as quickly as I could for a few hours on my own. I shook my head impatiently against the memories.

'Um – Mickey had been away for a few days; he'd been on a shoot for the *Romantic Retreats* brochure. He was meant to be coming back really late; and then he suddenly rang me in the afternoon, and told me to meet him in town. We went to see *Madame Butterfly*.' I was babbling. 'I'm not mad about opera but it was a last-minute work thing. A special gala night. His company arranged it. I hardly ever go out these days.'

'So who's Agnes?' Silver said.

My heart skipped a beat.

'What?' I must have heard him wrong.

'Agnes. Who is she, do you know? We've just got hold of Mickey's private online diary from someone called –' I heard him flick a page '– called Pauline. There's a meeting scheduled the night before Louis disappeared with someone called Agnes.'

'Are you sure?' I half-whispered. I remembered Mickey dashing into the box at the interval, straight off the train from the country, slightly sweating in the sultry evening heat, unusually ruffled for him. Deb was looking worried now.

'Got it here in black and white, Jessica. Can you shed some light on it? I need to eliminate everything I can asap, and I can't reach this Pauline on the phone right now.'

'Yeah, I can unfortunately.' My top lip was suddenly clammy with fresh sweat. 'Agnes is –' my voice cracked; I cleared my throat '– Agnes is Mickey's ex-wife. I thought she – she lives abroad, I think. I've never actually met her.'

'Right-o, kid—' He pulled himself up before he said it. 'Right you are. Know anything about it then, this meeting? I'm guessing from your tone of voice you don't.'

'Oh, well done.' I chewed a bit of skin right off my thumb, studiously avoiding Deb's concerned eye. 'As far as I know, Mickey hasn't seen Agnes since we met. I'm sure it's a mistake. Can't Pauline help you if she's back?'

'Let's see,' he said, and hung up the phone.

*

191

Two things were worrying me. One was that Pauline hadn't bothered to get in touch on her return. The other was far worse. Why the hell had Mickey been meeting his ex-wife behind my back?

'I'm going out for a bit,' I told Deb casually.

She ran a hand through her mop of hair. 'Do you think that's wise?'

I looked pleadingly at her. 'There's just someone I need to see.'

Her eyebrows shot up enquiringly. I was reluctant, but I knew she wasn't going to budge.

'Pauline. Mickey's PA. She's a friend, kind of. Apparently she's back from holiday. There are a few things I'd – I want to ask her. Not about Louis.'

'Well, let me come anyway. I'll keep you company.'

So in the end, I did. I called Pauline and invented some story about being in the neighbourhood, could I drop in for a cuppa; and then Deb drove me up to King's Cross. When we reached Pauline's, though, I wouldn't let her come in.

'Please, Deb.' I looked her squarely in the face, her cosy, friendly face. 'I need a bit of space on this one, yeah? It's kind of – personal. Is that okay?'

She squeezed my hand kindly, and I went up alone.

Pauline lived in a fashionable gated complex down by the old canal. I'd been there once before, to her fortieth bash last winter, just before Louis was born. I liked her a lot; she was sassy and young-looking beyond her years, small and sturdy with huge blue eyes, a no-nonsense Geordie, and absolutely Mickey's right-hand woman at work. When I'd first started at the office myself, I'd felt rather worried by her, threatened somehow, but once I'd started seeing Mickey I realised that, much as he leant on her for so much, it was strictly business – mainly because Pauline was as gay as you like. These days she shared her penthouse flat with her very posh and rather boyish girlfriend Freddie, and their slobbering mastiff Slobodan.

Pauline was waiting by the lift as the doors opened, tanned and fresh-faced from her holiday. She hugged me and I wondered if it was my imagination that her huge doll-eyes seemed strangely blank. 'I'm so sorry, pet.'

Slobodan wandered out into the corridor to goose me, and Pauline pushed him back inside. 'Sod off, Slob. In your bed, okay?' She led the way through the open-plan room to the galley kitchen, the big dog close on her heels. 'Just push him down if he annoys you. He's missed us, poor old thing. We only got in this morning.'

Through the open bedroom door I glimpsed half-unpacked suitcases and carriers of duty-free slung on their gaudy bedspread; heard the shower running.

'I was about to ring you, Jessica, but you got to me first. I'm so bloody sorry. I didn't have a clue about real life out on that boat. So isolated. Give me Ibiza any time, pet. Freddie might have grown up at sea, but me and sailing – nah.' She threw open the balcony door. 'God, it's hotter here than Greece.'

She made coffee while I perched on a chrome stool, summoning the courage to open the can of worms I'd tried to ignore for so long. There was a collage of photos in a frame on the wall that included a picture of Mickey, incongruous in a paper party-hat.

'He was pissed, pet,' she smiled, following my wistful gaze. But I could feel apprehension buzzing round her like a persistent fly.

'I gathered.'

'So, how are you bearing up, pet?' She handed me a steaming cup.

'I'm fine,' I answered automatically, and her forehead creased.

'Really?'

'Okay, no, actually, I'm bloody awful. Louis has been gone for –' I swallowed hard '– for nearly six days now. Mickey's still in hospital, not doing very well. I'm petrified.'

'Oh, pet.' She stepped towards me. I couldn't bear it any longer.

'Pauline, please. I've got to ask you something. And there's obviously – there's something on your mind, isn't there?'

The emerald in her nose glinted as a shaft of sun sliced through the glass and hit it. 'Yeah.' She put down her steaming cup. 'Yeah, I guess there is. And I suppose you weren't just passing, were you?'

'Hi.'

I jumped as Freddie plodded up behind me, wrapped in a huge scarlet towel, auburn crop all spiky and glistening from the shower.

'How are you?' she said. She looked at me very intently, her big face gentle, her carthorse frame bent towards me. 'I was – I'm so sorry about the baby.' Very baby-friendly, Freddie, for a dyke. I vaguely remembered her beneath the Christmas tree at Pauline's party, all drunk and maudlin, fondly stroking my bump; oddly familiar for such a stranger, though for some reason I hadn't minded. 'We're going to get one of these soon,' she'd told me, patting my tummy, though I hardly knew her. 'A baby. Just need to persuade her indoors.'

I didn't trust myself to speak now; so I nodded thanks as Freddie helped herself to coffee, grabbing her packets of tobacco and Rizla from the worktop.

'I'll leave you guys to it.' She dropped a kiss on Pauline's head. I thought uncomfortably of the last time I'd seen Freddie and Pauline together, at my house, a few months after Louis was born. Not a happy occasion in any way, although it should have been. The lavish bouquet they'd bought, the tiny Tiffany cup with Louis's name inscribed, the beautifully wrapped clothes from Baby Gap. The look of horror on Freddie's face when she came into the sitting room and found me and Louis howling on the floor, in total disarray. I pushed away the memory, pushed it really hard; watched Freddie plodding back towards the bedroom. Pauline sighed almost inaudibly, staring after her girlfriend with what looked much like longing.

'That nice northern policeman was on the phone just now, asking more questions,' she said eventually, looking back at me. 'You've spoken to him, then, this morning?'

I nodded. She went on.

'They wanted copies of Mickey's personal records – everything that only I had access to. I pulled it all off from here and faxed it over. And so you saw that –' She reddened a little. God. I wasn't used to Pauline being rattled. It freaked me out a bit.

'I heard he was – he was meant to be meeting Agnes,' I said bluntly.

'Well, I mean, I don't know if he did actually go that night, because I was in the middle of the Med by then, on that blinking boat.' There was hope in her voice. 'We'd already had words about it when – well, I thought it was such a crap idea, and I told him so.'

'When did you tell him?' I asked helplessly.

'When – when Agnes came to see him at the office before, pet. I thought he was, you know. Being a bit of a nutter.'

I plonked my coffee down and stood up; walked to the balcony door and pushed it back as far as it would go. I breathed in very deep, though there wasn't very much air to breathe.

'So, let me get this straight,' I said slowly, gazing down at the murky canal. A couple of Goth girls in inappropriate black swigged from beer cans as they passed below. 'Not only is my son missing, presumed kidnapped, but my husband has been seeing his ex-wife? The woman he hates so much that he can't even bear to say her name?'

I turned back. Pauline was anxiously twisting the stone in her nose.

'Look, pet, you've gotta try to understand. They had a very – tempestuous relationship. Very – what's that word? Volatile. Bit like me and Claudia did, you know, before Freddie. You knew that, didn't you, about Mickey and Agnes?'

My dignity was down the drain already. 'Do you know, Pauline, I didn't really. I don't know much about Agnes at all. Other than she was a ball-breaker at work, and came from somewhere cold.'

'Norway.'

'Norway, then.'

I was trying to absorb the news, to work out what I felt. No, I knew what I felt. Fury. No, worse. Misery.

'I mean,' I went on. In for a penny, in for a pound. 'He just didn't – doesn't talk about her. Ever, really. It's like it's always been too painful. And I'm not – I don't like pushing him. If he doesn't want to talk about her, that's fine.'

'Well, Mickey's hardly the type to wear his heart on his sleeve,' she admitted.

'You can say that again. But still –' my brain was ticking furiously '–why – I don't understand why he'd be seeing her now. After all this time?'

'I'm sure there's a simple explanation. I mean, there was no doubt they loved each other very much, but –' she clocked my scowl, held out a fluorescent-nailed hand. 'No, please – let me tell you, Jessica. It's better that you understand. They loved each other, but they were destroying each other by the end. It was completely shite. All they did was argue, pet. The best thing they ever did was separate. I'm sure Mickey was just seeing her to tie up some loose ends. It's just, he didn't want to discuss it with me. Which', she shrugged, and bit off

197

a piece of nail, 'was fair enough. I mean, the divorce only came through so recently, didn't it?'

Yeah, I knew exactly how recently. When I was seven months pregnant, vast as a small whale, waiting for Mickey to be free to marry me. Praying for him to be free. Flushed and occasionally ecstatic, my hormones bouncing happily on the good days when I wasn't sinking beneath the enormity of what lay ahead; lolling in a state of love and sexuality, all bound up with my own clever fertility.

'They had so much tied up in property and investments, you know.' Pauline paused to sip her drink. She was playing for time. 'I mean, Agnes – she's got a ferocious business brain. Canny as you like – top of her game, pet, that one. Had Mickey tied up in all sorts of deals. I'm sure there's probably still loads of paperwork and things to sort out, even now.'

But I didn't buy it. Mickey hated Agnes. She'd abandoned him, gone abroad, cleaned him out emotionally, so that when we met months later he was nothing but a walking husk of a man, although it was well-hidden beneath his facade. Fragile as an empty eggshell – although I didn't realise it at first, I could have crushed him with a single stamp of my foot. All that sadness I'd first seen: it sprang mainly from losing Agnes. And he'd only ever mentioned her occasionally to curse her memory.

I turned back from the window. I had to face facts.

'Pauline, we both know that Agnes was the love of Mickey's life.' There was no point denying it. 'Surely – surely if she'd said jump, he'd have done it?'

She shook her head vehemently. The dog yawned massively at her toe-ringed feet and began to dribble.

'No, Jessica, I don't think so. I don't believe he's that much of a glutton for punishment. It was over. He's an intelligent man –'

I grimaced. 'Yes, I know that. He's the cleverest person I've ever met – unfortunately. But since when did intellect make you sensible in love? God, if anything, it's likely to be the opposite.'

Valiantly, she kept trying. 'He loves you, pet. I know he does.'

'Do you? Does he really? Or does he just love Louis and the fact that I'm his mother?'

Pauline seemed to blanch a little as she leant down and petted her huge dog. Pain pricked my heart. It was what had worried me every night when I went to sleep, what had daily threatened to scar my happiness. I had been so in love with Mickey, and yet I felt I could never quite reach him.

When I fell pregnant with Louis so quickly and was worried about going ahead with it, Mickey and I had a huge row. It was almost the only time he mentioned his ex-wife, the first time that he ever raised his voice to me. Sick and greasy with early pregnancy, I was utterly confused. In the middle of some trendy Soho restaurant, he'd started shouting – much to the scandalised delight of all the other diners – shouting that he was surrounded by heartless women, that I was just like 'bloody Agnes. She's always denied me a proper family too.'

And it was that comparison almost more than

anything that goaded me into having Louis. That persuaded me against my better judgement. Initially I kept the baby because I loved Mickey so much I'd have done anything to please him. Blinded by my desire for him, my unflagging adoration kept me going for months – never mind that I was in no way ready for a baby; that I was frankly terrified. At twenty-seven, kids were the last thing on my mind. Never mind that I hardly knew the father-to-be, however hard I tried; or that Mickey hid himself away from me, even when he was right there in front of me. My desire kept me going until I grew to love my expanding bump on its own terms.

The pain and the pleasure of those days was the most intense I'd ever felt. It was like constantly pressing a huge knot in your neck; picking a scab on your knee that opened up again, all pink and shiny beneath the dark dried blood. The more I couldn't reach Mickey, the more I clutched on. Though he professed to want me near, I don't think I ever really believed him. And by the time Louis was six months old, by the time I was totally in love with my son, I was panicking that I'd made a huge mistake. That I'd married a man who'd never love me the way I loved him.

Sometimes, I'd feel Mickey watching me, and when I looked up he'd smile and my heart would be warmed enough to continue; but deep down, deep, deep down, I felt like a charlatan, living a life I didn't really fit. That didn't really belong to me.

And always there was Agnes, like a shadow in the hall, whispering through the rooms she used to live in, that she'd designed; the woman he'd hardly mentioned, whom he'd scrubbed religiously from his life. Who might almost never have existed, except in the dark autumn nights when I'd come down and find him hollow-eyed, drinking whisky on the back steps, staring out into the black. I wouldn't speak, I'd just hold on to him, and then he'd take me back to bed, and make love to me like his life depended on it. And I prayed that he remembered it was me who moved beneath him in the dark, that he didn't dream of *her*. And I never let him see the tears I cried in the early hours, first alone, then over Louis's fuzzy head, cried because my husband didn't seem to love me the way I needed him to. But at least by then I had my baby; I took comfort from the enormous love that, once it came, once I gave in to it, slowly grew and grew, until it threatened to burst me.

And now, I looked at Pauline sitting so discomfited, the least composed I'd ever seen her; and I wondered what the hell I had left from all this. I almost wanted to hug her, her guilt was so tangible.

'I suppose I should have told you. About Agnes, I mean.' But we both knew she'd never have done that. Her loyalty to Mickey was absolute. She loved him like her own, and I'd always respected that.

'Oh Pauline, it's not your fault. Mickey's a law unto himself, we both know that.' I tried to look on the bright side. 'And anyway, like you say, it's probably nothing. Probably just official stuff. He probably just didn't want to – you know, worry me.' But we both knew I was lying.

And then I thought I heard Freddie behind me again, and I turned quickly, embarrassed by Pauline's revelations – but she wasn't there. I must have imagined it. Only when I left, Freddie didn't bother to come out or say goodbye, but, heading towards the lift with Pauline, from the corner of my eye I was sure I saw the bedroom door closing gently. I guessed Freddie couldn't face me – but I went back down to Deb feeling somewhat perturbed. Something seemed a little strange; I just wasn't sure exactly what.

CHAPTER FIFTEEN

I was drunk. Not falling-down drunk, but getting there. I was swaying-can't-quite-right-myself drunk. Everything was rounded at the corners; nothing was quite where it should be. I was bendy, like a willow tree in a storm. I wanted to lean and keep leaning; all rubbery I was, like a jack-in-the-box.

I was verging-on-hysteria drunk. Shirl was not quite so drunk, I thought, though my reality gauge had gone rather off-kilter. I got up from the sofa and nearly fell, tripping over the rug, saving myself on the coffee table. For some reason this was hilarious. I started to laugh and I only stopped when I saw that Shirl had not joined in.

On the way home from Pauline's, I'd known I should go and visit Mickey, but I just couldn't face it quite yet. I didn't want to hear him say he still loved Agnes; I really couldn't bear it. I rang the ward from the car with apprehension, but when I spoke to the duty nurse she said he was asleep, and I was relieved. When I got home, I opened some wine; carefully making sure I was far too drunk to visit when he woke. I rang Mickey's web designer to nag him about my 'Looking for Louis' site. The idea that strangers might have seen my son without realising he was stolen crucified me; I needed to flag it up in any way, beseech people everywhere to look for him. The stories about lost children on the net still chilled me to the bone, but some compulsion drew me back to check time and time again.

Shirl came home and helped me through the bottle, and Deb tried not to look too disapproving; made me coffee, which went cold as I swigged away. I abandoned the computer after reading one horror story about a two-year-old who'd gone missing ten years ago; the mother was still looking, still posting desperate notes on her website. You'd look for all eternity, wouldn't you? Destined to spend a lifetime wondering if that nine-year-old you just passed playing football, that teenager on a bike in the street, that grown-up in the supermarket, was once your little boy.

Then Maxine came back and stomped up to her room, slamming the door behind her. I presumed the boyfriend wasn't Moldovan. I half-hoped that Silver might have dropped her off, but the car pulling off didn't look like his, even to my drunken eye.

'Stroppy cow,' Shirl said, 'I don't know why you put up with her.' She was sorting out her expenses.

'Oh, she's all right.' I was benevolent. 'She's got a good heart really. Somewhere. She loves Louis. And Mickey seems to like her.'

'Oh, does he now?' Shirl crooked a bushy brow. 'Even more reason to get rid of her, I'd have thought.'

'Not like that, you silly moo. I mean, Mickey thinks I need her.' I pretended to laugh. I wasn't going to let Shirl know how close to the truth she'd got. How I'd compared myself to the svelte Maxine as I struggled to get back to my old self; how I'd worried that my husband hankered after the freedom she represented.

Shirl sniffed. 'Mickey's got ideas above his station, I'd say.'

There was a pause, which went on until it became slightly uncomfortable. I wobbled over to put some music on; then I worried that it'd wake Louis. With a gut-punch, I remembered he wasn't here. I slopped more wine into my glass, spilling at least half in the process, looking round with guilt until I remembered it was my own house. Sort of. So I mushed it into the carpet with my bare foot.

'Shall we go out and look for Louis?' I suggested hopefully, trying not to sway.

'What – in that state? I think you're better off here.' Shirl sucked her teeth. 'Char, Jess! Your taste in music hasn't improved, I hear,' she said, as Nirvana blared out of Mickey's new-age speakers. I turned it up.

'We can't all be Bob Marley fans, now can we, Shirl?'

'That's a crass generalisation *and* a racial stereotype, my good woman.'

'But you love a bit of Bob,' I said, indignant.

'That's as maybe. But it's still a stereotype,' she replied regally, sipping her wine. 'Talking of which, do you think that nice police lady'd notice if I skinned up?' A

205

nice fat joint. Just what the doctor didn't order. Always made me sick.

'It's up to you.' My wine seemed to be going down particularly fast. I eyed it warily as I swayed half-heartedly along to Kurt Cobain for a bit. Then I said, 'Why don't you like Mickey?'

I'd finally asked the question I'd been scared to hear the answer to. My words came slipping, sliding sideways, from my disconnected mouth. I heard them from ten thousand miles away, not quite formed, unfinished. To her credit, Shirl didn't look fazed – or perhaps that's because I couldn't focus any more. I squinted at her through one eye.

'Well?' I slurred.

'I don't think we should go there really, do you, Jess?' she said, topping up her glass so she didn't have to look at me. 'I mean, he *is* your old man. There are some things that should remain unspoken, even between good friends. Know what I'm saying?'

I laughed, incredulous. 'But you make it perfectly obvious you don't like him.'

She shrugged. 'Yeah, but the poor man's in his bed, his sick bed at that. It's like – speaking ill of the dead, you know?'

'Oh come on, Shirl. Just say it. I mean, how long have we been mates?' Forever and a day, I'd say; right back to nits at junior school. 'You'd never normally bite your tongue. You never have before.'

'Yeah, but –'

'But what?'

'You went and married this one. You *do* know what

206

I'm saying. I know you do.' Shirl's patois broadened with her stress. But I wouldn't let it go, I was like a dog with a bone he's not allowed to have.

'Is it cos he can be a bit moody?' I tried. She lined her receipts up very neatly. They seemed neat, anyway. It was quite hard to tell in my current state.

'Cos he's rich?'

Her face was thunderous now. 'Do me a favour. You can keep his money.' But I'd got her goat now. 'In fact, it's gotta be the other way round, don't it?'

'What do you mean?'

'It's *you* who's landed on your feet.'

'What are you insinuating, Shirl?' I was outraged.

'Nothing.'

'I mean, if anything, I'd rather Mickey was poor.'

'Oh pull the other one.'

But it was true. Mickey's wealth made me anxious and beholden. I'd been used to having nothing most of my life; I was used to earning my own crust. Blearily I changed the subject before we had a row.

'Is it cos he's so bright?'

'No, Jessica, if you really want to know, it's because he doesn't love you the right way. Okay? Is that what you wanted to hear?'

'Oh.' I deflated like a geriatric balloon. 'That's not very nice, is it?' I drained my glass. 'What do you mean – right?' I began to feel like I was falling. According to the mirror opposite, I was still upright. Just about.

'Right. I jus' mean right. All right? You need a man who loves you for what you are, not what he wan' you to be. Not what you think you should be for him.

You change, man, around that Mickey. You know that. You're not yourself at all. Now leave it, Jess, please. Before we have some words.'

'But – what do you mean, "change"?'

'Jus' change. Not yourself. Too – deferential. Nervous. An' you know, you're a good-looking girl, you're beautiful, but you don' seem to know it. Any man worth his salt make you feel special, you know?'

'Oh,' I said again. Fourteen Shirls sat on the sofa now, weaving back and forth.

'Yeah – oh. I jus' wanna see you with a man who loves you for the fabulous person I know you are. Not all these – misfits for you. All these stupi' older men.' She got up, shaking her skirt out. 'You got a father complex, you know that, don't you?'

God knows why, I thought. I tried the one-eye trick again; apparently, it didn't work.

'And don't you go getting ideas about that tasty copper, either.'

'What?' I couldn't believe my ears. I couldn't actually focus any more. 'Tha's rubbish. How dare you.' I tried to conjure up some venom.

'I seen you, lady. I seen the way you looked at him the other day. Don't go there, Jess. That's the last thing you need.' She headed to the door. 'I'm going to bed, babe. I think you should too. You've had enough. You're going to feel rough in the morning.' She said 'rough' like a dog bark. Then she turned back. 'And remember, tomorrow is a new day. Forget the men. Tomorrow they could find Louis, yeah? I got a good feeling, you know.'

208

I nodded, mumbled something incoherent, slumping down on the sofa. I fell into a twitchy weird half-sleep where Mickey and a faceless Agnes were doing waltzes down our hall, and Kurt Cobain sang barefoot on the stairs, holding Louis in his arms. Something niggled me even in my drunken dream, and I couldn't think what... Then Deb woke me accidentally.

'Oh, sorry,' she stage-whispered, 'I was just coming to say I'm off now.'

I held my head in my hands; it was spinning so much I thought it might whiz right off. I (almost) realised how drunk I was. 'Deb,' I asked politely when the room slowed down a bit, 'can you take me to the hospital?'

'Sure. First thing tomorrow.'

'No. Now.'

'Now?' she repeated. She tried and failed not to look annoyed.

'Oh, don't worry,' I said brightly, 'I'll drive myself.'

I rarely drove. Even the idea of the expensive Audi Mickey had bought me made me rather nervous. I thought of Shirl's words – of giving up control. I vowed to drive it more. Then I had a great idea.

'Or no, I know what, I'll cycle to the hospital. I've won competitions, you know. On my bike. Nice night for it.'

And I had, in my teens. Right now, though, I couldn't have cycled round the block. So, of course, she drove me in the end – good old valiant Deb.

In the corridor outside the ICU, a young woman with a shaved head was pushing a buggy rather manically towards me. It was a Maclaren, just like mine.

209

Perhaps it was my Louis. Then I looked at the woman's face; she was sobbing. And the baby wasn't mine, of course; he was thin and fair, not fat and dark like my beautiful Louis. Poor lady; she didn't look happy at all. I shook my head sorrowfully. Most drunkenly.

Mickey was asleep when I got into his room. All this innocent sleep of angels, while I worried myself to death. I woke him up too roughly; I hurt him by mistake.

'Sorry, darling.' I was still slurring. 'Blimey, you were well away, weren't you?'

He took a moment to come round, rubbing the sleep from his good eye. He sized me up. 'I'm not the only one, I'd say.'

'What?'

'Not the only one who's well away.'

'Oh, I see.' I laughed – though I wasn't quite sure what the joke was. He was about to continue, but I had to get it out now or not at all.

'Mickey,' I asked, 'why've you been seeing your ex?'

He looked confused. His eyes were glittering manically.

'Don't lie to me, please,' I said. 'I thought you hated Agnes.'

'I do,' he said, but I didn't believe him any more. I began to cry; big body-racking sobs. I never cried in front of him.

'Oh darlin',' he said, taking my arm, pulling me down to him. He never called me darling. 'I don't like her very much,' he whispered, 'and that's the truth.' Then he kissed me gently on the mouth, and I felt that little shift inside, that Mickey feeling I could never escape. I kissed him back. I wanted to climb on the bed and bury myself inside him. I craved some kind of intimacy, any intimacy, now the closeness I'd had with Louis was gone. The sheer human warmth of holding my son – all gone. I moved against Mickey, and he groaned; more with pain than desire, I guessed hazily.

'I love you, Mickey,' I said, squinting down at him. If I looked through one eye I could focus better. 'I'm sorry if I've been weird.'

'You're drunk.'

'So what? Aren't I allowed to say it ever? Does it bloody scare you so much? You are the father of my child.' Hurt, I moved back, but he grabbed my wrist in his cool, thin fingers, pulling me down to him, and kissed me some more. My insides went all liquid. His eyes still glittered like disco mirror-balls, and I wasn't entirely sure he was quite there with me, but I didn't care. I just wanted to obliterate the pain I felt.

'Do you reckon anyone's ever done it in Intensive Care before?' I whispered, and he half-smiled.

'I don't know, Jessica. What do you think?'

I climbed up on the bed, pushing my skirt aside, straddling him. I dared not move too much in case I set the machines off bleeping. I rocked above him. I was thinking, while I could still think coherently, that this was what had always tied me to him, this thing that Shirl and all the others never saw, this urgent, hungry want. Though since Louis was born I'd been scared to come too near him very often, frightened by all the change.

211

And then I suddenly saw myself, as if I was hanging on the ceiling like a bat, watching me and my injured husband on the bed. What the hell was I playing at? I was giving into drunken lust like a drunken fool, while out there, somewhere out there in this sultry summer night, someone had my baby, was holding *my* baby while I just forgot him. No matter that I was desperate for any intimacy that Mickey could afford me now; I needed to focus on my son – on just my son. And I stopped stock-still, wide-eyed with horror at myself, at the indignity of my act, and I was utterly ashamed. I clambered down clumsily, far quicker than I'd got up. I straightened my clothes and pushed back my hair and prayed that no one had seen. I prayed that Louis hadn't sensed that, wherever he was, I'd forgotten myself just for a moment there.

Mickey whispered something and I couldn't quite hear it above the buzz and tick of the dim-lit room. I leant down to him and asked him to repeat it.

'I said,' and Mickey was panting now, ghost-like beneath the still-livid bruises, 'I said I never meant to hurt you, darling,' and he pushed my hair back from my face, kissing my mouth once more, only this time I stepped back because now the kiss felt wrong. But I did feel the effort that this all cost him and I clutched onto his hand. I wished vehemently that Mickey was better now; that he could get up and walk out of here with me, that he would help me look for our son. That together we would find our baby who needed us so badly.

And then, eerily, it struck me that Mickey was actually saying goodbye. There was a nasty sheen of sweat across his cold, cold body. Had I just nearly shagged him into relapse, I thought, and I was about to say it out loud and laugh – but he was struggling to breathe and something started to whir and beep, and he was shaking – fitting, it seemed – and then Sister Kwame was there and I was truly horrified at what I'd done. I held his hand like I was hanging on for life and his eyes began to flicker closed, and then he was out, and I was saying desperately, 'He will be all right, won't he? He's going to be okay? Have I killed him?' but I didn't like the way her jaw was set so grim and she ignored me.

The weather broke that night and I nearly broke along with it. I sat by Mickey's bed, clutching his hand, while they paged the small-eared consultant, who turned up very quickly, all bleary-eyed and mussy like he'd been sleeping in the broom cupboard, and they started to speak a bit like they do in *ER*, though not so fast and not so glamorous, and they said 'theatre' a lot, and I understood they might have to do something urgent to Mickey. Soon after that they rushed him off and left me there, bereft once more; worrying I'd hurt my husband, sapped him of his life-blood somehow.

And I went outside because they said, over distracted shoulders, that it might be a while, and so I sat in the hospital's entrance, beneath the neon signs; sat in the stark fluorescent light among the fag-butts and the nutters, and I watched the rain begin.

My brain was rattling like an Intercity train, and I

had this image of Mickey's Noddy consultant conducting an orchestra of nurses in the operating room, a scalpel for a baton, and I wondered why they called it theatre, was it all just a big game, a fantasy, to them; and then I thought I must still be drunk to think like this, and when some old lady with blood-stained fingers and a bashed-up Crocodile Dundee-type hat without the corks offered me her meths wrapped in brown paper, I didn't know whether to swig or cry, but I thanked her anyway as I said no.

And I realised that Mickey hadn't really answered my question, that I wasn't any wiser about Agnes, but the fact that we'd nearly had sex must make everything all right – mustn't it? And then I cursed myself because that was how eighteen-year-olds thought, not responsible married women with babies – missing or not – and then I thought I might start to howl, so I went back in the hospital and found the Ladies. I scrubbed my hands and face even though I was already soaking from the rain.

The strip lighting above me hummed and flicked as I stood staring at myself, lost soul, my face all ghostly in the mirror, and I realised I didn't know where I should go. Should I stay here and wait for Mickey to come out of theatre; should I go home – Agnes's home – and wait for Louis to come back? I fingered the new mobile phone that Deb had sorted out for me, and I thought of whom to call, and I didn't have an answer. I paced the corridor in front of the big board that declared where each ward was. My eye fell on the words 'Maternity Suite'; it was apparently on the third floor.

I walked into the lift and pressed number three; moved like a marionette, controlled by a higher force, pulled by invisible threads to where the babies were.

Outside the Delivery Suite an anxious father with very ginger hair talked quietly into an illicit mobile phone, pacing the well-worn lino that a hundred fathers must pace each week. Of course I knew this part of the hospital would be well-protected – all buzzers and inter-coms to get through and guarded desks and babies who were kept safely locked behind closed doors. But then a doctor slammed through the doors of the Neonatal Unit, there was some kind of crisis going on and somehow I managed to slip in behind. The harsh smell of disinfectant grabbed me round the throat as I stood at the glass; I pressed my nose up against that window like a small child outside a sweetshop and stared and stared at the tiny little bodies in their plastic beds, at all the wires, and my stomach somersaulted over and over again at the thought of what I'd lost. At the thought of the precarious hold on life these babies had; the utter vulnerability that had terrified me so much when Louis was first born and spent the first twenty-four hours in an incubator himself, the dependence that had aston-ished me. The fact that they relied on someone else for their first breath, for every sip and mouthful, every tiny bit of safe-keeping. And I found myself wondering how I could get into the room where the healthy babies were, the ones that didn't need all this constant medical care?

A woman stepped up behind me.

'They're so tiny, aren't they? So very helpless,' I said, sort of to myself.

'You'd be surprised. They're survivors, babies. Tough little things.' But I heard the desperation in her words. I looked at her. Eyes red-rimmed with exhaustion, she was pale and thin, wearing a huge cardigan despite the heat, twisting a hanky in her knotty hands. 'That's my John-John there.' She pointed at a tiny form, rather kitten-like in the corner incubator, a big blue light above him, a small fluffy bear watching him sleep.

'Is he okay?'

'We,' she swallowed, 'we don't know yet. We just keep praying that he'll hang on in there. He was so terribly early. Twenty-six weeks. But, like I said,' she attempted a smile and it nearly smashed my heart again, 'he's a little fighter.' She was hanging on to hope so fervently that it was palpable.

Inconsolable: the word inched into my head. I felt her gaze fall on my face now. She'd be inconsolable if something happened, it was obvious. If someone took her child away. Some God – or some madwoman. Some madwoman – just like me.

'Is your baby here?' she asked kindly. I stared at her blankly for a second.

'I wish he was,' I whispered in the end. 'I really wish I knew he was in such good hands.'

And she held out a hand to me – but then a nurse hurried down the corridor towards me and I knew that I must go. I clasped the woman's hand, just for a moment.

'Good luck,' I whispered, 'I'll think of you,' and I fled before I did something stupid. Before ... but deep down I knew I wouldn't now – not now I'd seen the

pain in that poor woman's eyes. How could l even coun-
tenance stealing someone else's baby?

And in the end I went back to Mickey's room and
curled up in the prickly brown chair, which was
comfortingly like the one in my old school library, and
I slept despite myself, because I was truly more tired
than I had ever been.

The sun had sunk and risen once again, and Louis had
been missing for six days. When I woke that morning,
stiff and cramped, still in the chair, they said that Mickey
would be all right, he didn't have the clot on the brain
they'd feared. As they weren't sure why he'd fitted,
they'd sedated him for now. So I sat helplessly beside
my husband, watching him sleep, and contemplated
the insanity of last night, when I'd actually considered
taking someone else's child to replace my own. And
this realisation made me imagine the desperation that
might have driven someone to take Louis; to pretend
that he was theirs. Somehow the knowledge just made
me feel worse.

Then Leigh came and took me to the police station,
where I did the eternal press conference. Only this time
it was DC Kelly who sat beside me, and thankfully this
time no one stood and mentioned bereavement or
child-trafficking. And nor did anyone mention potty
women who steal babies for their own solace, and for
that, today, after my moments of near madness in the
depths of last night, I was glad.

The room wasn't so crowded this time, the journal-
ists' air more harried and subdued than normal, and

I worried that people were forgetting. There had been some horrendous bombing on a London train that day, though, and so it was good, Egg-belly assured me, that anyone had come at all. And I tried to remember there was another world outside, but it was hard to visualise when every day I grew more desperate and wearier and more maddened by my loss. And I tried not to look for Silver, and I tried not to bite my lip too hard, but in the end I couldn't help but ask where he was. Egg-belly said he was tied up, and I had an image of Silver's hands tied behind his back, and then of him tied to me, and I thought I might be finally going mad. And Deb turned up and I was really glad to see her, and she looked all worried after she'd peered at me, and said did I want to see the counsellor again? And I did think about it this time, I really did, because suddenly I didn't feel I was coping well at all. I kept thinking Mickey was going to die, and I wasn't even the tiniest bit angry with him about Louis any more, I just wanted them both back.

Leigh got me some tea and she put lots of sugar in. We were just about to go to the car when Deb got a call on her mobile and I guessed that it was Silver from the way she spoke. She took me to his office and there he was. He looked like he hadn't slept for days; he actually seemed a little rumpled, and I resisted the temptation to remark on it. I thought it was time I got back to a strictly professional footing with him, especially now I'd been reconciled with Mickey. Especially since I'd nearly killed my husband. And then I caught Leigh making eyes at him, and I remembered how Leigh always got her man. But he asked to see me alone anyway.

'How're you doing, kid— Mrs Finnegan?'

'You're being very formal,' I said. I was suddenly aware that I hadn't had a shower for days; that I'd slept in this old dress; that I probably smelt of sweat and madness and Mickey still.

'Jessica, then. How are you? I was very sorry to hear about Mr Finnegan's relapse.'

I thought rather hysterically about making the nearly-shagging-Mickey-worse joke, then decided it was probably inappropriate. I sipped my tea instead. I played at being sedate. I said, 'I think he'll be okay. They said he will, anyway. It's all a bit –' I couldn't find the right word '–stressful,' I finished lamely. There was a photo on the desk that was turned more his way than mine, but it seemed to be of three smiling kids. They were tumbling over one another in desperation to reach the camera first, fighting to grin the biggest grin.

'Your kids?' I asked, over-brightly.

'Yes,' he nodded, but he didn't expand. It was the one thing he always seemed unhappy about whenever they came up.

'Are you –' I was embarrassed to mention it, kept staring at the photo rather than at Silver. 'Are you going to interview Agnes? Mickey's ex-wife?'

He shrugged. 'We're contacting her just to check her whereabouts, but from what I understand she's abroad anyway. Did you ask him if he did meet up with her?'

'I haven't – haven't really had the chance to talk to Mickey properly yet.' I had a sudden image of me above him on that bed last night. I coloured slightly. 'I guess it's nothing to do with Louis.'

'Well, I don't want to add to your stress, but I've had some slightly troubling news.'

My eyes snapped off the photo. 'About Louis?' I was on my feet immediately.

'No, no, don't worry. Nothing more about Louis, I'm afraid. I think we've got to keep operating on the understanding that Louis, whoever he's with, is fine. They obviously don't want to hurt him – they just want him.'

'Not as badly as I do.' I slumped back down again.

'No, obviously. But this is about Mickey and his injuries. We've had an eyewitness come forward, the landlord of a pub in Bermondsey, not far from where Mickey was found. He recognised the picture of Mr Finnegan from the papers.' Silver fiddled with the Venetian blind, snapping it open and shut.

'Actually,' he swung back to face me, 'our boys had been in there to question the landlord before, but he had previously been a little – reticent.'

I wished he'd just sit down.

'Seeing the baby was missing spurred him into action, though.'

'Not before time, I'd say.' I fiddled with my polystyrene cup.

'I just wondered –' He seemed apprehensive.

'What?' I said. If I had a pound for every person nervous of my reaction these days, I'd be a millionaire by now.

'Is Mickey in the habit of getting into fights?' he asked.

'Fights? Hardly. He's an artist, a businessman. Why would he go round looking for a fight?'

'It takes all sorts, Jessica. It's a funny old world.'

I ignored the cod philosophy. 'Anyway, what do you mean, "fights"? Surely Mickey was attacked?'

'Well, that's certainly what we'd been assuming – that whoever snatched Louis also attacked Mickey. Only what this guy at The Mason's Arms says throws a slightly different complexion on matters.'

'What *is* he saying?'

'That Mickey came into the pub on the evening that Louis disappeared, around seven p.m. He was highly agitated.'

Silver flicked the blinds again. I bit my tongue.

'Well, he would be, wouldn't he?' This was going nowhere fast.

'Yes, well, you would think so. Anyway, he kept asking to use the phone, but the payphone in the public bar wasn't working apparently. When he realised that, Mr Finnegan started to slam the receiver against the wall over and over again, until some bloke at the bar told him to stop.' Silver picked up his paperweight and began to lob it from hand to hand. 'The landlord was round the other side in the snug, but came round to see what was going on. By the time he got there, the first punch had been thrown – apparently by Mr Finnegan.' He waited for this to sink in.

'But – I don't understand. I guess,' I was thinking frantically, 'I guess that Mickey was just so stressed that he – he must have lost it a bit. Didn't know what he was doing. I mean, come on, that'd be natural, right?'

221

Silver shrugged. I chewed my lip. I'd chew right through it soon.

'Maybe. But, by all accounts, Mickey was pretty tanked-up.'

'You mean drunk?'

'I mean drunk, yes. Not that he'd been drinking in that pub as far as anyone knows. He just came in saying something about his son and using a phone, losing his mobile or something. After the punches started, the landlord threw both men out, but the fight definitely continued outside. Mr Finnegan – well, he took quite a beating.'

I winced. 'Obviously,' I said quietly.

'Yes, well. But then he disappeared, the other guy scarpered, and the landlord forgot all about it. Till now.' Carefully he replaced the paperweight on the desk. 'I'm trying to understand why your husband would pick a fight.'

It didn't make any sense. Why the hell would Mickey have been fighting when Louis was missing? Why was he drunk? I didn't believe it.

'It sounds like bollocks to me,' I said loyally. 'It sounds like this landlord bloke's got something to hide and he's trying to, I don't know – deflect attention. Perhaps he beat Mickey up himself?'

'Look, don't worry about that. Obviously we're checking him out, and the pub. There'll be other witnesses if what the landlord says is true. First and foremost we've got to find the guy who had the fight with Mr Finnegan. But I just wanted to know if you thought it was at all likely.'

I shook my head vehemently. 'No, I don't. Mickey's just not the violent type. Okay, he's got a temper, but to be honest,' I hesitated, 'to be honest, Mickey would think that fighting was below him.'

Silver raised an eyebrow. 'Right. So other than being overwrought about Louis, we've got to find a reason, a very good reason, for Mickey to pick a fight.'

'Being overwrought about your missing baby is a pretty good reason, I'd say. If that man's telling the truth,' I muttered.

'If that man's telling the truth,' he agreed.

I looked at the photo again. Definitely just three kids, no wife. Three happy, smiling faces. 'And what happened about Maxine's new bloke?' I asked.

Silver had the good grace to flush gently beneath his waning tan. 'Not Moldovan. Turkish. Bit dodgy possibly, definitely a bit flash, but no obvious links to any sort of gang.'

'Obvious links? That doesn't sound very reassuring.' I finished the last of my tea.

'Don't worry,' he stood up and stretched. 'It's all under control.' His pristine shirt came slightly untucked, exposing a strip of tanned skin. I stared down at my cup in discomfort, suddenly fascinated by the way my teeth left grooves around the rim when I bit it gently.

'We're bringing him in for questioning,' he went on. 'Maxine says that it's all over anyway; they had a big row apparently. She's a bit of a flirt, isn't she? Friendly little minx, that one.' He tucked his shirt back in meticulously, adjusted his snazzy tie in the mirror. 'Got a lift home?' he asked over his shoulder.

I was dismissed. I chucked the cup at the bin, but it fell short. 'Look at that,' I said, super-polite. 'I'm as bad at throwing as you are at reading character.' I opened the door. 'A "little minx", eh?' Then I closed the door behind me, a little harder than I might have.

Deb was waiting in the corridor, chatting to Leigh about some reality show that had started last night. I wandered off down the corridor. Then I stopped short. Deb caught up with me; Leigh was probably hovering for a look at Silver.

'Deb,' I muttered, 'I think I might need to talk to someone again.'

'DI Silver?' she said, wrinkling her brow.

'No. Definitely not him.'

She didn't understand, cocking her curly mop enquiringly. I lowered my voice to a whisper. 'You know, that nice lady at the hospital. The German one.'

'Oh, I see.' Deb was enthusiastic. 'The therapist. Yes, I think that's a very good idea.'

'Do you?' I hoped no one else had heard. I said as casually as I could without screaming, 'I think I – I threw her card away. Would you be able to help me find her number?'

CHAPTER SIXTEEN

It was Maxine's arse that I saw first. Storm clouds had gathered outside and the afternoon was dim, dark even, so when I opened the living-room door and saw those shining buttocks thrusting up and down, it took me a minute to focus. I couldn't understand quite what I was looking at; I struggled to adjust my eyes.

Maxine was riding her supposed ex-boyfriend Gorek like he was a rodeo horse – the boyfriend she'd just told Silver she didn't even like – on my expensive sofa. Agnes's £2,000 sofa. They were fucking soundlessly beneath the picture of Louis that I had begun to worship since he went. I was so angry that I couldn't speak, and then I sort of yelped and Leigh, who was bringing shopping in for me, dropped a bag. Something smashed as my sister came up behind me.

'What the hell?' she said, as Maxine slid inelegantly off the bloke, who was still prostrate, scrabbling with his trousers, swearing in what I assumed was Turkish. Leigh began to laugh. My prudish sister actually thought it was funny. Unfortunately, I didn't.

'This is the final straw, Maxine. Get the hell off my sofa and get your bloody clothes on,' I demanded, stepping over her scarlet g-string to get up very close. 'And then get the hell out of my house. If you want to fuck him, do it somewhere else, okay? Not in my living room.' I was practically spitting with rage, nose to nose with her, except she of course was taller. God, I was sick of being short.

'*Mais – pourquoi?*' she asked rather arrogantly, with a shrug of her bare, sloping shoulders. She reminded me of a gaudy butterfly that had shed its wings, leaving just its naked body behind. My skin crawled. Then she pulled her tiny little skirt on. 'I was doing nothing wrong. I have no duties right at this moment, *non*?'

For a moment I was stupefied. I could have punched her right then, right on her button nose. 'I don't care. I want you to go, now, please,' I said when I could speak again. Deb was beside me now, holding my arm gently.

'Calm down, Jess,' she said. 'Let's talk about this.'

'Could you pass me my underwear please, Jessica,' Maxine said to me, and then she smirked. So I did it. I slapped her right across her smug face: I don't know who was more surprised, me or her. She held her cheek, staring at me for a moment like some realisation was dawning. I thought uncomfortably about the first week she was here, and I turned away quickly.

Of course my brother chose this very moment to slink out from the kitchen.

'Blimey,' he murmured, clocking the still bare-breasted Maxine. 'What a pair!' And it was true. They were phenomenal – huge, pink-snouted and proud.

'Oh piss off, Robbie,' I said tiredly. He could always be relied on to appreciate the baser things in life. 'How did you get in this time?'

It was Leigh's turn to screech. 'What the flaming hell are you doing here?' She jabbed him in the chest. 'Did you invite him in?' She looked accusingly at me. Naturally he was still staring at Maxine's boobs, and Maxine was loving it, taking as long as she possibly could to put her lacy bra back on. Gorek scowled at Robbie's lingering gaze. Deb pushed us all back into the hall and shut the living-room door on the thwarted lovers.

'Why don't you go in the kitchen and put the kettle on? I'll sort these two out.'

'Yes, well,' I huffed, 'I don't want that bloke here, Deb. I'm sick of this. Please, will you ask him to go?'

In the kitchen I filled the kettle. My hands were trembling. There was a golden glass of very good whisky on the counter, a grease-stained copy of yesterday's *Sun* spread open on the racing news, bits of cheese and mayonnaise dripping from a half-eaten sandwich. It looked like it had been made from the last contents of my fridge.

'That's Mickey's.' I pointed dully at the scotch.

'Yeah, well, he wasn't here to ask, was he?' grinned Robbie. At least he'd had his front tooth fixed, I noticed.

Leigh rounded on him. 'Christ, and you wonder why I've got a problem with you, Robert.'

'Yeah, I do actually, Leigh. Blood's thicker than water and all that crap, eh?'

I flinched as he echoed my mum's words from the

227

other day. Leigh began to unload the shopping, slamming food into all the wrong cupboards. I could tell she didn't trust herself to speak.

'So how's it going?' Robbie looked at me. 'Any news?'

I took a deep breath. 'Mickey's had a relapse. No one's seen my son.'

'Still, no news is good news, yeah?' he said brightly.

Leigh kicked the cupboard door shut with her stiletto-toed foot as if it was Robbie's head. 'Can you really not come up with anything better than total bollocks?' she snapped.

Down the hall, the front door slammed shut.

'I'm trying to be helpful.' He shrugged indifferently.

'You're trying to help yourself, you mean.'

'Oh yeah? How's that then? How the hell can I help myself here?'

Leigh snorted with contempt, indicated the unfinished snack. 'Well, let's just think, shall we? I've been trying to work out why you've crawled back, but it ain't that hard really, is it, mate? You're nothing but a fucking ligger, Robert, nothing better than that.' Leigh never swore. 'You make me sick. Tell him to go, Jess.'

'Shut up, you silly cow,' he snarled at her. He knocked back the whisky in one go. 'I'll go when I'm ready – or when Jess wants me to.'

I stood helplessly between my siblings while their hatred crackled through the air, catching me the way static lifted your hair. I was shocked by Leigh's venom, shocked by Robbie's indifference. I had always been in between these two. Not much had changed, it seemed.

'What did you want, Robbie?' I asked quietly.

There was a pause. Leigh's fingernails drummed a mad rhythm on the worktop as we awaited an answer.

'Why do I need to want something to be here?' he asked plaintively. 'I just thought I'd make sure you were all right. I – I was worried.'

'I think you should go. For now, at least.'

A flash of lightning cut the sky in half. Guilt rose; I shoved it down. I was getting quite good at that now. No one spoke. Eventually Robbie sighed, pulling his heavy jacket over his torn T-shirt. His eyes were dull, lifeless even. The skin beneath them tired and spent, paper-like.

'Right. I will then.'

Thunder bellowed overhead. He paused, waiting to see how heartless his sisters really were. Would we let him step into the storm outside? Apparently we would. He grabbed the *Sun*, holding it aloft his greasy head, and ducked out the back door. Slammed it shut so hard I thought the glass would shatter in its panes.

'Thank Christ,' said Leigh. 'I bloody-well hope that's the last we see of him for a while.'

But as I crossed the kitchen, a shadow fell through the window. Robbie was there again. He mock-knocked, flung open the door and, scooping up the sandwich remains, jammed them in his pocket. I clocked the tattoo on his hand again, only this time I read 'Jimmy'. Something colourful and plastic dangled down for a split-second, before he shoved it back in along with the bits of bread.

'Needs must, eh, girls?' he said, with a cheerful grin. 'I had an idea, you know, Jess. An idea of how to help.

But if you don't want to know, well, that's up to you.'

And then he disappeared, along with the scotch. And it wasn't till an hour later that I twigged with horror what that plastic thing had been dangling from his pocket. It was a baby's dummy, bright and plastic, hanging from a ribbon.

Robbie's mobile was switched off when I tried to ring it. I paced the house with the phone clamped in my hand. This was the time I should finally shop Robbie to the police, I knew – but I wanted to speak to him first, give him one last chance to explain. Then Deb came in, making me jump: but she wanted to talk about Maxine, not Robbie. I thought the girl should go for good now – after all, I didn't need her any more, did I? I'd been keeping her there since Louis's disappearance as some kind of link to my son, I realised. If she'd left – well, it would have been like admitting defeat. But now even I'd had enough. Deb convinced me it was best that everyone stayed put while Louis was still missing; she persuaded me that Maxine and I needed to talk.

'Get some fresh air,' she suggested kindly, and so we walked over to the pub opposite the pond, and I bought us both a vodka. The rain had finally stopped and at last the air was cooler; the smell of the cut grass so lush and sweet it made me feel quite heady. Or perhaps that was the booze. Maxine was sulky, though she eventually apologised. I sensed that I'd done something to offend her.

'Why do you tell the police that my boyfriend is so

230

bad?' she finally ventured when I pushed her for the third time.

'Oh, I see.' I clinked the ice around my glass. 'Is that why you shagged him on the sofa? To punish me?'

She wrinkled her nose at me. 'Punish?'

'You know – to get back at me.'

'No.' She shook her head, but I could tell that she was lying. 'It was just – how do you say? The lust. We couldn't help ourselves.'

I would have laughed, but I'd lost my sense of humour.

'Oh, right.'

It dawned on me that Maxine genuinely didn't understand why I was so upset about the open sex, and I didn't have the energy to stay angry any more. Perhaps I *was* just jealous of 'the lust'.

'I didn't say that he was bad, Maxine.'

'If you didn't say he was bad, why was he arrested?' Surly, she wouldn't look at me, picking instead at a scab above her knee. Her skirt was so short I saw her knickers for the second time today. I felt exhausted.

'Because the police need to question everyone who comes to the house, Maxine. Surely you get that? And at the moment I can't cope with having strangers around, okay? Not who let themselves into my house, with my keys, and use my things, and especially not having sex publicly, on my sofa. It's not acceptable, it's just not.'

'Okay,' she shrugged.

'Until Louis is back I need some – some peace at home. Can you understand? I wasn't blaming what's-his-name –'

'Gorek.'

'Gorek. I just told DI Silver that he was around, and DI Silver made the decision to take him in, not me.' I remembered something Silver had said. 'Anyway, I thought you said you weren't that keen on him?'

She shrugged again; she really was so Gallic.

'I am drawn to him. Also, he has a very good job, *non*, at Harrods. He has money.' Always a prerequisite where Maxine's men were concerned. I knew that her own family were horribly poor; she had five sisters who were always turning up in London looking for a place to stay. Occasionally they'd arrive at our house, dragging cheap suitcases and plastic handbags up our stairs, short-skirted and bare-legged come rain or shine. I knew they'd grown up in two small rooms in the Calais suburbs where their father worked all hours down on the docks and their mother cleaned office blocks at night. It had always seemed quite obvious that Maxine was on the lookout for the main chance.

'And he wears the uniform on the door. He is – how you say – *je ne sais pas*. He turns me on.'

I blushed. God, when did I become such a prude?

'I can't help myself, though he can be *un peu* –'

'What?'

'Like the weather, you know.'

'Unpredictable?'

'*Oui*. Dangerous, perhaps.' She drained her drink, still worrying at the scab on her knee. This time I did smile. I remembered the stack of French Mills & Boon by Maxine's little bed, the battered *Angelique* novels too, and I understood that she celebrated what she would call grand passion.

'But you must not hit me again.'

'I know. I'm sorry. I lost my temper.'

'It is not the first time, *non*?'

'I've never hit you before. I've never hit anyone before,' I objected fiercely. I was feeling a bit drunk. The baby at the next table started to cry; I wanted to give it a cuddle. Maxine stared at me, then pulled the head right off that scab. A nasty feeling crawled up my spine. 'You're not talking about the time when Louis fell, are you?'

When Maxine had first arrived in London, I was in the midst of my worst time as a new mother. Struggling to adapt to Louis and my terror of messing up, the last thing I'd wanted was a stranger in my house, in Mickey's house, judging me – but he'd insisted I'd needed help. A Norland Nanny maybe, at a real push; a sex-mad French teenager with endless legs and attitude certainly wasn't what I had in mind. And then, in Maxine's first week, the day Freddie and Pauline came to visit, I fell asleep with Louis in my arms, and the baby rolled from the sofa onto the floor, and bruised his arm. Side-swiped by the broken nights, sluggish with the constant lack of sleep, firing on no cylinders at all, I was irrational and emotional about the slightest thing. Louis falling was the final straw; the guilt so immense; the fear something much worse could have happened rocked my already unsteady world. In the end it was a kind of paradox – it turned out to be a good thing, forced me finally, irrevocably to accept the sheer scale of my love

233

for him, to realise the breathtaking ends I'd go to now to protect him. I had to pull myself together before it was too late – and I had really begun to. But still, afterwards, although she had never actually spoken it out loud, I sensed Maxine's suspicion. Freddie too had eyed me anxiously that day, rushing into the room to find me howling above the sobbing baby – the baby who stopped crying far more quickly than I'd done, who was soon beaming happily at his new admirers while I apologised, shame-faced, to everyone.

'I didn't hit him, Maxine. You must know that. I'd never hurt my son. Never. I'd die first. It was a mistake, a complete mistake.'

'Okay. If you say so.'

We walked home in uneasy silence.

I spent the rest of the afternoon trying and failing to reach Robbie, and shuttling between home and hospital, where Mickey still hadn't stirred. Deb had arranged for me to see Annalise, the copper-haired counsellor, again. I cried bitterly through her box of starchy NHS tissues, and this time I let her hold my hand.

'I'm trying to keep strong for Louis, but it's hard,' I sniffed when I could speak. 'It's so hard. I can't face the thought of – of someone hurting him.' The thought made me want to scream. 'What – what if something's happened to him?'

'You can't give in to your imagination,' she said, patting my arm. I curled my fists to ward off my terrifying thoughts.

'I can't bear the thought that I should have stopped this happening. That I've let him down,' I whispered. 'And I'm frightened of something else now too.'

'What?' She peered over her glasses at me.

'It's just – my brother. He's so unreliable. I'm – what if he's mixed up in this?'

She frowned. 'Is he likely to be?'

'That's what I've got to find out.'

'Do you not think it's a police matter?'

'I think I can deal with him more quickly than the police can. He can be a bit – slippery. I don't want him to do a bunk. That'd be the worst thing.'

I didn't talk about my secret craving for the silence of the pills again. I wouldn't give in; wouldn't bend again. I wouldn't go the same way I'd watched my mother go.

In bed that night, I stared at the ceiling for ages before I even began to feel like I could sleep. I was racked with indecision over Robbie. If I couldn't track him first thing in the morning, I knew I'd have to tell Silver about my suspicions. I had to face the truth.

Finally, I started to drift. I saw myself and Mickey lying in the bed, Mickey reading the paper, or the *New Yorker*, me reading some art textbook he'd doubtless raised his eyebrows at. I floated into the morning Louis was born; waking early, my contractions starting, my gasps of shock and pain; the abject terror at what was happening too early coupled with the excitement of being about to meet my baby. Then I saw a three-month-old Louis lying in between us and me finally happier than I'd ever been – still too scared to admit

235

it in case someone came and took it all away. They say you only know happiness when it's gone, and I'd felt so very happy and prayed that this time it could stay –

And now I was falling – falling into –

With a shock I was jolted awake again. Despite the warmth of the night, I felt a proper chill; I had a sudden eerie feeling I was being watched. Slowly, I got out of bed and crept over to the window. I peered round the curtain, scanning the road outside, the heath opposite. Nothing, no one lurking. Just a stooped old man in a flat cap, with a fat little dog who was peeing against the postbox. The saplings danced in the new winds the storm had left behind. Despite my sudden fears and the threat of heavy rain again, l left my window wide open and the curtains pulled right back. In my gut, I felt Louis was near. If I left it open, that way I would hear him if he cried.

CHAPTER SEVENTEEN

I half-woke in the night. It was very dark, and I was sure I could smell cigarettes. Raising my head slightly from the pillow, I thought I heard a voice. The curtains stirred slightly at the open window. I froze for a moment; then I forced myself out of bed. I tried not to be frightened; Shirl was just next door – I hoped. Groggy, I stumbled; righting myself on the chest of drawers by the light.

I crept out onto the landing. Shirl's door was shut. Had she come back at all? I strained my ears and listened; everything had gone quiet now. Outside, a fox screamed time and time again. I peered over the banister; every-thing was black. Then, a sudden exclamation and someone opened the kitchen door in a rush of light, sending a huge spiky shadow down the hall.

'Who's that?' I whispered hoarsely from the safety of my vantage point. Silence. Then Maxine peered guiltily around the door, looking up. My stomach contracted in painful relief. She was holding the phone in her hand.

'Pardon, Jessica,' she said, 'I didn't mean to wake you.'

'No,' I said tersely, 'I bet you didn't.' I could just see the whites of her eyes glinting up at me.

'I was just speaking with *mon père*. He is home from the late shift.'

'Go back to bed,' I said. I went back to mine; slumping back into fitful sleep, escaping from my reality. Sleep was best for now. Sleep at least was safe.

In the morning I was woken very early by the rays of light that flickered through my room. The wind had cleared the sky, and little dribbles of cloud crossed the dawning sun. It was seven whole days since I'd last seen my son. One entire week. All my milk had dried up, and I lived every waking second in pure, unadulterated terror, on the verge of a precipice so steep that if I fell, I'd never climb again. The stark truth was, I wouldn't want to. I'd lost so much weight already my clothes were starting to hang off me. What I would have given to be fat and exhausted by Louis, and simply blissful to be with him again. The old refrain *What a difference a day makes* kept flitting through my head.

I lay and thought for a while; I remembered my drunken dream the other night, the faceless Agnes. Suddenly I realised why she had no face. I'd never actually seen her – I had no idea what Agnes looked like, I only had an image in my head. I got up and padded to Mickey's study in my bare feet and T-shirt. It was cool and dim in here, and I still felt like some kind of intruder, only now I didn't care. I searched the room from top to bottom for signs of Agnes. I found the expensive watch I'd given Mickey for his birthday shoved in a drawer, my futile attempt to stop him always being late.

Then, finally, just as I was about to admit defeat, I found one old snapshot in the back of his desk; scrunched and slightly out of focus. The woman I imagined must be Agnes was turned away from the camera, behind Mickey, holding his hand. They were at some kind of party; she was laughing at someone out of shot. She looked quite tall and very thin, but her face was almost impossible to see. Her hair was blonde and streaky and ridiculously straight, like it'd been ironed. She reminded me of someone. Mickey was grinning, toasting the camera. He looked almost Bacchanalian; his eyes glinting a bit like they had the other night before he'd passed out. He looked happy. I wondered why I'd never seen a picture of my husband's ex before. Was that odd?

Then I sat at his big desk and I rang Pauline. Freddie answered groggily; I guessed I'd woken her and apologised profusely.

'What's happened?' Pauline came on the line, struggling out of sleep. She sounded panicked. 'Is it Louis? Mickey?'

'No,' I said, 'it's me. I want to contact Agnes. Do you have a number for her?'

'I'm not sure,' she said, befuddled, voice thick with sleep. 'Do you really think that's wise, pet?'

'That's up to me, isn't it, Pauline?' I answered, as pleasantly as I could. 'Can you get a number for me soon?'

'I'll see what I can do,' she said. 'I doubt she's in the country though.'

'Where does she live?' I thought it was New York, among skyscrapers as tapering and elegant as I now knew Agnes to be.

'Between America and Amsterdam, I think. I don't really know now, pet. We're not in touch, you do realise that, don't you?'

Today, I chose to believe Pauline.

'I thought the police were going to track her down,' she added. I hung up, then thought of something else. I called back. She was trying hard to hide her irritation, but I heard Freddie mutter in the background.

'Pauline,' I said, 'sorry. I meant to ask you before. Why would Mickey have had his passport on him the day of our – the day Louis disappeared?'

'Did he?' she said.

'Yes, he did.'

There was a pause while she computed the question.

'The day after he got back from the *Romantic Retreats* shoot, wasn't it? He always has his passport on him on a trip, British or foreign. You know how anal he is, pet. Hire car, I should think.'

I hung up again, with relief this time. Then I went to my dawn kitchen, I sat and drank black coffee, savouring the fact that no one was around now, that I had my house to myself for a little while. I tried to think of normal things, like getting up early with my son, and watching him beneath the baby gym, or bouncing back and forth in his curving chair, kicking his chubby legs, sucking his fist. That little chair sat, stranded now, in the corner. I turned away from it; I felt now that I must take charge. It was too early to ring the web designer, Justin, who had promised to update Louis's website today, but in the end I did it anyway – and Justin was very nice about it, and promised to be round sometime later to show me the changes. If I had to sit and continue to do nothing for much longer, I would go quietly insane.

Around 8 a.m, I did what I had never done. I took a deep breath and I rang Silver's mobile. He'd always said I should call him any time, so I didn't know why I felt like I was calling for a date. He picked up quickly; there were squealing kids in the background, and he was pleasant, if a little distracted. I asked him about Agnes. Had he found her yet? Had he questioned her? Silver said they thought she was in Holland, where she lived now; they'd sent a local officer to talk to her. He'd hear back today, he was sure.

One of the kids started crying so near the phone I could hear the actual sniffs, something about Andy stealing the jam, and Silver excused himself. I felt a stab of jealousy that he was with his children; envy for the sheer normality. And then, sweating slightly, I told him about Robbie.

'We'll bring him in. I'll see you at the station for the appeal,' he said. I imagined a beautiful wife, buxom and dimpled, fixing him breakfast. He looked the type of man to enjoy bacon and eggs, the type of man who was waited on.

I was sitting at my dressing table, putting on mascara

in the vain hope I'd look less dead, when something crept through my aching brain and punched me between the brows. The Tate woman and Agnes. They might be one and the same? I was about to go and find the phone to call Silver back when the bedroom door flew open. Startled, the mascara wand shot up my eyelid. A steaming mug rounded the door, followed by my brother.

'Flipping heck, Robbie! Ever heard of knocking?' I said crossly, licking my finger to remove the black gunk. 'And how the hell are you getting in? I didn't hear the bell.'

'I brought you a cup of tea.' He was evasive as ever. 'Leigh's not here, is she?' he asked anxiously.

'She's hiding under the bed actually. I'm glad you *are* here, though. I've been trying to get hold of you. Did you get my messages? Why do you never answer your bloody phone?' I glared at him. 'And why the hell did you have a dummy in your pocket yesterday?'

Robbie plonked the tea down next to me; inevitably, it spilt onto the leather top. I watched his face closely. It was devoid of obvious emotion.

'What dummy?' Total nonchalance. He was always so convincing – that was the eternal problem.

'The baby's dummy I realised was hanging out of your pocket when you nicked Mickey's scotch. Well, I realised afterwards.'

'I don't know what you're on about.'

'Robbie!'

'I don't, honestly. Why would I have a dummy on me?'

'That's what's worrying me. Tell me the bloody truth, Robbie.'

'Are you saying you think I've got Louis? Don't be daft.' He sipped his tea casually. 'I must have picked it up when I was here without realising.'

'Louis doesn't have a dummy, he's never had one. I've never given him one.' Something I was proud of; a small victory in my hit-and-miss parenting. Leigh was a great advocate, and Maxine had tried occasionally when he was teething, but I thought they looked so ugly, stoppering the poor baby up like a used bottle.

'Oh God, I don't know. I swear, Jess, I swear I don't know where he is. You have to believe me.'

'Robbie,' I grabbed his face in both my hands and forced him to look at me, 'I swear I'll kill you if you've had anything to do with this. You do know that, don't you? I will tell the Old Bill if I think it's you.'

He put his hands up to mine. 'I swear, Jess, on my life, I'm as worried as you.'

But how much was his life worth to him these days? Still, he was starting to convince me. However low Robbie stooped, I didn't believe he had it in him to hurt me so deliberately. I started on my other eye.

'So how did you get in this time, Rob? And while we're at it, how the hell did you get in yesterday?'

He shrugged, unperturbed, and sat on the bed. 'Back door. Unlocked. You wanna be more careful. Never know who might be prowling around. This is nice and firm, isn't it?' He bounced a bit, smoothing the silk cover with a horribly nicked hand. I glimpsed a number tattooed on the inside of his wrist. I dreaded to think what it might mean.

'Right. Thanks for the advice.' I stuck the mascara-wand back into its holder.

'Jessie,' he started talking very fast, 'I really do think I can help you. I've been trying to say. I was up west the other day, and I met a bloke who reckons he can find Louis, and I –'

'Woah, woah, woah.' I stuck my hand out against the torrent. 'What do you mean, "find Louis"? If the police haven't found him yet, why would your mate be able to?'

Robbie sneered. 'Since when did you have so much faith in the Old Bill?'

I blushed.

'I mean, come on, Jess, they're not exactly doing a good job, are they? And, I mean, Christ, I would have thought that after everything we went through as kids you'd know not to trust them. Specially not since that bastard Jones. All that bird downstairs is good for is making tea, as far as I can see.'

'And there was I thinking you'd actually managed to boil a kettle. Don't be horrible about Deb,' I said hotly. 'At least she's here for me.'

He shook his head impatiently, didn't take the bait. 'Look, we're getting off the point.'

'Which is?'

'That I know people.'

I thought of that motley crew on the estate the other day. 'God, Robbie, do you know how ridiculous you sound?'

'Do you care what I sound like? Do you want my help or not?'

'Depends.' I started looking for clean pants. I really needed to do some washing.

'On what?'

'On whether it really is help or not.' There was a knock at the door. Maxine stuck her head around it.

'Did you call for me, Jessica?' she said. She saw Robbie; I swore she flushed gently.

'No, thanks, Maxine,' I said. 'I didn't.'

Maxine gave an almost imperceptible toss of her peroxide hair. 'Oh. I am sorry. I think I hear my name.' There was a slight pause before she closed the door behind her.

'You've got her well-trained, haven't you?' Robbie grinned at me.

'Hardly.'

'Look, anyway, I know this bloke who – well, let's just say he's got some dodgy connections.'

'What a surprise.'

'Just listen, okay? This bloke I'm on about, I mean, he's all right himself but he runs a bit of a racket down in Soho. Got a clothes shop too. Nice stuff. Anyway, I was talking to him the other day and he mentioned that he'd heard about these gangs –'

I sighed heavily. 'Robbie, Silver's checked out the gang thing already.'

'Who's Silver? Not that poncy cop with the flash suits?'

I reddened further. 'Do you have to slag off all the people who are trying to help me?' I asked angrily.

'Ooh, get you!' Robbie raised his eyebrows. 'Got a bit of a crush going on there, Jessie?'

I burned even hotter. 'Piss off, Rob.'

He laughed delightedly. 'I'm right! You have.'

'I have bloody not.'

'You bloody have.'

'Shut up. I haven't. I'm a married woman, thank you very much.' And a fraud.

'You forget how well I know you.'

For a moment I forgot myself too, and I actually laughed. I felt like I was sixteen again and my little brother was teasing me in our tiny shared bedroom about boys.

'He reminds me of that Merlin bloke.'

'Who?'

'Merlin – from the Frog and Forget-me-not. You know. I think his real name was Keith.'

'Piss off! Merlin had dodgy teeth and an eye-patch.'

'Yeah, well, that never stopped you. Mum caught you snogging him behind the garages that night, d'you remember?'

'No, I don't!'

'You bloody do.'

'Well, I'd had too much Merrydown, hadn't I?' We both collapsed into giggles. He lay back on the bed and waved his legs in the air as he guffawed. I felt a huge rush of love for him. In a beat, he ruined it.

'Seriously, though, Jess, this bloke. He says he can help. You know, he knows people. So, like, for a little consideration he –'

'There had to be a catch, didn't there?'

'What?' he asked, all innocent. He fished his tobacco out of his leather, started rolling up. His fingernails were filthy and broken; his nicotine stains spreading like canker down towards his palms.

'Oh come on, Robbie! For a "little consideration"?' I mimicked him. Crossly I pulled my pants on too fast and nearly fell; just in time, I caught myself on his knee. I stomped to the drawers and pulled out a clean vest-top, putting a pair of denim cut-offs on. 'What the hell does that mean, a "little consideration"? You mean if I give you some money you'll go and spend it on – on something you shouldn't have – and then you'll pretend you've given it to this geezer, and I'll never see it again. Or probably you, either.'

'You don't think much of me, do you?' Robbie said woefully. He had that delicate skin that flared and stained easily; his colour was high suddenly. He kept his eyes cast down as he concentrated on licking his cigarette, playing for time. I sensed that he couldn't decide whether to get angry, or be mortally wounded by my mistrust. He used to do this when we were kids, always choosing the path most profitable for him.

'I don't know what to think, Robbie.' Perhaps I was being disingenuous; perhaps we all did the same. It was so hot again, my mascara was already sliding beneath my eyes. I wiped it away furiously. 'If that's all you came to say, perhaps you should go now.'

'But I'm serious. I really reckon this bloke can help. And I'm not doing gear. I swear I'm not. I haven't done for – for years.'

247

'Yeah, right.'

'It's the truth.'

I looked at him. 'So what the hell were you doing in Elephant and Castle the other day? Drinking tea?'

We had never really spoken about the drug thing. The rest of the family used to pretend the problem didn't exist; it seemed easier that way – for my mother, anyway. I had tried to broach it once or twice after catching Robbie in awkward situations – but he'd always denied it stringently. I mean, I knew that he was up for anything as an adolescent – after the family's final shame – uppers, downers, vitamin pills. When we'd shared a room, I was always finding his stash of whatever-it-might-be-this-week, and chucking it away – much to his wrath.

'I was just doing some business.' For a minute, I thought he was going to cry. His voice had reached the pitch of an unhappy child who felt the world was against him. I forced myself to be tougher than my instinct said.

'Rob, look. If you really think you can help, I'd be grateful. But I'm not going to dole out money so you can hand it over to dodgy men in the Soho underworld. If you want to help, you give him the money and see what he comes up with. And we'll take it from there.'

'But –' His voice was nearly a whisper. I felt his sudden surge of desperation.

'But what?'

'I haven't got any money. I'm absolutely brassic.'

'What about what Mum sent you?'

'I haven't got it yet. Some problem with the bank account.'

'How did you afford the tooth?'

He looked at me blankly.

'Your new tooth.' I pointed at the gleaming cap. 'You've had it fixed.'

'I had enough for that. Couldn't go round looking like a minger, could I, Jess? What would the girls say?'

I didn't believe him, but I couldn't help it. Old habits died hard and all that crap. Opening the little drawer in my dressing-table, I fished out a twenty, a tenner and some pound coins stuffed between my higgledy-piggledy jewellery boxes.

'Here. For you, not the "bloke",' I said, thrusting it at him. I couldn't bear to look at him. My beautiful little brother – tattooed, dirty and desperate. Where the hell had it all gone wrong? He took it; he didn't look back at me either.

'Robbie,' I said, and this time it was me that whispered. 'Sort yourself out, mate, yeah? Please. Before it's really too late.'

He left the room as stealthy as a cat. He didn't look back.

As I headed downstairs, the phone began to ring. Deb came out of the kitchen, crossed the hall towards it. I hated the phone these days, it terrified me each time it rang, but now I skidded across the parquet to get there first. Too slow – Deb already had the receiver in her hand. I grabbed it from her as she lifted it to her ear.

'It's all right, Deb, I've got it.' I turned my back on her but I still felt her scrutiny. She frowned and walked away, headed into the living room where the telly was blaring away to itself. Subtly, she tried to turn it down.

As I'd hoped, it was Pauline, with Agnes's mobile number. I scribbled it down quickly, mumbling my thanks as Deb strained to catch the conversation.

'Who was that?' she called as I hung up. I shrugged, shoved the number in my back pocket.

'No one important. Just an old mate.'

She kept staring at me.

'What?' I said innocently, and shot into the kitchen before she could say anything more. I liked Deb but, God, I felt suffocated. My chest hurt. I kept picturing myself like a tiny cork caught up in swirling white waters, bobbing valiantly to keep myself above water, struggling not to get swept under forever.

Later, in the car, Deb tried to bring the phone call up again. I put the radio on loudly to drown her out. Some phone-in about terrorism, some hysterical female presenter. Some poor guy had been shot mistakenly by armed policemen.

'Doesn't give you much faith in the Old Bill, does it?' I said. I kept thinking about what Robbie had said, about the police when we were kids. About that bastard DC Jones. I didn't want to remember any of it – that final indignity after my dad had died. Not now, not ever. I switched over to a dance station. I felt about 900 – far too old for dance music – but I turned it up anyway. Deb gave in.

*

After the usual press affair, I was taken to see Silver in his office. He seemed psyched-up, trying not to let it show, perhaps, but his excitement was infectious. He was talking on the phone, waiting to be put through to someone. I daren't let myself get carried away.

DC Kelly came in and handed Silver a file. Silver scanned it, hung up the phone. 'Ian will explain,' he said, still reading, gesturing at Egg-belly, who was as unkempt and exhausted-looking as usual. Perhaps he was conducting the whole investigation on his own. He smoothed his tie – pointlessly. It looked every bit as rumpled as it had a moment ago.

'Do you have any particular connections with Soho?' he asked. He had a quiet, low voice, and I had to strain to hear him above the air-conditioning. His scalp was very pink between strands of greased-back hair. He repeated himself, meticulously polite as always.

I frowned as I considered the question hard. 'No. Well, not other than doing a lot of drinking there when I was –' I was about to say younger, but actually it was only last year. Just as I met Mickey, before I fell pregnant so incredibly fast. 'Not really. Not apart from Mickey's office being there, of course. Why?'

Kelly looked at Silver; Silver tapped his pen discordantly between his perfect teeth. 'All in good time, kiddo. Have a really proper think.'

I racked my brains hopefully, but nothing came to mind. Miserably I shook my head, but Silver smiled at me.

'It doesn't matter. We're following a lead, something the video guys have noticed from studying the tape, something we originally thought was a recording fault. Turns out it's more likely to be to do with where it was shot.'

The enigma just frustrated me much more. 'Please, explain what you mean.' I leant forward to Silver, but he just smiled mysteriously again. 'I will when I know more. I don't want to get your hopes up too early.' He chucked his pen back down on the desk. 'That's it for now, then, Jessica,' he said formally. 'Deb'll take you home.'

Kelly was up and out immediately. Silver walked me to the door. He looked down at me for a second, like I was a suspicious parcel.

'Are you giving her a hard time?' he asked quietly.

'Who?' I was surprised.

'Deb.'

Through the glass in the door, I watched her rubbing at an invisible mark on her skirt. She must have felt my stare because she looked up and waved.

'She's only there to help you, you do know that, don't you?'

I felt a twinge of guilt. 'Why, has she complained?'

'No, not at all. She likes you. I've just noticed that you seem a little – irritable with her sometimes.'

I'd hoped I'd hidden my short fuse better. 'Do I? Oh God, I don't mean to be. I mean, it's odd, having someone always there, checking up on me. But I'm really grateful, honestly, for all your help.'

'That's what we're here for.'

'It's just – I suppose I'm so desperate to get Louis back, and it's all moving so bloody slowly that it's like living –' I searched for the words. 'Like being on a knife-edge. Literally.' I would have been quite proud of my analogy normally. 'My balance isn't very good right now, that's all.'

'We're doing our damnedest, Jessica, I promise you. I'll be in touch.'

'It's been a whole week, you know. Seven and a half days since I saw my son.'

'I know.'

'Statistically I don't think that's very good, do you?'

His look was kind. 'I think every case is different, Jess. There's nothing hard and fast to say where or when kidnapped children are returned.'

I didn't want to leave. 'Sometimes, you know,' my words were tumbling over one another, 'sometimes I just feel like I'm going totally insane. Like I'm losing it completely. I don't know what to do with myself. I feel like I should be out there at all hours looking for him. But I also feel like I should be at home, waiting for him. I can't rest, I can't relax, I can't eat, I can't sleep. Oh God.'

Silver patted me like I was a small child. 'You've just got to hang in there, Jess. Leave the searching to us. You're doing everything you can. You're doing great, kiddo.' Then he herded me out the door; was about to shut it behind me when I stopped it with my foot.

'I was wrong about Robbie, by the way. I've seen him now, and I asked him about the dummy. It was a mistake, he said. But I – I want to know, have they spoken to Mickey's ex yet? Agnes?'

His eyes narrowed. 'Why are you so bothered? Are

you getting obsessed?' he asked, looking at me closely.

'No, I'm not getting obsessed,' I protested vehemently, but I squirmed under his gaze. 'I just –'

'What?'

'I just, I've got a funny feeling she may have been at the Tate that day.'

He nearly choked on his gum. 'You what? A "funny feeling"?'

This time I was on the defensive. 'Well, I'd never seen her till today. I found – I think I found a photo of her this morning. And well – she looks like the woman in the Tate. That weird woman who freaked me out. The one I did the photofit of.'

'Yes, I do know who you mean. Christ Almighty, Jessica, you've got to stop doing this to me. Have you got the photo with you?'

'Not with me, no,' I admitted, rather shame-facedly, 'it's at home. Sorry, I didn't think to bring it.'

'Hang on.' He went to his desk and buzzed someone. 'Did you speak to Mickey Finnegan's ex-wife Agnes yet?' he said. Then he laughed. 'Okay. Cheers, mate. No, that's fine for now.' The receiver clattered back into the cradle. 'Jess, I have to say, I don't see how Agnes can be linked to Louis. Kelly spoke to her on her mobile yesterday and she's been abroad, in the States I think. I'll let you know for definite when we've interviewed her properly, but we've checked all airport records. No Agnes Finnegan has travelled in the past seven or eight days. Apparently she's coming to London now, on business, anyway. But I really don't see how your women can be one and the same.'

My shoulders slumped. A gentle hand pushed me towards the corridor. 'Don't worry about it. We'll get to her very soon. And look, like I said, don't get obsessed. I know she's your husband's ex and all, but –'

'Who's obsessed?' I said staunchly. 'Just making sure you're doing your job, that's all.' But I still couldn't quite tear myself away. He raised his eyebrows as I hesitated at the door. 'Let me come with you,' I blurted.

'Where?'

'Wherever it is you're going to check out that tape. I'll be good, I won't be –' I chewed my poor split thumb again '– I won't be – you know, irritable, I swear. I'll know if Louis is near; I'll feel it, I know I will.'

But he shook his head again. 'I can't take you, Jessica. It's not wise. For your sake, as much as mine.' Very gently he removed my hand from the door. 'I'll be in touch, I promise, as soon as there's some news. Now, I must get on.'

He shut the door softly in my face. I was about to knock again when my phone rang. It was the hospital, a concerned Sister Kwame on the line.

'Mrs Finnegan, you really must tell your family not to upset your husband.'

'Sorry?' I was baffled. 'What family?'

'He really should not be having visitors right now. Only you. It is too much for him. Even when he is under sedation.'

'I didn't know anyone had been there apart from me.'

'I thought you okayed it. They both said you did.'

'Who?' I demanded impatiently. 'Which "both"? Who are you talking about?'

'He came last night, the man. He said he was a cousin. And the woman came today. I'm not sure of her name. She's still here, I think.'

'Hang on.' I rushed towards the doors, to Deb, fear pumping through my veins. 'Tell her to wait. I'm on my way.'

CHAPTER EIGHTEEN

I sat by Mickey's bed and listened to him ramble. His head tossed and turned this way and that; he was obviously feverish. They were pumping antibiotics into him; they didn't know why he wasn't recovering. They didn't actually say as much, but I sensed it in the air.

'Sorry,' he kept saying, over and again; and next, inaudible rubbish would spool out of him. Then 'Louis'. 'Louis' and 'sorry': they were the only two words I could make out.

By the time I'd arrived, Mickey's mystery visitor had vanished into the ether. The sister hadn't actually seen the woman herself, although she'd described last night's male visitor as dark and sweaty-looking, which made my heart plummet straight through the floor. And of course the staff nurse on duty who'd let the woman in had gone off-shift by now and couldn't be reached, however much I insisted I needed to speak to her. Biting my lip in frustration, I paced the room watching Mickey until, after a while, I couldn't bear the tension any more. I went outside for some fresh air. It was still very close and I felt in my pocket for my inhaler, but instead I came across Agnes's number from this morning. I stared at it for a moment, and then I fished the new phone Deb had got me out of my bag and I dialled her number. It rang like it was ringing abroad; she didn't answer. I left a message. I said that this was Mickey's wife, and I didn't know if she'd heard, but Mickey was ill and our son was missing, and I asked her to please call me back. Then I realised I didn't know what my new number was, so I had to phone her back with it. Afterwards, I went inside again, and listened to yet more of Mickey's insane ramblings, stroking his freezing hand.

When I left the hospital it was late afternoon. If anything, it felt hotter than before. As I turned my phone back on, the message signal bleeped frantically. I had two – one from Robbie, begging me to call him. The other was a cool foreign voice I'd never heard before. Agnes. She sounded just like I'd imagined that she would: Transatlantic, glam. She had just landed at Heathrow, she said, and was on her way to the Sanderson Hotel in central London for business meetings. I could call her on her mobile if I wanted to speak.

Deb was down in the car park, sorting out the ticket. I didn't stop to think about it, I just ran to the side of the road and flagged down a cab, launching myself guiltily into the back before Deb could witness my flight.

Apart from my brief jaunt to the opera the other night, when my son was still safe, I hadn't been into town for months. I was amazed by all the noise, the sheer amount of people; the eternal red and white roadworks. Sirens like I imagined on the mean streets of New

York. I sat behind a taxi driver as round as a billiard-ball; his bald head matt, like he'd just powdered it. He wanted to talk about terrorism; I nodded politely and contemplated Agnes. What the hell I'd say to her. 'Are you screwing my husband?' seemed a bit of a non-starter.

When I got out at the Sanderson, which looked exactly like some drab old office-block, the driver said, 'Don't tip me, love. Not in this time of crisis.' Which crisis? I nearly asked; and tipped him anyway before flip-flopping my way anxiously into the hotel. Weird fish floated in the spherical reception desk, and I asked the immaculate girl sitting above them for Agnes Finnegan. It didn't register; nor did I know the company she worked for. By this time, despite my polite smiles, the receptionist was staring at me like something the Sanderson's prize Siamese had just dragged in. She knew I didn't belong here. The lobby was cram-full of people wanting to be seen, busy pretending that they didn't. I flashed 'misfit' like it was stamped in neon across my head.

I was about to ring Agnes's mobile again when I suddenly spotted her striding through the doors. The woman in Mickey's photo; white jacket draped over bronzed, coathanger shoulders, a pile of Louis Vuitton and a sweaty porter in tow. Her hair was scraped back severely from a strong-jawed face. She was very striking – beautiful, in fact. My heart plunged absolutely. Of course Silver had been right. She wasn't the woman from the Tate; they looked nothing alike. She wasn't even blonde any more; her hair was more of a tawny shade now. I glanced down at my shabby cut-offs and wondered nervously when I'd last washed my own tangled curls. I forced myself to step forward anyway, intercepting her before she reached the desk.

'Agnes?' My voice faltered. I drew myself up to my full height. She wasn't all that tall herself, I realised now, but in spike heels she had a great advantage. Strappy leather sandals so expensive I could practically hear their flesh mooing softly while being trotted across a lush emerald field to die humbly for Agnes. She looked across at me; she stopped; she tilted her head rather like a cockatoo.

'You must be Jessica,' she said, after a studied moment. She pushed her sunglasses up into her hair. 'I wasn't exactly expecting you here, I must say.' Cool as a December day, as the snow plains that she hailed from – despite a degree of obvious exhaustion. I offered my hand as graciously as I could, but inside I shook like jelly. My rival, I thought uneasily, as she slid her own hand calmly towards me. Her skin was very cool and dry; I was sure mine was all clammy. I watched the porter fall over himself to take her trolley as she suggested a drink at the bar to me.

We swayed on ridiculously uncomfortable high chairs. With impeccable but frosty manners, she ordered a Manhattan; I opted for water, then swapped to vodka at the last minute. My mind was scrabbling like a spider in a filling bath. I kept seeing her in bed with Mickey, him ripping off her flimsy underwear, their lithe bodies twined round each other. Pauline's words came back to smack me in the face: '...they loved each other very much ... destroying each other...'

Agnes lit a cigarette without offering me one. 'So,

what's up with Mickey? I heard he had an accident, no, but he is all right?' She inhaled deeply.

'He was attacked. Our son's been –' I tried not to choke on the words; I was determined not to cough as I breathed her smoke in. '– kidnapped,' I managed eventually. I'd never said that word out loud before. I clenched my hands very tight between my knees.

'My God!' she said, paling. She looked properly shocked now at least. She tapped her ash very carefully into the ashtray. The vodka whacked straight up into my addled brain.

'I'm so sorry. I didn't really understand your message. I had a call from a policeman too some days ago. DI Silver? He is also coming to meet me here.' She inhaled again. In my vodka blur I could see her and Silver now, writhing around. Agnes looked like she writhed. I shook my befuddled head sharply.

'Are you okay? Is –' For the first time, she hesitated. The way she talked was slightly odd, stilted even. 'Is Mickey okay?' She eyed me closely. Her irises were grey and flinty; like a cat's. I hated cats – they always made me wheeze.

'I'm fine, thanks. It's my baby I'm worried about. And my husband, obviously.' I emphasised the 'my'.

She shrugged her stylish shoulders. 'Mickey, he's a survivor, no? He will be okay, I think. I hope to God.'

I bet you do.

She sipped her drink, and I felt her check the clock behind me. Cold as ice, she was, and almost as brittle. Her nails were beautifully filed, but I noticed that her manicure was rather chipped. It was now or never.

'Why have you been seeing him?' I asked, with the utmost civility.

This time it was her that almost choked; then the choke became a cough, a proper smoker's rattle. When she had composed herself a little, she looked at me, and now she didn't bother to hide her disdain.

'Excuse me?' Her perfectly plucked eyebrow curled into an elegant question mark.

'You heard, I'm sure,' I answered bluntly. 'Why have you been in touch with Mickey again?'

She was about to protest, but I cut her off. 'I know you have, so don't bother to deny it, please. Pauline told me.'

Agnes smiled sardonically, running a finger round that beautifully glossed mouth. Inhaled, exhaled, like some old dragon. 'Ah, Pauline. The dolly lesbian.' Inhaled again. Then, 'Do you really want to know?'

'Yes, I do actually.'

'Well, you should ask your husband perhaps.'

'I can't. He's out cold in the hospital.' She paled again. 'That's why I'm asking you.'

'Out cold?'

'Unconscious.' Her eyes narrowed. I relented a little. 'He'll be okay.'

She sized me up for a second. 'It's – been very hard, you know, Jessica. Can I call you that?' It seemed like she was searching for words; she twirled her cocktail stirrer round and around her glass again. 'When you have known love like mine and Mickey's, it's hard to not – how can I explain it? Not to pursue it, I guess.'

'Pursue it?' I had a sudden image of Mickey running

around our garden, chasing a laughing Agnes. I pushed my vodka away.

'Yes, pursue. He won't leave me alone.'

My stomach hit the floor with an almighty thump. Then I looked at her, and something in the way she fidgeted very slightly made me question her honesty.

'You're lying,' I challenged.

'Oh yes? You think?' She stood up. 'I don't want to talk to you now. I am sorry for you, but really, why have you come here? To rub my nose in it?'

'Rub your nose in what?'

'You have it all now, don't you, Jessica? My man, my house. Leave it at that, okay?'

'Agnes,' I said wearily, 'please, I don't want to upset you. But I need to know the truth. About you and Mickey. I need to restore some order to the chaos that my life's become. You must understand that? Please, finish your drink at least.'

Reluctantly she sat down again, taking a careful sip of her vibrant cocktail. I felt her make a decision. 'Okay. I tell you the truth – and then you'll go, yes?'

'Yes,' I agreed.

It was rather like a safety valve had flown off somewhere. 'I have tried to leave him alone, I tell myself I must get on with my life, and I do for a while. But then I can't help it, I need to speak with him. So I ring him. I say, look, you are married again. What about your new wife? Is it the same amount of love we had?'

I refused to flinch. I pulled the vodka back to me, *oh, what the hell,* and gulped at it, holding the glass

263

too tight until it made my old wound sore. The icy liquid trickled down my throat.

'I have even changed my home number recently, you know, so if he did want to ring me, he couldn't. So I didn't wait by the phone all the time.'

So that was why Silver couldn't reach her at first. She was fiddling with an expensive-looking lighter; it bore an inscription that I couldn't quite read. My stomach lurched, the vodka sloshed. I swallowed hard. 'So why did you see him?'

'When?'

I did the calculations. 'Last week. Sunday. Pauline said you were meant to be meeting.'

She laughed huskily, but her eyes didn't even start to smile. They were flat, cold. 'I didn't see him in the end. I stayed in New York. He rang me some days before and he said he was working. I think he only arranged it in the first place because he –'

'What?'

'It is hard to be honest with you, Jessica, about my feelings. It's very – private.' She said my name like it made her feel quite sick.

'Well, try,' I suggested.

She shrugged again. Her poise was faultless, but I sensed an anguish lurking somewhere deep. She looked away, over at a table of laughing City boys. One of them winked lasciviously at her, and she received it like a woman used to eternal attention, basking in their desire. She looked back at me. For a moment I thought there were tears in her grey cat eyes, but she blinked them away damn fast. I found myself almost smiling encouragingly.

264

'Well, I guess, Mickey chose you – didn't he? But, he knew – he felt – my sorrow, so we arranged that dinner when I last went into his office. Then he changes his mind. He wants to be the family man now, he says. He feels sorry for you.' Any pity I'd felt for her dissolved entirely; my smile vanishing as my heart sank sickeningly. 'And so he cancelled it.'

'Sorry for me?' I echoed.

'You had that – how do they call it? Postnatal depression, no?'

'No, not really.'

But she knew that I was lying; she looked utterly contemptuous. 'I wouldn't know, anyway. I don't have kids.'

I looked at the sheen of her, the sheer time-consuming perfection. 'You don't say.'

'Not my thing at all,' she purred, looking me up and down with subtle malevolence. I bit my tongue. *What would you know about sacrifice*, I wanted to ask, *with your Prada clothes and your platinum credit cards*. But I didn't.

'When did you arrange this dinner?' I pushed. I just wanted the facts, and then I wanted to get the hell out of there.

'I really don't remember, Jessica. Some time when I was last working in London.'

'Why did you go to see him originally?'

'To sign some papers to sell a property we owned.'

I glared at her. She stared back unabashed. 'Oh, all right then. If you really want to know – to tell him we should still be together. And we should, you know. But he – I think he – doesn't want another broken marriage, not again.'

Oh, how magnanimous. I didn't trust myself to speak immediately. She smoothed her chignon, her hair as crisp as it was in that old photo, and checked her jewel-encrusted watch. I fiddled with my own hair self-consciously, then wondered when I'd last shaved my exposed armpits, and clamped my arms to my side. I didn't really get it, but she was so different from me there seemed little point starting with comparisons. I was sure that lighter said '*Love forever, your Mickey*' on its side, but it was still the wrong way round to read properly.

'Now if that's all, I'm really very tired, and I don't have much time. And it is painful for me to see you, you must understand that?'

For the first time, she smiled at me – and I saw why men might worship her. She leant towards me and, briefly, she touched my hand. In different circumstances I could have been captivated.

'I am sorry for you really, about your baby. I mean, it's terrible – but I guess he will be okay, no? I hope you see him soon. British police are very good, I think.' With great deliberation she checked her watch again. 'So – you know, I'm only here one night. I have a lot to fit in, meetings, you know.' She sighed, stubbing her fag out. 'And I guess I have to see this Silver too.'

'Fine,' I said stiffly. What else was there to say? 'Well, thank you for meeting me.' I sounded like a schoolgirl and I winced inside as she gestured for the bill. I started to dig round in my bag, but she waved me off. 'Let me.'

'Thanks.'

I was finishing my drink as her phone rang. She answered it, fussing at a small mark on her jacket shoulder. I could sense her growing annoyance, though she masked it pretty well.

'Ahh, DI Silver. Yes, I am in the lobby bar. With a little friend of yours.' If Silver caught me here, he'd have my guts for garters. I didn't even want to begin the explanations. And for some reason I didn't want him to see me beside the stunning Agnes. I leapt up. 'Thanks for the drink,' I stammered again, draining my glass; then I headed for the doors.

'Good luck,' I thought she called to my departing back, and I tried to smile as I shot out the door. She'd been so together, she was like some bloody ice maiden. So cold I felt like I'd got frostbite.

As I waited for a cab, Silver's car pulled up metres from where I stood. I saw him check himself in his mirror, straightening his tie, before flashing his badge at the valet. I tried to merge into the pillar, willing a cab to hurry up. I really didn't want him to find me here. Silver swung his legs from his car. 'Come on,' I pleaded silently to the God of cabs, but Silver was still heading my way; surely he couldn't miss me… A cab pulled up just in time. I had absolutely no idea where I was going now.

'I hope you're man enough to get her measure, Detective Inspector,' I muttered, throwing myself onto the back seat.

In the cab Robbie called me again, and this time I listened to what he was suggesting. I'd think about it, I said. The cabbie dropped me in nearby Soho and at the first café I came to, I chose a pavement-table and ordered coffee, strong black coffee, and a croissant. I needed to sober up; and I was more shaken by my encounter with Agnes than I wanted to admit. The faceless woman had become flesh – and too-flipping-perfect flesh at that.

I felt like I'd just put my head in the washing machine, on the extra-fast spin-cycle. Perhaps I was being too hard on Robbie. After all, he was my little brother. Perhaps he really did care. Leigh was always bound to say that he was out of order. They'd never been close, and he'd really burnt his bridges with her when he'd vanished the last time. Leigh hadn't forgiven him for nicking Mum's engagement ring and Nana's gold chains and her own bankbook; for disappearing from our lives without a trace. Leigh saw how much he hurt Mum, how once again we'd been left to pick up the pieces, and her anger had festered over the years he'd not been around.

And I just couldn't sit around and wait much longer. I felt like I was bouncing off the walls, and Silver's team was losing my trust by the minute. It was days since that video arrived, and Louis seemed no nearer. I was running out of time; Louis was running out of time. If I didn't find him soon he might forget me. Or worse. What if his captors got bored with him? What if he cried once too often? Or laughed once too often? What if they could never bear to part with him?

Dusk was falling. The theatre crowd thronged the streets, the out-of-towners conspicuous in their best gear. Tight T-shirted sons and smiling, floral-clad mothers queued behind Australian tourists for the Abba musical opposite, while young girls glued to mobiles sashayed down the road, brown bellies swelling gently over low-slung skirts. I smothered the croissant with blackcurrant jam and forced it down, trying not to feel jealous of two handsome boys beside me, ordering Martinis, smiling into each other's eyes.

With a thump, I realised how lonely I was, and it forced me into a decision. I made a phone call and then ordered more coffee. My eye was twitching, up and down like a jumping bean. Despite my exhaustion, I felt all rushy and hyper from the caffeine. I dug out my compact, checked my tired face. Behind me, a shadow crossed the little mirror, then my brother slunk into the seat beside me.

'God, you made me jump! Don't do that, Rob.'

'Sorry.'

'I'm already enough on edge.'

'I said sorry.' He re-lit his roll-up, spooned sugar into the espresso I'd ordered him. 'He needs a grand.' He was really twitchy, much less upbeat than this morning.

'Nice to see you too. A thousand pounds? For what, exactly?'

'That's just what it costs.'

'What, just for a bit of information?'

He shrugged. His hand shook as he stirred his coffee. 'I don't set the price, Jess.'

I stared at him, but he was looking at something over my shoulder. Then he slugged his coffee back in one.

269

'Don't you? Are you sure about that?' A nasty thought inched slug-like through my head. 'Robbie, were you at the hospital last night?'

'What hospital?' His stupid roll-up had gone out again.

'Were you trying to see Mickey?'

Robbie struck a match just as I grabbed his hand, burning my fingers. 'Robbie, bloody look at me! This isn't just some kind of blackmail, is it? Some money-making scheme? Do you know where Louis is?'

His face was coated nastily with cold sweat again. Under the twinkling little lights of the bar-canopy, his normal pallor had a greenish tinge. His dark curls were greasy, the clothes he'd been in for days were quite filthy, the row of tiny silver hoops up his left ear tarnished and dull. When he finally looked me in the eye, his were filmy and glazed. He didn't answer.

'Robbie!' Hope fluttered in my chest like a fledgling attempting its first flight. 'Answer me, for God's sake! Do you know where my baby is? Look,' I grabbed his wrist again desperately, 'I won't be angry, I promise. Just tell me the truth.'

He shook me off. 'Of course I don't know where the bloody baby is, Jess. Christ!' Then he saw my face, and guilt crossed his. 'Sorry, sorry. But you know what I mean. Of course I haven't seen Louis.' He was still peering nervously over my shoulder. 'I thought we'd been through all this. I'm your brother, Jess. Even I draw the line at some things.' He attempted a joke, but he was so distracted he was making me feel even more anxious. I turned around, scanned the street behind me.

'What is it?'

'Nothing.'

'Well, what do you keep looking at then?'

'Nothing, all right! I thought I saw someone I knew, that's all. Just leave it, will you?'

I sighed heavily. The bird in my chest crashed and burned.

'I think we should get on with this.' Robbie was on his feet already, dragging his heavy leather back over the skanky old T-shirt.

'D'you know, I'm not sure any more,' I said listlessly. I was exhausted, dirty and sweaty. I just wanted to go home and wash and think of a new way of finding my son. Robbie's appearance hardly filled me with confidence for his scheme. I didn't trust him any more; I was struggling again with the thought that I should ring Silver and shop my own brother right now.

'Jess,' his face was livid in the dusk light, his thin skin high with colour now. 'Don't mess me around, all right? I've set this up now, we've got to go and meet this bloke.'

I stared at him. He must have sensed my discomfort, because he softened a bit. 'Look, he might solve all your problems, Jessie. It's worth a try, isn't it?' He was pleading now. I sighed. His downfall had always been his knack of persuasion.

'I suppose I've got nothing left to lose.' I fished out my last tenner. 'I expect the coffee's on me, is it?'

Robbie's sense of relief was unmistakable as he shepherded me through the crowds outside the café. All the time we walked, he kept glancing back. Then I caught

271

his face, lit up by a streetlight, and I realised he actually looked scared. More than scared. He looked like he'd seen the dead.

The shop, closed for the night, was on the corner of Berwick Street and a murky little alley, the kind that men piss down when they've had one too many – or when they're just that type of man. A smell of putrid fish and fruit hung heavy in the air as I picked my way behind Robbie through squashed strawberries and mouldering cabbage leaves that squelched between my flip-flopped toes. Someone had dumped a tray of blackening avocados on the shop's front step; in the humid night air they swarmed with tiny flies.

The bloke that let us in looked like he would never care where he peed. A supercilious smile played round his bloodless mouth when he saw my brother, and he slicked his scrawny little rat's-tail back with a flick of a skinny wrist. Then he saw the rotting avocados and, scowling, kicked them into the street. The frog-green flesh splattered the tarmac; smeared his heavy boot.

Robbie was pitifully quiet, deferential even, to this man who led the way through racks of male clothes that screamed Millwall-on-a-Saturday. Heavy dub throbbed through the ceiling above, and I shivered involuntarily on the stairs, wishing fervently I were anywhere but here.

The room above was utterly dark apart from the television and the neighbouring strip-shows' neon signs that flickered eerily through the blinds; like heavenly traffic-lights, they illuminated the squalor of excess scattered all around. It smelt dirty, decadent; the kind of place watched by a thousand hidden eyes. Mine were still adjusting to the gloom when a shadow on the long leather sofa reached lazily behind him. A blinding light flooded our faces, and my brother clamped my hand between his sweaty palms. 'All right, General?' he coughed nervously. Rat's-tail had disappeared.

Very slowly, the man on the sofa lowered the lamp, his gaze skimming me unnervingly. His thick brown hair was like crimplene, the light behind casting an odd halo round his head. He had the sneering face of an ugly angel; almost carved, he looked, so waxen and defined was his curling top lip. His feet were thrust on a table strewn with overflowing ashtrays and empty bottles. A dusky girl with *Charlie's Angels'* hair and a sinner's body curled into him possessively, smoking weed, her ashtray balanced on a stack of glossy porn. She looked over, bored, and then away again. Expectantly, I waited, but Robbie just hung there in the doorway and something in his manner made me cringe.

'Get our guests a drink, will you, Tan?' the man called General said, smirking with what he apparently mistook for benevolence. Tan was going to argue until he slid his hand inside her skimpy vest and squeezed her nipple, hard. Embarrassed, I looked away, but she seemed undaunted; took a long toke on her spliff and ambled off towards the door, freeing tiny shorts from her voluptuous bottom as she went.

General turned back to the football on the TV, and Robbie still hovered like a fly unable to decide which bit of crap to land on, until suddenly he pushed me forward, catching me off-guard. I snagged my flip-flop on a jagged board, almost landing in General's lap. *An offering from the Gods* flashed ridiculously through my head.

'You're rather forward, dear!' His voice was rasping, as ugly as him. He indicated that I should sit beside him on the sweaty sofa. I looked imploringly at Robbie, but he just leant there, shivering in the sub-tropical heat, struggling with his roll-up. Oblivious. Slowly, I sat. I waited.

'This is my big sister, Gen,' my brother eventually mumbled. 'Jessica.'

General looked me up and down. Under the gaze of his pale eyes, the kind that could freeze your very soul, I suddenly felt naked. I clutched my bag in front of me, like it was a small child to hide behind. Like it was my Louis.

'Hardly big, darling,' General deadpanned. I tried really hard to smile, but the atmosphere was thickening with every second. Soon I'd be able to pick it up in both hands and smash it on the wall. I was about to speak when Tanya sauntered in with dripping beers. She'd almost reached the table when General drove a sudden booted foot into her stomach.

'I've changed my mind actually, Tan. Get the bubbly out, yeah? Special guests and all that.'

'For Christ's sake, Gen,' she pouted. He dropped his foot so she fell against him hard; pulled her forward by one plump arm, grabbing her chin between spider-haired fingers.

'You what, darling?'

She winced as she pulled free. 'I'll get the Bolly,' she muttered.

General took a long, hard slug of beer. He was still smiling, twisting a thick gold ring round his little finger, round and round it went. I decided he was mad.

'So,' he said in that sandpaper voice, eyes glued to the football on the telly, 'Robert tells me you're missing a baby. Oh, you fucking twat! What the fuck was that?' He gobbed a mouthful of beer at the screen. 'Fucking Ferdinand.'

Missing a baby.

I nodded miserably. Sweat trickled down the front of my vest, trekked slowly down my back.

'And you fancy a little help, yeah?'

'Do you think you *can* help?' My voice came out all funny.

'Do I think I can help? I'd say so, darling. I could help most people if I felt like it.'

'Really?' I said politely. My skin prickled.

'Yeah, really.' He leant over me, too close, to relight Tanya's joint. I could smell his acrid sweat beneath the cloying scent. He was the kind of white man who thought he was cool, street and black. All my instincts screamed bully; louder, they screamed 'leave'.

'But only if they've got the money, yeah?' He blew a clumsy smoke-ring in my face. 'A grand up front, that's what we're looking at. That's right, ain't it, Robert?'

Robbie nodded. He wouldn't meet my eye as Tanya returned with a pretty black boy shambling behind her,

275

a cracked ice-bucket in his hand. For the first time since we'd arrived, Robbie became alert. I caught the wanton smile the boy flashed at my brother as he passed, and I realised it was the same boy from the other day, from the estate in Elephant and Castle. Perhaps it was my poor vision in that dark room, but I swore his fingers brushed my brother's balls. Tanya shoved the bucket on the table, dislodging rubbish that fell with a bang.

'Thought you'd be pleased to see your friend,' General leered at Robbie. With utter indolence, he popped the bottle. Robbie slunk out behind the boy.

'Robbie,' I began, and then gagged as General stuck a thick, champagne-sodden finger into my unsuspecting mouth.

'Nice, yeah?' He moved nearer me. 'Don't tell me you don't like champagne now, hey, Jane?'

'Jessica, actually,' I mumbled. I wanted desperately to wipe my mouth, but I really didn't dare.

'Jessica. That's a nice name, ain't it, Tan? Very pretty.'

'S'pose,' she shrugged sulkily.

'Oh, come on now, Tan. You forgot the glasses, you naughty girl.'

Oh don't go, Tan, I silently intoned, but with a scowl she slouched back out. We were on our own. General contemplated me for a slow moment, swigging from the champagne bottle, then thrust it between my bare legs. The freezing glass made me gasp.

'You know something, Jessica, you're a very good-looking girl,' he leered. 'Bit of make-up, few nice garms, some rocking T-rex, yeah? Soon sort you out. Know what I mean?'

I took a massive swig to avoid answering, and promptly choked on all the fizz. Champagne cascaded down my front. 'Sorry,' I stammered. Oh God, don't touch me. 'Bit clumsy.'

His cold eyes swivelled.

'The thing is, General – can I call you that?' I rushed on. He moved his stinking pit-bull body closer again. 'The thing is, I don't have much time. Everything's a bit – it's all a bit frantic right now. You know. I'm sure you understand. It's been over a week since –'

'Well, *my* thing is, Jessica,' he pulverised the joint into the ashtray. 'My thing is, I need as much time as it takes me. And I've been waiting for a long time now, yeah?'

Tanya banged the glasses down on the table, then plonked herself on the other side of her boyfriend and started to dig round in his pocket. I was finding it increasingly hard to concentrate. The heat was unbearable; the booze made my tired head swim again. 'Sorry, what do you mean, "time"? To find Louis?'

'Who's Louis?' General poured the champagne. Tanya retrieved a small gold case that she lovingly flipped open.

'Louis is my son. My missing son. The reason that I'm here.' This was complete bollocks. I stood up, too fast, and immediately felt sick. 'Look, there's obviously been a misunderstanding. I thought Robbie said you could help; that you might, you know, know people who might be able to –'

His arm shot out and grabbed my wrist, clamped it vice-like and pulled me back down. Tanya was racking out huge lines on the cover of *GQ*, curving them neatly between Angelina Jolie's cleavage. I fell heavily on the sofa, and she tutted as tiny clouds of white powder flew up into the air.

'There's no misunderstanding, darling.' Menace curled elegantly through his words. I took a huge swig of champagne, then another, brain racing. Where the hell was Robbie? Tanya snorted long and hard, leant back, eyes closed gratefully, holding her nose, her great golden breasts flopping from her top.

'But – you – you didn't know who Louis was,' I mumbled desperately.

'You want?' General pointed at the coke. I shook my head vehemently. I wished to God he'd stop grinning like some crazed fool; like everything he said was some sort of tea-party pleasantry.

'Louis-shmouis. I'm not good with names, yeah? I just need the money up front, darling – then we can talk names.' Down into the coke, up again with an encrusted nose. I stood up quickly once more; edged away around the table.

'Look, thanks for the drink. I need to get the money anyway, so I'll sort that out and get back to you, okay?'

With a whoosh of pure relief, I saw he was about to agree. 'Do you know what, Jessica?' he said, looking at his hands. My name sounded sordid in his mouth. Fastidiously he dug a bit of dirt out of his thumbnail. 'I'd love to say it was okay, darling, but the thing is, it really ain't at all.' He flicked his find towards my feet. 'The thing is, your useless piece of shit brother promised you'd deliver.'

'Deliver what? I thought it was you who was going to deliver?'

Tanya's eyes snapped open in surprise at my raised voice. Her nose was running. General stood, and I took a quick step back.

'Jessica,' he sighed, 'Jessica, Jessica, Jessica.' His mad grin dripped with malice now. 'This is starting to get on my tits, yeah?'

I clamped my hands behind me so he couldn't see how much they shook.

'Look,' I played frantically for time, 'can I just use your loo quickly? I'm busting. Then – then we can sort this out,' I said. I hoped my voice was steadier than I felt. Somewhere, a phone began to ring. He stared at me then he shrugged idly. 'I suppose. Tanya, take the lady to the toilet, yeah.' He walked towards the steamy window that ran with sweat behind the blind. 'What?' he rapped into the receiver.

I followed an undulating Tanya through the debris to the door, my heart pounding in time with the dub music still echoing through the flat. I looked desperately for Robbie through each open door we passed, but he was nowhere to be seen. All I could think now was that I had to try to reach Silver. He might still be up in town, but I couldn't think if I even had his bloody number on me.

'I'll wait out here, in case you get lost.' Tanya stopped at the door of a filthy bathroom. Maroon paint peeled from the suppurating walls, the bath encrusted with God-knew-what. She leant against the wall outside, scarlet-tipped toes tapping frenetic time with the beat.

'Thanks.' The stupid lock was bust, so I leant heavily against the door, fished my phone from my bag and scrolled urgently through the numbers. *Just remember to keep breathing.* My hands were so clammy the mobile slid straight through my fingers and bounced off my foot, clattering to the floor. I froze, waited with baited breath for Tanya to knock, but the music must have saved me. Eventually I found what I prayed was Silver's number stored in my call history – but I had hardly any signal. On the third go, the phone connected, but the signal bar kept flicking in and out. Finally, about to give up all hope, Silver answered. I was whispering frenziedly – but he couldn't hear me anyway.

'Hello, hello?' he kept saying like a bloody parrot.

'It's me.' I tried not to shout in desperation. 'It's Jess.'

'Hello, hello? Jessica, is that you?'

'Of course it's bloody me.' I was practically shrieking now, the music throbbing through the door.

'Jessica, I can't hear you. Call me back when you've got a proper signal.' He hung up. I was nearly crying with frustration. *You stupid bloody fool, Silver, the one time I ask for your help...* I tried to ring again, but this time it didn't connect at all. I started to text him a vague address, but the message wouldn't send.

'You died in there or what?'

I jumped, whacking my head on the old cabinet above the scummy basin: Tanya, cross and bored, up close against the door. Oh please, just bloody send, I prayed silently to my mobile. I held it up as high as I could stretch while still holding the door shut, staggering on tiptoe, searching for a signal. Tanya began to knock loudly. 'Come on, mate. I don't wanna stay up here all bleeding night.'

'Yeah, yeah, all right,' I called, 'let me pull my knickers up, at least.' I licked the sweat from my top lip, shoving the phone back in my bag without seeing if the message had sent, and opened the door.

'Sorry,' I lied shakily, 'I'm not feeling too good. Too much booze, you know? This heat.'

She shrugged and wandered past me to reapply her dark lipstick in the flyspecked mirror. 'Have a line then. Sober you up.' I shook my head, leant nonchalantly against the filthy, saturated wall. I could feel my body shaking; Tanya's eyes never off me in the mirror.

'You know, one thing I'd say to you. Don't fuck General off, okay? He's got a nasty temper.'

'Oh really?' I said. 'Thanks. I was just hoping – well, you know, my brother suggested he might know something, that's all.'

'Ah, yes, your brother.' She smacked her lips against each other. 'He's a naughty boy, that one, ain't he? You want some?' She offered me her lipstick and I acquiesced this time. Anything to keep her on side. My hand shook as I traced my mouth with 'Black Narcissus'. 'Great colour,' I enthused manically. It made me look like I was dead.

Back downstairs, Robbie was still nowhere to be seen. General was apparently glued to the football again. 'Had a bit of time to think then, yeah?' He didn't look at me.

'A little, I guess. The thing is...' I smiled at him, racking my brains, 'actually, can I have some more champagne first? It's going down a treat.'

He topped up my glass with a meaty hand.

'Thank you. You're so generous. So,' I sipped flirtatiously. The lipstick left a dirty mark as I drank. 'How did you meet Robbie?'

He smirked. Tanya's eyes were slit with suspicion.

'I don't think you really want to know, darling.'

'Oh.' I sipped again. *Come on, Jess. Think of Louis.* 'The thing is, I'm not really sure what you're offering.' I patted his knee; I felt as sexy as a dead fish. Tanya's nose was properly running now as she opened the gold case again.

General shrugged. 'If you want help, I'll give it to you. At a price, yeah?'

'Yes, but what kind of help? I mean, the police are helping. Do you really know things they can't find out?'

He laughed without mirth. 'What do you think, darling?'

Tanya was snorting straight from the case now. General swore and muttered something to her I didn't catch, but she ignored him and carried on. Robbie appeared suddenly in the doorway, stumbled slightly on the small step into the room. He slumped beside me.

'All right, Jess? Has General explained the deal?' He was slurring now. With a sinking heart, I realised my brother was totally gone. He began to rock vaguely back and forth. General giggled, sensing my despair.

'What do you expect? They're as bad as each other.' He nodded at his girlfriend, her eyes popping as she chewed on her lip. 'Not like you and me, eh, girl? So, if you, like, give me the money, I'll help him, yeah?' He looked at Robbie with contempt.

'What do you mean, "him"? I thought this was about me – about my baby?' Finally, *finally*, I'd had enough. First Agnes, then this. Why was everyone playing me for a fool? My patience ran out.

'Look, have you got any idea at all about Louis or is this all just pure bloody bullshit?' I pushed away from him and stood up again.

'This baby, you mean?' General reached lazily into his jeans pocket, held something crumpled out, something I couldn't quite see at first. I peered. A photo of a baby. A photo of Louis. 'This little darling? He's so like his mum, ain't he?'

I sprang for him. My nails caught his jaw as I scrabbled for the photo.

'Where the hell did you get that?' I lunged for the arm that taunted me, that held Louis's image just out of reach. Using his full force, General slapped me then, his ring catching the edge of my lipsticked mouth. As I went flying back, the photo fluttered in the stultifying air, landing face-down on the filthy floor. I fumbled for it, but General grabbed me by my hair and pulled me back, slammed me against the wall.

He wasn't tall but he was much bigger than me, thick-set like a fighting dog. The air around him spoke of evil, and when the neon lights flicked through the window, they caught his piercing eyes and I saw that they were empty. He pressed up against me; I felt the heat emanating from his body, so near his chest hairs tickled my neck. I tried not to gag again.

'Robbie,' I gasped out, but my brother wasn't there. I thought about a time a bit like this ten years ago, about how my little brother had leapt to my defence then. Now, though, now he just sat swaying on the sofa, eyes closed, gouching out. Tanya too was in her own world, filing her scarlet talons. Just biding time; waiting for her bloke to do whatever it was he had to. General shot her a look, and she got up and left.

'Please,' I wheezed, but in response he rammed an insistent knee between my legs, forcing them open. He ran a hand down my arm and then grabbed my breast, the other hand manacling my wrist. I was in real pain now, but I was damned if I'd let him see.

Coming in still closer, he whispered, 'There are ways to make me help you, you little tart, and we both know what they are, yeah?'

I read the vicious lust in his look. His breath was warm and sour as he moved the hand from my breast, and it lingered cobra-like – until he shoved it between my legs. For Christ's sake, was he going to rape me here before my doped-up brother; rape me while his girlfriend waited patiently outside?

I struggled frantically, panting with the effort, but with every move I made his cock got harder, digging into my hip. The more I fought, the more turned-on he was. So I stopped fighting and stayed very still. I could feel my chest tightening, closing; I must try not to panic. I looked him in the eye and licked my lips; Black Narcissus tasted like crap. I could hear my wheezing loudly now.

He thought this was his moment. He reached to my mouth, and I tried not to flinch. He brought my blood away on his finger, licked it lingeringly like a lover would. My stomach lurched queasily but he read my stillness as a signal, and he lunged down. I summoned every bit of hatred I felt for everyone involved, every person trying to hurt me and my son, and I kneed the filthy bastard where it'd hurt him most. With a yelp, he let go.

Free of his weight, I fell forward onto my knees, spilling my bag across the floor. All I wanted was that photo of Louis. I scrabbled in the champagne sputum and the fag-butts for it, but General was back on his feet now, grunting, grabbing for me, and so I left the photo, I left Louis there, and I made a run for it. Vaguely, I thought I heard knocking downstairs and I ran towards the noise, gulping in air, praying I could keep breathing without having an attack. Rat's-tail pushed past me on the stairs. 'Oi, Gen! The fucking pigs are outside.'

Silver – a little too late for me. I went flying down, taking two steps at a time. Robbie hadn't even opened his eyes as I'd gone. I resisted the urge to shout into my brother's face; instead, with a sob, I pummelled my way through the clothes standing sentinel to the madness going on above, sent a rack of trousers flying, grazing both knees as I fell. I was up again; the door was locked but I scrabbled with the bolts, the keys that Rat's-tail had left swinging there, and I let myself out into that stinking alley, came out flying like a bat from a literal hell.

Silver and DS Kelly were outside, a couple of uniformed men behind them. Silver, barking out orders to the others, tried to grab me as I passed but I slithered through his grasp, I couldn't bear the thought of any touch right now. I thought I saw Deb sitting in an unmarked car on the road; in my confusion and my shame, I turned back the other way. I passed some middle-aged couple grunting in a doorway, his trousers round his knees, his arse pearly in the moonlight; I was halfway down the murky little alley before Silver caught me up. God alone knew where I was headed.

'Jess, wait!' he called, and his hand came down on my shoulder.

'Get off me, please,' I whispered, sliding away. I was seventeen again; I was locked in my old living room with that sweating rabid policeman. I needed my inhaler.

'Jessica! Just wait a minute. What happened? Are you all right?'

'I'm fine, I'm fine,' I intoned. I found my puffer, stopped to use it with blessed relief.

'I must say that lipstick doesn't do much for you, kiddo.' He'd caught up with me. Then he peered closer in the half-light. 'Is that blood?'

I smeared the lipstick across my face with my hand; I was quite delirious with fear. 'That bloke in there nearly –' I heaved '– he nearly raped me and you're making jokes.'

Silver's face went very still. 'What happened?'

'He had a photo of my son and he's just – he mauled me. He wanted money,' I sobbed, dry-eyed. 'He's an evil bastard. It's him you need to get, not me. I'm fine.'

'You're not fine, you're hurt.' His face was still inscrutable, but his fingers tightened on my shoulders. 'Let's get you checked out now.'

'Don't worry about me. Please, Silver, you need to find him. He might – I think he knows where Louis is.'

'Jess, they've arrested him. He's not going anywhere. Please, come with me now, will you?'

I pulled away, bending to try and breathe. 'I called you and you hung up. I needed you, Silver. You said any time, you'd be there – but you didn't come.' I started down the alley again, stumbling in my flip-flops that bent beneath my crazed, sore feet, and Silver reached out to steady me, but I was too fast for him. I ducked away but he was on my tail.

'I couldn't hear you, Jess. The line was too bad. Don't be ridiculous.'

'Oh, sorry – I forgot you were busy.' Anger began to pulse through me like a strobe until I was gibbering with hurt and fury and pure terror. 'Did you fancy the lovely Agnes too? I expect you did. My husband still does, apparently. She's very beautiful, don't you think?'

And suddenly my anger turned to ice, and a chill went through my body, pervading my very bones. I had never felt so sad and lonely in my life. The streets around me were filled with people: party-seekers and kids searching for cheap fun; City boys scoring Tanya's coke; parents rushing home to relieve babysitters after a rare night out – but me? I was utterly alone, caught in the middle of the most abject misery, the hardest, most unrelenting misery I'd ever felt. The only thing that was ever really mine had gone; had been snatched from me; my reason to breathe each morning was out of reach. Unconsciously, I'd waited all my life for Louis, and when he'd come I'd woken from my slumber. Now someone else had got him. Every day it got harder to believe in him, in his fuzzy peach face and his crooked gappy grin.

The tears came at last. I doubled over and I cried like I was dying; I sobbed the air in like I was taking my last breaths. I went down on my knees like I had that first night Louis went, and slowly and deliberately I banged my head against the pavement.

'Stop, Jess, please. You'll really hurt yourself.' Silver was down beside me, holding me, restraining my head, rocking me like a little child, and I struggled for a while until I couldn't any more. I rested my bleeding head on his chest and covered his smart shirt with tears and blood and Tanya's dodgy lipstick, cried and cried and sucked at my inhaler, trying to breathe before I collapsed forever under all the pain. I hugged him like I hadn't really hugged anyone since my dad had gone. Eventually my wheezing slowed, and the tears began to trickle less, and then he wiped my face with the pristine pocket-handkerchief that someone had ironed for him, and he half-carried me to the waiting car. He did it all so kindly and so gently that I nearly forgave him for not being there when I'd needed him. Nearly, but not quite.

CHAPTER NINETEEN

I stood in the shower and it was truly freezing, so cold it took my breath away, making my teeth ache in my throbbing head. I was sore and bruised; my forehead was grazed from where I'd hit it on the pavement, my legs cut from falling in the shop. I was dirty all over, filthy from where that man had touched me. But the physical pain faded rapidly beside my longing. I desperately craved some solace, but I didn't know what would do it.

My world was crashing round my ears. I took a pill again, I really didn't care now, I would take lots; and I went to bed with Shirl lying beside me. I couldn't be alone, not now, not ever again, so she held my hand and promised it would work out – but I didn't believe her any more.

Deb tiptoed in as I was drifting off and leant down to say they'd taken General and my brother into custody, and that made me want to cry again; but I fell asleep before I found the energy for more tears.

In the morning I got up early again and crept out of my room, leaving Shirl muttering, rolling in my warm spot, snoring softly. I opened the back door and heard the birds, and thought how hollow their hopeful sound suddenly seemed. I made coffee so strong it was thick and oily, I piled it with sugar, and then I sat on the floor of the living room and watched our few tapes of Louis, right from when he was born. I traced his face on the screen, and sobbed until my eyes were nearly swollen shut with tears.

I thought of how I'd felt back when he was born, felt that I was playing a game, playing at being a grown-up. How for weeks after my terrifying vision in the hospital of losing my new love, my baby son, I'd watch Mickey, who would just sit and gaze at him. 'I just want to protect him,' he'd say, but I was panicking. I'd turned away because I was so scared. I thought now of my useless parents and how frightened I'd been that I'd be just like them. I remembered the day when Mickey wasn't there any more, left me with my son, alone; the day Louis looked up at just me, stared me in the eyes, and cooed. I'd looked behind me – but no one else was there. It was the day my heart began to thaw. It actually made me smile now.

Eventually I switched off the TV and fetched more coffee and then Deb arrived, yawning. She saw my reddened eyes, but she didn't mention them. We sat at the kitchen table, companionably quiet now, eating our toast. My mouth was sore and bruised from General's ring. I wondered what I should do next. And then Deb's phone rang and it was Silver, wanting to speak to me. He told me he'd had to let Robbie go; he'd committed no offence that they could charge him with, and secretly

I was relieved. I knew my brother was no danger really, that he'd only lost his way. Mostly I was relieved that they were keeping that other bastard General in.

Then Silver said he was going to Sussex for the day.

'I must come with you,' I pleaded.

'No.'

'Sorry, Silver, but it's non-negotiable. If you don't take me, I'll go alone. I'll just follow you.' And I would. Finally, he agreed. I passed the phone back to Deb.

'Right, sir. See you there.' She hung up. 'DI Silver wants me to take you to meet him now. They've got some sort of new lead.'

Hope shot through me yet again, making my hands tremble. I told myself it was the caffeine. Though I didn't speak it, Deb must have sensed my surge of energy.

'Just –'

I was already dashing out the room when she grabbed my arm. 'Just don't get your hopes up too high, okay? These things can take time.'

But how much time did they want? It was over a week since I'd seen my son.

'I won't,' I agreed. But I was lying. This was it, I was quite sure. 'But I've got a good feeling about it, you know, Deb. It's that General bloke. He's told them something, hasn't he? I mean, how did he get that photo of Louis if he's not involved? God, he was foul.' I shuddered as I looked back at her from the door. 'You know, my Uncle Jack always did say I had a touch of the psychic about me. And I feel – I do feel like something good is about to happen. Finally.'

Deb smiled despite herself. 'Well, let's hope so, Jess.

You deserve it, don't you? I'm crossing all my fingers.'

She drove me through the suburbs that sprawled beyond Blackheath, through the cut-price bathroom stores and the Chinese takeaways, past cherry-cheeked girls pushing smart prams bought on the never-never, out to Sidcup, where Kent begins. It was hardly the Garden of England it proclaimed to be. We met Silver at a petrol station; he came out of the kiosk drinking Diet Coke, without his jacket on, and I felt uncomfortable again. It was a bit like seeing your favourite teacher naked. I dumped my stuff on the back seat of his car while he and Deb muttered together. Then he opened the passenger door for me.

'Looks like you're with me,' he said, as I waved her off. 'No puking this time, right?'

'I can't promise anything,' I said breezily, squeezing past him. 'I do get very carsick you know.' I plopped into the car seat. 'And Diet Coke's really a bit gay, don't you think, for big butch policemen, I'd say.' I grinned at his expression.

Silver kept trying to read the map while he was driving. Finally, as he took yet another bad corner and I smacked my bruised head against the window for the umpteenth time, I lost my patience.

'If you just tell me where we're going I can read the map for you.' I grabbed the atlas from the dashboard where he was attempting to hold it open with one hand.

'Eastbourne. South Downs. Near Beachy Head,' he said.

'Beachy Head?' Alarm bells rang. 'Beachy Head, as in the most notorious suicide spot in England? Fantastic.'

He ignored me, opened another can of drink, spraying it across the car.

'But why there? Why would anyone take Louis there?'

'Look, Jessica, I'm not saying he is there. You have to prepare yourself for that. But there are a few positive leads which are worth really checking out. And', I couldn't read his look, 'the change of scenery might do you good.'

My world drew in, grew smaller as he spoke. My head was in that clamp again.

'I'm meeting Kelly and the Sussex lads down there.' He popped another stick of gum in as we swerved precariously round a poor dead badger who looked like he'd just forgotten to keep moving.

The countryside was too gorgeous for the occasion. We swept down tiny, lush green lanes, trees hugging above our heads. Red-bricked oast-houses with roofs like snowy curls of foolscap flanked the bigger roads, and, in the woods beyond the lanes, saplings stood bristly as a hairbrush. It all seemed strangely familiar.

Silver's phone rang. He answered it as he drove. Perhaps policemen were allowed to do what normal people weren't.

'Don't cry, kiddo,' I heard him say. 'Please don't cry.'

I stared out of the window trying not to listen, trying not to feel a little envious as he reassured another woman.

'I'll be there next weekend, I promise. And if I can't, I'll get Mum to bring you down, okay? Yes, she will. She will, Molly, if I ask her to. We won't, kiddo. I promise; no more arguing. What – why?' His face went dark as he listened to his daughter. I felt terrible for my envy of a moment ago.

293

'He hasn't said anything bad, has he? Well, then. Look, I know you don't like him much, but you'll get used to him.' He took a deep breath. A tic went in his cheek. I stared at my hands. 'You will. He's not that bad now, is he, Moll? I thought he bought you that nice book about the ballerina?'

He swapped the phone to his other hand, the car veered very gently. 'I love you too, sweetie-pie. Of course you can stay. I've got the marshmallows in already. Oh, and Moll? Don't forget to bring the picture you did of – yes, that's the one. I've got a frame for it now. Pride of place, that's right. Above the telly. Yeah, big kiss to you too, my bonny lass. Big kisses all round, all right, kiddo?'

Inexplicable tears pricked my tired eyes. He flung the phone down, glanced at me quickly.

'Youngest daughter,' he said quietly. 'Struggling with her mum's new fella.'

'Oh, right.' I felt so sorry for him at that moment that I sought desperately for something soothing to say. 'I expect it's, you know, very hard –'

'It is.' He spat his gum out of the window almost violently, and turned the stereo on. I shut up.

'Silver,' I said meekly, a short time later, when he was a bit more composed. I remembered last night's hysteria with a shudder.

'Yes,' he answered idly, one hand on the wheel, the other arm casual on his open window. For the first time, I noticed a small scar beneath his left eye.

'What did you really think of Agnes? Did you –' I cleared my throat '– do you think she's very beautiful?'

'Cold fish. And her eyes are too close together,' he

said. Then he turned the radio up, his arm brushing my bare skin. 'No competition,' I thought he muttered quietly. Perhaps it was in my head. I thought about Mickey, about how he would have been riled just by me asking the question.

We didn't talk much the rest of the way.

Outside a newsagent's near Eastbourne Pier, DC Kelly was leaning on his car, eating a pork pie and reading the paper. Behind him in a marked Panda, a uniformed copper I didn't know was talking on the radio. Kelly's stomach had swollen back to its original size, a convenient shelf for all the crumbs he was dropping as he ate.

'All right, Guv? Mrs Finnegan.' He waved his lunch at us. If he was surprised to see me, he didn't show it. Silver looked rather squeamishly at the greasy pie and fished his tie from his pocket. 'Any good?' he asked.

'Not bad, Guv, thanks.'

'Not the pie, you fool. The witness.'

'Oh, sorry, sir. Well, not sure really.' Kelly shot me a swift look. 'Same thing – long hair, metallic car, screaming baby. Shopkeeper thought it was really odd that she didn't seem to know what sort of baby milk to buy. Very flustered, apparently. Had seen the story on TV. Jogged his memory.' Kelly gestured to the newspaper flapping gently in the mild sea-breeze.

'Only trouble is, this bird –' another quick look at me. 'Sorry – this woman was dark. Other two said blonde. Constable's getting the artist down.'

Silver sighed. 'I'd better have a word. You all right here, Jessica?'

The two men went into the shop. Full of apprehension, I took over Kelly's spot, glancing at the local paper he'd left behind. My story was on the front page, a description of the woman, another photo of Louis. I imagined the smile and blur of a thousand little faces whizzing through the presses; the photo of my son reprinted infinite times. How weird it was to have my life in strangers' hands, people I knew nothing of trying to help. A harsher truth, perhaps – people I didn't know simply doing their jobs.

When they came out, Silver wanted to meet the first two callers from the other day. He wanted the artist's impression done right now, again. Why hadn't it happened already? We drove too fast round Eastbourne, above the azure sea, past the floral displays gaudy with mismatched splendour; revved impatiently behind lavender-haired old dears in ageing maroon Metros, never topping twenty on the clock; past peeling, white-fronted B&Bs with their endless 'VACANCIES' signs.

Each time Silver got back in the car I felt his tension increase. The last time, out in Meads village with its elegant townhouses festooned with fading hollyhocks, he simply couldn't hide it. The student witness had apparently been stoned and incoherent. 'I've got half a mind to book him,' he muttered to Kelly, who tried to pacify his boss with a conciliatory mumble that was ignored.

'That flat reeked. Bloody students.'

Apparently we'd finished. We dropped the tubby copper back at his car.

'Hungry?' Silver asked me tersely. I was too disappointed to care about food. 'Guess so.'

'There's fish and chips somewhere this way, apparently.'

I didn't bother to ask about the interviews; I could read the defeat in his posture. He seemed tired, grey beneath his suntan, as if he felt guilty for taking me on some wild goose chase. I felt his frustration almost as keenly as my own.

We headed out of Eastbourne on the coast road that climbed up from Meads village. As we wound across the gently billowing downs, past the ice-cream vans and the wedding-cake white cliffs of Beachy Head, we didn't speak. A few skinny clouds wisped across the still-cobalt sky as dusk slowly descended, heavy with heat. Forlornly I stared at the evening walkers, families packing picnics up, couples with their bounding dogs. How could you tell if someone was simply admiring the view, or just about to jump? And why would you choose here to do it? I supposed if you decided to die, it might be only right to do it somewhere literally breath-taking.

The sun was setting dramatically as we pulled in at a small beach called Birling Gap. Silver went to buy us chips from the Seventies' eyesore that called itself a café, and I wandered across to the rather bleak row of cottages that leant towards the sea. I had that strange sensation I'd felt on the drive down. I rested my elbows on the old wall, and stared at the houses until Silver appeared behind me. 'All right?'

'You know,' I said slowly, taking my chips from him. 'This place – I think I've been here before.'

'Really? Recently?'

'No. I think – I think we came here with my dad. On holiday. A long time ago.'

'When?'

I deliberated for a moment. It was a hazy memory – necessarily so. 'Dunno. Just before my dad went down for the last time.' Getaway driver for a crap team in a clapped-out old Fiesta nicked from the station car park. Got away as far as the first corner from the bank before the police pulled them in. Although some of them had scarpered, my dad was well and truly nicked, of course. Couldn't even do that right. 'I guess I'd have been about – not sure. Nine?'

I felt him calculating. 'Who came, Jess?' Silver asked, and there was a new urgency to his tone. 'The whole family?'

'Yeah. The whole family.'

'Your kid too?'

'Robbie? Yes,' I said, even more slowly. 'Why?'

Silver thrust his phone into my hand. 'Can you ring your sister and check? See if she remembers.'

Leigh took ages to answer. She was getting the girls' tea, could she ring me back? I cut through her chatter. Leigh confirmed it crisply. Yes, Birling Gap, of course. How could I forget, she remonstrated. The place where it never stopped raining; where my mum kept crying. One of the very few family holidays. She brought the girls here sometimes, for the day. She was about to say something else but I saw Silver's face, and said I'd call her later.

Silver strode off to make some calls. I stood there with my chips and counted the cottages again. There were four. I was sure we'd stayed in the one nearest the sea; I vaguely remembered it being an inappropriately cheerful colour, primrose-yellow perhaps. Now it was a sort of dirty beige, stained by years of sea and salt. I paced up and down the row until I realised the cottage that we'd rented all those years ago was no longer there. The cliff's edge was crumbling, propped up by scaffolds. Our holiday hellhole must have slipped quietly into the water. I stared out at the stripy little lighthouse far out to sea.

'Reminiscing?' Silver returned, shoving his phone away as he bleeped the car doors unlocked.

'Oh yeah.' I turned away from the ramshackle little row; remembering my dad's lies and my mum's never-ending tears. 'Top times we had down here.' I drifted towards the car, clutching my chips. 'You know what I remember most?' Apart from all the fights. He shook his head. 'That lighthouse.' I pointed with a chip, then popped it in my mouth. The vinegar scraped my cut and made me wince. 'When we were having our tea, the lights would come on. We thought it was well exciting. Like being in *The Great Escape*.'

He looked puzzled. 'I don't follow,' he said. 'What do you mean?'

'You know, like the Nazi searchlights. Sweeping through the room, searching out the escapees.' Hiding under the table with Robbie during the interminable August rain, playing Daleks, while Leigh stuck her rattling old Walkman on and ignored us, read *Jackie* on a scratchy little sofa. We were hiding mostly from my parents' pain, as much as playing a game. Sheltering from their screaming in the kitchen. I left out those bits.

'It's operational then?' He was thoughtful, enlivened even.

'I don't know about now, but it definitely was back then. Robbie even wanted to be a lighthouse-keeper for a while.' God, I wish he had followed that dream.

'Wait here.' He crunched across the car park to the Information Point. It was shut. He came back and tried the Coastguard's office. All locked up. Cursing, he fished out his phone. I sat on the bonnet in the dying sun and finished off my chips, watched him talking, but couldn't read his lips. I didn't have the energy to get excited again. Too many false starts already today. Eventually, he gestured for me to get in the car.

'How do you feel about staying down here tonight?' he said, turning on the ignition. I had a feeling I didn't have much choice.

Silver took me to a small hotel on the seafront, not as posh as the nearby Grand looked, but quite smart in an executive sort of way. Sitting in the empty, mute-toned bar, I watched him through the glass door of the private lounge, barking down the telephone. I ordered a vodka and tonic and rang home, spoke to Shirl; rang the hospital, spoke to Sister Kwame. Mickey had come round again, was sleeping peacefully now. They were pleased with his progress. Hanging up, I wondered why my husband seemed so very far from me now. So far in every way.

Some Technicolor police drama wobbled on to itself in the corner of the room, followed by an inane chat show where vacuous celebrities ran down huge jelly-like stairs before patting each other lovingly on the back and telling jokes. I flicked through brochures for a local zoo, painfully imagined Louis's face lighting up at the funny llamas. We hadn't really started day-trips yet; the Tate had been the first, and – I ordered another vodka and knocked it back.

A while later, a pretty WPC turned up with a carrier-bag of toiletries.

'I got you a spare pair of knickers too, hope they're the right size,' she murmured. She passed me the bag, but she was actually looking through the door at Silver. He glanced up and gave a cursory wave; she flushed, and I felt annoyed. Most irrational, I warned myself quite strictly.

'Very fetching. Did Silver ask you to get these?' I asked her dryly, pulling a large pair of sensible white pants from the bag.

She looked vaguely embarrassed. 'Not sure who the order came from. Is there anything else you need?'

'An explanation would be good, actually,' I said, articulating most carefully. 'Can you help at all?' I was warmly slicked with vodka now; I felt like I hadn't felt for ages. An odd kind of exhilaration mixed with nerves.

'I can't really, I'm afraid. I'm sure they'll fill you in soon.' She obviously knew little more than me. Silver suddenly swung through the door. I shoved the pants hastily back into the bag.

'Thanks for that, WPC –?' he said. She flushed puce again.

'Martin.'

301

'WPC Martin. Any idea what's happened to your bloody boss? I'm still waiting for his call.'

'He's on the Doherty murder, out at Peacehaven. It was pretty full-on. I think he'll be there till the early hours,' she said shyly. There was a brief silence, then almost reluctantly she said, 'Well, if that's all for now?' and he flashed her one of his brilliant smiles.

'Yeah, cheers, kiddo. We'll see you tomorrow.' He turned away and headed towards the bar. For a moment she looked stranded and my heart went out to her.

'Thanks so much for the stuff,' I called after her departing back.

Silver came back to my sofa with something dark in a glass, and another vodka for me.

'Shall we go outside? It's stifling in here.'

I followed him out into the small walled garden that fell down to the sea. 'Nice umbrellas. What's that?' I pointed at his glass as he settled at a table on the deserted terrace.

'Coke,' he took a sip. 'Why?'

I shrugged. 'Just wondered, you know.' I looked out to sea for a second. There were tiny lights at random points, bobbing in the blackness. Fishing boats? 'Why are you drinking Coke?'

'I don't drink alcohol.'

'Oh. Sorry.' I thought back. 'Why not?'

'Because I used to. Drink – too much. Much too much. And then,' he fiddled with his gum-wrapper, 'then I lost what really mattered because of it.'

'You mean your wife?'

'I mean my kids.' He tossed the wrapper on the table.

'So I don't any more.' In the darkness he looked almost saturnine. 'And I'm nicer if I don't. Much nicer.' Then he pulled himself together. 'So, no trying to get me pissed, all right, kiddo?'

Under the multicoloured bunting from some forgotten garden-party, I suddenly felt glad of the darkness. The little flags flapped lightly in the gentle breeze, and I changed the subject. 'So, are you going to tell me what's going on?' The tonic fizzed into my drink.

'Sorry,' he said, loosening his tie. 'God, it's a relief to get this off sometimes. Especially in this bloody heat.' He chucked it on the chair beside him. 'It's the lighthouse thing. I was trying to get out there tonight, but apparently the tide's turned and the coastguards won't approve it now. We'll have to wait till morning.'

'What lighthouse thing? Why d'you want to go there at all?'

'It was what you said at the beach that made me think. The sweeping light. Do you remember on the video there was a strange flicking?'

I thought of the ghostly light. I nodded slowly.

'It was something we just couldn't quite work out – the forensic team kept looking at it; we guessed it was lights from some kind of club flashing outside, you know, through a window in the room. Like at General's gaff. But the colours are wrong for his. When they went back and timed it on the tape earlier, they found it went round every two minutes. Just like a lighthouse beam, apparently.' He looked at me triumphantly, and raised his drink. 'And the nearest working lighthouse, as you so rightly pointed out, is out by Beachy Head.'

'You mean,' I stared at my glass as if it were some kind of crystal-ball, searching for comprehension. The ice had melted already in the dense night heat. 'You mean, you think Louis could be in the lighthouse?'

'Jess, like I've said before, it's impossible to absolutely know anything. I've probably told you too much already. And I never want you to get too excited. But it's a – a possibility, kiddo.'

I shoved my drink onto the table and stood. 'Then why the hell are we sitting here? Why aren't we out there looking for him?'

'I've told you, there's a dangerous rip-tide now, and we can only land in a very small boat. It's not safe, apparently.' He put a hand out to me. 'Sit down, please. I'm as frustrated as you, honestly.'

'I doubt it, Silver,' I snapped. 'For God's sake, if it means getting my baby back, I'll swim out there. Sod the bloody tide. Let's go.'

He stood up too, came towards me. The stars behind him filled the cavernous sky above the treacle-black sea. The night went on forever.

'We'll go first thing, I promise you. At dawn. It's all arranged. It's not much longer to wait. Try to be patient, Jessica.'

'How? Where the bloody hell do you suggest I find any more patience from?' I took a slug of vodka, paced away onto the grass carpet, then back. The springy lawn thrust up soft and firm between my bare toes. 'I'm so sick of waiting, Silver. I've done nothing but wait for over a week. I feel so – so useless. So absolutely redundant. I'm a mother who should have protected her son, but I didn't. Instead, I let someone else take him and now, now I'm – look, I'm just sitting here sipping vodka with some – some silly flash policeman.'

'Thanks very much.' He seemed unperturbed. 'Don't be so hard on yourself.'

'Well how do you expect me to be, for God's sake? I mean, how would you be? Can you imagine how you'd feel if it was one of your kids?' I challenged him. 'You wouldn't just be sitting around waiting, would you?'

He shook his head slowly. 'No, I can't imagine. I can only think it must be hell. I miss my kids like crazy, but at least I know where they are.' He held me lightly by my shoulders. His face was in shadow, but I felt the compassion in his gaze. 'Look, you're doing brilliantly, kiddo. I know it's horrible, frustrating. I understand how hard it is – but it will be over, Jessica, soon – I swear to you. We will find Louis.'

'I'm starting to think –' My voice cracked, I breathed hard and deep to retain my cool. 'I'm starting to think I might never see him again.'

The words echoed emptily in the dark night air, smashed to the ground between us. His grip on my shoulders strengthened a little.

'You will see him again, I'm sure. You have to believe that.'

'I just feel so – so weird all the time. Like it's not really me it's happening to, like it's a nightmare I'll wake from, and Louis'll be there beside me again, and someone will say I dreamed it all.' I tried to get my breath. 'And nothing prepares you – I mean, no one ever tells you what to do. What am I meant to do?'

He pushed my hair back out of my eyes and he didn't remove his hand, and I didn't want him to. Instead, he reached a thumb up and stroked the side of my face softly. I couldn't bear to look at him; I couldn't quite breathe. I looked down at my bare feet caught between his booted ones and I waited. Like I was on a cliff about to jump, I held my breath almost painfully; I curled my toes over, teetering on the edge.

'You're not alone,' he said quietly. 'I'm here, aren't I? I'm not going anywhere.'

And then he tried to make me look at him, but I wouldn't – I couldn't. I mustn't. You shouldn't let this happen, a little voice kept saying inside my head, whatever 'this' was. You shouldn't even want it. But there was something so safe about Silver, something that made me just want to fling myself into his arms forever and take refuge. I knew that if anyone could find Louis it would be him. And he made me feel so calm now – most of the time. None of the slamming up against each other like me and Mickey, the crashing in midair as we met, the violence of that lust. This was quite different. For one brief, glorious moment, I let myself forget it all, imagined melding into Silver, thought of nothing except the present. In the dark, starlit garden, only we existed now. I breathed him in, he was so near, and he smelt right somehow.

I thought I heard his breathing quicken a little and I felt myself start to fall headfirst into my own longing. My glass went slipping to the ground. And then –

And then I caught myself. Just in time I caught myself. What in hell's name was I doing?

'Not yet, you're not,' I said unsteadily, pushing away from him.

'What?' he said, and his accent seemed a little harsher, more pronounced than usual.

'Not yet, you're not going anywhere –but you will be. And I'll have to deal with things on my own. That's what I'm used to.' I picked up the glass shakily so I didn't have to look at him, and shoved it back onto the table. I moved back towards the hotel, away from him. I felt the hot, ugly plunge, the emptiness of unfulfilled lust. 'And anyway, there's Louis. I must just concentrate on Louis. We both must.'

'Jessica –' he started but I ran away. I ran from him and me, I ran inside. 'Wake me in time to go, please,' I whispered over my shoulder, and I launched myself into the lift before he caught up with me, willing the doors to close. I glared at my tousled reflection in the yellow-lit mirror, my mouth all swollen still with General's bruises, finally with some colour actually in my cheeks; I stared at myself and turned away. I went to bed and lay sleepless and terrified, sweating under my sheet for what seemed like hours.

Sometime soon after I lay down, Silver knocked gently on my door and called my name, but I put a pillow over my head and blocked up both my ears, like a little kid would do. Eventually he went away.

CHAPTER TWENTY

I am dreaming of Louis, my little Louis: a shirtless Silver is holding him aloft, but he keeps putting him down and I run to pick him up. Each time, Silver gets there first, mockingly moves him further on, so I never quite reach my son. Then my mum and dad are standing in the doorway of that tumbledown old cottage which is gone now, arm in arm they stand grinning inanely, like the wooden couple in a cuckoo clock who pop in and out, and it is that rainy summer from my childhood.

I woke up drenched in sweat, the sheet twisted around me like a shroud. Freeing myself, I scrabbled for my inhaler, trying to block that pathetic holiday from my whirring mind. The holiday that ended abruptly when my mother suddenly discovered my dad was due back in court the next day for sentencing. That he'd only been let out on bail because his cancer was malignant. The beginning of the proper end.

I realised someone was knocking on the door. Blearily, I blinked at the luminous alarm display. 5.32

a.m. The morning of the tenth day. The day we'd find my son...

'Jessica, we need to go.' It was Silver, and I was immediately anxious, and I felt like he was on the wrong side of the door, but also the right side, and I realised that however much I fought it and knew it was wrong, that I still wanted him to be near. I sank back into the bed for a hopeless moment.

'I'll be down in a second,' I called brightly after a second, but there was no reply.

I got dressed. I pulled on the gleaming white underwear that young policewoman had brought; I cleaned my teeth and splashed my face and thought that if the hollows under my eyes got any darker they'd start to look indelible. The grazes on my forehead made my face look kind of dirty, and I wondered why I'd even think that any man would ever want to kiss me again.

Silver was waiting in the foyer, pacing in front of the yawning receptionist, tapping his phone against his leg. He was tie-less, and his shirt was undone. For the first time since we'd met he was unshaven, dishevelled even. I felt quite shy.

'Breakfast?' the receptionist asked politely, trying to stifle her yawn. 'I'm sure we can rustle something up.' She indicated the dining room, but there was no time. Silver shoved a paper cup of coffee into my hand, a packet of biscuits from his room's tea-tray. He propelled me out into the car park without actually touching me. Something like hostility emanated from him. I tried to smile, but he looked grim.

'Just for the record, Jessica,' he plucked open the car

door without looking at me, 'I'd never try it on with anyone I worked with. Never.' He slammed the door before I could speak. When he slid in the other side, he studied me, just for a second, almost sorrowfully it seemed. Then he said, 'I just want the best for you. The best result.'

I tried to formulate my thoughts, to think past my son, past being a 'result', and after a while I began to talk, but he didn't want to hear now.

'Just leave it, will you?' he said curtly. He turned the radio up, opening the window very wide so I shivered in my thin summer dress, and had to hold my hair back with my hand. It was best if I was quiet anyway. I didn't want to admit the feelings that had pulsed through me last night.

The sun was coming up over the sea, and I watched a little white yacht smooth over the horizon, and thought, *This might be it – perhaps I will see Louis now, please God*, and a new kind of longing penetrated my bones.

The red and white lighthouse was on a small promontory, cut off by the tide for hours each day. Pretty as a storybook illustration, it glimmered tantalisingly out in the water as we slid down the sloping stony beach. The sun was still low, clouds dribbling gently over the horizon; no one around yet apart from a random dog-walker.

It was quite obvious who we were there to meet. The small cluster of men waiting at the water's edge looked as conspicuous as donkeys on Derby Day, uncomfortably suited and booted in the early-morning heat. The eldest man detached himself from the huddle to greet us, his incongruous shiny brogues blemished by the treacherous chalk pebbles, bespectacled and grim-faced. He nodded perfunctorily at me despite my hopeful smile, addressing Silver directly over my head.

'The boat'll be here any sec, Joe.' On cue, a small police-craft chugged round the headland towards the beach. 'The lady staying here, is she? Williams can wait with her.'

'I'd like to go too, please,' I said, as calmly as I could. Glasses cocked an eyebrow at Silver. Women, hey, pal? his sympathetic look read.

'It's not really procedure, madam,' was what he actually said.

'I couldn't care less about procedure, frankly. I just need to find my son,' I replied carefully. 'I'm sure there's room for me on the boat if we all squeeze up.' I didn't wait to see if Silver exchanged his look.

In the end we went on foot because the tide had finally turned, slipping out far enough to let us walk. I stumbled and slid across the seaweedy rocks in my old sandals, frustrated by the time this precarious hike was taking, stoutly refusing hands whenever one was offered. Especially Silver's suntanned one.

'My dad told me the seaweed was the mermaid's hair,' I said to no one in particular. I imagined my bow-legged father there on the beach behind me, shrimping-net in hand, willing me on. Was he watching out for his grandson, somewhere near, grinning the ubiquitous grin he'd had for his little girl?

311

'Sounds like a bit of a dreamer, your dad.' At last, Silver smiled at me.

I returned it weakly, my father still flitting through my mind. 'You could say that.' We were silent for the rest of the walk, speeding up as we neared our goal; concentrating on our individual hope, we were, I guess.

At the foot of the lighthouse, I looked up at the hundreds of stairs, trying not to feel daunted, then took a great breath and climbed as fast as I could manage. I followed Silver's giant strides, driven by a rising, frantic beat that echoed in my chest. I thought I heard a baby – and I nearly cried out with joy. Then I realised it was just the mewling of a solitary gull; I bit down painfully on my lip. I hoped beyond all hope that this would be the end now; I saw my Louis chuckling at the top, happy and unharmed, eyes wide with wonder at it all – and I climbed a little faster. By the time I reached the final level, my breath was ragged and I needed my inhaler. I couldn't deny the sinister silence above me – but still I burst into the room at the top with a final stab of sickening hope.

It was painfully obvious that no one was here. The place was deserted. My devastation was so complete now, I wanted to rail at Silver for letting me get my hopes up again, but I bit my tongue, and sat down heavily, sat before I crumpled where I stood. I struggled to retain my composure; I couldn't look at anyone. Silver smacked the window in frustration.

'Local kids, I'd say.' Glasses hadn't even broken a sweat. He kicked a pile of rubbish in the corner, and lit a smelly cheroot. It was apparent even to an uneducated eye that someone had been doing drugs here. On the old wooden table that rattled every time someone passed was strewn the works – old foil, matches, a bent teaspoon. In the corner, a syringe rolled spent beneath Glasses' foot, along with fag-butts and a discarded packet of Golden Virginia tobacco. There was a flagstone floor very like the one I remembered from the video, and a small pyramid of chalky stones stacked on the windowsill. But there was no sign of a baby having ever been here. No sign of my little baby.

The forensic team – the SOCOs as Glasses called them – arrived in their crackly paper jumpsuits, and I trudged behind Silver back down the stairs, across the sand that shone like plate-glass in the morning light; hobbled back over the smooth stones on the beach, up the wooden steps. Following Silver back to the car, I felt limp with a new, unprecedented despair.

On the way back through the twisting lanes, a light rain began to fall. Wistfully I remembered the fairy grottos my dad had whispered of as we'd driven so hopefully through the night, packed into the old Cortina for that one last summer holiday. Before my family fell finally and irrevocably apart.

Silver put something suitably tragic on the stereo, some aching blues, and he still wouldn't really talk to me, apart from a murmured 'Sorry'. I did try rather feebly to engage him once or twice, but eventually I gave up. I drifted into a light and flicky sleep as Silver drove, and my dreams were filled with giant syringes, and images of my brother, who suddenly looked just like my son. When I woke with a start, we were almost home and I'd been dribbling. I checked to see if Silver had noticed but his eyes were fixed on the clogged-up road in front. And I couldn't push Robbie from my mind, my baby brother and his glazed look, his empty eyes narrowed to nothing but a pinprick in General's flat the other night.

But something else was worrying me. I kept thinking about the empty Golden Virginia packet in the light-house this morning. I'd seen a packet of tobacco some-where else recently, other than in Robbie's hand. It was driving me quite mad now that I couldn't recall where.

CHAPTER TWENTY-ONE

There was something different about the front of my house as we pulled up outside, but I wasn't quite sure what. It took me a moment to realise that my car wasn't there. For the first time since Louis's disappearance it had gone; someone else had parked haphazardly in its place. For a weird moment I thought Mickey must be back. Then I thought that maybe Louis had been brought home in that strange car, and I stumbled wildly towards the door.

Kelly and Deb came out onto the path together like some odd welcoming committee. Something was most definitely up.

'Is Louis here?' I shouted hopefully, but Egg-belly looked all mournful.

'Sorry, no,' he said. For once, he wasn't eating.

'Did you give Maxine some time off?' Deb asked me, rather anxiously, and I shook my head. 'Why?'

'She's done a bunk, and we rather think – we think she may have company.'

Silver stuck new gum in his mouth. 'What kind of company?' he snapped, and Deb looked a little flustered and said, like an apologetic mother, 'We think she may have gone off with Robbie.' She couldn't quite meet my eye.

Silver swore under his breath. 'I told you to pick him up again last night, didn't I?' He looked at Kelly, but he was as mild as ever, entirely unruffled by his boss's anger.

'We were intending to, Guv, and we will – once we find him.'

My brain felt slow, full of mush. I turned to Deb. 'I don't understand,' I said stupidly. 'Maxine and Robbie? Together? Why?'

She gave a little shrug, flicking a nervous look at her boss. 'I'm not sure yet, Jessica.'

Silver glanced at me, then jerked his head at Kelly. 'We need to get on,' he said, and he got back in his car without a word, drumming his fingers impatiently on the wheel. I looked at him; he couldn't see me from where he sat now, and I thought, I'm doubly sad now – sadder even than when I left here yesterday. Then I shook myself like a dog coming out of cold water.

'I need to see Mickey, Deb,' I said quickly, because it seemed like a sensible, married sort of thing to say. It covered my doubts, papering across the cracks a bit. I grabbed my things from Silver's back seat and fled into the house without a second look. I heard him berating Kelly as I went.

'Why the fuck wasn't I told of this?' were the last

snarled words I caught. Silver was finally losing some of that cool.

Now what?

Two things, that was what. Leigh had caught Maxine and Robbie together in my bedroom last night, and had called Deb up in panic. Deb wanted me to ring my sister now; she thought she should be the one to explain.

Within twenty minutes Leigh turned up, wearing a horribly lurid pink tracksuit – presumably to match her truly foul mood. She'd been at home spring-cleaning, a true sign of her stress. Her hair was lank and swept back, and tension pulsed through her slim frame.

Deb made us tea – eternal tea lady that she was, poor woman – while Leigh stood by the back door and chain-smoked. She was really rattled. Apparently, she'd turned up unannounced last night to see if I was all right, and had seen the lights on in my bedroom. Getting no answer at the door, she let herself in with the key I'd given her and went upstairs, thinking I'd fallen asleep. Instead she found Robbie attempting to shag the au pair in the middle of my bed, without much success, it seemed. To Leigh's horror, Maxine had been tied to the bedposts with various things, mainly Mickey's belts and ties apparently, while Robbie snorted something off her back as he straddled her from behind. Both of them had been completely wasted; whisky and worse – blood – spilt across the sticky silk bedspread, fag-butts on the floor, in wine glasses; foil and spent matches in the en-suite sink, an open jar of pills strewn across the floor. My pills.

'The mess,' Leigh kept bemoaning now, as if that was what upset her most. 'I was going to take your bedspread to the cleaners today,' she said almost apologetically, lighting one fag from the other, neatly standing the last butt on the windowsill to fizzle out, 'but Deb said I should leave everything alone.'

Leigh had screamed at the pair in horror, and then rung Gary who'd come screeching round, and Deb, who wasn't far behind. By the time they'd both arrived, though, Robbie had disappeared and Maxine was unconscious on my bed. When they'd ascertained that she was actually still breathing, had just overdone the booze, they'd untied her and carried her to bed, deciding that Deb had better stay the night – just in case.

When Deb woke this morning, to her lasting embarrassment, there was no sign of Maxine in the house. On further inspection, most of Maxine's clothes were gone, along with the stereo, and my car (later I realised my jewellery box and Mickey's redundant Rolex were missing too). As Maxine had never been known to drive, the suggestion was that someone else had whisked them both away in my motor. That left – Robbie.

'The worst thing about it,' said Leigh very quietly, and she looked out into the garden as if she might find solace there, 'the really worst thing was that I don't think he even knew me, Jess.' She turned to me and her fists were clenched. 'Robbie didn't even know who I was last night when I walked into that room. He was so fucked, so off his bloody stupid little head, he – he just looked straight through me, like, it was weird – like we'd never even met.'

With some alarm, I saw her eyes flood with tears. Leigh *never* cried.

'I can't bear it, Jess. What the hell went wrong with him? He was such a gorgeous little boy.' She sniffed hard, wiped her nose on the back of her hand, where the fake tan was beginning to streak worryingly. 'I mean, we didn't turn out so bad, did we?' She looked at me for some reassurance.

The problem was she'd never dealt with the true Robbie, not really, not once he reached his teens. He was so lost, but she'd always just shut him out, written him off, valiantly fought my mum's battles for her, no matter how soft my mum had been on him. Leigh had fought *all* her battles, in fact; and she hadn't made space in her head to accept the real Robbie like I had. And even when we three had dealt with the last crisis, the one we never spoke of now, the three of us facing my father's final ignominy in death, squaring up to the police, trying to hide it from the neighbours, holding my mum together – just about together, even then – it didn't bring my siblings any closer.

And eventually, inevitably for us all, there was no escape from Robbie's truth; a truth that even I was only realising now. I could see how much it hurt Leigh as the sadness of his situation finally smacked her in the face.

I stood and put my arms around her tough little body. 'No, Leigh. I'd say we've done all right. And you never know, Robbie might come through this okay.'

We looked across the overgrown garden, at the last blowsy white roses fading on the bushes. In silence we listened to the little clinks of domesticity that filtered through the dozy afternoon. Someone was watching cricket, applauding merrily. The smell of sausages lingered in the air; a child laughed nearby, ready for his dinner, and the joyful noise sliced me like some kind of paper-cut. Tiny, but painfully deep. I tried to find some comfort in the familiar household noises that told a hundred unknown stories. I stood there with my sister, outside my silent house, my house that had stopped clinking altogether. We both knew that my hope for Robbie was unlikely to come true.

My chest was really tight, and my bedroom still an utter tip as I hunted for an inhaler. I was running low; I must remember to refill my prescription soon. I was less bothered by the mess than Leigh; after that flat in Elephant and my night at General's, nothing much would surprise me about Robbie any more. But I was confused. Robbie and Maxine together seemed very odd. I remembered the tattoo that read 'Jimmy' on his hand, remembered the pretty black boy and his voluptuous look.

Was someone else pulling Robbie's strings? General's nasty leer passed through my mind; at least he was still locked up – as far as I knew. Silver had said that if I pressed assault charges it would hopefully keep the bastard out of harm's way, for now at least.

I was about to change my clothes when the phone rang downstairs. As usual, hope was as ever swiftly followed by stomach-clenching fear. Wrapped in just a towel, I peered anxiously over the banisters. I could just see the top of Deb's curly head. *Come on*, I willed silently – and then she looked up at me and smiled. A smile big enough to show she thought it was good news, though not big enough to mean Louis.

'The hospital,' she covered the receiver, 'pick up the phone.' And there was Sister Kwame's gentle lilt saying what she thought I longed to hear – that my husband would soon be ready to come home. Mickey was finally on the mend again. With a sort of weary relief, I slumped on a chair by the phone.

I felt more than a little odd, shivering despite the heat and sort of flushed with panic, which I pushed down resolutely. I shunted the thought of Silver to a corner of my mind. I smiled with Deb; I tried, I really did. I mean, I *was* glad that the aloneness would soon come to an end; that together Mickey and I could hunt for Louis. I was incredibly relieved that my husband was finally okay.

We could get back on track now. I tried to forget the way my stomach had plunged initially at the thought of his brooding presence back home again. And then I thought, feeling like some kind of traitor, I thought that if I had to choose between Mickey or Louis coming home – well, there would be no choice to make. The crisis hadn't brought us closer in any way; if anything, it was driving me away. We had bridges to build when Mickey came home. We needed to start straight away.

CHAPTER TWENTY-TWO

The next day, everything around me started to speed up, until I felt like I was on a merry-go-round of hope and horror. The fact that Robbie and Maxine had done a bunk was seen as some admission of guilt; descriptions were put out along with an all-ports call, and my car numberplate. Leigh was convinced that our brother had taken Louis; she hardened up again. My mum called from Spain, crying pitifully, waiting to be consoled. I dug deep and found some soothing words. But, deep down, I wasn't so sure about my brother; I didn't know what to think. Much as I prayed for the riddle to be solved, why would Robbie have taken my son? There'd still been no ransom demand – what was his motive if it wasn't money? And oddly it was Maxine I felt more betrayed by. I'd taken her in; I'd been nice to her, at times against my better judgement – and look how she'd repaid me.

Mickey was conscious and recovering fast, but frustratingly he still had little memory of the day that Louis went. I wanted to talk to Annalise about my doubts, about my fears that my marriage was under too much strain to bear, but I was frightened to admit it, to say these things out loud, so I took a pill instead. Then I despised myself. I pored over photos of Louis, but still every time I walked past his bedroom I had to avert my eyes. The door had been shut tight since the night he went, the door with the little wooden letters, the multicoloured leopards and oranges and sunshines that spelt my son's name out. Silver stayed away. He was busy, I supposed.

I paced the house, thinking, thinking, always thinking what I could do. Should do. Eventually I got my bike out. I had been a champion cyclist in the old days. It had gone unused for so long that cobwebs hung across its burial place, out in the garage. It took me some time to retrieve it because it was so tightly wedged behind the heavy old lawnmower and some posh deckchairs we never used. The front tyre was a little flat; I pumped it up and then I rode the bike out onto the heath, cycling round and round in ever growing circles. It made me breathless; it made me want to fly from here, wind streaming through my hair, like I used to before I met Mickey. But I daren't go too far. You never knew, Louis might be back at any minute now. I thought about cycling down the hills to Silver and asking what he was doing next to find my son.

And then Robbie rang. He called my mobile, and his voice was tremulous and distant. He sounded really strange.

'I know what you're thinking, Jess,' he started, and I shook my head in sorrow. I sat astride my bike, and I sighed quite hard.

323

'Do you, Rob?'

'Yeah, and I haven't. I swear I haven't got him.'

'D'you know what?' I said slowly. 'I think I believe you, Robbie, deep down I do. Only it doesn't look good to all these coppers, know what I mean? Doing a bunk. It really doesn't, mate. And they'll find you, Rob, even if you don't tell me where you are.'

He laughed unsteadily. 'Yeah, well, that makes sense. But I wouldn't – you have to believe me, I wouldn't take him.'

I strained my ears, detective-like, for background noise, for a clue, but there was nothing discernible. 'Where are you, Robbie? Are you with that – that girl?' I couldn't bring myself to say her name.

He laughed again, without feeling. 'Yeah, I am, and that's why we went. Cos of her old man.'

'What? Her dad? I thought he was in France?'

'Her boyfriend. Gorek. He's nasty.'

It was my turn to laugh. 'Oh, come on! You're mixing with those tossers up in Soho, and you're frightened of her bloke? Pull the other one.'

I thought I heard a mewing in the background. 'What's that noise, Robbie?' I demanded. 'Have you bought Maxine a love-kitten?'

He ignored me. 'It's true, Jess. It's him the pigs wanna check out. He's got a nasty temper. You should see her bruises.'

'From what I hear, Robbie, from all that mess, it's you who she –'

'Jess,' he intercepted brutally, 'I'm sorry, yeah? I –'

'What?'

324

'I'm just – I'm really, really sorry.' There was a tiny pause – I thought he'd hung up. 'And look, Jess, if I do find out anything, I swear I'll let you know, yeah?'

'Robbie –'

It took me a second to realise that he'd gone. Wearily, I cycled home. As I rounded the corner past the bay-windowed pub, I saw Silver's car outside my house. My heart pumped extra hard, my stomach rolled uneasily.

Silver looked fresh. He'd recovered himself now, was as shaved and fragrant as he'd ever been. He even smiled, though I wasn't sure it reached those steady, hooded eyes. I told him what Robbie said; he raised an eyebrow as he leant against the kitchen worktop.

'He could be telling the truth, I suppose. Gorek didn't strike me as a particularly nice lad. But there is no reason for us to suspect him, no hard evidence at all. We'll put a trace on Robbie's call now.'

I brushed past Silver as I reached up to the cupboard to get a glass. My skin almost hurt where it had just touched his. 'Did Deb offer you a drink?' I asked courteously, like we were at a party.

'Forget that.' He turned me round, and I flinched from his hands. 'Look at this.' He shoved a brown envelope in front of me. A Polaroid of Louis's smiling face; another one of him sitting propped in some baby seat, his double chin creased beautifully as he looked intently down at something he held, a dewdrop of dribble caught for all time, tumbling from his bottom lip.

'Oh God.' I staggered slightly as I gripped the photos. I felt like I was falling headfirst into Alice's burrow, like Silver was the White Rabbit who led me through this insanity, always hurling me towards more madness. The shock was too much; tears flooded my eyes, and silently I wept. But I knew Louis was still alive, I really did. Whoever took these pictures had bought him things. He was dressed in clothes I'd never seen; he was playing with toys I didn't choose. Whoever took these pictures loved my son. They'd brushed his silky hair so carefully; they'd taken time to make him smile.

Silver stepped towards me, and I stepped back.

'Where –' I sniffed hard. 'Where did you get them?'

'Bloody courier again. Picked up from a doorstep of a Knightsbridge shop this morning at dawn. Dropped at one courier firm, delivered to me by another.' He looked at me and grinned that lopsided grin. 'We're closing in, Jess, I promise you. It won't be long now.' He rattled his keys in his trouser pocket, fishing out his mobile phone and tapping in a number.

'We've managed to keep David Ross in a little longer – General, you know him as – again, in the light of Robbie's disappearance. I have to say, though,' he broke off as someone answered his call, then came back to me, hand over the receiver, 'my gut feeling is the bastard's not involved.'

Into the phone: 'Kelly. I want to speak to Gorek Patuk again. Find him.'

With a sinking feeling, I realised they were just going round and round in circles – like me up on the heath just now. It was down to me. I'd had enough. I was going to have to find my son myself.

*

In the early hours I woke, and it was so close in my room that I couldn't get back to sleep. Eventually I slipped out of bed and went downstairs. I checked Louis's website, and added the date: *DAY TWELVE* – it looked so stark in black and white. There was nothing new apart from a few postings from a weirdo or two, and a woman who posted every day now, whose husband had taken her children to Pakistan, rambling on and on about parental abduction. Nothing that would help me. I unlocked the kitchen door and breathed in deep, felt the stillness almost solid around me. Nothing in the garden moved, no breeze stirred, not a leaf. I felt stifled by the lack of air, by my longing, by the eternal wait. I leant against the door and closed my eyes. I felt that Louis was closer now; my son was near, I sensed it.

In the morning I sat by Mickey's hospital bed. He wanted to know where my bruises had come from and I mumbled vaguely about General; I didn't want to worry him unduly. I distracted him with copies of the pictures of Louis. Mickey smiled with huge relief, and stared at them.

'I miss him terribly,' he said quietly, tracing Louis's face, and I loved him then for understanding what I felt. I felt our bond strengthen now; invisible but there. I told him about Maxine and Robbie, whom he'd never met. I muttered that I couldn't believe my brother was involved, and Mickey squeezed my hand.

'Sure, you might have to accept it, Jessica, however much you love your man there,' he said. I hated the fact he could be right. Then he apologised again for not remembering more. 'They say my memory will come back, they just don't know when.' He was doleful.

'Are you looking forward to coming home?' I said, with a buoyancy I didn't quite feel, and I thought I caught a flicker around his mending eye. He looked away.

'It's just – Louis, not being there,' he muttered, and I had a nasty feeling he might cry. My mind scrabbled round in panic.

'It'll be fine,' I said, falsely bright, 'he'll be home soon.' If only I believed my own words. 'Like you. And I should let you rest now, shouldn't I? I need to get on anyway. You know, check the – the police reports and things.' I fiddled nervously with the flowers on his bedside table. I still found it so hard to face his emotion. An uneasy feeling kept pounding through my exhausted head again and again: *Without the sex, without my son, what actually existed between Mickey and me?*

He grabbed my hand, pinching the skin painfully. I pulled back and frowned, rubbing my sore fingers.

'Ouch! That hurt, Mickey.'

'I wanted to tell you. About Agnes,' he muttered, 'I think she's in town.' He cleared his throat. 'I think she tried to see me when I was out.'

'Out?' I said blankly.

'Unconscious.' He was impatient now. An icy claw crawled across my gut. I stuck a spiky dahlia behind a bit of green stuff.

'I saw her,' I mumbled.

'What?' His mouth set hard and cruel, like it did when I said something stupid in company.

'I saw her.' I was defiant; I had to be. 'She's very beautiful, isn't she? I wanted to know why she'd seen you. I did ask you the – the other night.' It came out in a rush. *Before I nearly fucked you senseless, when I was mad*, I didn't add, staring at my feet like a naughty child.

'Did you? I don't remember. And I don't remember seeing her either.' He looked hard at me, and his eyes were very dark, and glittered, as if he had a fever still. 'And so?'

'She said you had a love like no other. I don't know. Some bollocks like that. I didn't like her, Mickey.' Steadily I met his look.

'No, well,' he was first to drop his eyes. 'Why would you?' He sighed, a rattling sigh full of self-pity. A large nurse with a fat, shiny face bustled in, followed by the consultant with tiny ears, and behind him a sweaty porter with a wheelchair.

'I'm sorry, Mrs Finnegan,' Noddy said cheerfully, and I was sure one little ear twitched, 'but it's time for us to take over. We need to do a final MRI, a scan, you know, before we can release him into your loving arms.' They started to wheel Mickey out.

'I'd say just one thing, Jessica,' Mickey murmured as he passed me. 'Don't trust my ex.'

'What do you mean?' I called urgently, but the lift had swallowed him already. His consultant smiled at me benevolently from the door.

'The sooner we get on, the sooner you'll have him home,' and then he was gone too. I was left alone in the funereal room. Picking up my jacket from the chair,

I dislodged the Harrods Food Halls bags Pauline had crammed with goodies for Mickey when she last visited. They fell like green and gold dominoes at my feet. I stared at them.

'Knightsbridge.' I smacked my forehead with my hand. 'Bloody Knightsbridge.' The photos of Louis left in a shop doorway. How could I have been so dense? I thought of missing Maxine and her penchant for uniform – the uniform in particular of a Harrods doorman. I ran out of that hospital like I was Linford Christie.

CHAPTER TWENTY-THREE

DS Kelly met Deb and me down in Greenwich, near the language school. We had no idea if Gorek would be there; they'd tried to bring him in last night but apparently there'd been no sign of him in the house he shared in New Cross, although they'd rounded up two of his brothers.

Silver came running up the stairs from the school, chewing almost fanatically.

'Do you want to wait inside, Kelly? His mates say they're expecting him, but I'm not so sure.' Silver twisted the spearmint wrapper in his hand and checked his watch. 'Let's get a quick coffee next door.'

'Sir.' Deb muttered something in his ear. He grinned at her. 'Of course. See you in – what?' He checked the time again. 'Thirty minutes?'

I followed him into the greasy spoon. A patrol car and three uniformed coppers sat outside the school. My coffee was so hot I scalded my tongue.

'I'll say this for you, Jess.' He put sugar in his tea. 'You're nothing if not diligent.'

'Any mother would be, surely?'

'Shock affects people very differently.'

The past twelve days streamed through my head. I flinched at the image of myself in the hospital after all those pills; I was truly ashamed I'd been so weak.

'You mustn't be so hard on yourself.'

I stared at him. 'Are you a mind-reader too now?'

He smiled. 'No, but I know that guilt is every parent's first emotion – and that's when everything's fine and dandy. And women feel it worse than men, I'd hazard a guess?'

His phone blipped.

'Yes?' He winked at me as he listened, before chucking the phone back on the table. 'They've nearly caught up with Gorek. He was with his wife and daughter in Bow this morning.'

'Any sign of –'

He placed his hand over mine where it was curled desperately around the coffee cup. I'd forgotten for a moment just how hot the china was. 'No sign, no. And apparently he got the sack from Harrods days ago. So it's unlikely he'd have been in Knightsbridge anyway.'

I swallowed hard. I tried to make light of my latest disappointment. 'Wife? Blimey. I wonder if Maxine knew?'

'Would she have cared if she did?'

I shrugged. 'Probably not.'

He picked up his phone again; my hand felt suddenly naked where his fingers had been. 'I've got to get on, Jess.'

'Okay.'

Deb was outside the window now, waving, a carrier from the local chemist in her hand. She took me home.

The evening was balmy, more comfortable at last. Out in the garden with Shirl and Leigh, we opened a bottle of Mickey's expensive wine. Shirl had lit a huge spliff, long legs resting on the tabletop; Leigh, carefully re-tanned, painstakingly painted her nails a seashell sort of pink, splaying her fingers periodically to admire them. I fiddled with my newly washed hair, put it up, took it down again. With some apprehension I was about to bring up the ex, the perfect Agnes, to seek a bit of female advice and solidarity, when the news came.

Deb appeared from the porch steps; immediately, I noticed the vein throbbing beside her eye; like a warning-drum, I knew that it spelt trouble. Egg-belly Kelly wasn't far behind. Politely they overlooked Shirl's joint. With casual ease she tossed it, still smoking, into my scrunchy-headed petunias.

'An unexpected turn of events,' Deb called it. They'd intercepted another delivery, this one addressed to me. A package with another tape, a note typewritten and misspelt. 'A ransom demand.' They, whoever 'they' were, were now demanding money. I could have my son back if I stumped up £50,000.

'Is that all they want?' I said, incredulous, and I laughed out loud, a laugh that bubbled up from some-where very deep. The others all looked suspiciously at me; suddenly, I felt like dancing. I looked joyfully at the evening's last sunrays refracting in my glass of golden wine, so rich and oily it slicked the glass like Fairy Liquid.

'It's good news, don't you see?' I glanced around, smiling encouragingly. 'Fantastic news. Fifty grand – well, it's bloody nothing, is it? Not these days. Not in the greater scheme of things. I'd pay anything for him, of course I would.'

But Deb looked concerned; her vein still throbbed.

'I suppose –' began Leigh cautiously.

'It means I'll get him back. If that's all they want, I'll have him back in no time.' I toasted the others excitedly with my drink.

'But why –' said Shirl quite slowly, and she wasn't really addressing me, she looked over at the police, puckering her lips in thought, '– why has it taken them over a week to ask for cash?'

'For God's sake, Shirl!' I snapped, and I slugged some wine back. No one was going to taint my optimism, not now, not when I'd waited so flipping long. 'They're probably just realising what hard work a baby is,' I joked hopefully, but no one else joined in. I pushed my chair back in frustration. 'I can't believe you're being like this.' I was starting to feel cross. 'It's good news – I'm sure it is. It has to be.' I looked at Kelly, impassive as ever. 'It is, isn't it? What does Silver say?'

Kelly shrugged noncommittally. 'He's with the boss, Mrs Finnegan. I'm sure he'll be in touch.'

Boss. How strange. I'd always thought of Silver as the boss. 'Well,' I was more than a little flushed with drink, 'I'll ring and ask him myself.'

I went inside and did just that. 'Can you come round,

please? I really need to talk.' I was bold with alcohol.

To my mortification, he declined. 'I've got to stay here, Jessica. Work on the logistics. You just sit tight.'

'But,' and I was floundering now, falling from my high, 'what should I do?'

'Sit tight, kiddo,' he repeated, and my heart began to sink. 'We think – well, we need to be very circumspect about what we believe at this stage. You should prepare yourself to – it might just be a hoax, Jess.'

There was a pause – a silent, deathly pause. He carried on. 'I don't see any reason for someone to put a ransom demand in now. But do talk to your husband about the possibility of raising the money, by all means. It's good to be prepared, if the worst comes to the worst.'

To my husband. The worst coming to the worst.

'Okay,' I said stiffly, and I reached for my almost empty inhaler, which I squirted rapidly in short, fast bursts. Then I finished up my wine. 'Thank you. I'll do that. I'll talk to my husband.' I put the phone down rather hard. I stood in my living room and I gazed at my Louis on the wall. 'I'll get you back soon,' I promised him, 'I'll bring you home if it kills me. If it's the last thing I ever do.'

There had to be a clue somewhere, something that had been missed. The police had already mounted a full-scale operation to find Robbie and Maxine; they were on the tail of Gorek – but still I couldn't rest. What Mickey had muttered earlier kept coming back to haunt me. 'Don't trust Agnes,' he'd said – but why?

I went upstairs and dug out her number. Her mobile went straight to answer-phone, so I left a message asking her to call. Then I crept back into Mickey's study. I took one deep breath, and then I pulled the place apart. I hunted again for traces of Agnes, some clue to her history with my husband. Nothing. Mickey had told me once that he'd destroyed everything, and he hadn't lied. That photo must have been it.

Suddenly the door opened and a long shadow fell across my lap. I nearly jumped out of my skin. But it was just Deb, who stood there looking down at me, surrounded by files and folders and old diaries. I felt like a small child with my hand caught in the biscuit jar.

'You okay?' she asked, and I realised how dishevelled I must look, hot and sweaty from lugging boxes down from shelves, from rifling frenetically through Mickey's private papers, searching for a sign.

'I'm fine, thanks. Just looking for something,' I said, trying not to sound guilty. I pushed my damp hair out of my eyes.

'I'll be off then. I'll see you in the morning.' She lingered for a moment, like she had something else to say. 'Have faith, Jessica, won't you?'

I snorted a bit like a horse. 'Faith? You're not getting all religious on me, are you, Deb?'

'I didn't mean it like that,' she blushed. 'I meant, in us. I know it must seem like ages but – look, we're doing our very best, I swear.'

'Well you shouldn't, should you?' I said.

'I shouldn't what?' Her brow wrinkled.

'Swear.'

'I wasn't –'

'Oh ignore me. It's the wine. I'm just being facetious.'

She smiled indulgently and stepped towards the door.

'Deb?' I said it quickly before she could turn round. 'I do – I really appreciate you so much, Deb. I don't know what I'd have done without you, really.'

We grinned at each other bashfully. 'You're welcome, Jess.'

'Deb?' I said slowly.

'Yes?'

'Silver – he's a good cop, isn't he? Do you think – will he find –' The words caught in my throat.

She smiled. 'He's the best. I really do believe that, Jess. He really cares. He'll find Louis for you, I know he will.'

'Oh,' I said. 'That's what I thought.' We left it at that.

I lay in bed, sleepless yet again – but I'd given up on pills for good. Every time I closed my eyes, I saw Louis in another woman's arms. I pulled the sheet over my head, and then, however hard I pushed it away, the scene with Silver in the hotel garden replayed time and time again. And I thought of how safe he made me feel. Like when you're exhausted, and you finally lie down where you belong, you sink down and relax, and the relief, the prospect of rest is immense. That's what nearly letting myself melt into Silver had been like. The prospect of rest at last.

I turned over, searching for a cool bit on my pillow; scribbled Silver's name out in my brain; thought longingly of Louis. Suddenly I had an idea. One place I hadn't looked. I sat bolt upright in bed; got up and padded out onto the landing.

'Shirl?' I tapped quietly on her door. Silence. I tapped harder.

A grunt. 'Whassermatter?'

'Shirl, listen, mate. I just –' I stuck my head into the gloom. 'I need a hand. Sorry, but would you mind?'

Eventually, she stumbled grumbling into the light, her afro as huge and hectic as a dandelion-clock ready to blow.

'Can you help me get the ladder down? I need to get into the loft.'

'Jessica, it's –' she squinted at her watch '– one in the morning. Can't it wait?'

'Not really, no.' I was hopping from foot to foot now.

'All right,' she yawned vastly and her gold fillings glinted. 'But you better not be expecting me to sit up in no loft. Once you're up there, you're on your own, you hear me now?' Muttering, she stretched on tiptoe from the chair I held, and swung the ladder down.

'I ain't sitting in no loft in the middle of the night, not for no one. And don't you come complaining about ghosts or some such nonsense. You're on your own.'

'I won't, I promise.'

But, of course, she didn't leave me. She lay with her head on a roll of old carpet and her long legs folded elegantly at the ankle, struggling to keep one eye open. Within minutes she was snoring gently while I went through all Mickey's neatly stacked junk. To be honest, I was glad of her company. I'd never been in the attic before; Mickey had shoved a few bits and bobs belonging to Louis up here as he grew out of them. 'For the next one,' I'd said, rather apprehensively, from the landing, and Mickey had just smiled.

Half an hour passed, and I had nothing to show for it but grimy hands and cobwebs in my hair. Finally, just about to give up, just as I felt that I was mad to have even begun, I came across something wrapped tightly in Mickey's moth-eaten graduation gown, wedged into the corner. Eventually I freed it, falling backwards with a bang. My heart was racing again as I unwrapped it. It was a big smart folder, a leather affair, marked with a tiny *A.F.* in gold leaf. Agnes Finnegan. And God, how neat it was. My heart pounded as I flicked frantically through the inner leaves – but crashing disappointment quickly followed as I realised how very dull its contents actually were. Store-card bills from shops like Harvey Nichols and Selfridges. Some papers about pensions, and statements of a PEP that she'd cleared out. And finally, tucked in the back, a medical file. Indecipherable notes that I didn't understand from a doctor in Harley Street. A glossy leaflet on how best to recuperate from an operation. Holed up in an expensive spa, by the looks of this. Frowning, I tucked it all back in its plastic sleeve. Then I shook Shirl gently awake, and followed her mad barnet back down the ladder to bed.

I woke at the crack of dawn again, permanently on Louis-time. In the kitchen I waited for the kettle to boil, staring vacantly at a bluebottle dead on its back beside the biscuit tin. He looked like he'd died mid-flight.

Blearily, I cleared a space at the table for my coffee cup, stacked up the letters, bills and magazines that lay everywhere. Mickey's folder from his last shoot fell open, and I flicked idly through the sheets of contact prints. Little cottages on cliffs; an old glass lighthouse; a laughing couple walking hand-in-hand down a tiny country lane. I peered closer at the girl, tall and thin, blonde hair streaming behind her. *The girl.* My coffee went down with a bang, burning my hand. I blinked hard and looked again.

'I don't bloody believe it.' I stared at the picture. There was no doubt about it. The girl with streaming hair. The woman from the Tate.

Hands trembling, I rang the ICU. They said Mickey was sleeping and refused to wake him, despite my pleas. Absolutely no visitors until nine; I knew the rules by now, surely? So I hunted for Pauline's number. It just rang and rang. I left it five minutes, and called again. Eventually Freddie picked up, grumpy with sleep.

'I don't know where she is. She left her mobile last night. Try her bloody work. She's snowed under already.'

But when I rang, the phones at Mickey's office were still on divert. I looked at the clock; it was only seven. So I threw on my clothes and nicked the keys to Shirl's old banger – left her a scrawled note, shoved the contacts folder into my bag, and drove up into town.

Soho was just awakening, lazy as the white-thighed girls who'd later adorn the doors of dim-lit clubs. I dumped the car and made my way to Mickey's building on Wardour Street. Crossing past the strip-show on the corner, not open yet, I suddenly realised how uncomfortably close to General's shop I was. His waxy face loomed huge in my mind and I felt a spasm of disgust; with vigour I stamped him out and buzzed Mickey's office intercom. Nothing. No one answered. I cursed my impetuosity. As I turned away, I got a faceful of spray from the pavement-washing machine trundling up the road like a baby elephant.

'God's sake!' I muttered, wiping my face.

'Hello?' A disembodied Geordie accent wafted suddenly from nowhere. Pauline.

'It's Jess. Can I have a quick word?'

She let me in, coffee in hand. Dishevelled and baggy-eyed, she looked like she'd just got in from a night on the town; all done up in some strange cowgirl ensemble, hair in little braids, seemingly still half-asleep. I was sure I could smell booze.

'Can I get you a drink, pet?' she asked, stifling a yawn as she led me across the big open-plan room. I passed the desk where I'd first sat as a design assistant and I thought with a lurch how things change. There was a blanket on the office sofa; the weight of a body still imprinted in the leather folds. I looked closely at her. Had she been sleeping here? Was that why Freddie had been so curt?

Pauline opened the green glass door to Mickey's private office and ushered me through as I scrabbled in my bag for the folder – and then my heart was in my mouth. Propped against Mickey's desk were huge boards

341

of blown-up photos – and there, right at the front, larger than life, smiling enticingly from the doorway of a quaint thatched cottage, was that bloody woman.

'Pauline, who the fuck is that girl?'

'Sorry, who?' She looked up from kicking the wedge under the door, slopping her coffee on the floor. She flushed beetroot when she saw who I meant.

'Oh, you mean Claudia. They're good, aren't they? They're still awaiting Mickey's approval though.'

'Yeah, but who *is* she, Pauline?'

'Don't you remember her?' She seemed surprised.

I shook my head again. 'No, I don't. She was at the Tate that day.'

'That's Claudia Bertorelli. Sorry, what day, pet? You've lost me.'

'The day Louis disappeared.'

'Oh.' Pauline looked truly puzzled.

My heart was galloping. 'Pauline, is Mickey – are this girl and Mickey –' I couldn't go on. It just got worse and worse.

'What?'

'Are they, you know –' The words stuck in my clamping throat. 'Do you know if he's been –'

She laughed. She actually laughed.

'Please, don't laugh, Pauline.' I twisted my bag-strap tight around my finger until the circulation stopped. 'This is deadly serious.'

Immediately, she stopped; she put her hands up dramatically as if I might attack her. 'All right, calm down, pet. It's just – no they're not – an item, if that's what you meant.'

'And how do you know? Are you sure?'

'Yes, I'm sure, Jessica.' She looked suddenly weary. 'I'm sure because she doesn't do men.'

'She doesn't –' Her meaning filtered through my brain.

'She's my ex. Do you really not remember her?'

Vaguely, *vaguely*, something trickled into my over-wrought head.

'You've met Claudia, I'm sure you have. I was seeing her when you first came here. Before I met Freddie. Before you were with Mickey.'

'Oh.'

So what the hell had she been doing at the Tate that day?

'Mickey uses her a lot for his brochure work, you know. She hasn't got the typical model look, she's a bit more real, isn't she? Very photogenic though.'

'Right.' I felt the backwash of an adrenaline slump. I sat heavily on the edge of Mickey's desk. 'Sorry, Pauline. I just – I found these photos this morning and I've been panicking.' I held out the folder to Pauline and she took it. 'This girl, well, she was in the Tate the day Louis disappeared. Really freaked me out for some reason. Only I didn't know who she was. It makes sense now. Mickey said he'd bumped into someone from work and – and she said to me that I looked familiar. I've been trying to work out who she was all this time.' I looked at her. 'She's a suspect, you know.'

Pauline laughed again, though she didn't look particularly amused. 'Claudia? Why, for God's sake?'

343

I shrugged. 'Because she was so into Louis, and then he – disappeared. Because she was – strange.' Had she really been strange, though? Or was it my highly charged state, my exhaustion at the time that made it seem so?

'Well, she probably was into Louis.'

My heart soared. 'Yes, that's what I –'

'Claudia loves babies. She's just had her own. About six months ago. Emily, I think she's called.'

'What?' I didn't follow. 'Her own?'

Pauline sighed. 'Jessica, pet, just because you like shagging women doesn't mean you don't like babies. Doesn't mean you don't want to be a mother.'

I thought of Freddie. 'No, I guess not.' I was truly embarrassed now.

'In fact, it's part of the reason me and her,' she jerked her head at the smiling model, 'it's part of the reason I binned her off.'

I didn't understand.

'Why we split up, I mean. She was about to try to conceive with her mate Josh. I wanted to give us a chance first, you know, before babies – but she wouldn't wait. Couldn't wait, she said.' Pauline walked to the door. 'So you see, I doubt Claudia's going round snatching babies, pet, what with her own wee bairn at home.'

'No,' I said foolishly, 'no, I guess not.' I thought of Silver, shuddered at having to tell him I'd made such a big mistake. 'I suppose – oh God. I'd better let the police know who she is then. Have you got her details – her number or something?'

'We don't really talk, you know. It didn't end on a good note.'

My face was pleading. She was gruff. 'All right. Hang on. It'll be on the photo-shoot call-sheet, I expect. Wait there.'

A few of Mickey's staff were drifting slowly into the open-plan office now, deadlines obviously looming, flinging iPods and *Independents* on their desks, chatting cheerfully. The smell of coffee filled the air. Someone switched the radio on. I waved politely at the few faces I still knew, then turned my back on their inquisitive eyes. Stared at Claudia's laughing face. Pauline came back with a number on a Post-it note.

'Thanks,' I mumbled. 'I'm sorry if – you must think I'm a fool.'

'Hardly. Don't be silly, pet. You must be bloody frantic.' She squeezed my hand kindly. 'Everyone's a suspect, I guess, until you know they're not.'

She walked me to the door, telling me that she'd been relieved by Mickey's state when she'd visited him – she'd been so worried. Then she kissed me on the cheek, stinking of stale drink, and told me to take care. I felt discomfited by my former desperation.

'And you – are you all right, Pauline?'

'Oh aye, I'm grand, thanks, pet, just grand.'

But she looked like she might cry, and the lines around her eyes were deeper etched than ever before. She flicked her braids back defiantly, straightened her sheriff's badge.

'It's just me and Freddie – we're, you know. Going through a bad patch. The sailing holiday was meant to be a new start but, well, you get home and it's still all the same, isn't it? All that sea-sickness for nothing –

and all this bloody relentless baby stuff.' She gaped at me in sudden horror, her hand creeping to her mouth.

'God, sorry, pet. I mean, between me and her. Her clock's ticking so loud, you know.' She pulled the door open, and the noise from the street trebled. 'Trouble is, mine's just not. Perpetual problem of mine, apparently.'

'I'm sorry. I hope you sort it out.'

But as I got back into the car, something somewhere rang false. And Mickey was the only person who could tell me what it was.

I drove straight to the hospital, parked the car badly in a disabled space for want of any others, and ran into St Thomas' like my bloody life depended on it. Through the yellowy corridors, up in the antiseptic-smelling lift, down the hall to ICU. I rang the bell frantically. Sister Kwame came to the door.

'Mrs Finnegan,' she began; I shot straight past her. His room was empty, the bed stripped. 'Where is he?' I was nearly shouting now.

'Don't fret, Mrs Finnegan.' Her milky brown eyes held mine and calmed me with their will. 'He's on the ward, on the main ward now, downstairs. Out of Intensive Care for good. Such good news, yes?'

'Where is it, Sister? The ward. I need to see him now.'

'Is everything okay?' She was frowning now, perturbed by my panic. 'Is there some news of your baby?'

'No,' I shook my head vehemently, 'there's never any bloody news. I just need to see him – Mickey – now. Please.'

'Come, I take you,' she said kindly, and she put her arm around me. 'This is very stressful for you, yes? Poor Mrs Finnegan.'

I leant into her for a second without answering.

We tracked back the way I'd come, down in the lift, onto the fifth floor. Marcia Banes Ward was the last on the corridor; I was trying not to break into a run. We reached the door of this ward, and rang yet another bell. I felt like I was doing my social rounds, should be leaving cards for all those I called on.

The fat-faced nurse from the other night appeared. She was so large she shone; glossy skin pulled taut, housing fat that pushed beneath the surface and threatened to burst out. Sister Kwame gestured at me. 'Deidre, Mrs Finnegan is looking for her husband. I told her you were taking good care of him.'

The fat nurse crinkled her brow – with some difficulty as her skin was stretched so tight. 'Finnegan? From the ICU? Of course we will. When he arrives.'

It was Sister Kwame who frowned now. 'But we released him this morning. He was brought down by the porter.'

'Oh really?' Shiny said. She strode Sumo-like to the nurses' station and grabbed a chart, scanned the names. 'I've only just come on. Probably some mix-up with the – ah, hang on a second.' She counted down a column. 'Finnegan, you said? Yes, we've definitely got a bed for him. Let me check with someone else.'

A young Asian nurse was crossing to the station, plump plait swinging, a roll of bandage in her hand.

'Sunita, have you dealt with Mr Finnegan from ICU this morning?'

The girl considered for a minute, then shook her head, plait flicking snake-like across a bony shoulder. 'Doesn't ring a bell. Checked with Sally?'

'Oh, for God's sake!' The involuntary protest slipped from my lips. The nurses all looked up, across, then down again, ignoring me.

'Sorry,' I muttered self-consciously, 'I just really need to see him.'

But he wasn't there, wasn't anywhere. Eventually they managed to get the porter on the phone. Shiny nodded, um-ed and ahh-ed like she was ever so important, then hung up with a flirty 'Swing by later if you've a mo.' I tensed my fists in my pockets.

'Eddie brought him down,' she announced conspiratorially, 'but then Mr Finnegan said he'd rather walk from the lift. Wanted to stretch his legs. Said he'd see himself to the ward. Eddie was late for the O.R. so he let him go.' She looked round as if expecting applause. 'Well, Mr Finnegan's a grown man, isn't he? I mean, Eddie can hardly be blamed in the circumstance.' She checked her watch, sunken beautifully between rolls of fat. 'Only about forty minutes ago, Eddie said. He's probably gone for a little wander, pleased to be back on his feet, you know. They get cabin-fever, some of our boys.'

Any minute now she was going to break into a pompous rendition of 'We'll Meet Again'.

'Thanks.' I headed swiftly for the door again. 'Just –

can you ask him to ring me as soon as he appears.'

I stood at the lift with a sickening sense of déjà vu, the old Clash song reverberating round my dazed head. Should I stay or should I go? Should I search the hospital for Mickey, or should I just cut my losses and leave, trust that he was getting coffee, reading the paper somewhere, relishing five minutes of normality? Should I just get on with looking for Louis?

In the end, of course, Louis won out. He always would.

CHAPTER TWENTY-FOUR

Shirl's car was gone.

'For fuck's sake!' I shouted, to no one in particular, to the pale blue woolly sky, to the ugly concrete ground. Why would anyone nick such a dodgy old banger? The car-park attendant hurried towards me, a ferrety little man. He wanted to commune with me over my loss – those bloody tow-trucks, he began. Smiling grimly, I fled.

I was like the water building up behind a hosepipe's air-lock, suddenly unleashed. Propelled forward by an unseen force, launched out into the street, pushed by an almighty hand, driven by fury and longing. I contemplated calling Leigh to collect me, to keep me company, but it'd take her too long to get here, so I hailed another cab, climbed in, realised I didn't know where to go. My impulse was to return to Sussex – I didn't know why, but something drew me there. I would go home, borrow Leigh's car, drive down, find Louis, I decided. I was muttering to myself, the cabbie caught my eye in his mirror, looking hastily away. He thought

I was mad, I suddenly realised, and I nearly laughed hysterically. Perhaps I truly was.

My phone rang, shocking me back to reality. It was Shirl.

'Listen, Shirl,' I started, 'I'm so sorry, mate. I'll get the car back. I just haven't –'

'It's Mickey,' she said baldly.

'What?' My heart flipped over and withered. He was dead, I was sure. That was it. I tried to breathe. 'What's happened?' I croaked.

'He's here.'

'What? Where?'

'Here. At home.'

A pause while I absorbed this.

'In your house, stupid.' She was impatient now. I didn't understand.

'Are you sure?'

'Sure I'm sure. Char, man, I haven't even had a spliff yet today. Get your arse back here now. He don't look well, Jess. Not well at all.'

'Put him on the phone,' I begged.

There was another pause; I heard her calling his name; doors were banging. She was back. 'I would if I could get him to sit still. He just keeps muttering about Louis, running about he is. Get home, Jess. I've got to go to work, I'm late already – but he's acting – kind of odd.'

'Shirl,' I said, very firmly, 'get him to ring me back. I'll be there as soon as I can.' I tapped on the glass divide. 'Can you go any faster please?' I said.

'It's not *The French Connection*, love,' he muttered wearily.

'Yeah, I know that. But it is a matter of life or death,' I implored before slumping back in my seat.

When I got home Shirl was standing by the open door, agitated. I fumbled with my change, calling over my shoulder to her. 'Where's –'

'He's bloody gone. He said he tried to ring you, but he couldn't get through.'

I swore loudly, running into the house as if my feet were on fire, but of course it was true. He wasn't there.

'What was he doing? Where's he gone?' I demanded frantically.

'Changing his clothes. Getting money or something. He's gone to look for Louis, he said. I think – I thought he was, you know, off his head. Feverish, he looked. I tried to get him to sit down and have a drink, to wait for you, but he just kept rushing round.' She was pulling on her poncho now. 'To be honest, Jess, I was a bit scared. He looked kind of – crazed.' She put some lip-gloss on, talking to my reflection in the mirror. 'Look, I'm really sorry, but I'm going to have to go. I'm so late already, and I've got my first client at midday.'

Then she stopped, shiny stick poised above her generous mouth. 'Why were you in a cab?' she said slowly. 'Where's my motor?'

I flushed guiltily.

'Jessica?'

'Ah,' I said, playing for time. 'Umm – I was trying to tell you on the phone but I got a bit, you know, distracted. It – er – it got towed at the hospital. I didn't park it very well,' I confessed.

'Jess! You bloody fool!' She slammed her gloss back in her bag.

'I'm really sorry,' I said imploringly, 'I'll get it back. Look, get a cab and I'll pay for it, okay?'

I was talking to her back now as she swung her over-sized bag across her shoulder.

'I'll take your bike. We'll sort it later,' she said. Heading out to the garage, she looked back. 'Just find Mickey, Jess, quickly. He isn't well.'

I flopped down on the stairs and tried to think. My mind was spinning like a rabid hamster in a wheel. I'd better call the police about Shirl's car; should I also let the hospital know about Mickey? I was just wondering when the house-phone rang. I jumped, then rushed down the hall to snatch it up. It was Mickey, thank God.

'Jessica,' he said, and his accent had gone all IRA, which meant the stress had finally conquered him. 'Jessica, I'm sorry I rushed off. I couldn't wait. I've just got to find our boy.'

He sounded like he was standing in the middle of a motorway, but he couldn't be, could he – he'd only just left the house.

'Where are you, Mickey?' I asked. 'Shirl said you didn't look well. Come back and we'll go together, yeah?' It felt like trying to talk someone down from a bad trip.

'Jess, I'm going after –' The bloody phone started breaking up, his voice fading in and out. '– I don't –' but he'd gone again.

'What? Mickey?' I said urgently. 'You're breaking up. You're going after who? Just tell me where you are.'

'I'm on my way to –'

I heard the back door creak very slightly. The hairs on my neck stood up; I glanced behind me. 'Shirl?' I called.

There was no one there. A gentle breeze sighed through the hall, wrapping itself round my trembling legs.

'Mickey,' I said again, 'just tell me where you are, okay? I'll come and meet you –'

There was a footstep in the kitchen. I froze.

'Who's there?' I whispered, and goose-pimples appeared all pointy up my arm. Mickey was talking now, saying something about knowing Louis would be okay, but I wasn't listening properly, I was on tenterhooks, straining to catch the noise again. Someone was in the house.

'Hang on, Mickey, there's someone here I think,' I croaked, and I was about to turn again when I saw a shadow fall down the hall past my own. Then I felt a blow, deafening pain upon my head. I cried out, my neck crumpled to my chest and I was going down – I was spinning – spinning – spun.

When I woke I couldn't think where I was. My face was stuck to something; when I moved it made a noise like fresh bacon peeling from the packet. I was drooling like an idiot, a pool of something warm and sticky cradling my cheek. Why was it so dark? I tried to raise my head, but it pounded so hard that I collapsed back down again.

After some time, I tried again. I realised I was lying

on the floor; my hall floor – and the darkness was the heap of coats that had fallen on me as I'd pulled the coat-rack with me as I went. I put my hand to my cheek and brought it away, trying to focus on the wet that stained it. Some of it was dark. Some of it was blood.

There was a phone ringing somewhere very far away, and then the answer-phone clicked on and there was my jolly voice again, my falsely jolly voice accompanied by Louis's little gurgle, and then Deb was talking in the distance, asking me to ring her; why hadn't she heard from me today? She was worried. There'd been developments – I must call her when I heard this.

And then I realised there was knocking in my ears, someone was knocking, and I tried to get up, but it hurt so bloody much it nearly made me sick. I pulled myself to sitting, and after a while I croaked out 'Hang on, I'm coming,' and I got there after an eternity, I sort of limped and I sort of crawled and when I got as far as the front door I used the handle to pull myself up, and I managed to open it – but the doorstep was empty.

Wheezing, I slumped down again and I knew I should try to reach the phone, tell someone what had happened, but I really couldn't face the pain that thudded across my head each time I moved.

And then I heard the back door creak open once more, and my guts went to water. I promised a God I hated that I really would behave now if he could just protect me. Shuffling as fast as I could towards the phone table, I had some vague thought of picking up the lamp that stood there, of arming myself and hitting

355

back, but the kitchen door swung ajar a little before I could even get there, and a shadow tumbled down the hall.

Then, finally, the door opened enough to let me see that standing above me, towering over me where I cowered, stood Agnes.

Agnes wanted to call the police, but I wouldn't let her yet. I had some questions of my own first.

'How did you get in?' I asked her, groggy and puzzled as she helped me up.

'I looked through the letterbox when you didn't answer; I saw you lying on the floor. I went around the back, and it was open, thank God.' My weight made her stagger in her stilettos as she pulled me up to sit on the hall chair. 'I used to live here, remember?'

How could I ever forget?

'What happened, did you fall?' she asked, and then looked at her hand, horrified. 'My God, you're bleeding!' She was so near I could see the tiny flecks of mascara beneath her eye.

'I don't know.' My head was swimming and I bit my lip with pain. 'Someone – someone must have hit me, I think.'

She looked at me like maybe I was making it up, and I started to doubt myself. I was desperately trying to collect my thoughts, which was proving horribly hard. Agnes said she'd put the kettle on, so then I called Deb, though it took me a long time to find the number, to think where it would be, where Deb would be, whether it should be her or Silver I should ring. When

I did get through, Deb was in a meeting, so I left a message.

In the downstairs loo, I leant against the basin for a long time to stop myself from being sick. Then I attempted to wash some of the blood off my neck, and found some painkillers in the cupboard. I swallowed them thankfully, and went to face my nemesis.

She made me a cup of tea in my own kitchen – the kitchen that was once hers. The way she moved around it – almost balletic she was, moving on the balls of her high-heeled feet – you would have thought it still belonged to her. The thing that unnerved me most was the way she knew where everything lived: the teabags, a spoon, the cups. I made a mental note to change things round immediately.

Perhaps it was my confused state, but she seemed a little less perfect than last time we'd met; tired and dull beneath her slick make-up and her suntan. I sat on a kitchen chair and asked for three sugars in my tea. I was still shaking. All the time I could feel her brain ticking as if she was about to say something – and then she'd change her mind again. But finally it came out.

'I want to see Mickey,' she said, keeping her back to me. 'Would you mind?'

'He's not here,' I said dully. I didn't exist past this raw and sickening pain deep in my skull.

'No, I know that. In the hospital. I need to speak with him, Jessica.' She plopped my tea down ungraciously before me. 'I can't really tell you about what.'

'Well, I wasn't asking actually,' I retorted. I stirred the black liquid round, and thought vaguely about milk. 'But you've already seen him in the hospital, haven't you?'

She washed up a teaspoon vigorously. A delicate pink stained her cheeks. 'Yes, okay, I have. But he was sleeping. We did not talk.'

'Oh,' I said. 'Well, I don't know where he is, actually.'

For the first time, she sort of smiled. 'Has he – have you left him?'

'No, I haven't bloody left him,' I snapped. 'He's gone to find our son. I don't know where Mickey is, he's not at all well, though, and –' My head gave an almighty throb, and I gasped in pain. She looked worried, stepped towards me, but I recoiled. I couldn't bear the thought of her smooth flesh near mine.

'I'm fine,' I said, 'honestly,' but my eyes kept watering, and we both knew I was lying. 'Why are you asking my permission anyway?' I asked in between the throbs. 'You weren't bothered before.'

'Because I have met you now. Because I – I respect you, Jessica. As a woman, as Mickey's new wife. I see you as a person now; before you were just a shadow in my life.'

Blimey. Too much therapy, I'd hazard a guess. I watched, horribly fascinated, as she gazed distractedly into the garden.

'I love those roses, don't you? The white ones. I planted those when we first came. When I had such hope for everything.'

I really didn't want to hear about the lovechild flowers of Mickey and his ex; about the hopes they'd shared. A magpie bounced across the lawn – one for sorrow – beady eye set far into its blue-black skein as it searched for all that glittered. I willed Agnes to go now.

'You must miss your baby very much, do you?' She didn't look at me.

'Of course. I can't really,' – *I can't really function* – 'I can't really think of anything else. Until I find him again.'

'I wish I could help you.' She kept staring at the roses, then she turned and smiled at me. She really was a beautiful woman. Just a little, sort of – hollow.

'Thank you.' I tried to smile back. 'Look, I'll tell Mickey you want to see him, okay? Frankly,' and I realised it was true, 'frankly, Agnes, I don't care if you talk to him. For whatever good it does you. All I care about,' I clutched my pounding head, 'all I care about, actually, is getting Louis back. So,' with some great effort I hoicked myself from the chair and stood, 'if you don't mind, I should get on. Thanks for the tea,' I finished rather lamely. The phone started to ring, but by the time I found it the caller had hung up.

She stood too.

'Yes, I should go,' she said. I nodded with relief, trying not to throw up as my skull cracked with pain, concentrating hard on a tiny scratch just by her left eye.

'Good luck with everything,' she said formally, and she was almost awkward. She picked up her bag and took out her car-keys, gestured to my head with an elegantly tapering hand. Any minute she'd start pirouetting across the hall, arms in demi-bras. 'You should get that looked at. It must be very painful, no?'

'Yeah, it is. Very bloody painful. I will.'

And then she was gone.

Deb was absolutely horrified at the cut on my head, and whisked me straight to Lewisham A & E, where I was X-rayed and patched up. 'A touch of concussion,' they said to Deb, as if I were a child, 'don't leave her alone for long,' and they gave me painkillers so strong I felt like I was flying.

Back at home, Leigh arrived with the girls and stuck them in the sitting room with *Harry Potter* and some Happy Meals. My sister's standards were slipping: the tracksuits, this fast food, the streaky tan, all meant deep, unspoken stress.

'I'm staying here tonight,' she said, compressing her mouth until it all but disappeared. I was secretly pleased; the kids brought me some kind of comfort as I watched them fighting over their chips.

I went upstairs to change, idly activating the answerphone as I passed it. First Deb's old message from earlier played out, then, halfway up the stairs, someone new, whispering quite frantically. I stopped, and turned, and rushed back down. I pressed replay, and listened again. That mewing I'd heard the other day suddenly became clear. It was seagulls – of course it bloody was. And those frantic tones – my little brother Robbie.

'Where are you, Jess? Answer the phone. I know where Louis is,' he said. 'I know where he is, Jessica.'

CHAPTER TWENTY-FIVE

I was pacing the hall floor when Silver screeched up outside – it'd all gone a bit *Sweeney* suddenly – and I snatched the door wide open, and for a split second, we stared at one another without words. I fought the impulse to fling myself into his arms; I felt like we'd come so far, and finally this was it. He'd tried to protect me, despite the ups and downs, he'd done his very best. But I just said, 'Well come on then,' grabbing my bag, and strode out to the car.

Kelly was sitting in the vehicle behind, and I waved a funny little wave – we were old mates now – and he waved back, and almost smiled. Then I climbed into Silver's front seat. Deb came out before him, and I hoped she'd get in Kelly's car – but she slid in tight behind me, and inwardly I couldn't help but groan.

And my sister was on the doorstep, hugging her youngest daughter to her side, biting her lip and calling out, 'Good luck, we'll be waiting. Call me as soon as you've got news, won't you?' and Silver patted her arm soothingly as he passed; then we were off.

The light was falling as we travelled through the suburbs; the clouds glowering across the motorway said that summer's card was marked. My tummy was jumping, rolling like fighting puppies did. I was rather breathless, and I clutched my inhaler in my pocket; I thought of Louis and I smiled. Then Silver was talking, cutting through my daydreams; wanting to discuss exactly what Robbie had said, again.

'But you just listened to the message, didn't you?' I asked, disconcerted by the interruption, and he nodded his head.

'Yes, but I'm trying to work out if Maxine's with him.'

I shrugged. 'I guess she must be.'

'We had Gorek in for questioning this morning –'

'Brilliant!'

'It wasn't brilliant, Jess. We had to release him because frankly–' He overtook a rusty old Nissan straddling two lanes. 'That's not bloody fit for the road,' he muttered, ever the copper.

'Frankly what?' I was impatient.

'Frankly, there's still nothing to link Gorek to the crime, nothing apart from Maxine.'

'There must be, surely.'

'There isn't.'

'Well, if Gorek's not bloody involved, who is?'

An ominous silence settled throughout the car. My head was really aching still.

'You don't think – you're not imagining that Robbie –' I couldn't quite say it out loud.

'Jess, you're going to have to accept your brother's involved.'

'I'm not. He isn't.'

'Don't be silly. How can he not be? He's just rung you and absolutely incriminated himself.'

'He rang to help,' I objected desperately.

'That's as maybe, but it doesn't change the facts. I mean, who else knew about the location – your holiday home? It's too much of a coincidence.' He turned his sidelights on, glancing down at me. I stared stubbornly away from him.

'Look, I'm sure – I know it's really painful, but it's also unavoidable,' he said.

I was literally lost for words. Deb chimed in softly from the back, placing a warm hand on my shoulder. 'Jessica, it's going to be okay. Let's just try to keep calm, shall we?' I should keep calm, she meant. 'We'll see Robbie soon, and you'll get a chance to talk to him.'

But I felt a constriction in my throat, and though I swallowed painfully several times and gritted my teeth quite hard, a hot tear trickled from my eye, swiftly followed by another. Trading Robbie in for Louis, that's what it amounted to, apparently. Silver didn't speak, but he must have seen the tears that plopped plump onto my jeans. He rested his hand briefly over mine, but I couldn't even savour the warmth. I sat there numbly until Deb shifted slightly in the back, and he took his hand away again.

The car crunched across the gravel and pulled up at the exact spot Silver and I had eaten fish and chips only a few days ago. I was suddenly bowled over by horror at how near I must have been to Louis. And I hadn't even felt it. So much for maternal instinct. The guilt that whacked me now was quite immense.

The car park was much emptier than it had been the time before; evening was drawing in, and the temperature had dropped dramatically in the past few days. The holidays were coming to an end.

Squad cars were parked at random around the garden wall of the cottages, and uniformed coppers milled about looking serious, intent. Police-tape was already flapping in the brisk sea breeze, and a small crowd of locals had gathered, vulture-like, to pick over unfolding events. As I got out of the car, Silver's phone rang and he hung back to take the call. I wanted to ask him why they hadn't looked here before, but Deb was already shepherding me through the crowd.

Glasses stood in the scrubby front garden, slightly apart from a clique of uniforms, smoking a cheroot. He clocked Silver first and raised a hand, then saw me in the crowd. I couldn't read the look that passed over his rather lugubrious face; quickly he ground out the fag and barked an order to a nearby female officer. She walked briskly into the cottage, and my heart leapt. Was she going to fetch my son? I rushed forwards, but as I reached the tape an officious young copper held me back. I was about to barge past anyway when Silver caught up with me, flashed his badge and propelled me into the garden.

And then the policewoman came back out, empty-handed, and muttered something in Glasses' ear, and he stepped forward to greet us, shook Silver's hand. I could hardly curb my impatience, but my heart was in my mouth because something was not right, that was obvious, and I tried to speak but my voice wouldn't come out at first, and when it did it was cracked and hoarse.

'Louis?' I begged. 'Is Louis here?' and I saw Glasses hesitate, and fear engulfed me absolutely; I became a human time-bomb of angst. I was shaking and my knees might not hold me up much longer, they were going to tell me something bad, I could see, and I whispered, 'What is it?' and Silver was staring hard at Glasses, and Deb had her arms round me now.

Then Silver spoke and said, 'It's not Louis, Jess. Louis is not here,' and I didn't know whether to laugh or cry, because at least they hadn't said what I expected, that Louis was dead, his little body stiff inside that small damp house, his arms flung up to save himself. He must still be safe somewhere – but Silver was still speaking, he'd moved in front of me, and he was holding both my hands now, and taking me apart from the group, and Glasses turned like it was all slow motion, and his shoulders slumped, and Silver said,

'It's Robbie, Jess. I'm so sorry. Robbie's dead.'

I started laughing then, because he must be joking, and I said, 'Don't be stupid. Of course he's not dead. He just rang me, didn't he?' and Deb's arm clutched tighter, but I pushed her off and I looked at Silver and said 'Don't lie', but then I saw he wasn't, and I doubled over as if he'd punched me in the stomach, I couldn't breathe, my breath had gone all strained, and then I thought I would be sick. I was panting with the effort not to, and I didn't care who saw. I gripped onto my knees, and took a minute or two to right myself, but eventually I did.

I started to move like I was in a dream; it surely was a dream. I stepped towards the cottage, and I said, 'Where is he? I want to see him,' and Silver said, from somewhere behind me, 'I don't think that's a good idea, do you?' but I shouted at him, 'Just let me see my brother. I want to see my brother, please,' and I stumbled towards the cottage, and so they followed me.

There was noise and voices from inside, and I even heard some laughter – before they saw me in the doorway. How wrong was that – the dead weren't even cold, and people here were laughing?

And there on the floor, on the old floorboards that could have done with a proper good scrub, lay Robbie, and he looked like he was asleep. My little brother sleeping on the floor like he had done when we were kids, just used to curl up anywhere, my Robbie did, and snooze awhile. I stood in the doorway and just looked down at him, through the haze of police photographers and men in those ill-fitting jumpsuits, dusting things; they looked at me and one by one melted away, until it was just him left in the musty room. His legs were bent up towards his chest with one arm flung out, and he looked like he was five.

And I walked towards him slowly, and knelt by him, and I took his head in my hands, and laid it on my knee. I couldn't bear to think that he had died alone, because he'd never liked the dark, my big strong little brother, and I leant down and kissed him on the lips, only they were truly freezing now. I cradled his dark head in my arms, and I whispered, 'Wake up, Rob, it's me.' Only he didn't wake, he didn't stir, he didn't move at all. He was just cold and still.

'Wake up, Robbie, wake up, please,' I said again, more urgently, although I knew he wouldn't now, and dry-eyed I stroked his tousled curls, staring down at him. And it was only then that I saw there was a syringe beside him, and his arm was tied with a tourniquet and was black and bruised, but he sort of looked at peace, I thought, and I laid my head down next to his and eventually the tears came. I cried for my childhood mate who'd gone and left me now; I cried for the baby I used to feed a bottle to, so proud I was, pushing him in the park, though the pushchair was twice my own size. My baby brother who sobbed beneath his bunk-bed when my parents fought, he thought we didn't know; who had run shrieking with me in fun so very near these walls. My little brother with whom I'd shared Mr Whippies for our tea, because our mum was too spaced-out to cook; who'd hidden behind the saggy sofa with me when Tom Baker fought the Cybermen on Sunday afternoons, holding sweaty secret hands, until Leigh caught us and laughed out loud. I held on to him now like I'd never let him go, and I felt a sadness that cracked my very heart, a mourning for all his dreams that came to nothing, for the waste that was my Robbie's life.

Eventually, Silver knelt beside me, and very softly said, 'Come on, Jess, we should let them get on, shouldn't we?' but I didn't want to leave my brother here, where it was so cold and lonely, where the wind was whipping up outside.

'Please,' I whispered, 'I can't bear to leave him,' and Silver said, 'I know. But they need to do their work, and then they'll move him somewhere better, I promise you.'

'Will they take him somewhere light?' I said, utterly forlorn. We both knew that the light was gone forever now for Robbie, but still he nodded and said, 'I expect so.' And so I took my jumper off, and laid Robbie's head back down, laid it on my jumper as gently as I could.

Then I kissed him once again, kissed him for the last time, and let Silver lead me from that dark room, back over to the car. Deb brought me hot sweet tea and wrapped a blanket round my shaking shoulders, and hugged me to keep me warm while I mumbled rubbish.

'I should ring Leigh,' I was just starting to say, when Silver came back again.

'It's gonna be okay, kiddo,' he said, and then the policewoman who'd been with Glasses arrived with a plastic bag. As she gave it to him, I saw her shoot me a look so full of pity it was almost obscene.

'Why didn't you find him before? When we were looking at the lighthouse? I told you about the cottage the other day,' I asked numbly.

'They weren't in this cottage at the time, Jess, I swear. It was searched from top to bottom; they all were. We think they were in another rental property over the road.' Silver pointed at a cluster of buildings behind us. 'We're tracing the owner now. I know you're in shock, Jessica,' he went on, 'but I need you to be strong, all right? Can you cope with helping me some more?' and I nodded dumbly because Louis was still gone, and I still had to get him back, and then Silver pulled something from the clear bag he held. A long, blonde wig. Then something else: a tiny knitted cardigan that had been in Louis's changing bag when he'd disappeared.

'That's Louis's top,' I mumbled through dry lips, and Silver nodded and said, 'We thought as much,' but when I held out my hand for it, he held it back and said, 'I'm sorry, kiddo, we need it for Forensics,' and suddenly I couldn't breathe.

I tried, oh God I tried, I fought for breath but my chest felt like someone had knelt on it, and I spilt my tea all down myself. I scrabbled for my spray but it wouldn't work this time, and I was wheezing like a steam train, and Deb was trying to help me, but I still couldn't breathe, someone was smothering me, squeezing all the air out, and then just for a second it all went black.

For the second time that day I couldn't think where the hell I was, and when I tried to sit upright the oxygen mask across my face held me back. A paramedic with a kind, bovine face leant over me and smiled at me and said, 'Don't panic, love. You're in the ambulance with me.' He removed the mask and said, 'Good to see you back, girlie. How're you feeling now?' and Deb was suddenly there, taking my hand. And then I remembered that Robbie was dead, like a huge cosh round my head again.

The paramedic checked me over, and said he

thought I'd be okay, and Deb could take me home again. But I didn't want to go to my empty house, not while Louis was still gone, not while he might be so near. Not with – I balked at the thought. Not with Robbie lying alone in some dingy mortuary down here. So Deb went off, and came back to say they'd take me to the hotel where I'd stayed the other night. She said Leigh had been informed about Robbie's death; a colleague had been round to see her and then Deb had spoken to Leigh on the phone, and she was going to let my poor mum know. My mum. I couldn't even bear to imagine her pain.

At the hotel, Deb ran me a hot bath. I tried to sneak a beer out of the rattling old minibar while she ordered us some sandwiches but Deb wouldn't let me drink it; she thought it'd make me ill on top of the painkillers I'd been given. So I lay in the bath, a bath so hot it scalded me, as if it would purge me somehow, strip me of my sorrow; and all I thought about was Robbie. My eyes were gritty and unseeing now above the steam; and what I felt was guilt. The most terrible, gut-wrenching remorse and guilt.

When I finally clambered out of the water, so red I looked like I'd been flayed alive, I felt sick to my stomach with grief – and I was far too scared to go to bed. How could I ever sleep again; I'd just keep seeing Robbie lying in the dark, or Louis hidden in some cupboard. So Deb stayed with me, and we sat together on the double bed and drank more tea, and watched some rubbish TV for a while. And finally I rang Leigh. I'd put it off because I couldn't bear to say the words, to hear them out loud. She was sleepless too, chain-smoking, frigid with shock at first, just like I'd known she would be. She'd spoken to my mum.

'She's coming back with George. She's – well, it's not worth you trying to talk to her now, Jess, anyway. You've got enough on your plate. She's in bits. At least –' Leigh's voice faltered and I knew she was trying to hold back her tears.

'At least what?'

'At least', her lighter clicked again, 'he might be at peace now.' She took a deep and steadying draw in. 'Christ, Jess. I can't believe how much he fucked it up.'

'Leave it, Leigh, for now – can you?'

'But –'

'But what?'

'I feel so bloody guilty, Jess,' she whispered, and I heard her voice break.

'I know what you mean,' I said. And then there was a pause, until she cleared her throat. 'And Louis?'

I took a sip of my tea; I steadied myself. 'I dunno. Silver's out there still, they're all out there looking for him. Did Deb tell you, they found his cardigan?'

'Yes, thank God. So they know he's near at least.'

'Or –' My throat constricted.

'What, Jess?'

'Or at least, he was near. Maxine's completely vanished.'

'Bloody bitch.' Then, in a small voice, she said, 'I wanted to tell you something. I did try the other day. It was – I took Maxine down there, you know.'

I didn't understand. 'What? Down where?'

'Down to Birling Gap. A few weeks ago, you remember, when you went to have your hair done. When I took the kids and Maxine to the seaside for the day.'

I thought of all the sand rattling round the baby bag at the Tate. 'Oh, I see. Oh God, Leigh. Do you think she was planning it then?'

'I don't know, babe. Christ, something else for me to feel shit about.'

'Don't be stupid. If it hadn't been here, it'd have been somewhere else.'

'Yeah. Suppose. I've told DI Silver anyway.'

Another pause. I couldn't bear to hang up. 'Oh God, Leigh. I can't get Robbie out of my head. I'm never going to get him out of my head.'

'I know, babe. But you've got to keep on being strong, for Louis's sake. Not long now, I'm sure of it. Just think of that.'

There was silence on the line then, but it was a nice kind of quiet. Eventually we said goodbye. I had to face my demons some time.

'After all,' I said to Deb, 'if I'm getting Louis back soon, I'll need my sleep.'

She tried to match my false smile, but I felt the concern behind the kindly façade. She hugged me quickly. 'Try and get a good night's sleep.'

I grimaced.

'Just try. I'll see you in the morning. Call me if you need me, though.'

'Thank you.'

And so eventually I lay on my bed, in the dark, with

372

just my headache for company. Through the open curtains I watched some little lights that flickered quite frantically out at sea, up and down they went, bouncing up and down. A storm was surely brewing. I thought of Robbie and my stomach twisted; of how cold he'd felt, and an awful pain gripped my heart. I should have known, I should have seen. I could have saved my brother. I'd been so caught up with Louis, I'd let poor Robbie down. Grief roared in my ears until I was on the verge of screaming to drown the sound – and then, suddenly, there was a gentle tap on the door.

Silver stood there, silhouetted, yawning.

'I just came to see if you were all right.' His short hair was ruffled. 'Can I come in for a sec?' he said, but he was already in by now. I went back and lay on the bed; I didn't speak because I didn't know what to say. He hovered by my feet.

'We're getting closer, Jess, I swear,' and I turned over so he couldn't see my face. Slowly, he took his shoes off and, without speaking, he lay down on the bed. He was tentative; he was fully clothed. We lay there side by side, and I stared at an invisible ceiling with hot, dry eyes, tensing my body against his anticipated touch, a touch that in truth I really longed for; and then, finally, he moved. He gathered me into his arms, and I was still as stiff as an ironing-board, considered turning away, but in the end I didn't. Couldn't. Couldn't turn away from him. Was I betraying my loved ones – Louis, Robbie, Mickey? I didn't know – I didn't care any more. I just knew it felt curiously right to be lying here with Silver.

Spindly rain began to lash the windows, and gradually I gave in, muscle by sore muscle, and gently he just held me until I'd relaxed a bit. I buried my face in his shirt, which smelt faintly of lemons, and tried to close my eyes, to block out the ghosts that whispered through my brain.

'I should have helped him, Silver. I could have done,' I said, and then the tears came. 'I can't believe he's gone.'

Silver murmured 'Shhh' into my hair, until I'd sobbed myself to sleep.

CHAPTER TWENTY-SIX

My mobile was ringing. My eyes seemed to be glued tight shut, and I knocked the phone to the floor in my effort to reach it. When I answered and said 'Hello', it was Mickey's voice that replied. I sat up fast, which made my head thud painfully, and I looked around with guilt, but Silver was long gone, and I was apparently alone.

'Where are you?' I asked, still groggy with sleep. I wondered what the time was. A weak sun trickled through the unveiled windows, saturating the clock's digital display so I couldn't read it. It looked like dawn had already been.

'At home. Where are you? Are you all right? They told me – I heard about your brother. I'm so sorry, Jessica.'

It was like a huge hoof to my stomach, like finding out again that he was dead. In these past two weeks, each time I fell asleep and woke I had to come to terms with a hideous reality once more. Now Robbie was gone too.

'Thank you,' I said numbly. 'What time is it?'

'About eight, I think.'

'Where were you, Mickey? You should still be in hospital. I was really worried.'

'I'm sorry, Jessica. I don't know what happened – I lost it there for a while, I guess. I panicked.'

'I'll say. They found Louis's jumper you know. Where – where Robbie was.'

'I know. I spoke to your man there – to DI Silver – this morning.'

My face in the mirror opposite was a sight. 'Oh,' I said. 'Did you? When?' I tried for innocence. *Your man there.* I was innocent, of course.

'About half an hour ago. He said they're getting nearer. I'm coming down.'

Why did that make me feel so strange?

'Do you think you should?' I said. 'Have you been checked out? You're still meant to be in recovery, aren't you?'

'And aren't you, my girl? Honestly,' there was a pause; I heard something being poured, a drink, 'we're a right old pair, are we not?'

Not. Not really a pair, no. Not now.

'Yes,' I said dully. 'A right old pair.' Then I thought of Louis, and a bubble of anticipation swelled up inside. 'Oh, Mickey,' I said, and I got out of bed. I forgot my anxieties about my marriage. I even forgot Robbie for a minute. 'I've got a feeling this is it. We're going to get our Louis back today, I know we are.'

'I hope you're right.' His tone was fierce, vehement even. 'I do know – I know how much it's hurt you,

Jessica. Are you sure you're all right? I'm sorry you've been so – well, left so alone to cope. I'll be there soon.'

'Oh yes,' I said, 'I'll be fine, I expect. Call me when you're near, okay?' Then I thought of something else, and I said, 'Mickey.'

'What?'

'I'm sorry that –'

'You're sorry what?'

'I'm sorry if it was Robbie. That took him. I didn't want to believe it, but I guess – well, you know.'

'Yes, I know.'

'It makes me feel – sort of, responsible somehow.'

He laughed dryly. 'I don't think that for a minute, right?'

'Right,' I said. I hung up, and then I rang Silver to find out what to do. I was a little tongue-tied.

'Jess,' he said, and he was distracted, 'I can't talk now. We've had a positive sighting. I'll send a car.' And then he was gone. The sea outside the window was white-peaked and rough, the clouds that scudded past were foreboding. I got dressed, sick with excitement and terror. I clutched my breasts and wondered whether milk ever started again, and in response I felt a dull deep tingle.

'Louis,' I whispered, and I stared at the photo I carried in my purse. I stroked his tiny face. 'I'm coming, baby. Mummy'll be there soon.'

Deb and I were sitting in the back of an unmarked car that was going much too fast, even by my desperate standards. We'd travelled across the bosomy South

Downs, parched and brown from the long, hot summer, then trailed down the narrow coast road behind dawdling tourists and armies of OAPs until our driver stuck a siren on the roof and overtook on every blind bend until we arrived in the dump called Newhaven. We swung by the rundown ferry-port, taking such a sharp right that Deb and I banged heads as we went sprawling across the back seat.

'We'd like to get there in one piece please,' Deb snapped at the driver, hauling herself up with dignity.

He just laughed, and put his foot down. 'Two pieces, don't you mean? Sorry, girls.' He didn't look the least bit contrite. 'Orders from the boss, get you there quick smart.'

'Not to kill us, were they, those orders?' Deb retorted, but he just smirked. Halfway up a narrow street that led to the sea, we slowed at a roadblock, and I sighed with silent relief. The policewoman who'd brought me those pants the other night leant down to the driver. 'You'd better park up, Frank,' she said. 'No cars any further.'

At the point where a terrace of scruffy houses ended, a gaggle of plain-clothed coppers loitered, looking uneasy, muttering into radios. In the distance, bright but shabby fishing boats bobbed in the water, old nets and pots stacked neatly along a dilapidated jetty. Rusting anchors stained the concrete where they lay, and the air above was full of gulls, crying tragically. They made me think of Robbie; coupled with the over-powering stench of seaweed and rotting fish, my stomach lurched queasily.

I spotted Silver behind a small group of men, chewing his ubiquitous gum, talking to a broad-shouldered, grey-haired man in a long blue coat. Squat and bulldog-like he was, this bloke, and from the way he held himself I guessed he was Silver's boss. Despite their distance, the tension in both men was obvious from where I stood. I put my hand up to wave – and then my heart stopped. A team of armed police marksmen trotted past, up to some oil-drums where they took cover, guns relaxed across their shoulders, slung idly in holsters, laughing and joking like it was business as usual.

Deb clocked my face, and took me by the arm. 'I think we should wait here,' she said, but I was frightened now, more frightened than I'd been this entire bloody time, all these fourteen days.

'What the bloody hell's going on now, Deb?' I demanded. Without waiting for her answer, I marched round the marksmen to where Silver stood.

'Jess,' he said, and he didn't smile. He seemed anxious, really tense.

'What's happening, Silver? Why all these guns?'

'Precautionary, love,' said the other man, 'just a precaution at this stage.' He stuck his hand out, little grey hairs sprouting below each knuckle.

'Jessica Finnegan, DCI Malloy.' Silver made the cursory introduction.

'Hello,' I said politely.

'I'm sorry about your brother, love,' said Malloy gruffly, 'very sorry.' For a moment our eyes locked. Very bright eyes, they were, boring into me, and it seemed like his sentiment was real. And then Silver crumpled his drink can in his hand, and cleared his throat, rather awkwardly.

'I think you should know, Jess, the tox screen for Robbie just came back. It looks a bit – odd.'

'Odd?' I repeated numbly.

Malloy glanced at Silver.

'Yeah – odd. Heroin levels were enough to kill an elephant. Robbie was a regular user, wasn't he?'

I shrugged. 'I don't know really. He hasn't –' I took a breath '– he wasn't exactly being straight with me, recently.'

'I know, and I'm sorry to ask. But the amount he had in his system would suggest he either had a serious death-wish, or –'

'Or what?'

I watched one of the marksmen, a young bloke whose ears stuck out at funny angles beneath his cap, making a roll-up from his packet of tobacco. He held his green Rizla packet between his teeth, laughing at something a colleague had just said. It made me think of Robbie. It made me think of –

Suddenly their radios crackled into life, and I lost both men's attention. The marksmen were straightening up, chucking fags down, pulling hats back on.

I repeated myself frantically. 'What's going on, Silver?'

'We've had various reports from local residents: a woman and a baby were seen boarding a boat at the harbour here in the early hours. These boats aren't usually inhabited; the harbour-permits are strictly for fishing. We don't think anyone's disembarked again; they certainly haven't sailed because it's been so stormy. Now there's a gale-force warning.'

'Maxine?' I asked Silver. Adrenaline surged through me.

He shrugged. 'We don't know yet, but it'd make sense. Blonde, apparently, and tall.'

And then I was gripped by panic. A sense of … impending doom, perhaps.

'Silver, the guns –'

'Just a precaution, Jess, like we said.'

'But I really don't want guns around my baby. It's not *Miami Vice* or something you know.' An unbidden image flickered through my head; a bullet slicing straight through Louis's heart, him floppy and doll-like in my arms, cold like Robbie had been yesterday. Me screaming like I'd never stop. I clapped a hand to my mouth. Silver looked down at me, took a small step closer.

'Just keep calm, Jess. It'll be all right.'

But I didn't believe him and he knew it.

'I'm going to try to get onto the boat in a minute. I won't let anything bad happen, I swear.' He grasped my hand and squeezed it tight, so tight the bones cracked painfully. Then Glasses made his way towards us, followed by a man in some kind of nautical uniform.

'Bet they're feeling seasick now. Don't think that fucking boat looks seaworthy myself,' remarked Glasses cheerfully, pulling his cheroots from his pocket. Then he noticed me. If he rued his pessimism, he didn't show it. 'Oh – hello.'

I didn't even attempt a smile. A dull drone in the background was getting louder; and then, between the houses and the seawall, a speedboat came in sight, a big, expensive-looking beast, gleaming cabin perched on top. DCI Malloy had his binoculars out; the boat was heading into shore.

The harbourmaster frowned officiously. 'Don't know who that'd be. You need a special permit to moor here, you know.'

Malloy looked at Silver and jerked his head. 'You'd better get a move on, Joe. We haven't got time to waste.'

And so we all watched quite helplessly as Silver detached himself from the hidden group, and made his way down to the sea. I'd never noticed what a lolloping gait he had, and I wanted to shout 'Good luck, good luck' but my mouth felt like it was full of feathers, full of sawdust now, and anyway I knew I must keep quiet. And for the first time in my life, I wished I smoked, just to have something in my hands, some-thing to do. Instead I sought my inhaler out and took a squirt, and I felt Deb eyeing me warily. She took my arm and held it protectively, almost possessively, like your best mate does at school.

We were all desperately spying through any gaps we could find. The speedboat had cut its engine now, and was throwing down its anchor, still out to sea. And then all eyes were drawn to a figure, a woman, who staggered out onto the deck of a faded green boat called *Miranda Jane*. The woman waved at the other boat with obvious relief. A mutter went through the police, and Malloy swiftly switched his gaze to her. She was wearing some sort of hooded sweatshirt, the hood snugly up against the wind, and I couldn't see her face from where I stood – but in her arms she carried something carefully, and my heart soared right up to the moody sky. Louis! Then she turned slightly, and I saw it wasn't him at all; just a heavy bag that she was clutching in her arms.

And then Silver reached the jetty and called out to her, and she jumped and dropped the bag. She fell against the boat's side and her hood slipped down as she turned, and I saw it was Maxine. I took an involuntary step forward, but Deb was quicker, and held me back.

'Maxine Dufrais, sir,' Deb muttered to her boss, who nodded curtly. And Silver was talking to her, but all we heard was the sharp cries of mewling gulls, and the distant slap of the ever-roughening sea against the wall, against the boats. And as we watched, Maxine looked around quite desperately, wondering where to go. Nowhere, was the answer – there wasn't anywhere to run – but I couldn't see how Silver could get onto the boat unless she let him up. We could see he was trying to reason with her; a lot of gesticulating was going on, and occasionally she looked towards the small gangplank, raised up on the deck.

'Where's Louis? Just get Louis out, please God,' I was muttering aloud, and Deb took my hand and squeezed it, and then Maxine was peering out to sea, and moving round the deck. A burly figure on the other boat waved at her, almost carefree he seemed, whoever this man was.

And now Silver was walking away, then he turned back to her and said something else, and she was obviously crying now, pleading with him frenziedly, starting to look hysterical as she saw she had no way out. She paced back and forth across the tiny deck as the wind whipped up higher, chopping the water even more now; and she stumbled badly as the boat lurched once more.

The man on the speedboat, almost just a little matchstick man from where we stood, he was waving and gesturing more frantically too.

'What's the silly bugger doing?' grunted Malloy, training his binoculars on the man. 'He don't seem to have a Scooby that he's in big trouble if the baby's with the blonde.'

And then, suddenly, all hell broke loose. Maxine turned from Silver and made a dash for it; she went diving awkwardly into the sea. As one, we all surged forwards. And, almost at the same time, Silver ran the other way and he grabbed a tatty plank lying between the lobster pots, and hurled it up to the boat. By some feat of genius, God knew how, he was up that precarious walkway, onto the deck. We couldn't see where Maxine was now, she'd gone over the side away from us so she was hidden from the shore, and I was thinking, 'This is it, thank God, this is it,' and I broke into a run. I skirted the lumbering Malloy and dapper Glasses and left Deb behind, falling over my own feet, and I went down once into the grit, but got up again; my hand was bleeding now but I didn't care because Louis must be in my sights –

And then Silver was backing down the deck, and

there was someone else there on the boat. A figure standing just inside the cabin, so I couldn't quite make them out. And Silver put his arms up in a sort of conciliatory way, and I realised, with my heart almost in my mouth, that the figure was pointing what could only be a gun, straight at Silver's chest.

'Stay there, Jess,' he shouted, and I skidded to a halt at the foot of the plank. And the figure, who was wearing some sort of hooded cagoule, laughed and shouted back. And the tobacco and the mentions of seasickness, those little signs, those clues that had so eluded me, all spun together, came together in that one moment – and now finally I knew it. Who it was who'd stolen my son. So desperate for a baby she'd do anything – even sail right out to sea with him. I pictured her face as she opened the door of my sitting room and saw me sobbing on the floor above my bawling baby, and I remembered the fear that had crossed those benign features. It had been followed swiftly by something else, something fleeting that I'd shut out – but nevertheless it had been there. Anger. No, not even that. Jealousy.

'Freddie,' I gasped, but no one else could hear. The figure was talking again now, waving the gun at Silver.

'No, tell her to come here. The rest, they can stop right where they are,' and I felt the pack behind me slow down and stop, and I thought, I know that voice, and then she stepped outside onto the deck and I realised I'd been wrong. This woman moved elegantly, was much too slight of build. She wasn't tall enough. It wasn't Freddie at all...

'Is Louis there? Have you got my son?' I shouted, and my voice went kind of wobbly. How could I have been so wrong? It was my nemesis who'd taken Louis – of course it was. My rival in love and luck – the indomitable Agnes.

'Maybe,' she sneered, without looking at me. Her gaze was fixed on Silver, his gaze was on the gun. And then there was a terrible commotion in the water, and I could see Silver and Agnes both look down into the sea. The man on the speedboat was yelling now; I still wasn't near enough to hear his words but I realised he was pointing frantically at the water, and Silver said to Agnes very calmly, 'Let me just throw her the lifebelt, Agnes, okay?' and Agnes curled her lip disdainfully, and said, 'If she's so stupid as to jump, she should pay the price, I think.'

Silver kept trying to cajole her, but she ignored him. He glanced at me, and I could have sworn he winked, just once, and then suddenly he dived into the sea.

'For Christ's sake, Silver,' I yelled, but it was too late. Now he'd also vanished from my view. And Agnes trained the gun at me, and said icily, 'If you ever want to see your son again, come here,' and so I obeyed. I glanced down towards the road, and I saw the little huddle of coppers frozen there. Deb looked like she was going to cry. I turned my back on them, and walked the gangplank to my fate.

I didn't care if she shot me dead; I didn't care at all right then. I didn't care about anything but seeing that Louis was still alive. The boat creaked and swung in

386

the wind, and I tensed my feet against the tarry deck, and sought my sea-legs. The gulls were so bloody loud, it was almost impossible to hear much else, but I strained and strained to listen for my Louis.

'Have you got him? Is he here?' I demanded, as I faced her on the deck now. She looked terrible; her hair frizzed out beneath her cagoule hood, her face all smeared with engine-oil. Worse, a tic was going in her cheek, jumping up and down it was, uncontrollably. The gun she held was big and bulky, not an ordinary gun, but one to shoot distress flares from, I guessed.

'Have you got my son?' I asked again, a little louder now, and she shrugged almost nonchalantly, though defiance blazed in her flinty eyes.

'Maybe, maybe not.'

'For Christ's sake, Agnes, stop playing silly-buggers. There's no way out of this, you know.'

Perhaps I should have been more scared; rationally, I'm sure I should, as she stood there so deranged, cocking some old gun at me like she was Clint Eastwood. But an amazing sense of calm suddenly suffused me; the knowledge that I'd die gladly for my son – take any punishment I must. My heart was going so damn fast it almost hurt, but I could sense that Louis was near, I knew he was, and every maternal instinct I'd ever felt rang its bell; kept on ringing till I was almost deafened.

She kept the gun pointed at me, but her hands were shaking now and it seemed to weigh her down. Her face and body spoke of utter exhaustion and defeat. It had begun to rain; a thin harsh drizzle stung my face, and I almost savoured getting wet.

387

'Why did you do it, Agnes?' I asked quietly, and I took a little step towards her.

'Why not?'

'That's a bollocks answer, and you know it.'

'Because, okay? Why should I explain to you?' and she was spitting venom now, pushing her hood back, the rain drenching her angular face. I sensed an internal battle in her head, but she looked me squarely in the eye. 'Because you had it all, and I had nothing any more, okay? Because I wanted Mickey's baby and I wasn't – I couldn't do it.'

'Why?' I scoffed. 'Because you didn't want to give up your designer lifestyle?'

She looked at me like I was mad, drew herself up. 'What are you talking about? I would have given anything to have his child.'

'Well, why didn't you then?'

'Because I couldn't.' Her lip curled. 'Surely he told you that?'

I thought back, my mind scrambling over the obstacle course of recent events. 'No. He said you didn't want to.'

She looked like she was going to cry. She straightened up the gun. 'He never said that, you liar. He never would have said that.'

I didn't like the steady gun, and the look on her face was quite mad now. 'No, all right, he didn't say exactly that,' I agreed quickly.

'I wanted it more than I've ever wanted anything in my life. But I couldn't do it. I was – unwell.'

'Unwell?' I shook my head uncomprehendingly.

'We tried for years. I couldn't. In the end, I had to – ' she glared at me '– I had an operation.'

I remembered the folder in the attic. The Harley Street doctor. The advice on recuperation after major surgery. The penny finally dropped.

'I had a hysterectomy. So that was that. You see. Nothing. No child of my own. Impossible.'

'But,' I tried to gather my thoughts, 'Mickey said that you – you *wouldn't* give him kids.'

I thought back to that horrible scene in the Soho restaurant and my heart sank. I realised it was only how I'd read his words, not what he'd actually said. I saw his angry face, unusually flushed, his dark eyes snapping with pain, his long fingers crumbling the bread-roll into a thousand tiny crumbs.

'And you said they – weren't your thing. You told me that yourself,' I persisted, but I was wincing at my naivety now. 'When I met you at the hotel.'

'Why should I tell you the truth? I hated you. Why would I tell my enemy the thing I wanted most?' She dashed back rain – or tears, I couldn't tell – with the back of her hand, and I felt a sudden and unexpected sorrow for her. Poor, perfect Agnes, who had everything money could buy and more, defeated by the one thing she desired more than life itself. My anger finally dissipated.

'But this isn't the right way to get a child,' I said, and I hoped desperately that I sounded soothing. 'It's mad, Agnes. It was hardly your only option, surely? I mean – you didn't have to do this – this stupid thing, did you?'

'But I didn't want *a* child. Not any child. I wanted Mickey's baby – and that was all.'

'Yes, okay. I understand it must have been horrible for you.'

'You don't understand. You became pregnant without even trying – apparently.' Her tragic eyes flooded with tears again.

'Okay, you're right.' Instinctively, I put my hands out, trying to placate her. 'But I can sympathise.'

'I don't want your sympathy. You know, I'd worked so hard to make everything so perfect, but it wasn't. Because in the end, well – I knew Mickey, you see. Oh God, you have no idea how well I know that man.' She pushed her hair out of her face, and I saw that her nails were chewed down to the quick now. The gun-hand was wavering again, tired and unsure. 'Mickey would never take another man's child into his house. He's not like that, you must know that yourself. He is too – proud.'

My frown deepened. 'I suppose I don't know really. I guess he might be.'

'Well, I did know. By getting pregnant, you gave him the thing he craved. That I craved. The thing I could never manage. He wouldn't even discuss adoption, you know.'

'You had his love,' I said quietly, and it was true. Mickey had never loved me like he'd loved her. I felt it in my bones; I'd known it from the start. Right in the very heart of me, I'd recognised the truth – and chosen to ignore it. He would never love me like he loved this woman, this crazy, maddened woman.

'But I didn't think that I could keep it,' she said, and she was crying properly now. 'I couldn't keep his love, not on my own. It was tearing us apart. I had to give him more. He needed his own family. He was always searching to replace his little brother.'

I thought of my own little brother. Had she –

Agnes went on. 'It ruined us in the end. The emptiness. Our house; it was so empty.'

'So you thought you'd just take mine? *My* family.'

She was racked with sobs, shaking, the hair whipping round her face. Slowly I put my hand to my bruised head.

'Did you hit me, Agnes? Was that you?'

'I am sorry. I needed Louis's passport; Maxine couldn't find it when she looked. I thought it must be in the house. And then I was worried how much I'd hurt you. I didn't mean to do it so hard, I just panicked when I heard you.'

'So you came back?'

'So I came back. You know, I didn't understand real love until I had your Louis,' she whispered, and I craned a little nearer so I could hear above the wind, above the gulls. The boat pitched sickeningly, pushing us closer together.

'I could only imagine it,' and she looked me in the eye, above the quaking gun. 'If I'd realised how much anyone could love a baby, I don't think I could have done it. I didn't know how much it would hurt you, Jessica, taking your child.'

And I realised that she meant she loved my son, and for one strange out-of-body moment I was almost glad she'd had the chance to. And then I heard a small cry, and I tensed up; for a tiny second I thought my ears were playing tricks, I thought it was another needy gull. But there it was again, and my heart literally flooded with joy. It had to be my son. Every tiny hair I owned stood up on end.

'So,' and I took a final minute step; I couldn't get much nearer without swallowing the gun, 'can I have him back now, please? Can I have my baby back?'

Her face quite literally collapsed – quite ravaged, it became. I'd never seen such desperation in my life; I don't want to see it again. Her beautiful features were etched with grief so pure, and her eyes went sort of blank, emptying themselves suddenly of life. It was like a cloud had passed before the sun, draining her of light and being. Her soul was being sucked out as I watched. We stood there on that creaking deck for what seemed like an eternity, and I felt her frantically calculate. I saw her lose all hope, grow old before my eyes, like a crumpled shadow of her former self.

And I was just debating grabbing the gun, and preparing myself to do it – when suddenly she found strength from somewhere deep, and she gathered it all up. She levelled the gun right at my head, and her hands, I saw they weren't shaking any more.

'So, let's see now,' she said, and she seemed very calm. She took a step towards me; my heart was about to bang right through my aching chest. 'Should it be you or me then?'

Don't kill me before I see my son once more, I prayed, that's all I ask. I tried to speak but I was truly terrified, frightened to my very core and I found my voice had shrunk to nothing. Feverishly I tried to think of something – anything – conciliatory to say, but my mind was blank – and then it was too late.

'Who gets the baby, hey, Jessica? Who should have him now?' She pushed her hair out of her eyes with one free hand, the other still trained at me. 'He needs you, I see that now – much more than he needs me. More even than I need him,' she said.

And then very fast and with such elegance, she pointed the gun back towards herself, slipped it in her mouth before I knew what she was doing, and I shouted 'Agnes', but before I could move to stop her, before I could even look away, she blew her beautiful tortured brains out.

CHAPTER TWENTY-SEVEN

Louis was sleeping as I bent to pick him up. There was a huge commotion outside, but still he slept, just like a baby, as they say.

Malloy and his team were on the deck in seconds, but Agnes was already gone; there was nothing anyone could do for her. And I trod carefully round her, concentrating on what came next, stepping down into the cabin, and there was my little baby, sleeping on a stained old camp-bed, beneath a cashmere blanket.

I was about to scoop him up, but first I stared at him and I couldn't quite believe his beauty, his perfection. One chubby hand was flung behind his head, and in his sleep he made little sucking motions with his rosebud mouth, and I wanted to stroke the tiny curve of his top lip, just where the pink met the pale of his creamy skin, and I wanted to hold him to me so tight that he'd become part of me again, but I didn't. I just stared and stared at him, because I couldn't believe he was mine.

And then the boat jerked again, and I could hear

the water slapping harder against the bow, the wind wasn't dropping and I knew it was time to get him safely out of here. Gingerly I lifted him, and he muttered, and at last he woke. His gold-tipped lashes fluttered against his fat cheeks and then his dark eyes opened and I could have sworn he smiled at me like he knew I was his mother. He was so warm and solid and he smelt of milk. He rested his heavy little head on my shoulder, all feathery, still half-asleep he was, and I breathed him in. I stuck my face into the curve of his smooth neck, and I absorbed him through my pores. I'd got my son again, and that was all that mattered.

By the time I got back up on deck, they'd covered Agnes up. On the quayside Deb was smiling, fit to burst, as she helped me down the plank that had finally been secured. She chucked Louis under the chin like some fond aunt, and I smiled and smiled at her, at him, I held him in my arms like some precious china doll, and I was looking round for Silver; I wanted to show Louis to my new friend Silver.

But I couldn't see him, though I kept looking all the time, and eventually I began to panic. I clutched Louis a little tighter, and then I spotted a dripping, trembling Maxine sitting on an ambulance step, wrapped up in blankets. As if it were a dream, I saw Egg-belly handcuff her, and the man who was on the speedboat was talking French very fast and loud to him. The mild-mannered policeman just looked back at him, bemused, and I heard her say 'Papa' imploringly, over and again, and I wondered if the poor man understood just what his daughter had involved him in. But I found I couldn't bear to look at her. I turned away as her betrayal smacked me between the eyes, and I hunted for Silver in the throng. Oh God. What if he'd drowned?

And then a car sped down the road just as I spotted a dark-haired figure who was also sopping wet, rubbing his short hair with a pathetically small towel, his fine suit all untucked and ruined, seaweed like boiled spinach draped around his collar. Barefoot. Nice feet, I thought disjointedly; they were long and thin and handsome. I felt a rush of relief so huge it almost bowed my knees, and I moved towards him smiling, and he was smiling back and unbuttoning his soggy shirt and he said, 'So this is the famous Louis, eh? Suits you, Jess, a baby on your hip,' and I clutched my son tighter and said, 'Thanks very much for abandoning me out there,' and I felt simultaneously cross and shy and so happy I couldn't stop the smiles.

Silver removed a bit of seaweed from his cuff and said, 'You had ten marksmen backing you, kiddo, guns all trained on Agnes. Anyway, I knew you could handle her,' and I didn't know whether to punch him for being so bloody complacent about my life, or kiss him for just being alive – but before I could decide, suddenly there was Mickey coming full-tilt from the car; he was running up towards us and he reached me and Louis and drew us clumsily into his arms.

I knew I should be happy that my family was back together, but over Mickey's shoulder I kept staring at Silver. And he stared back, just for a minute, and we locked eyes, and then Silver stooped a bit, and fished in his pocket for his gum, but of course it was sodden too. So he chucked it into the gutter, and this time I knew he winked. Then he turned away, and I closed my eyes and succumbed to Mickey's hug. I pushed the sort-of-bereft feeling down, and just thanked God for my Louis.

It was me who had to tell Mickey that Agnes was dead. I don't know what I expected really, but he took it stoically. At first he kept saying, 'I never realised she was so desperate,' but after a while he didn't mention his ex-wife again.

There were lots of unanswered questions, of course, now Agnes was gone. In custody, Maxine had apparently tipped over into complete hysteria, and was little help to the police. I spent the next few days in a complete haze of unadulterated love for my baby son, mixed with utter grief for my brother – and in a strange way for Agnes too. I had never warmed to her, it was true, even before I knew what she'd done, but I felt sorrow for the lengths her desperation had driven her to. I found I could forgive her, could be benevolent, now I had my Louis back.

Leigh had opened Louis's room up again, and let in all the light. She'd thrown back all the windows, pulled up the blinds and put flowers everywhere. And so I retreated to the old rocking-chair in Louis's room and licked my wounds, both physical and mental, and held on to my son. Though it did have to be said that pretty soon he was bored of all the clutching, and the crooned inanities. He began to wriggle, trying to get down, to explore his old world on his own.

And though I searched intently for the slightest scratch or bruise on his plump and downy skin, there was little doubt he'd been treated properly. Agnes had taken good care of him: the best, perhaps? Louis was wearing expensive new clothes when I got him back; the stripy cashmere blanket I'd found him under even had his initials embroidered in gold thread, I noticed – before throwing it in the bin. He seemed fatter than when I'd last seen him, his little tummy gently rounded above his nappy like a miniature beer-belly. I imagined Agnes carefully ordering things for him online; pretending he was her own. I saw her feeding him, looking down at him with painful, aching love while he guzzled a bottle in their hiding place. Unable to show him off as her own, hidden away, her love had been, through desperate necessity, hidden right away. Overwrought, I found myself sobbing in the bath one evening at the thought of poor wretched Agnes; my own agony distilled by time.

For a while the press turned up outside again, looking for an angle, but eventually they tired of us and disappeared to the next tragedy. My mum and George flew into London the day after we got home, but they went to stay with Leigh. Robbie's funeral would take place when the police released his body. I spoke to my mum on the phone; I promised to visit soon. Her lack of support had affected me more deeply than I'd realised – and I felt the yearning void between us that meant she didn't mind not seeing me yet. I had to prepare myself properly for my mother's loss; I couldn't quite envisage her pain. It was too near what

I'd dreaded, what I'd just about staved off for those two weeks.

Silver turned up unannounced one cool September evening. I was upstairs putting Louis to bed when he arrived, and Mickey let him in. By the time I came down, the two men had sat themselves as far apart as they could politely manage; my husband had found his offer of a celebratory drink refused, of course. Mickey himself swirled a glass of heavy golden scotch in his hand as I wandered into the room without realising who else was there.

'So, when did the girl get involved?' Mickey was asking, leaning back to turn Puccini down with some reluctance. Silver's unexpected presence made me feel quite flustered, unable to meet his eye as I grinned hello at him. I crossed the room as casually as I could. Some white roses Mickey had bought me when we'd all come home were losing their petals in a mini-snow-storm, and I busied myself with collecting them, my back towards both men.

'Sit down, Jessica, will you,' Mickey said, and automatically I obeyed, hovering on the edge of the sofa near my husband.

'We're not absolutely sure to be honest, Mr Finnegan. It's proving hard to get a straight answer from Maxine, especially since her English seems to have abandoned her entirely since her arrest.' Silver took a gulp of his orange juice. 'One thing's for sure, though. Her poor old dad didn't seem to have a clue what was going on. Seems Agnes had splashed out some unholy amount to hire the speedboat, and for him to bring it over to Newhaven. What's most difficult –' he finished the drink and shoved it on the coffee table, where it left a big wet mark. I suppressed a smile as Mickey flinched. 'Yeah, what's most difficult,' Silver went on, apparently oblivious, 'is the Robbie scenario, I'm afraid, Jess.'

Did Mickey turn his head slightly at the small intimacy of my name? Silver fished gum out of his pocket, offered it around. Mickey refused it, hardly able to hide his disapproval.

'Yes, please.' I felt a surge of loyalty for the predictable Silver. My voice seemed rather loud. 'What do you mean about Robbie?'

He handed me the packet, and his fingers grazed my hand. I shot back on the sofa.

'It's proving very difficult for pathology to tell if he administered that dose of heroin himself. There's no doubt, like we said, that the levels were inordinately high. There's also little doubt that he could have injected himself. But', he shrugged very slightly, 'there was definitely something odd about the way he was lying when he was found. Awkward. Like he'd almost been placed there. And the huge dose seemed strange – unless he was definitely suicidal. Do you think he was, Jessica?'

He looked at me, very direct, and I saw the little yellow flecks in his hazel eyes. 'I don't know, Silver. It's so hard to say.' I thought of Robbie's recent behaviour. 'There was no doubt he was in a bit of a mess. But suicidal – I don't know.' It made my belly hurt. 'I think – I like to think I would have known.'

'He always was a waster, though, your man there, was he not?' Mickey chimed in. 'Once a junkie always a junkie, don't they say?' He took a big swig of his fiery drink.

'Excuse me,' I was astounded, 'but that's hardly fair. You never even met him, Mickey.'

'Thank God,' he muttered into his drink.

'What did you say?'

'Nothing. Forget it. I'm sure he was a grand guy. Just decided to steal our son, that's all, your man there.'

'Mickey,' I stood up, fists clenched, 'if you're looking to apportion blame, it was your bloody ex-wife who took our son. I don't for one minute think Robbie was involved until later.'

Silver seemed slightly uncomfortable now.

'You don't, do you?' I looked at him.

'It does seem unlikely, kid— Jess,' he pulled himself up. 'We questioned Robbie extensively, Mr Finnegan, before he ran off with Maxine. I don't think it was until he got involved with her that he had anything to do with Louis's disappearance, and I think that was only an unfortunate coincidence. We did go down a dead-end with Robbie's unfortunate friend – "General" David Ross – but it came to nothing. Well, nothing to do with Louis, anyway.'

I shivered. Silver shot me a quick glance and ploughed on. 'The two things we're trying to ascertain right now are –' absent-mindedly he took his gum out and rolled it between his fingers '– at what point Maxine entered Agnes's pay, and whether there was any foul play over Robbie's death.' He chucked the ball of gum in the leather bin; it landed with a small splat. Mickey winced; Silver went on regardless.

'Don't get upset by this, Jessica.' I steeled myself. 'But it seems that Agnes worked on Maxine by telling her you weren't a – a fit mother. That you might have been – abusing Louis in some way.'

'I was what?' I couldn't believe my ears. Then I thought of that hideous first week again, when Maxine had first arrived, of all my guilty nightmares about that fall. Even so, I couldn't believe that Maxine would have believed Agnes's lies.

'Plus Maxine was furious that you implicated her boyfriend Gorek. So that all meant Maxine's guilt was absolved a bit.'

'So much for staff loyalty,' joked Mickey.

I glared at him. 'All right, darling,' he said softly, taking my hand. 'I'm only teasing.'

'I know it's tough to hear, but Agnes was obviously a very desperate lady.' Silver looked at me. 'Look, forget about it. We all know it's complete crap. I'm more concerned with how they met. Would Maxine have had any opportunity to meet Agnes before Louis disappeared?'

'Mickey?' I looked at him accusingly. It was strange – almost like I was seeing him for the first time. He pushed his dark floppy locks back with long fingers, apparently exasperated.

'I was hardly in contact with my ex-wife before all this happened,' he snapped, and then he caught my eye. 'I wish I knew more, honestly,' he said. 'But I don't.' He squeezed my hand now. I fought the impulse to move away, to move towards Silver, sitting in the dusky light that sliced the room in two.

'I mean, it was only that once that I saw Agnes. When she came to the office to sign some papers.' Mickey clutched at his skull suddenly. 'Jesus. God, my head aches. I still get these terrible pains, you know. You should excuse me – it makes me a bit ratty,' he explained to Silver. 'Getting a check-up tomorrow, you know.'

Silver nodded. 'I'm sure it's been very hard for you, losing so much memory.' He stood up and shook his trousers out a little. The creases were razor-sharp as ever. The vanity of the man, I thought, with affection. 'I can't imagine it really. Anyway, I'll let you know what we discover as we progress.'

Don't go, I screamed inside, but what I actually said was, 'I'll see you out.'

'Cheers,' said Mickey, and he raised his glass in the other man's direction. 'I do appreciate all your help, mate. For getting Louis back. We owe you one.' Then he wandered over to the stereo and whacked up the music that still played softly in the background.

'Oh,' Silver said, turning back to Mickey at the door, calmly raising his voice over Maria Callas. 'I thought you'd be interested to know, we just tracked down the guy who attacked you in Bermondsey the night Louis disappeared. Kelly's bringing him in as we speak, I hope.'

Mickey looked steadily at Silver, who looked steadily back. Then Mickey smiled. 'That's great,' he said, 'well done. Sort the bastard out. And it might fill in some gaps for everyone, I guess.'

'Might do,' said Silver, 'you never know. Bye for now.'

Mickey raised an indolent hand as I followed Silver's shadow down a hall that sparkled again with Jean's polish, my bloodstains gone forever.

'Well, thanks,' I said uselessly, hanging behind Silver. 'Thanks for everything. I don't know what I would have done – well, you know.'

'Yes, I know. And you're very welcome. I knew we'd get him back. I'm just sorry it took so long.' He turned to open the front door. I felt something was about to finish, something I didn't want to end.

'Oh, I brought you this,' he said, turning back to hand me a scruffy bit of paper. It was rather stained and dirty, folded many times. It had those tiny little squares on it; looked like it had been torn from a French exercise book.

'What is it?'

'A note to you. From Robbie.'

My heart twisted painfully. 'Oh God.'

'We found it in Agnes's stuff.'

'Have you read it?'

'I had to, kiddo, I'm sorry.'

'No, it's fine.'

'Unfortunately, it still doesn't solve the suicide riddle – it's so ambiguous. But – it might make you feel better. Well, a bit better, anyway.'

'Thanks,' I muttered, staring down at the folded scrap. 'I might even have to start liking the police now, mightn't I?'

'Well, yes. That was the other thing.' His hand was on the latch now.

'What was?'

'I did a bit of delving, about your dad.' I felt the colour flood my cheeks. 'I just wanted to know what it was we did – the police did – that had so upset you. I didn't think you were ever going to tell me. And I just want to say, now I know – I'm truly sorry. It must have been very hard.'

He didn't know the half of it. I tried to smile. 'It was. But it's over now. It was a long time ago. I've got to move on. I've known that for a while really.' Determined not to cry, I stared down at my feet, and then suddenly I felt his hand upon my chin. My stomach did a slow somersault. Gently, he lifted my face to meet his eyes.

'And I also want you to know that I reckon you did brilliantly, kiddo, these past few weeks.'

Oh God, don't leave me, I prayed silently, but on the outside I just blushed. 'I don't think I've cried so much in years. Like a bloody – I don't know. Like a silly old weeping willow, I've been!'

'You had a lot to cry about. And you're pretty tough, I'd say. In a good way.'

'Yeah, well, you hardly met me at my best. I'm sorry if I was, you know, a bit – stroppy sometimes,' I said, scuffing my bare foot against the doormat. My toenails needed painting.

'Sometimes?'

I looked up quickly; saw he was teasing. Sort of.

'I wish –' I stopped, glanced quickly over my shoulder. The sitting-room door was still shut. Silver followed my gaze, then looked into my eyes like he was searching there for something.

'You wish what?' he prompted quietly.

'I just wish –' I whispered '– well, perhaps you know.' My face was on fire.

'Yes, Jess,' he said, and his thumb shifted very gently against my jaw, 'I do know. I really do.'

Silver leant down and kissed me gently on the mouth. And then he was opening the door, and walking down the path, and whistling softly, opera it sounded like, something more jolly than bloody suicidal *Tosca* though. When he got to the end, to the garden gate, he looked back. And then he was gone, and I was alone with Mickey and Louis, in Agnes's old house.

Like a squirrel hoarding stolen nuts, I took the note up to Louis's room and sat on the little sofa to read it while he slept. Robbie's pen must have run out halfway through, and the last bit was written in pencil so faint I had to hold it above Louis's starry nightlight to even see it. My brother's voice echoed down the years, through the scrawled words, the dreadful punctuation, and I imagined him sat all louche beside me, smoking roll-ups, his trainers filthy, twisting his earrings as I read.

Jessie,

I don't know what to write really. You know me, always crap with words. I suppose – all I really want to say is how sorry I am. What a mess. I expect it's hard to believe, but I swear I had no idea that Maxine was mixed up in all this. When I came down here with her, I thought we were just getting away from that bastard boyfriend of

406

hers, away from shitty London. You must have realised I owe a bit of cash – I'm sorry about all that General stuff too. I'm gonna clean up my act. Anyway, we get on okay, you know, me and Maxine. I swear I didn't know that Louis was anywhere around – when she suddenly turned up with him a few hours ago I got a nasty shock. I phoned you straight away – I tried you a few times, I swear that too. It's like Max doesn't know what she's doing either, though I expect that's no consolation to you. I think someone else is giving the orders, but I haven't worked out who yet, and she won't say. I've told her that I've rung you and she was pretty pissed off but I don't care. I think someone might have told her some bad lies about you. I'm sorry, Jess. I really am.

Max's gone to get some nappies and stuff before we drive home to you. I've made her leave Louis with me. She didn't want to but I said she weren't going to take him anywhere without his uncle now. He's wicked – dead cute. Looks like you. And a bit like Dad (poor bugger)! I think he quite likes me too. He keeps smiling at me – though he did puke his milk all over my jacket. I'll send you the bill, ha ha. I wanted to spend a bit of time with him now cos I'm going to have to leave him on your doorstep with this note. I don't fancy facing the pigs now. Not after this. Sorry.

I'm sorry about the car too. It's a good drive, though, you flash cow! I said you landed on your feet, didn't I – I always knew you would. I'm glad, though. You deserve it.

God I feel sleepy now.

There was a small doodle here of a cartoon Robbie

lying in bed with lots of 'Zzzzz' above his snoring head. It made me smile through my tears. My little brother could have been so good at so many things if he'd really wanted to have been.

I should be more honest, shouldn't I? That's my new resolution. Okay then – I'm a bit fucked. One last time, and then a new start. I swear.

Oh God. I wiped my eyes fiercely on my sleeve.

It's really weird being here – I think we came here with Mum and Dad, didn't we? Maxine said Leigh brought her here, which was weird. Do you remember dropping your Mr Whippy on that geezer's head, down the beach-stairs? That bald bloke? What a wicked shot! I've never laughed so much in all my life. I've never laughed again that much anyway, not that I can remember, now I think about it. That's a bit sad, isn't it? We did have a laugh, though, didn't we? You and me? That's what I told Maxine. Am I rambling? My bloody pen's running out now…

Found a pencil. It's a bit blunt. By the time you'll be reading this, I'll be long gone, and you'll have Louis back. Please just know I'm sorry I let you down again. I know you always believed in me. I fucked it up, though, didn't I? Royally, as Dad would have said.

Please tell Mum and Leigh I'm sorry too. Give Louis a kiss from me. And warn him not to turn out like Uncle Robbie, or I'll come and get him!

All my love, Robbie xxx

I just sat there in the dark, clutching the letter to my chest, an eight-year-old Robbie next to me in the shadows, my baby brother, playing Donkey Kong, his fluffy parka hood like a halo round his tousled head; my dad beside him ringing horses in the paper, sucking his stubby pencil, whistling 'Wild Thing', feet up on the coffee table. My flesh-and-blood baby asleep across the room, breathing deeply. Breathing safe at last.

CHAPTER TWENTY-EIGHT

The police returned my car, so I drove over to see my mum at Leigh's, and I took Louis to try to cheer her up. I took Louis everywhere these days; we were inseparable. As I drove down the dual carriageway, I kept checking that he was really there, constantly looking over my shoulder in wonderment, to say hello. I swerved so often and so unnervingly that eventually I had to stop it before we crashed.

One look at my mum's ravaged face, though, one glance at the overflowing ashtray and the large gin glinting beside her in the dying light, and I realised this battle was one I'd never win. The air was thick with fag smoke and a grief so palpable it almost trickled down the walls. She barely registered a chuckling Louis. Nothing was going to shake her from her sorrow. I showed her Robbie's note, but it just made her purse her lips against yet more tears, and then light another fag.

'Mum.' I took her hand. I noticed with a jolt it was starting to look old, the skin turning soft and wrinkled on the back now. 'I'm so sorry, Mum. I don't – I can't say I know exactly how you feel,' I felt the dull pain throb beneath my ribs, the pain that had been there since Robbie died, 'but I've got a pretty good idea.' Losing my brother was bad enough. The idea of losing my child sliced me to the bone.

'What did I do wrong, Jessie, eh?' She looked at me and I saw the unshed tears glinting in her eyes. 'I let you all down, I know that now. I wasn't much good as a mother.' She took a deep drag of her fag, the lines around her mouth creasing deeply as she did so. 'I've known it for a long time. I messed it up.'

'You didn't, Mum. You did your best.' She probably had at the time.

'Did I?' She looked at me with gratitude. 'I did, didn't I? I did try. It's just – your dad. It was quite hard, you know. Coping with all that.'

And I knew the truth; knew however much I'd loved my dad, how hard it must have been to be married to him.

'I should have told him to go a long time before the end. I should have told him to sort it out. Only –' She almost smiled. A wistful, almost dreamy look crossed her face. 'There was something about your dad, you know. Something about Roger – something I never could resist.'

I thought about Mickey and me, how hard I'd fought the attraction back at the start; how I'd fought and failed. I squeezed her hand – my mother's ageing hand.

'Oh God, I loved your dad. And I know you understand that. Always were his little favourite, you were,

Jessie. You and your mad curls.' I searched her face for the old resentment – but it wasn't there today. She stated it like fact. She swilled the remains of her gin around the glass, staring into the mists of time. 'I can see you now, you three. You were beautiful kids, really gorgeous. I was so proud of you, you know.'

I was surprised. 'Were you? You never really showed it.' Not to me, she hadn't.

'No, and I should have done. Too wrapped up in your dad. God, he was the death of me.' The living death of her. She dragged hard on her cigarette, like it was her very last lifeline. 'I was too hard on you, Jess. I know that now. Perhaps you reminded me of myself –'

Oh Christ. I really hoped not.

'You know, I see you now with Louis, and Leigh with the girls, and it seems like it was only yesterday you three were small, and I think, God, where has the time gone?' Her face crumpled like an old paper-bag. 'And oh, God, my little boy. Oh God.' Those tears spilt over now, those huge unshed tears, tracking down her sun-leathered cheeks. 'I can't –' a shudder of despair racked her thin frame, 'I just can't believe he's gone. I can't believe I'll never see him again. My little boy.'

I clutched her hand tighter. 'I know,' I whispered. 'I can't either.'

We sat there in silence, and I watched the ash from her cigarette grow into a curving arc until Louis let out a sudden squeak from the centre of Leigh's sheepskin rug, shaking the soft bear he was holding so the bell rang inside its tummy. The baby crowed with delight

412

at his own genius and shook it again before offering it to us.

'Da,' he said profoundly. My mother looked at him. She gave a great sniff and then she stopped crying.

'Come here, darling,' she crooned, holding out her arms. Louis stared up at her very seriously, his little moon-face rapt with concentration. Then he toppled onto his front and pulled himself towards his grand-mother, crawling commando-style.

'You know, Mum, if it hadn't been for Robbie, we might never have got Louis back. In the end, it was him who saved the baby.' I watched my son's gargan-tuan effort to cross the rug; the solemn commitment written across his small smooth features, his solitary tooth all pearly white and lonely in his bottom gum. I held back my own tears. I'd known my little brother would come good eventually.

'That's right, isn't it? Isn't it, angel? Your Uncle Robbie saved you.' My mum scooped the baby up into her arms, jumping him up and down on her knee until Louis gurgled with laughter again and clapped his hands. I resisted the urge to snatch the poisonous ashtray out of his grasp. I should just let them be for a while – the baby a tonic for my tragic mother.

Leigh was washing up in her immaculate white kitchen, Capital Radio droning blandly in the back-ground. Her marigolds whisked around the sink, flashing like small pink seals in the sea of suds.

'All right?'

'Getting there, you know.' I helped myself to a Jammy Dodger from the tea-tray.

413

Leigh pushed her hair back with a soapy arm. 'It must be amazing to have Louis back again.'

'It is. I keep pinching myself. I'll never moan about a sleepless night again. But you know,' I finished the biscuit slowly, buying some time to compose myself, 'I just can't stop thinking about Robbie.'

'Well, I guess he vindicated himself in the end, didn't he? I feel crap about the whole thing. More than crap. I should have trusted him more.' She looked so sad. Eternal regrets.

'Oh, Leigh.' I sighed heavily. 'I think we're going to have to let it go, you know?' I licked my finger and collected the crumbs from the biscuit plate. 'Otherwise we'll never rest.'

She slapped my hand with the J-cloth. 'That's quite tough, from you.'

'Well, there's only so much we can blame ourselves for, isn't there? He made his choices. I suppose he had to deal with what that meant.' I handed her the plate casually. 'Silver found out about Dad, you know.'

She wrenched the plug out of the sink like it was a live thing. 'Oh yeah?'

'Yeah.' I'd been longing to say his name for days. Silver. It was another small bereavement, losing him from my life. 'I thought it was about time I faced up to it.'

'I've said that for ages. Years.'

'I know. But then it's not every day your dad's body gets dug up, is it?'

'No,' she agreed, peeling her gloves off with a vigorous snap of rubber. 'And they should have told us

414

before they did it. But, you know,' she switched the kettle on again, 'they were only doing their job. Even if they did do it very badly.'

'I suppose.' She hadn't been there, though. She was already married, already safe in her new life. I remembered the absolute mortification, arriving home from my first mock A-level to find my mum a tranquillised soggy heap, the neighbours whispering in the walkways, the headlines in the local rag the next morning: '*Convict's Family's Fresh Shame*'. The bullet-headed copper in charge now trampling his way around our new flat, around our supposed new life, shouting about ill-gotten gains, furious the dug-up coffin held nothing but old bones, pulling our home apart again and again – furious at finding nothing. My Uncle Jack – the grass – limping round after dark, before he left for Florida: trying to explain this last betrayal. To get them off his back, he'd told the police my dad had hidden the wedge from that final job until he died, that it had been buried with him for safe-keeping till the time was right to retrieve it; that the undertaker, who'd since passed away himself, had taken a bung to cover up the stash. Of course it was all rubbish. We'd never seen a penny, though Jack, on the other hand – well, his shoes were new and shiny, just like his big new car. A fourteen-year-old Robbie, full of futile rage and hormones, seeking vengeance for his devastating role model – our sorry father – went after our supposed friend (too late). When my brother eventually came home, he was wasted for the first time – but sadly not the last. My mum sobbed inconsolably as the priest blessed my poor dad's remains as they finally went back into the ground. Secretly I think she'd been hoping Jack might take her away from all this – but now he was gone too.

But none of that hurt me as deeply as what had happened next. With a great shiver, I thought of DC Jones. I'd tried to block him from my memories, but he was always there, lurking in the background. That friendly middle-aged copper who'd fooled me into thinking he cared about my welfare; that he had the best interests of my wounded family in his oily heart. He took me in for questioning, alone; sat too near me on the Panda's back seat, stinking of Brut; stood behind me in the police station with one possessive hand upon my shoulder. I'd actually felt protected. I thought that I'd imagined his fond fingers nudging my teenage breast, his red hair slicked back with something that smelt quite sickly. It was only when he suggested so subtly that if I *'helped'* with the inquiry, suggested with a cheeky wink – *well, then he could help me, hey, little lady?* – I began to realise the hideous error that I'd made.

'Don't act the innocent with me, you little bitch,' he'd hissed, leaving bracelets of bruises round my wrists and a coating of spittle across my face before the WPC came back with cups of tea and told him to back off. Lucky escape, I thought, and went home to forget it.

And then Jones turned up at our flat one night – to apologise, he'd said. My mum was at the pub, but I let him in eventually because he swore he'd come to clear my father's name. I actually fell for it. I made him tea and he nicked a nip of my mum's gin; he made a joke about mother's ruin – I remembered it forever and I could never drink the stuff. And God I was so stupid, so trusting still, even when he kept inching nearer to me on the old settee, I just inched away, until I practically hung right off the end – scared to hurt his feelings, desperate to believe he could exonerate my dad. He felt guilty for his actions, he said – I reminded him of his daughter – and then when he'd lulled me into trusting him again, he'd launched himself at me, on me, and I'd struggled under his heavy weight until I'd nearly given up – and then Robbie ran screaming through the living room and whacked Jones with my mum's favourite glass elephant, which shattered on his bald spot. *That* breakage took some explaining when she got home.

DC Jones had gone by then, and my mum never knew he'd ever been. He'd threatened to press charges against Robbie for assault, but thank God he already had a reputation within the force. Later I found out he'd slunk off to deepest Surrey – taking early retirement to play golf there with his chums. The damage to us kids was done, though. Why would we ever trust the police again?

And then I met Silver. I thought of his kindness; of his devotion to the case. Of his warmth and reliability; of the way that, for the first time in my life, I'd come to depend on a man who hadn't actually let me down. I'd let myself lean on him, and in the end it had felt right to do so. I thought of Silver, and I felt a great sorrow that he'd gone now. I told myself it was because he was like the kind of father mine had never been. I knew that was a lie.

As if on cue, I heard Louis start to cry in the other room. 'Coming,' I called through to my mum, to my baby. 'I'm just coming.'

My mother was weeping again, clutching the confused baby to her bony chest, weeping and weeping over his little swirly head. He blinked at me and smiled. Oh, the oblivion of utter innocence.

'She'll be okay,' whispered Leigh as I left with Louis firmly on my hip, firmly where he belonged. I clasped my sister tight and thanked her, while George gave me a shaky thumbs-up from the conservatory. I prayed that Leigh was right.

CHAPTER TWENTY-NINE

Mickey suggested that after Robbie's funeral we should go away for a while. I didn't want to fly; my feet were hardly on the ground again, so in the end Mickey booked us a cottage in the Lake District. For some reason I fancied the north, and for once my husband acquiesced. Something in me yearned for the sheer savageness of nature, the anonymous beauty of a place I'd never been.

The week of the funeral, Mickey stayed at home. Pauline and Freddie had apparently split up, and a heartbroken Pauline was more than willing to distract herself with work, so Mickey threw himself into family life for once. We talked about redecorating; he bought me lots of glossy interior magazines and said I could choose any colour scheme I liked. He drove me and the baby up to town and bought me clothes from Harvey Nichols; he spent a fortune, holding a squirming Louis on his knee while I tried on dress after skirt that I didn't really want. But I knew I shouldn't protest. This was Mickey's way of saying that he loved me.

Only once did we talk of Agnes. Her body had been flown back to Norway. One afternoon, Mickey told me he wanted to ring her parents and asked if I would mind? I chose to stay upstairs with Louis while Mickey was on the phone; I didn't want to hear. Afterwards, he came up to the bedroom where I was building towers for the baby, towers which he promptly and proudly knocked straight down again.

'Okay?' I asked. Mickey looked utterly bleak.

'You can imagine. They're devastated.'

God, all this never-ending grief. The complete desperation that had caused the well of pain; that had brought such a bittersweet ending for me.

'Mickey,' I said carefully. He was staring out of the window, his hands thrust deep in his jean pockets.

'Mmm?'

'Why did you see Agnes again?'

He looked round, surprised. 'When?'

'I don't know. Whenever you did.'

'I told you, Jessica, it was only once. She came in to sign some papers.'

I stacked the coloured blocks one above the next, lining each edge up exactly. 'Is that the honest truth?'

'Yes it is.'

'So why didn't you mention it at the time?'

'Because,' he sighed deeply, and ran his hand through his thick hair. 'Because I knew you wouldn't like it.'

'*How* did you know?'

He gave a gentle shrug. 'Okay, I guessed.'

'I'd have liked it much more if I'd actually known about it. If you hadn't hidden it from me.'

He stooped down and kissed my forehead. 'Okay. I'm sorry. I know that now.'

We left it at that.

Robbie's funeral was a few days later. It was the most distressing experience of my life so far, apart from losing Louis, worse even than attending my dad's burial, when my mum had been so out of it she'd staggered on her heels, precariously near the open grave, and had to be supported before she fell in. In the crematorium, I sobbed over Louis's head as Robbie's coffin slid forever between those grim red curtains. I imagined my brother running free now, chasing me across the playground in the park until we both collapsed in giggles, lying on our bellies in the afternoon light, trying to play the best tune on blades of emerald grass, rolling down the hills, squinting joyfully at the sun, making our one bottle of precious Seven-Up last all day. And then I thought of Agnes, of her ruined body, thousands of miles away, being lowered into the cold ground, and I clasped my son even tighter to me and cried harder than I ever had before.

The day before our holiday, I cooked Sunday lunch for everyone. The funeral had been so devastating that, when I'd finally managed to contain my grief, I'd decided I needed to take action. To do something positive now to mark the next bits of our lives – to mark the good bits –Louis's return, us as a family.

As I sweated over roast chicken in the kitchen, assisted by a hung-over Shirl, Mickey made a huge effort with my mum, and I was grateful for it. He turned off the opera and put on Roy Orbison – though he drew

the line at actually singing 'Pretty Woman' to her, thank
God (Julia Roberts was my mother's heroine of all
time). Mickey sat next to her at the head of the table
and never let her glass go empty, gave her the chicken
breast ('the best bit, hey, Carol – for my best mother-
in-law') and even pulled the wishbone with her, let her
snap it and win. His sympathy was genuine; I knew he
was imagining his own mother back when Ruari
drowned; that he was truly sorry for all my mum's raw
and suppurating pain. I watched Mickey charm her
easily, complimenting her on the green blouse that
'matched her eyes' (red-rimmed and sore, actually, from
all the tears and fags, I noticed, finishing my wine rather
faster than I'd meant to). I watched Mickey and I
remembered why I'd fallen for him in the first place,
fallen so hard. And I thought, now we're tied together
forever by our tragedies, by the loss of both our
brothers. Across the table George and Gary were
arguing about snooker as only they knew how; Leigh
was telling my mum about the latest hairdresser that
she loved. I watched the girls feeding Louis slivers of
carrot and laughing as he pulled funny faces and spat
them out again. I looked at them all and thought I'd
never imagined anything like this; and then I caught
Mickey watching me, his dark eyes veiled. He toasted
me with his wine glass. Then I caught Shirl watching
Mickey toasting me.

I went to make the custard. A few minutes later,
Shirl followed me in with a stack of dirty plates, staggering slightly on her platform heels.

'So it's good to be back together, babe?' she asked,

helping herself to the last roast potato in the dish. 'Mickey seems very loved-up.'

I flushed. 'God. Does he?'

'Probably what he needed, a nasty shock.'

'Shirl!'

'I don't mean Louis, stupid. I mean –' She popped the rest of the potato in her wide mouth contemplatively.

'What?'

'Oh, never mind.'

'What are you on about?' Standing at the hob, I briskly stirred the custard but it wouldn't seem to thicken. 'Why's this so runny? God, I never can do bloody custard.' I topped up a glass with the dregs of the wine left on the sideboard and downed it. 'Fancy some soup *à la* Jessica with your apple pie?'

'Yeah, well, last of the domestic goddesses you are not, my girl.' Shirl peered over my shoulder. 'So, you're going to make a go of it, are you? Here.' She whisked the spoon out of my hand and beat the custard into submission.

'What do you mean?'

'With Mickey. You're back on track?'

'Why wouldn't we be?' I said, very carefully.

'Oh, no reason.'

'Spit it out, Shirl, for God's sake.'

She cast a rather theatrical look over her left shoulder. 'Oh, it was just that nice policeman. I thought you might be sad to see him go.'

I opened the dishwasher and started to stack the plates very fast. 'So what if I was?' My hair swung across my face conveniently.

'I just thought you might have – you know. Wanted a bit more.'

Sometimes, you know, I wished my best mate wasn't quite so candid.

'Shirl,' I straightened up, 'Silver is the one bloke in my life who's ever done what he actually promised. Why would I want to go and fuck that up? And anyway, even if I did like him, which I don't, and he did like me, which I'm sure he doesn't – well, Mickey and me – we're good.'

'Glad to hear it.'

'I don't think you are.' I pushed the dishwasher door home with one hip.

'I am, Jess, really. I see that Mickey appreciates you more now. I see how he looks at you. It's just – I want you to have some –' She snatched the pan off the heat in the nick of time. 'Whoops. Nearly.'

'Some what?'

'Some peace in your life. What you deserve. And maybe now you get it anyway with that man out there. Maybe I was wrong all along.'

'You were.'

'I'm sure I was. Now, where's the custard thingy? This is looking jus' fine.'

'You growing the apples out here or what?'

God, I jumped. Mickey put an arm around me and squeezed my shoulder.

'I've just been chatting to your folks.' He smiled at me, then cast his benevolence towards Shirl for once. 'You'd make a good godmother, don't you think?'

'Char, man. The best.' She poured the custard neatly into the jug.

'I don't follow.' I pulled the apple pie out of the oven. The far edge had burnt a little. I prodded it sadly. 'Bollocks.'

'Your ma thinks we should have Louis christened.'

'I thought you hated the church? You didn't want to get married in one.' I started to cut the charred bits off the pie.

'That was different.' For the first time today he looked like the Mickey of old. Guarded. A bit cross. 'I couldn't. I'd been married before. You know that.' Like I said – surprisingly Catholic. 'But in the circumstances I think it might be nice, don't you? After everything we've been through. Good excuse for a party.' He kissed my forehead. 'We could maybe –' Did he look almost bashful? 'We could maybe renew our vows too. So your family could be there this time.'

'If God approves.'

Were the fault-lines starting to shift? Mickey raised an eyebrow.

'I think it's a great idea,' Shirl cut in. I raised my eyebrow at her now, but she ignored it. 'Now, this custard ain't gettin' any better for hanging around. Shall we?'

When everyone had gone, and Louis was in bed, I found Mickey sitting in the near dark, nursing a whisky and staring at the Emin print he'd bought me all that time ago.

'You look sad,' I said, leaning over the sofa-back beside him. He reached his arm up and stroked my hair.

'You know the real reason I liked that picture, whatever I thought of the artist. It reminds me of you. My sad little Jess.' He let go of me and pulled himself up. 'Let's go to bed.'

And he took my hand and led me up the stairs and then in the bedroom he silently undressed me, almost like he worshipped me. My final thought before sleep came was, *This is going to be okay.*

In the night I woke and Mickey was lying next to me, and it took me a moment – and then I realised what was wrong. We would have to leave this house for good, to free ourselves of all the ghosts, forever. It was the only answer, I saw that now, the only feasible way to make a fresh start. I got up and padded round the packed suitcases ready for tomorrow, into Louis's room, and I held my breath as I looked into his cot, just in case he wasn't there again, just in case he'd –

But he was there, of course, deeply asleep, legs curled up like a little frog's in the warm night, breathing softly, in, out, in, out. I reached down and stroked his face very gently so he wouldn't wake, remembering how I used to hold my breath in terror sometimes, hold one anxious finger before his tiny nose to feel the heat when he was a newborn, when I was still so scared his breath might just stop. My milk hadn't returned, but it didn't seem to matter any more; Leigh said I was lucky I didn't have to wean him from the breast, it was done for me, and I loved my sister more for looking on the bright side. It had brought us closer together, all this, and that was one good thing about those fourteen days of hell.

I lay on the sofa in Louis's room and I stared at the moon that filled the room with pale white light, and it suddenly all fell into place. I thought about waking

Mickey now, and telling him my decision. And then I thought how much I did hate talking, and while I was thinking all these things I fell asleep again.

In the morning I woke quite early, before Louis even, a luxury these days. I had the strange feeling someone had been looking down at me, but I shook it off. Stiff from the sofa, I showered in the guest room so I didn't wake Mickey up. I switched the radio on and it was tuned into one of those old hit stations, and I was humming along to a song that reminded me of Dad. 'Nice legs, shame about the face,' he used to shout out the window of that old Cortina at all the short-skirted girls we passed, if Mum wasn't around; me and Robbie and Leigh screaming with laughter and ducking behind the seats when the flustered girls whipped round.

And when I stepped out of the shower, I felt revived. It was time to start things afresh, I felt optimistic and, wrapping myself in a huge white towel, I went back to check Louis – only he wasn't in his cot. So I padded over to my bedroom, still dripping wet, to see if Mickey had put him in our bed, only they weren't there either.

So then I called downstairs, and there was nothing, no answer, and I ran down, just as Jean was coming through the front door, and I said hello as I slammed into the kitchen, and the back door was swinging open. I stepped into the garden, shouting, 'Mickey, where the bloody hell are you?' but he didn't answer, and the garden was empty, just Agnes's bloody roses shedding their last tears, and I shivered in the September breeze as I realised Mickey had gone and taken Louis with him. And I was filled with fury, more angry than I'd ever been before, because wherever he'd taken him, Mickey knew I couldn't cope with this, not now, not any more. It was a visceral pain now, like Louis had been ripped right out of me again, and I was panting with the effort of just staying calm.

I ran through the house still in my towel, and I saw that Mickey's car wasn't in the drive, and with a sinking heart I cried to Jean, 'Did you see Mickey leave?', but she shook her head and looked terrified again – and so was I, just like the bloody last time. Just like the bloody last time.

I threw on my clothes in seconds, began to dial Mickey's mobile. Then I saw it sitting redundant on my dressing table.

'Don't do this to me, Mickey, don't do this, please,' I muttered, taking the stairs three at a time. But I had a feeling, I just had a feeling I knew where they'd be.

I floored it across the heath, turned the car through the great wrought-iron gates into Greenwich Park, parking near the bobble-headed Observatory, where we always joked we'd like to live. I set off at a jog across the grass, Henry VIII's old stomping ground, wending my way beneath the chestnut trees, crunching over their spiky conker-shells littering the leafy ground.

I couldn't see the statue from here – Mickey's favourite in all London, apparently – an early Henry Moore, balanced on the top of the steep park hill. Finally, as I reached the longer grass, it came in sight – but the bench where Mickey liked to sit was still shielded from my view by an old couple doing Tai Chi under the watery sun.

And then I spotted a tall figure in the distance and my heart began to pound. It was Mickey, I was sure of it, it had to be, and in his arms – there in his arms, thank God, was Louis. Standing stock-still by the statue, they were looking down at London through the trees, gazing towards St Paul's – towards the Tate, I realised with horrid irony. And I ran faster than I'd ever run before, and by the time I reached them I really couldn't breathe.

'Mickey.' I was behind him now, panting, trying to catch my breath. He didn't turn. 'What are you doing here?'

Louis looked at me over his father's shoulder and smiled, happily oblivious, his one tooth sticking up all pearly, but still Mickey didn't speak.

'We're meant to be going this morning, aren't we? Have you changed your mind?' I panted, still gasping for air. 'We don't have to, I don't care. Let's stay at home.' I was rambling with nerves. 'It was your idea.'

And then he looked at me, finally turned and looked at me, and his lip went back wolfishly. And something in his face made my stomach plunge, like a leaden weight, like a pendulum that won't swing up again. A cold realisation was creeping slowly through me, icy in my veins.

'Why are you looking at me like that?' I whispered, and everything finally began to slot into place. 'What is it?' But I think I already knew. I stared at him, an utter stranger now. I'd been so stupid, so frantic with worry I hadn't seen the truth.

Mickey was walking away from me, taking my son with him. He seemed so calm it was surreal.

'Give me my son, Mickey,' I said quietly. I held my arms out for the baby. But Mickey kept moving; like a wild animal, he slunk just out of reach. 'So,' I said, and I moved too, 'how long did you know for?' I tried to catch his eye. 'When did you realise, Mickey?'

The vital thing now was to keep my wits about me. I stalked him, keeping Louis in my sight the entire time. Mickey reached his bench, and then he sat, sort of settled on the edge, like he was contemplating flight. Louis was struggling slightly now, and grizzling a little, but his father reached in his pocket and dug out a broken biscuit. Louis grabbed it with chubby dimpled fingers, pacified for a while at least.

'You're going to have to tell me the truth sometime, Mickey, you know,' I said quietly.

It was very quiet as I waited for his reply. A lone dog barked in the distance; a far-off helicopter chopped the air.

'Yes,' eventually he sighed, 'I suppose I am.' He ran his hand over Louis's silky hair. 'You know, I thought it'd be okay, we'd make it work, you and me, once Agnes was gone. Only then,' he looked at me accusingly, 'only then I saw how you looked at your man Silver the other week.'

'What?' Slowly, oh so very slowly, I was edging ever nearer. 'Don't try to blame me. This is about you and Agnes, isn't it?' Tentatively I sat down too, careful to keep to the opposite end of the bench. I daren't make any sudden movements.

'Was. Sure, it was about us.' Another pause. His voice

was very quiet now. 'You know, I was shocked at how distraught you were.'

'When?'

'When Louis disappeared.'

I laughed incredulously. 'What, you thought someone could steal my son away from me, and I wouldn't care?'

'Oh come on now, Jessica,' he said harshly, staring down at the top of Louis's swirly little head. The baby was nodding off. 'You were hardly a natural mother, were you now?'

I was about to argue, but of course it was true; I hadn't been. I'd had to dig extremely deep to uncover my maternal instincts, so shrouded in doubt and uncertainty they'd been. Mickey, on the other hand, had been besotted by Louis from the word go.

'Maybe not at first,' I admitted quietly. 'But it's different now. You know that.'

'Yes,' he said sadly, 'yes, I do. Too late, I do.'

I looked down the hill. 'So,' I said warily. A girl in tight leggings jogged across my view. 'So, when did you find out that it was Agnes? And why the fuck didn't you do something about it?'

'I did. But it wasn't easy from that bloody hospital bed.'

A knife was twisting in my gut. 'I loved you, Mickey. I believed in you.'

'Did you?' He turned and held my gaze. 'I don't think you ever really did.' His expression was unfathomable. 'I think you knew it wouldn't work, if you're honest with yourself.'

431

I was desperately trying to piece it all together. 'You didn't just see her once, did you?' The words stuck in my craw. 'Did you – were you sleeping with Agnes again?'

I couldn't read his look.

'God. The *whole* time we were together?'

He looked away.

'Just bloody tell me, Mickey.'

'No.' He was quick, finally contrite. 'No, I swear I wasn't. It was only when you – when you were really pregnant, when you went off me, sure it was.'

'Off you?' My face scrunched in surprise. 'I didn't ever go off you. I just felt – odd. Self-conscious. And –' I thought back to those days, of being huge, the weight, the pressure of my unborn child. Of feeling like I was about to split open down the middle, like a great ripe watermelon. I flushed. 'And I was uncomfortable. I'm sure that was – that is quite normal. Not wanting to be touched all the time in pregnancy.'

'But you know, sex was all we really had, Jess,' he said softly, 'it was the glue that held us together.'

'Oh, was it?' I retorted angrily. But deep down I knew he was probably right.

'I'd say so.'

I reflected for a minute. 'And so Agnes...?' I prompted.

He was getting irritated. 'We had a quick drink to sort out some property we'd owned. Ages ago, when you were still pregnant. I didn't want to see her, but I had to get a signature, and then – well, one thing just led to another.'

Pauline's words echoed fatally in my mind. He went

on. 'It wasn't planned, Jessica. It just happened.' He really wanted me to believe him, I could see that. 'We couldn't help it. We tried. I tried. I ended it again – I didn't see her for a while after Louis was born.'

'How considerate.'

He was talking to himself now. 'And then – it all just fell back into place. I couldn't keep away.'

The knife kept pushing deeper. 'I thought – I thought you hated her?' My voice cracked painfully.

'Loved her so much I hated her too, I guess. Couldn't –' he looked at me, eyes hard and glassy, 'couldn't live without her, no matter how I tried.'

Swift jab to the soft bit of my belly. 'And so you knew she was going to take Louis –'

'Don't be stupid,' he snapped. 'I may be a bastard, but I'm not that mad. Not that heartless. She planned it on her own.' He was so intense, I saw his fingers turn white where he grasped the baby. 'I swear she did.'

'Oh, well. That's a relief.' I watched the jogging girl cross back the other way.

He shrugged. 'It was like a – a sort of joke we had. We'd – you know. Run off with the baby, the two of us. I just never realised she'd take it seriously. I thought she was kind of – over the mother thing.'

'A joke!' I couldn't believe he'd actually said it. 'A fucking joke, Mickey? Stealing my son?' I snarled, and stood, stepped towards him with arms outstretched. 'Give me Louis, Mickey, just give him to me. I don't care what you do, I really don't. I just want my son back.'

But Mickey just sat, totally implacable, our sleeping

433

baby cocooned tightly in his arms. 'Not like a funny joke. I mean, like a kind of fantasy. You know – a daydream.'

'Mickey,' I said wearily, and I clutched the back of the bench for support, 'you're just making it all sound even worse.'

'But,' he looked at me intently, and he was stripped bare at last. Freed from his usual arrogance; the naked man beneath the haughty veneer. 'I need to explain. I feel – well, I don't feel good about it, Jessica. I'm a guilty man, so I am, I realise that.'

'You don't say! God, Mickey.'

'What I mean, what I'm trying to say is – I guess I played down your love for Louis for Agnes's benefit, I suppose. I just didn't realise she'd take it all to heart.'

'Mickey, I really don't need to sit and reminisce with you about your and Agnes's bloody pillow-talk, all right?'

'But it wasn't like that, I swear. It was –' He looked at me, eyes manic, lips drained of colour. It dawned on me that he was holding out for sympathy. 'Before it happened, she was already collapsing inside. She'd lost all hope, and – I was – I was frightened she'd do something stupid.'

'Like steal a child?' I glared at him.

'Like kill herself. I was trying to make her feel better.' The finality of his words shocked us both, I think. God, he looked sad. I thought of Agnes and the gun, the swiftness and the beauty in her last movements. A release. A gift for Mickey. She couldn't give him a child, but she gave him her eternal protection. She left him her silence. With some effort, I pushed those awful final moments from my mind.

'So?'

'That day in the Tate, she just appeared.'

I thought about Mickey disappearing for a while as I ate his cake. What if I hadn't been so greedy, I'd wondered a thousand times; what if I'd just stayed with him in that exhibition and not tried to be all art-loving and independent.

'I had to promise to meet her – she was going to tell you everything. She was already hysterical when she turned up. So I slipped off with Louis. I thought you'd be ages looking at the pictures. I thought you'd – you know, just get a coffee and wait.'

I shook my head in utter disbelief.

'I wasn't thinking straight, I realise that. I just wanted to get her away from where you were before she made a scene. I went to meet her down by the river. We went to some dingy pub, she got me drunk. I think she might have put something in the whisky. I don't know, I felt very odd. She kept going on and on at me to leave with her. Eventually I went to try to ring you outside, to tell you I was on my way back, but I couldn't get an answer.'

'You had my bloody phone, that's why.' Or she had, anyway.

'Anyway, when I went back to get Louis, they'd both gone. I nearly had a heart attack.'

'So why didn't you get the police then?'

'I thought I'd find her. I looked everywhere.'

I saw myself running round the Tate while Mickey hunted the streets so near to me. Louis's frantic parents.

'I had no idea that she'd really take him, that she'd just disappear.'

435

'Christ, Mickey.'

'Oh, I know it might sound ridiculous now, Jessica,' he said softly, 'but when I was with Agnes, I would have done anything for her. She was suffering so much. She couldn't come to terms with her fate at all.' Louis muttered, shifted in his father's arms. 'I'm truly sorry, that you must believe.'

'Why must I? You let some nutter run off with my child.'

'I didn't mean to. I got into that stupid fecking fight and that was it. I was so hyped-up, and I'd been nipping whisky with her, and then when she disappeared my bloody mobile ran out and eventually I went into that pub to use the phone. I was still trying to ring Agnes, and then I *was* going to ring the police, I swear, if I couldn't reach her. I didn't realise what had happened for days after I ended up in hospital.'

'So you really lost your memory?'

He had the decency to look ashamed.

'You bloody didn't, did you?'

'I did, initially I did, I swear,' he said, 'but eventually it started to come back. I was – you know, I had to play for time. I was trying to get Agnes to take the baby home to you; I thought it would be safer if I did it. Only once she had him she was truly besotted and I realised she wasn't going to do that, whatever I said. I realised – she loved the baby more than me.'

'Tragic for you,' I said bitterly.

'Yeah, well, everyone has their limit, don't they, I guess.' It wasn't a question.

'You should have come clean.'

436

'I couldn't. She –'

'What?' I whispered.

I could see he found it painful to say. 'She – she threatened to hurt Louis if I turned her in. I didn't think she'd ever actually go through with it – but I just couldn't take the risk. You must see that.'

'Christ.' The very idea made me feel physically sick. 'She was completely mad, wasn't she?'

'Not mad. Just desperate. And so I thought I'd have to get him back myself. I did try to warn you.'

'A bit bloody late, Mickey. And, I don't understand. The police kept saying she was abroad.'

'She had two passports, Norwegian and British – two names. She must have travelled under Hohlt. They were looking for Agnes Finnegan.'

A lone leaf drifted down by my feet. I thought of something else. 'And Maxine? I mean – it was all a bit – matey, wasn't it?'

He had the good grace to look abashed. 'Well –'

'What?'

'Maxine caught Agnes and me –' He stopped.

'What? Oh God, Mickey, don't try to protect me now, for Christ's sake. It's a bit late to spare my feelings, don't you think?'

'I'm not proud of it, sure I'm not. Maxine caught Agnes and me in bed together at the house.'

Numbly, I stared ahead of me.

'She was threatening to tell you, taking the moral high ground, you know, so Agnes bribed her instead. I didn't realise that Maxine was in on Agnes's plans. To be fair, I think she just thought Agnes was going to take Louis away for a few days. And the amount of money Agnes was offering – well, think about it. You know how desperate Maxine was to better herself. She wasn't going to turn it down.'

She always had been grasping. 'Especially if you played up my unreliability as a mother, hey, Mickey?'

'I'm truly sorry about that.' But his eyes were mad. 'I must have mentioned it once to Agnes, and she obviously used it as ammunition.'

I shivered, slumping back on the bench. We sat in silence for some time, and he let me reach out my hand, gently smooth my son's hair where the breeze had ruffled it. The church clock on the nearby hill struck nine. A raw-faced man with a brown Labrador raised his cap at me. Louis stirred a little; Mickey stared into space. He was gone forever; I knew that now. I'd already known it, deep down, a long time ago.

'I'm truly sorry, Jessica.' He broke through the silence, making me jump. 'I – oh God, I know it's a cliché. But I never meant to hurt you, really. I just wasn't thinking when I was with Agnes. You always seemed so – so tough. Agnes was the vulnerable one.'

I thought of Agnes's beauty, her apparent perfection. I thought of Agnes's absolute misery.

'When I realised what she'd done, when she rang me in the hospital to try to get me to come to her, I was still delirious. I said if she didn't bring Louis straight back, I'd shop her – and then she made her threats. But at least she sent you that video, those photos.' He looked almost imploring. 'So you'd know he was alive.'

'Big of her.' I was still trying to absorb what he'd said. 'Tough? Why does everyone keep calling me tough?'

'You're a survivor, that's why. I knew that when I met you. You never said – you never talked about how you felt. You never said you loved me. Agnes – well, she wore her heart on her sleeve.'

'I loved you, Mickey. Oh God, how much I loved you. I just never said it because – we weren't like that. Because I – I was frightened, I suppose. Because – because I'm tough.' In the distance, Canary Wharf blinked at me. The sun danced on the red-brown trees that swayed gently down the hill, and he seemed genuinely surprised. I thought briefly of Silver. Perhaps none of us are as innocent as we'd like others to believe.

'I didn't know,' he said quietly.

'You chose not to know.'

'That's not true. You're quite a closed book, you know.'

'Not that closed. So, did you never –' I swallowed hard '– was it all, like, pretend with me then?'

'God, no.' He looked at me again. 'Jessica, when I met you I was in a really bad place. But I couldn't keep my hands off you. You and that petticoat.' He tried to smile at me.

'Please, Mickey, don't. Just don't.' It broke my heart to even think of it.

'You do know that much.'

I didn't speak. I couldn't.

'Don't you?' he persisted, almost angry now. 'It's just – I met you too soon after Agnes.'

439

'Yeah, well,' and the pain that had been festering began to rise, 'that's quite apparent now.'

'I just mean that if it had been different – later, if you hadn't got pregnant so quickly, it – it might have worked.'

The straw that broke the camel's back. 'Don't do me any favours.' I'd had enough, as a horrible thought occurred to me. 'And what about Robbie, Mickey?' I stood up now. 'Did he just get in everyone's way too?'

Louis's head fell back, heavy with sleep. His father cradled it back onto his shoulder as he stood too, pleading with me now.

'You have to believe me, your man there had nothing to do with me. I never even met him. Him and Maxine – well, Christ knows what was going on – but that was between them. Nothing to do with me or – or Agnes.'

'Oh, you know that, do you? For God's sake, Mickey, it was you who told me not to trust her. So why should you?'

'I just know that death wasn't what it was all about. It was only ever about Louis.'

'Oh, right. So what about that almighty whack on the head she gave me?'

'I don't know, Jessica, but I'm sure she wasn't trying to kill you. Just wanted to stop you. She'd truly lost it by then. I think she was looking for Louis's passport. She must have heard us on the phone, and she knew I'd tell you the truth. She was trying to stop you hearing.'

I paced away from the bench. My world was still like Alice's Wonderland. Growing and shrinking, shrinking and growing.

'And that woman in the Tate? The model, Claudia? Was that really just a coincidence?'

He shrugged. 'Sure it was. We'd been talking about Hopper on the photo-shoot, and Claudia was intrigued. I did tell you I'd seen someone from work, I'm sure I did.' He looked down at Louis then with such love. 'Look, do you think – I hoped there might be a chance we could –' He was beseeching; Mickey, who was never humble.

Swiftly, I cut him off. 'What – a chance for us? Don't be so fucking stupid. Just give me Louis, Mickey.' I pushed my hair back off my face, sweaty with fear. 'It's over. You must realise that. I want my son back – right now.'

Mickey moved quickly – but I followed him. I'd fight him tooth and nail for my son; I'd kill him first, this madman I didn't know. He stood on the edge of the hill, staring down, and I steeled myself. He looked at Louis, waking in his arms, grumbling away. What did others see? The perfect portrait of a happy little family, enjoying the last of the September sun.

'Don't even think about it, Mickey.'

He hesitated. My gut said he surely loved Louis too much to do what he could now do, but his position was so precarious, teetering on the edge of the grassy hill, a virtual precipice. He was desperate and, if he gave Louis up, ultimately alone now. Adrenaline and fear were coursing through my exhausted body, sorrow following not far behind. I held out my arms, tried to keep them steady.

'You owe me this much, Mickey, surely,' I said softly.

He looked at me then, and his dark eyes filled with tears.

'What will you do?' he whispered.

'I don't know. I'll think about it. I need some time to take all this in.'

'I am so sorry, Jessica. I would have got him back for you, you know. I swear I would. I wouldn't have let her keep him.'

I stretched my arms out further, and Louis swung back towards me in Mickey's grasp. The baby was about to wail, I could sense him building up to it; his bottom lip was trembling. And then, slowly, sadly, with absolute tragedy scored into his thin face, Mickey relinquished his priceless cargo into my shaking arms. Our fingers touched as I took the baby, and the pain it caused him was solid in the air – but I couldn't think of Mickey any more. It was my time now, my time with Louis.

I grasped his solid little weight and clutched him tight against me. I didn't look at Mickey now; I couldn't look again. I just looked at my baby; I drank him in, his curving cheek, his fat little moon-face, his milky baby smell. And then, very carefully, with the gentle breeze ruffling my hair, with Louis tucked into my coat, I began to walk away. I walked towards my freedom, and I took my son.

ACKNOWLEDGMENTS:

I would have been very stuck at times without the help of some extremely talented people. Thank you to Tiggy, my first reader, for trying to guess who did it; to Flic Everett for her inestimable brushing-up, and to the rest of my Goldsmiths group, Judy Mcinerney, Guy Ware and Pyllice Eddu for providing invaluable feedback, as well as lots of wine and even more crisps. Thanks to Lou for answering my invasive questions, and to my mother for all the full-stops (you were right about Jess in the hospital, after all!).

Profound thanks to my heroically tenacious agent Teresa Chris for believing in me so early on, and to everyone at Avon, particularly Maxine Hitchcock for her insightful editing and for counting those infernal days with me time and time again; and to Keshini Naidoo for reading between the lines. Last but never least, thank you, Tim for all the domestic bits (e.g. meals) - and for wandering off so spectacularly in the first place. Thank God you both came back!

Enjoyed *Lullaby*? Then read on for an exclusive extract from Claire Seeber's new novel *Bad Friends*, to be published in 2008.

PROLOGUE

I breathe hard onto the window and watch the fug slowly spread before me. Tracing the small cloud with my finger, I write my name across the middle like a schoolgirl. A single tear tracks downwards from the M. I make a fist and vigorously rub myself out again. Cocooned in this muggy warmth, I'm struggling to stay awake. Far off in the drizzle a tiny house twinkles with beguiling light. I gaze wistfully after the enticing image but we are truly hurtling now, a sleek capsule slicing the M4's black, and the house has vanished already; a safe haven gone long ago.

I hold my breath as my teenage neighbour bobs his head shyly; as he uncurls his awkward new height from beside me scuttling with odd spider gait to watch the film up front, I exhale with audible relief. Now he has gone there is some space for my sadness, some room to acknowledge the pain of what I've just come from. I feel utterly raw, stripped down; a bit like I've been flayed alive. The truth is we've gone too far this time, I can't see a return. I think we said it all; we let the floodgates down and we got truly flooded. The fury and the anguish leer out at me;

I close my eyes against them, shrug down under my scraggy little blanket of grief.

An abandoned can of Strongbow rolls under my feet; I let it rattle until it starts to annoy me then I retrieve it, stick it firmly into the net on the back of the seat; fighting the urge to lick my wet fingers, drying them instead on the knobbly cloth beside me. I wish I'd had the foresight to buy myself some alcohol before I embarked, to kill the ache. The throbbing heartache. I wish I had my iPod, the *Sunday Times*, some means – any means, in fact – of forgetting. I wish I wasn't travelling alone. I wish I'd known I would be.

My eyelids droop inexorably until my head bangs against the thick cool glass.

'Ouch.' I jerk up, feeling foolish, force myself upright again. I don't want to sleep here, don't want to surrender to the inevitable nightmares surrounded by these strangers. So I watch the woman across the aisle, a mousey hobbit who mouths each word of *Northanger Abbey*, scanning each page fervently, her pale lips oddly stiff despite their constant movement. The couple in front lean into each other, the tops of their heads touching, their hair almost entwined as he whispers something he wants only his partner to hear. Right now, I think tragically, it's unlikely I'll ever feel that pleasure again; that anyone will ever want to whisper anything to me again. I almost smile at my self-indulgence. Almost – but not quite.

Eventually I succumb to sleep; rocked by the lullaby of voices that murmur through the dim coach. I don't notice the dark-haired girl as she passes by to the loo, though later the girl swears that she saw me in my seat; she liked my hair, the girl says (God knows, it's hard to miss). Says she knew I was a kindred spirit. But I do notice the tall man who bangs my knee as he stumbles past, jolting me uncomfortably back into wakefulness. I am startled again, glancing up befuddled. My heart stops; I think it's Alex. My heart flames with pain; my belly corkscrews.

I won't catch the man's eye, although I can feel he wants to speak. He might see what I'm trying so hard to hide, so I turn away, attempting a smile to show that I'm OK. I find my fists are clenched. I twist my hair into a nervous rope, tucking it behind one shoulder. Even in my shadowy reflection I can see the red of it, the flame I can't escape and –

I see something else, something beyond the window, out there in the dark. I hold my breath in shock.

What I see is fear. Pure and undistilled; the face I gaze into is mad with it, big eyes rolling back into the head until they are all white; a nightmare vision. The nostrils drip and flare in panic, the huge teeth bared in a grin of frothing terror, the mane flying in the wind. For one small second snatched in old time, the time that will soon become the time before – the safe time – I find I'm not scared. I want to stretch my hand through the window and smooth the trembling flank; to ground this rearing beast. But then my own terror crashes in around me and I feel very tiny. I think his great flailing hooves will surely pierce the coach's metal side; frantic, I press back into my seat.

The chance to find my voice, to shout a futile warning, has already passed. The lullaby is building to a shriek. The passengers are screaming, have begun to scream as one because the coach is tilting on its axis until it cannot right itself again, until finally it topples. It skids across the road in hideous scraping chaos; on its side now – and still the coach keeps moving. I am level with the road now; blue sparks fly up before me as if a welder was torching the ground. Then I roll, slam hard into a body so all the wind is squeezed out of me.

I cannot see. My hands flail at the blackness. Panting with terror, I am thrown against some metallic edge, a flash of agonising pain fills my left shoulder as I crack it on the ceiling. A child cries piteously – but I cannot find him to offer comfort. Someone's foot grinds into my gut, a fist pummels my mouth in fear. I claw at my face as something oddly intimate drapes itself across me, something soft that chokes and sickens me. I struggle to free my mouth, to let some air in. I panic that I am blind. We are still moving. Why the hell don't we stop moving?

A huge whump: the central reservation goes down as the coach crashes through, on its back now. It's slowing, and someone near me won't stop screaming, on and on –

A terrible metallic crunch ends the voice. The coach is jerked by force into the fast lane. The crunch of the first van as it hits us head on, and folds: then the next vehicle, then the next. Finally there is silence – almost silence. Just a single horn blaring into the complete darkness, a first horn then, soon, another: a petulant electronic chorus. Closer to me, a whimpering that spreads like forest fire. We have finally stopped moving and now there is nothing. Just darkness. Just the sob of my own breath as I clasp myself and wonder – is this death?

CHAPTER ONE

I am not ready for this.

I was about to change my mind when the girl came to get me.

'Maggie Warren?'

I smiled. Such a false smile, it nearly cracked my face.

She was a new girl; she must have started since the – since I'd been away. She was supremely confident. More confident than I ever had been at her age. She was young and blonde and walked with a swish of paper-straight hair and an empty click of the long leather boots that promised – something; I wasn't quite sure what. Exactly Charlie's type.

'I'm Daisy,' she threw over an immaculate shoulder as I tried to keep up. I was already unsettled, and her swagger unnerved me more. Did she know something I didn't? Painfully I followed her down corridors, trying to keep up, banging awkwardly through the doors, even more clumsy than I used to be. Waiting for her to speak. Waiting – but she didn't. I searched for something to say, I contemplated myself in her position, remembering all the inanities I'd ground out since I'd started. The punters have earned it just for being here, it's the least I can do, I always thought. Not in Daisy's book though; apparently, I hadn't. But perhaps I was different.

I felt the need to fill the silence in; the silence that was the click of her dominatrix boots. She awarded me a thin smile as she pulled open the next set of doors, waiting for me, not quite tapping her toes, her pity obvious – the smile said, 'This is a smile of superiority; because I know things you have no idea of; because I am leading you like a lamb to your slaughter.'

I said, 'Have you worked for Double-decker before?'

She shook her sleek head. 'Came from the Beeb.'

I loathed people who said 'the Beeb'.

'Graduate trainee.'

Didn't like them much either: the graduate trainee who invariably thought they knew it all. She was remarkably flat-chested for one of Charlie's girls, I noted as I passed by her.

'Oxford, you know.'

'Ah, Oxford,' I nodded sagely. That would explain it. Charlie had a penchant for posh, 'specially the Oxbridge ones.

Before I could struggle any further to be her 'friend', just like, I realised uncomfortably, all those punters in the past had tried to be mine, we had arrived. *Pull yourself together, Maggie*, I told myself firmly. But my hands were actually shaking. It was so odd to be here on the other side. The green room was alive with people and light, the buzz and hum of adrenaline and apprehension palpable. Everyone was bathed in the horrible neon light that yellowed the skin and made the eyes look dead. The banks of croissants and sandwiches were already dry and curling; the orange juice was spilt on the white linen. What was I doing here? Would they see inside me; know I'd sold my soul? I looked for Sally, then for the wine, but Charlie found me first.

'Maggie, darling;' the emphasis on *darling* as he kissed me on both cheeks, his face lingering a little too long next to mine. I tried to step back imperceptibly but I was so unwieldy these days with my silly foot.

'I could murder a drink.' I was just a little too bright. I contemplated him for a moment. Then I leant forward and asked, quietly, 'You are sure about this, Charlie?'

He clasped my hand, a little too hard. I winced. 'Not going to back out now are you, darling?' It wasn't a question. 'Daisy, get Maggie a drink, would you?' Kinky-boots smiled at him and fetched me a drink. Begrudgingly. She'd go far.

'What?' Now Charlie leant in to catch my words. Had I spoken aloud?

'Oh, nothing. God, I'm nervous. This is so –'

'Exciting?'

'Weird, I was going to say. I'm really not sure that –'

'Don't be silly.' He looked impatient. 'We've been through all this. It's your big chance.'

'Hardly,' I began, but then a tense-looking Sally peered round the door. I was so glad to see her that I cried her name too loudly. She smiled back at me, but stress was definitely winning the day.

'Hi babe.' Her eyes flicked round the room. 'Daisy,' Sally found her target, gestured frantically, 'has the anti turned up yet?'

'What anti?' I frowned.

'Oh don't worry. They're not for you.'

I didn't believe her. This was the exact reason my job had lost its allure; the deception of those we relied on to provide the entertainment. With a nasty lurch, I realised I was the entertainment now. 'Sal, I really don't need a row on air. Charlie promised. I thought this was a neutral show.'

But I lost her attention as Rita swept into the room, pausing by the door for maximum effect. She knew exactly how to work it. There was a brief lull as heads turned and she started her rounds. She didn't always bother these days, but this was a big one – the proper scoop, and a ratings winner, if they did it right. This year's greatest tragedy so far. I shuddered. Sally was off again.

'Sal', I hissed after her, 'I'm not having a row with anyone. Charlie did promise.'

A shadow flitted across Sally's face. 'Bear with me alright, Maggie? Daisy, get the rostrum tape of the headlines into the gallery. Now, please.' Then she was gone. I downed my drink in one huge gulp. The headlines. That overwrought outpouring of horrified voyeuristic – what? Delight? A glut of hysterical sympathy for our terrible misfortune on that coach. Blame, shame and sorrow. I wasn't sure I could cope with seeing them again: I'd managed to avoid most of them the first time. Only occasionally a nurse had forgotten to bin –

I skidded the memory to a necessary halt. I wanted a cigarette badly. I wanted to get the hell out of here more badly. I must have been mad to agree to this. I inched toward the door as surreptitiously as my bad leg would let me; then Daisy was by my side. Clamped to my side, in fact. 'OK?' She smiled that horrible thin smile again.

'I need a fag.' I tried to smile back. Someone stopped Daisy to ask where they could change and that was it; I was off down the corridor as fast as my crutches would carry me. But I wasn't going to make it outside in time. I veered off to the loo. Perhaps they wouldn't look here (they always looked here. I was hardly the first guest to hide behind a locked door). The end cubicle was free; I stood against the door and fumbled for my cigarettes. My skeletons weren't so much rattling the closet as smashing down the walls. Two women were discussing Rita over the divide between their cubicles. 'Such pretty hair,' one cooed. If only they knew. Normally I would have smiled, but right now I felt more like crying. Everything was out of kilter. Worst of all, I despised myself. I hadn't realised quite how hard I was going to find this. I didn't know if I was more scared about being on the other side for the first time in my life, or of talking about – it. Digging up the past. Would they manage to mine my depths for secrets long untold? I inhaled deeply. The women clattered out, tutting about passive smoking. My leg throbbed and I searched my bag for yet more pills.

'Maggie?' The deep tones of Amanda, the floor-manager. 'You in here?'

I held my breath but then the smoke curled up my nose, and I tried to stop it but I coughed anyway.

'Maggie? Is that you?' The relief in Amanda's voice was tangible.

'Ten minutes, darling.'

It was useless. 'Just coming,' I whispered miserably.

'I'll wait for you.'

'Great.' I took a last deep drag and dropped the fag into the toilet-bowl. Wiping my sweating hands on my jeans, I opened the door and awkwardly manoeuvred out.

'Darling!' Amanda hugged me, sniffing the air. 'Smoking, you naughty girl? How are you, you poor old thing?' I felt like her pet Labrador.

'Oh, you know.' Naked under her caring gaze.

'Look, do you want to come through now? Take the weight off your poor foot. Is it very sore?' She glanced down at my leg like it might snap. My crutch got caught on the sink, and I stumbled, just a little. I winced as Amanda grabbed my arm.

'It's OK,' I said, and I heard my own voice very bright, very false, ringing outside my own ears. 'It's just the wine.'

She frowned.

'I'm not pissed'. Absolutely I was pissed. 'Don't be silly. True professional, me.' I hadn't eaten anything apart from painkillers since God knew when. 'But I might just have a quick top-up before –'

Amanda took my arm, gliding me swiftly through the door towards the studio. She was like a little wiry foxhound and I was clenched between her teeth. I debated bashing her over the head with a crutch and making a run for it.

'No time, darling.' She assessed me with speed. 'You should have been to make-up. You're very pale, Maggie.'

'Pale and uninteresting,' I joked. Nobody laughed. Anxiety set in again.

'Amanda.' This was the point of no return. I took a deep breath, pulled her to one side. 'I'm really not sure – I really don't think I can do this actually.'

''Course you can, darling. Gosh, if I had a pound for

everyone who nearly changed their minds before we started, I'd be a millionaire. And they all come off loving it. All wanting more…'

'This is me, Amanda, remember?' I muttered. The old platitudes would not wash, of that I was quite sure. Pissed or not.

She had the grace to flush slightly. 'Look, I'm going to get Kay up here with some blusher for you. And you,' she poked Daisy with her clipboard, 'get Maggie another drink. Stick some wine in a water bottle. Just don't let any of the other guests see, for Christ's sake.'

We were at the studio door. It was so hot in here already. Sally had taken the floor now to do her bit and the audience was laughing at some feeble joke. Charlie rushed in, rushed to my side. He too was utter consternation now. 'Alright, Mags?' No-one ever called me Mags, least of all Charlie. Unless I was his star guest.

'Oh you know,' I repeated like a well-schooled parrot. 'Fine and dandy.' Who was I kidding? Charlie smiled, his teeth shining toothpaste-white under the bright lights. Suddenly headlines from the days after the accident flashed up on the studio monitors. My heart began to race as I was compelled to read them. The *Sun* screamed 'CRASH COACH CARNAGE', the *Express* enquired politely 'HORSES ON THE MOTORWAY: WHO IS TO BLAME?'; the *Mail* screeched 'GOVERNMENT'S ROADS CAUSE TRAGEDY'.

I tore my eyes away just as Daisy arrived with the water bottle. I took a huge swig. Now Kay was here in a fug of sweet scent, in a cloud of powder that always made me think of my mother.

'You alright, ducks?' I loved Kay. I wished she was my mum.

'Just a bit of blush to brighten you up, a dab of powder to stop the shine, OK?' She moved round me in a fragrant flurry. 'Oh, just look at those baby blues, Maggie! You can manage without mascara, lucky girl.'

Pete the soundman rolled up to check my mike. He adjusted it slightly, taking pantomime care not to delve too deeply down my V-neck, and winked at me. 'Funny to see you on this side. Break a leg.' Then he backed into my cast and went quite puce.

And now Rita arrived. She swept on to set like the true diva she was and the audience went mad; they loved her so. They had no idea of the blood and sweat we poured out for Rita, of the tears (ours) and the tantrums (hers) and, and –

She held her hands up for quiet. Silence dropped like a blanket across the studio. Now Rita was talking. Oh, I knew exactly why she was so captivating. She drew them in – she was every man's friend, every woman's confidante. Like fish on a line she reeled them closer until they were prone with ecstasy. She dropped her voice, inviting them to lean in, to – lucky things – share her world.

And in this trice, as I listened, as her words washed over me, I began to relax a little. I still felt the surge of adrenaline, but I could play Rita at her own game; I knew exactly how to do it. God knew I'd been in this business long enough. Once I was as naïve as our audience; a true innocent believing everything we revealed on television was for the greater good. Now I was hardened and desperate to escape this trap, so I'd done my deal with Charlie. This

457

morning I knew what they all wanted and I had to give it to them. For me – I had to remind myself – this was a one-time, only-time thing, to be on this side of the cameras, with my make-up done and under my blue armchair the drink no one but me knew was there. No one except Amanda and Daisy. I had a final swig, and took a deep breath, remembering Charlie's threat. I remembered Charlie's promise. I just had to ensure I didn't reveal too much. I thought of being on the running track at school, my dad shouting encouragement as I drove myself forward – and I was ready. Whatever Rita threw at me, I was ready.

Rita was delivering her final droplets of wisdom and waving her final wave before she left the floor. Kay gave my hand a last squeeze and Charlie stood behind the curtain and sleeked back his hair before giving me an obsequious thumbs-up. Amanda was counting us down, the titles were up on the monitors and the sweat had started to run down my rigid back. And then Rita was on the floor, waving, the audience cheering and clapping until she snapped on the gravitas this subject required and a hush fell.

It was then for the first time that I noticed the girl. She was sitting two chairs away from me, on the other side of the eminent trauma psychologist Sally had wheeled on, and she was stunning. A cloud of dark hair framed a little heart of a face and she held her arm, her plastercasted-arm, gingerly in her other hand, and as if she felt my stare she turned and blinked and smiled at me, a smile that filled those big violet eyes, eyes like bottomless buckets of emotion, and I felt very odd. Like, what do they say? Like someone had walked over my grave.